Sleeping Dogs
Don't Lie

Sleeping Dogs Don't Lie

by

Michael McCoy

Sastrugi Press

Jackson Hole

Sastrugi Press / Published by arrangement with the author

Sleeping Dogs Don't Lie by Michael McCoy

Sastrugi Press
PO Box 1297, Jackson, WY 83001, United States
www.sastrugipress.com

Library of Congress Catalog-in-Publication Data
Library of Congress Control Number: 2017939195
McCoy, Michael
Sleeping Dogs Don't Lie / Michael McCoy - 1st United States edition
p. cm.
1. Fiction 2. Native American 3. Archaeology
A young Native American man comes of age while pursuing his passion of archaeology and hunting down the person who murdered a beloved friend and workmate.

ISBN-13: 978-1-944986-15-5 (paperback)

Printed in the United States of America
10 9 8 7 6 5 4 3 2 1

Dedicated to the memory of my mother,
Mary M. McCoy, 1917–2017,
who instilled in me a love of language.

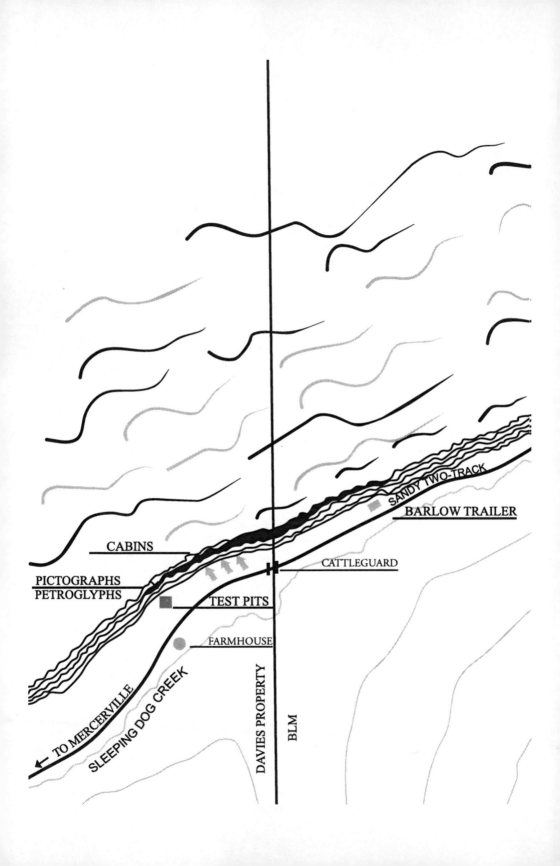

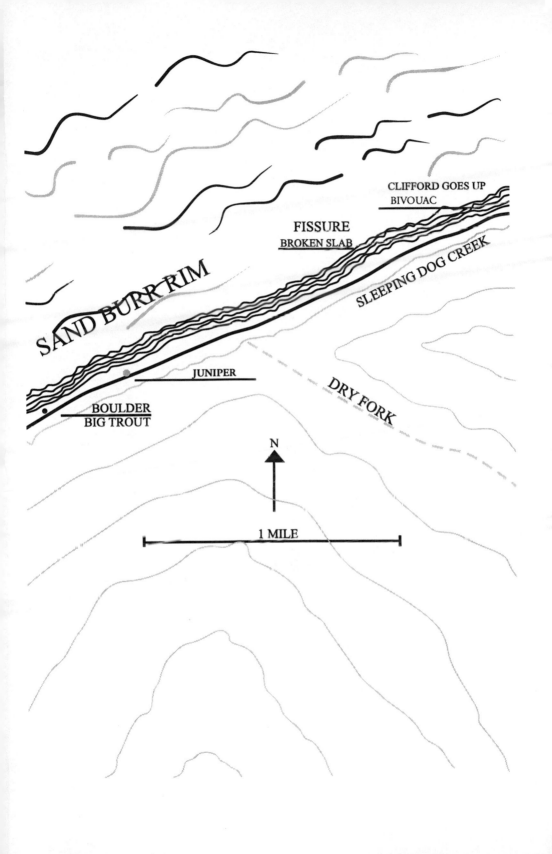

PROLOGUE:
OCTOBER 6, 1973

Clifford Gustafson gazed out over the sun-bleached autumn vast-ness of the Big Horn Basin. Though the lugged soles of his bulky leather Galibier Super Guides rested on Beaver Butte's table-flat sum-mit, his mind and spirit dwelt elsewhere, centered on the kaleido-scopic chain of clashes and passions he had experienced over the previous four months. Thinking about it caused Clifford's heart to rise and return to the young woman who, in such a brief period, had become his friend, his love... his lover.

"Bobbi!" Clifford cried, looking skyward. Then he fell to his knees and crumpled to the ground in a sorry mass of grief.

Gathering himself, Clifford glanced at his watch: ten before noon. *Enough of this foolishness*, he thought. He stood, re-slung the strap of his deer rifle over his shoulder, and tried focusing on his surround-ings, on being in the present. He watched arrowleaf balsamroot leaves, brittle in the breeze, click-clacking at his shins. He listened to ravens cackling overhead, breathed in the pungency of sage, felt the cool breeze of fall on his face.

But before long his concentration faltered again, as the delicious Indian summer sun drew his face and body to it, seducing him. He stumbled drowsily across the broad top of the butte and into an open park of fat-trunked ponderosa pines. Choosing the beefiest tree in sight, Clifford leaned his rifle against it, removed his rucksack, and crashed to the fertile duff, nestling his backside against the tree's rusty-orange base. With his hand he flipped his long raven ponytail off the front of his shoulder, placing it back behind his head where it belonged. He emptied the contents of his pack onto the ground, then unwrapped and tucked into his sandwich of chunky peanut butter and raspberry jam on a hamburger bun. To wash it down and to quell his mighty thirst, he guzzled the entire contents of his plastic quart water bottle.

It was a comfortable place to be, an oasis of autumn. The air felt cool and dry, the sun warm on his skin. No mosquitoes or flies buzzed around, biting or otherwise annoying him.

Any recent hatches no doubt got themselves flash-frozen last night.

The bright sunlight made Clifford squint. He found it easier keeping his eyes closed, but that rendered him helpless to resist the gravitational pull of slumber. As he slipped into the strange gray world that bridges sleep and wakefulness a fleeting thought told him, though he wasn't yet sleeping, that at this juncture he couldn't return to the world of the conscious if he tried.

Lightly dreaming now, Clifford joined the raptor whose T-shaped profile he had spied against the infinite ceiling of blue earlier that morning. Sinking deeper, he *became* the bird. Angling outspread wings just so, Clifford Gustafson the red-tailed hawk caught a spectacular thermal that lifted him high into the sky, higher, higher still. Permitting the wind to have its way with him, Clifford soared hard to the northeast, gliding across the Big Horn Mountains' desiccated western foothills, over the prehistoric Medicine Wheel, above the Castle Buttes of the Pryor Range. Looking down, he recognized a dot on the landscape as the homestead of the great Crow chief Plenty Coups, a place he had visited just months earlier.

Continuing his airborne journey, Clifford the hawk soared upstream along the course of the Tongue River, passed over a windswept corrugation of rippled dry ridges, and entered the watershed of the Rosebud. Then, unexpectedly, the man-bird began losing elevation. In little time and through no effort of his own, Clifford touched down a couple of miles north of Lame Deer, Montana, where, nearly two decades earlier, in a horror of heat and flames, he had been torn from the Cheyenne Indian Way. Almost forever. He could see the fire, feel its heat. He smelled smoke and his own singed eyebrows. Screams pierced his skull.

The latter part of this vision Clifford had dreamt countless times over the years, a fact he semi-understood when trapped inside the dream. But never on awakening could he conjure any details. Rather, a hazy apparition would encompass him like a ground fog—undeniably there, but impossible to grab hold of…

PART 1
THE MIGRATION EAST

1
THE FIRE

Thomas Backway stormed in from the moonless Lame Deer night through the big double front doors of the tribal community center, aka the Gray Building. The bright lights of the Stella Yellowcolt–Freddy Old Bull wedding bash blinded him. After his eyes adjusted some, Backway found who he'd come looking for: John and Ellen Whitetail, out on the dance floor, dipping, twirling, and grinning to the electric sounds of the Cheyenne Cowboys. Backway ran up and forced himself between the couple.

"Thomas, what the heck?" the bulky John Whitetail queried of his hired hand.

"John, it's your house!" Backway yelled, looking up at Whitetail while attempting to out-shout the band, whose singer was yodeling something about muleskinners. "It's burning! I called the firehouse. You gotta get out there, quick!"

John drew Ellen close and spoke into her ear. Hand in hand, both wearing grim expressions, the couple raced out of the Gray Building and over to their white Ford F100 pickup. After slamming his door shut, John turned the key and revved the engine. The truck's rear tires spat gravel at parked vehicles as he peeled out of the lot. Taking his eyes off the road, he glanced to his right at the northern sky.

"Holy cow," he said. "People are gonna think the northern lights have come south for the night."

"Is it from our house burning?" Ellen's voice quavered as she spoke.

"I'm afraid so," John said. "I just hope the kids are okay."

After covering half a mile at twice the posted speed limit of twenty-five miles per hour, John turned right just past Dino the green dinosaur to begin banging north out of town along the pot-holed Rosebud Road. Backway hugged close behind in his own F100. Inside of a mile, the small motorcade caught up with the fire truck, one of a pair of used '46 GMC pumpers the reservation had acquired earlier in the year at auction in Billings. The road powder kicked up by the pumper obscured his view, and John didn't dare try passing the truck on a dirt road.

"Normandy," he said.

"What?" Ellen asked.

"That siren reminds me of Normandy," her husband said. "D-Day. Eleven years ago, but seems like the day before yesterday. Death and dying. I don't like thinking about it, but there it is."

Two miles north of Lame Deer, the Whitetails followed as the fire truck turned east onto the family's half-mile-long, two-track driveway. The north wind whisked the road dust southward, and the couple could see, for the first time, the conflagration their home had become.

"Jesus in Heaven," John said. Ellen made a soft whimpering sound.

Parking fifty yards away from the small house, with Backway right behind, the Whitetails immediately spotted six-year-old Mary silhouetted against the fire. She clutched her Raggedy-Ann close to her chest with both hands, as if it were life itself.

"Why did we ever leave them alone, John?" Ellen said. "Even for just an hour?"

The fire department's other truck had arrived earlier. Four volunteer firemen, two Indians and two whites, had the hose rolled out and were showering the house in a token, futile effort. Once this tanker and the one just arriving ran dry, no more water would be readily accessible. The Whitetails hauled drinking water from town in fifty-gallon drums, and they obtained their washing water from Looney Creek—when it was running, which it wasn't at this late autumn date. Regardless, even if every acre-foot of impounded water in Rosebud and Big Horn counties combined somehow became available on the scene, that could not have spared the house at this point.

"Mary, where's Clifford?" Ellen demanded of the tiny girl, shaking her by the shoulders.

"What, Momma?" Mary said, looking up into her mother's brown eyes with an eerie calm.

"Thank God, Mary!" John Whitetail yelled. "But what about Clifford? My boy?" John's thick hair, black as the night and slick with Brylcreem, shone from the fire. Flames reflected in his dark eyes, making him look crazy and frantic.

"Haven't seen a boy!" bellowed one of the firefighters. "Just the girl. Couldn't go in the house by the time we got here."

"I'm goin' in for 'im!" John cried.

"Don't do it!" countered the firefighter.

"John, no!" Backway yelled.

The wind-driven flames roared like a tornado. The Whitetails' trio of mutts barked up a clamor, running around wild and useless amid the thick smoke and suffocating heat. Like a spooked cougar negotiating a tall pine, the stocky man moved across the dirt yard and slipped into the terror of the small frame house.

"No, John, wait!" Ellen screamed. For at that instant, in the corral to her right, she saw John's Appaloosa mare Nezzy lift her head and neigh, then nod toward Clifford, who was emerging from the grove of stunted aspens behind the house. His dirty tan blanket trailed on the ground behind him.

A mighty updraft of fierce heat carried Ellen's words starward into the dark night sky. She could see that they had failed to reach her husband's ears, so she ran in after him.

Neither John nor Ellen Whitetail emerged alive from the crackling inferno that devoured their longtime abode.

***

A bare bulb hanging from the ceiling lit the dank, windowless room situated off the hallway beyond the lobby of the Bureau of Indian Affairs office in Lame Deer. Clifford and Mary Whitetail sat on card-table chairs, hands folded in their laps, eyes directed forward at the unembellished white wall, their gaze held still. Jacket collars hugged high on their necks. A mouse scratched somewhere within the bowels of the building. Accompanied by plenty of record crackles and speaker pops, Billings radio station KGHL blared from the ancient Wurlitzer Navaho in the lobby, sending Hank Williams' nasal twang down the hallway and into the room where the children sat:

"Kaw-Liga was a wooden Indian standin' by the door,
He fell in love with an Indian maiden over in the antique store.
Kaw-Ligaaaa…"

In the adjacent room, Randy Jackson and Eugenia Looksbehind stood close, gazing intently into one another's eyes.

"Genia, I just don't see what else we can do other than put 'em up for adoption. Father Kaufman thinks that'd be best, too."

Jackson spoke in the passive, fatalistic tone of one who has seen too much, can no longer be surprised, and never could change the course of things much, anyhow. His slender fingers brushed back what remained of his red-turning-gray hair, as they habitually did when he was saying something he didn't like saying, which had been often enough during his twenty-six years with the B.I.A. A soft rural Virginia drawl revealed Jackson's roots. As he spoke, he lowered his chin and looked over the top of his reading glasses down at Eugenia, who stood a full eighteen inches shorter than he.

"The last time I saw Ellen's brother he was in Billings, face down on the sidewalk, playing welcome mat in front of the Bucksnort Bar. Who knows where her sisters are? And I don't have to tell you John was the only one who ever amounted to a great gray's hoot in his family."

Tears welled in Eugenia Looksbehind's bottomless black eyes. Gathering herself, the ordinarily reticent woman spoke forcefully, though her voice had a patina of resignation.

"Randy, we've lived within shouting range of the Whitetails since Arnold and John got home from the war. You know that."

"Sure I do," Jackson said. "And how Arnold and John went ashore at Normandy with the Cheyenne Rebels army detachment. Maybe someday they and their fellow warriors will get those Medals of Honor they deserve." He paused and winced. "Posthumously, in their case."

"Arnold and John, well, they were like brothers," Eugenia continued. "Me and Ellen were the same, like sisters. And sometimes when I'm not concentratin' too hard, I still can't remember right away which kids are mine and which are hers. That might sound strange, but it's a fact."

Jackson thought back on the tragedy of it all; how, a couple of years earlier, on the morning before Armistice Day, at just thirty-one years of age Arnold Looksbehind had suffered a heart attack and died while felling a tall lodgepole pine he'd intended to peel, stain, and put into service as a flagpole. Now, today, Jackson understood Arnold's widow was feeling things becoming further unraveled, as Indians throughout Indian country had been experiencing for a hundred years or more.

"I'm afraid you're right, Randy" Eugenia said. "As bad as I want to, I don't think I can care for Clifford and Mary much longer."

"I'm well aware you're stretched thin, Genia," said Jackson, who knew she was struggling to raise her own brood of three on a meager tribal allotment and Arnold's veteran benefits. Food supplies were sparse, and so were firewood and clothing. Jackson himself had offered to bring Eugenia a hind quarter of cow elk just a week earlier, and she hadn't refused it, as the proud woman characteristically would have done.

Eugenia Looksbehind, short and thick, stood her ground, staring up at Jackson.

"Okay, Randy," she said finally. "I'll cry every night for Clifford and Mary. I'll pray to God in heaven for them. Maybe getting off this cursed reservation is the best thing for 'em. Maybe it'd be the best thing for us all."

"Father Kaufman told me he can get the kids linked up with the Lutheran Welfare Association, which he thinks is the right thing for them," Jackson said. "Find 'em a good home, he said."

Eugenia's eyes widened.

"I know, I know. It doesn't seem quite believable, does it?" Jackson said. "Let's just say Father Kaufman isn't your typical priest. But you know that as well as I do. Seems he used to play golf with the head of the Lutheran group when he was serving up there in Great Falls. Thinks the world of the man and his program. He told the father he can find a good Lutheran family or two that'll allow the boy and the girl to grow up Catholic."

Two days later, Eugenia Looksbehind drove Clifford and Mary Whitetail into the center of downtown Lame Deer, where low clouds had squeezed the November morning into the clenched fist of a late-autumn cold snap. At eight-thirty sharp she helped load the children and their duffel bags onto a Greyhound Courier to begin the long ride west and north to Great Falls.

Eugenia waved long and slow as the blue-and-white bus pulled away. Its windows were frosted over, so she couldn't see if the kids were waving back. To her, the skinny, stretched-out dog adorning the side of the bus looked cold and out of place. Roaring and spewing diesel fumes, the big vehicle created a ground blizzard as it kicked up the light snow that overnight had dusted the street and sidewalks fronting the mostly vacant buildings lining Lame Deer's main avenue of commerce.

"Have a good Thanksgiving!" Eugenia shouted, not a soul within earshot to hear her.

2
THE FARM

After movement from that direction caught his eye, Eric Gustafson turned his attention to his distant farmyard.

"By golly, she looks so young," he murmured.

He shut down the red International Harvester Farmall he was using to plow deep black furrows in his undulating spread of fertile Minnesota prairie. The warm, humid morning air washing over him, coupled with the spectacle of a younger version of his wife hurrying his way, provided a rush of spring fever like he hadn't felt in years. The red-and-black skirt Martha wore flapped like laundry on the line, and her long, still-blonde hair fell over her shoulders, in liberated contrast to the tight bun she tended to imprison it in these days.

For reasons yet unknown to the farmer, his wife had reverted to the fetching gal he'd met and immediately fallen in love with twelve years earlier at the Midsummer Day solstice celebration up Beaver Falls way. He continued watching as Martha covered the quarter mile between their house and the tractor, running through the churned-up, sticky loam with grace and apparent abandon.

"Oh, I bet I know what this is about," Eric whispered, finally grasping it all.

"Hey there, Needles," he said, grinning, attempting to subdue the tension he felt mounting.

"Needles?" Martha asked. "Where's that come from?"

"Why, that's the three-year-old that won the Kentucky Derby last weekend."

Martha looked at him as if she thought he'd lost his mind. She shook her head, trying to steer her train of thought back on track.

"Gus, we're getting a *boy*," she blurted, underscoring the word "boy" by uttering it in a pitch half an octave lower than her other words. Hearing it so spoken grabbed at Eric's own vocal cords in such a way he felt he would either start bawling or stop breathing. He jumped down from the tractor and turned away from Martha. His dam of reserve failed.

"It's okay, Gus," Martha said, laughing.

Only slightly embarrassed, he turned around and came face-to-face with his wife, who stood on ground a bit higher than his, so that their noses were separated by a fraction of an inch.

"We're getting a boy, Gus."

Martha smiled through her own tears, then took him in her arms and didn't let go. They held their embrace, not saying a thing, for the better part of a minute. As they did, their ever-nosy neighbor Erling Bergstadt inched by on the gravel road skirting the Gustafsons' field. The bachelor farmer honked the horn of his faded blue, rust-eaten '41 GMC flatbed and gestured with his arm out the open window.

"Gus, we've never put on a public display quite like this," Martha said, giggling.

"I know," Gus said. "And I apologize."

"You sure don't need to do that."

"I mean apologize for not doing it before. I will get hell about it for some time to come," he added, "what with old Bergy catching us in the act. But I don't care. He can go to hell himself."

"Gus, you don't talk like that!"

"Not very often I don't."

A few weeks later, on June 14, 1956, four-year-old Clifford Whitetail arrived at his new home. His travels had taken him by bus from the Treasure State's Electric City to Havre, then by train across the Montana Hi-Line and the plains and prairies of North Dakota and Minnesota. From the Lutheran Adoptive Services state head-quarters in St. Paul, he'd been chauffeured to the modest-sized farm just outside Red Earth, Minnesota. There, several days later, once the adoption papers were all stamped and notarized, he would earn distinction as the only raven-haired Gustafson in Red Earth County.

After the driver pulled up and stopped beside the farmhouse, the passenger door swung open and out popped Clifford. He just stood there, beaming up at Gus and Martha. Against his dark skin and coal-black hair, his was a white, tooth-filled grin bigger than the Bighorn Canyon and more honest than Abe Lincoln.

"Oh, Gus," Martha gasped, putting a hand to her mouth and glancing at her husband. Gus winked at her, then looked down at Clifford and gave him a wink, too.

✶✶✶

"Clifford, breakfast is in ten minutes!" Martha stood at the kitchen doorway, aiming her words up the narrow staircase leading to the second floor of the Gustafsons' farmhouse.

"Okay, Mama!" came the shouted reply.

"He's just the best boy, isn't he?" Martha said, smiling. "In the three months he's been with us, he's done anything we've asked of him, without question or hesitation."

"And he rarely speaks unless spoken to," added Gus. "A trait I admire. But there's this seriousness, this sadness, about the boy that we've talked about. I wish I could rip it out and cast to the wind out there." He nodded towards the window and the leaves of the elm trees beyond, which were fluttering in a passing breeze.

"It'll take time, Gus," Martha said. "Be patient. I think you can do it."

"By golly, I'm gonna try my darnedest."

Gus and Martha did not know what trauma Clifford had experienced, or even that he had an older sister who had been adopted by another family. They knew only that Clifford's parents had perished. Such were the hush-hush policies of the Lutheran Adoptive Services. And Clifford hadn't mentioned Mary, not once. Such was his reserved nature.

Clifford clomped down the stairs and pulled his chair up to the kitchen table, wagging his head against the stiff new collar abrading the skin of his neck. His glossy black hair lay plastered flat against his head, thanks in large part to his adoptive mother's liberally applied elbow grease.

"So, the big boy starts school today!" said Gus, looking up from the sports page of the *Mankato Free Press*. He took a sip of coffee.

"Yeah, Papa," Clifford mumbled through a mouthful of pancakes.

"Five years old last month—quite the young man!" Gus looked at Clifford and smiled.

For most of his ensuing public-school career, Clifford would board a big yellow bus to ride the five miles northwest to school. Today, however, on his first day of kindergarten, both Martha and Gus "coincidentally" remembered reasons they had to go to town, so together they drove Clifford into Red Earth.

Gus pulled the family's burgundy Bel Air four-door up in front of Brennan Grade School as Martha licked her palm and used it to rub hard on the back of Clifford's head, trying to tame his resurrected cowlick. She opened the car door and stepped out, letting him out from between her and Gus.

"Do what the teacher asks of you, Clifford," Martha instructed.

"Okay, Mama."

"Give 'em what for, Cliff," chimed in Gus.

"Okay, Papa."

Clifford turned around and joined the jostle of kids bouncing up the walkway toward the two-story, tan-brick schoolhouse. Gus and Martha watched as his black head of hair bobbed along like a dark log in a flowing stream of blonde and light brown water.

***

Later that day, at a quarter before one p.m., Clifford waltzed through the back door of the Gustafsons' white Queen Anne-style farmhouse. "I'm home, Mama!" he yelled, letting the screen door slam.

"Clifford, hi! Did you have fun at school?" Martha came around the corner from the living room, where she'd been ironing clothes and chortling at the antics of Wistful Vista's *Fibber McGee and Molly* crackling over the radio.

"Yeah, I liked it," Clifford said.

"Where's Papa?"

"I dunno."

"What? You didn't ride home with him?"

"No, I rode the bus."

Martha half-frowned, half-smiled.

"Come on, Clifford," she said at last, grabbing a jacket and the keys to the pickup truck. "We'd better get back to town quick and find Papa. I'll bet he's waiting for you in front of the school and about to have a cow, if it's not already mooing."

3

CASSIDY

Stuart Cassidy was squatting in the rain forest with his pants down when the initial explosion shook his world. He had consumed something that disagreed with him, or maybe contracted a tropical intestinal bug. Whatever the cause, a painful case of diarrhea had sent him on this trip, his fifth of the morning, to a makeshift kaibo in the forest, downslope from the others in his work detail.

The deafening blasts of heavy artillery above made him feel like he was watching a violent movie, witnessing something but detached from it. Then he heard the assault-rifle fire and *rat-a-tat* of machine guns commence. He knew he should grab his own M-16 and climb into the fray. Instead, he sought safety, descending another couple of hundred yards, watching out for signs of camouflaged pits that might harbor bamboo punji sticks. When he figured he had gone far enough, he hunkered down beneath the three-tiered forest canopy. And prayed.

Fifteen minutes after the shooting began, the jungle went quiet. Cassidy waited another quarter hour before standing to start up the slope. He sensed no movement and heard no human sounds. He continued toward the place where his detail of forty soldiers had been working to clear the way for a new tank road. Arriving at his destination, Cassidy saw dead men strewn about everywhere. He could find no survivors. His Dog Company peers, his superiors, several members of a CIDG Mike Force team composed of local indigenous Montagnards, had all been slaughtered.

Cassidy's existence had turned blood red at its core.

Panicked and in shock, he fled the scene, and just kept moving. His journey took him from the Central Highlands south of Dak To in western Kontum Province through northern Cambodia, then into southern Laos. He battled thick jungle, traveled past bamboo groves, waded through snake-infested rice paddies. Resting and hiding by day and traveling and scavenging by night—never knowing whom, if anyone, to trust—he proceeded west. For how long, he had no idea. Time escaped him.

This Cassidy did know: he had to run, and keep running. Maybe never stop.

4

SPORTS

The school bell clanged, startling Clifford. He looked up at the clock hanging high on the wall above the classroom door: five past eight. The time marked minute number one of his first day as a high school sophomore.

Earlier, when Clifford entered the room, he had noticed his new American history teacher, Mr. Hennessey, staring at him. With brown hair clipped military-style in a flat-topped burr, Mr. Hennessey had stood chest-out erect, his eyes focused on Clifford. So it had seemed to the young man, at least.

"Good morning, people," Mr. Hennessey finally barked with obvious self-importance. He banged his wooden pointing stick on his desk to further ensure the capture of everyone's attention. "And welcome. Today we're going to talk about Jamestown. Does anyone know the significance of Jamestown?"

No one volunteered that he or she did, so Mr. Hennessey proceeded to spout his first-semester, day-one lecture about the settling of Jamestown, how "disease and starvation and attack by the Red Man destroyed the first permanent white settlement in America…" It was the same lecture he had recited on a similar day in early September in each of the previous seventeen years.

The bell ending the period rang at nine o'clock sharp.

"Okay, people, that's all. Now you know everything anyone who's anybody needs to know about Jamestown."

The students stood, grabbed their books, and filed out of the room. All except for Clifford, whom Mr. Hennessey intercepted near the door before he could exit.

"Clifford... Gustafson, is it? Did you just move to town, son?"

"No, sir, I've lived here since I was four."

"Since you were *four*? Didn't you play football last year?"

"No, sir."

Mr. Hennessey paused. "I knew you didn't. I admit it. I always acquaint myself with the names and faces of every boy on the junior-high roster. How come you didn't play?"

Teacher and student were approximately the same height. The former's unwavering green eyes stared straight into Clifford's eyes of deep brown. *I'm trapped*, Clifford thought. He tried looking away, but that felt even more uncomfortable than making eye contact with his elder.

"I don't know. I just don't play football. Never thought about going out. I don't think I'd be too crazy about butting heads and tackling people. Anyway, I'm out for cross-country."

"Cross-country! Running?" Mr. Hennessey's revulsion for cross-country as a weenie sport was obvious. "You're too big to run."

"But I like to run."

"You can't be very fast."

"I don't know... but I like it. I was a pretty good runner in junior-high gym class."

"Well, you must have grown some since then."

"That's true, I guess," Clifford acknowledged. In fact, over the past year he had gained four inches in height and thirty pounds in weight. If fashion model Twiggy was a wisp of willow, the new and improved Clifford was a century-old oak. Six feet tall and solid as a bison's hump, he exuded athleticism.

"I have to say, my mind was on the subject matter less than usual today," Mr. Hennessey continued, softening his demeanor some. "When I saw you walk into the room, I thought, 'I bet nothing short of a runaway Peterbilt could knock that kid to the ground.' Then I remembered last year's three-and-five record. It was my first losing season, you know, in seventeen years as head coach at Red Earth High. I wondered how I might take advantage of this sturdy Indian-looking kid—that would be you—to help reverse that record before it threatens to become a trend.

"You know, the first game of the season, against Beaver Falls, is this Friday," Mr. Hennessey went on. "There's no time for me to whip you into shape and have you worth anything for that game. But I think maybe, just maybe, you could become an important part of the ticket to a winning season. I've developed a second sense for these things. I'll get you suited up today at two and then over to the field. We'll run through some drills.

"Let's walk over to my desk here," he added. "I'll write you a permission slip. You don't mind getting out of school early, do you? We can rearrange your class schedule if necessary."

"Okay. I guess not."

"And Gustafson?" Clifford didn't know it yet, but those whom Mr. Hennessey addressed by their last names were members of a small, select fraternity: his football players. The same privileged few who addressed him as "Coach Hennessey."

"Yes, sir?"

"The girls go nuts over football stars."

"I s'pose so," Clifford said, blushing. Easy-going, he'd do just about anything an adult asked him to do that wasn't illegal or un-ethical. And certainly he didn't mind getting out of school early by legitimate means. Maybe football wasn't so bad, after all, if practice always started at two. Cross-country training didn't begin until three-thirty, so no school-day-shortening privileges there. *But the idea of girls falling all over me? Ridiculous*, he thought. Any atten-tion Clifford recalled receiving from females in the past had hardly been of an amorous nature. They mostly seemed to want to kick or hit him.

Slow on the uptake in matters of the heart, Clifford Gustafson hadn't yet figured out that this was the odd way certain girls had of showing they *were* interested in him.

"Cross-country," Clifford heard Mr. Hennessey muttering, as the younger man headed for the classroom door and the hallway.

That afternoon, Clifford came to an understanding: his high-school autumn athletic future was sealed. As always, he did what he was told, and Coach Hennessey was a pro at barking orders. It seemed to Clifford he wasn't as winded as most of the other boys as they ran their warm-up laps around the field. He felt smooth when he ran, natural, so he thought it odd when the coach yelled: "Gustafson, pick it up, you run like a gol-danged elephant."

Under the lights that Friday night, Coach Hennessey gambled and put the green Clifford in at defensive end with a minute remaining in the fourth quarter. On his first play ever in an organized football game, Clifford chased down the Beaver Falls quarterback, who had snuck through the line, after starting ten yards behind him at the fifty-yard line. He brought the ball carrier down at the Red Earth fifteen, preventing what looked to be a sure touchdown. The Redskins went on to hold Beaver Falls, Red Earth's fiercest rival, to a gain of just one yard over the next three plays. The Beavers missed the field goal attempt, and the game ended in a 12-12 tie.

"Good game, Gustafson," Coach Hennessey said as he, the team, and the support crew streamed back toward the school and the locker room.

***

The sun lay low above the western horizon by the time the Gustafsons finished their supper of breaded pork chops, baked potatoes, home-canned green beans, and apple pie. Stuffed, Clifford sat and watched *The Huckleberry Hound Show* with his dad. They both laughed, loud and often. Gus even slapped his knee once during the "Pixie and Dixie" segment.

After the cartoon show ended, Clifford excused himself. "I'm gonna go running, Papa,"

"Okay, Clifford," Gus said. "Where do you get all the energy? Don't tire yourself out too much. You have a game day after tomorrow. I didn't tell you, but I ran into Coach Hennessey at coffee on Saturday. Said he thinks you're going to be a real asset to the team."

"I won't." Clifford bounded up the stairs three at a time. On reaching his bedroom, he disrobed and donned his running gear: Red Earth red-and-green team gym shorts over a jock strap, plain white T-shirt beneath a red sweatshirt with green sleeves, and ripple-soled New Balance Trackster running shoes over thick gray-cotton sweat socks. On a whim, he grabbed the round, metal-encased stopwatch from the top of his dresser before bouncing down the stairs and out the front door. "Come on, Ralphie!" he called. "Let's go running."

Sir Ralph the Wonder Dog, Clifford's three-year-old yellow Labrador retriever, stood up from beneath the big oak tree he'd been lying under and shook, his tags jangling and ears flapping. Together, boy and dog walked through the gate in the Gustafsons' white picket fence, up the long unpaved driveway, and onto the gravel road fronting the property. After jogging northward for a few minutes to warm up, Clifford began running in earnest, Ralph keeping pace.

Though September had nearly run its course, it still felt like summer. A powerful humid front had pushed its way up from the Gulf of Mexico, staving off the cold air that, according to the six p.m. television weather report, was squeezing its way down from the north. It didn't take Clifford long to begin sweating. He stopped, stuck the stopwatch in his mouth and clenched it between his teeth, then whipped off his sweatshirt, grabbed hold of the two sleeve ends, and flipped it in circles before tying the tube of a shirt around his waist in a square knot.

Clifford resumed running, stopwatch in hand. A dry August and early September had allowed the area's corn crops to field-dry, enabling an early harvest. Already stripped of their fruit, the dry stalks rattled and clacked in the gentle breeze, which carried on it the mature, earthy scent of autumn, and the even earthier smell of the Johnsson Hog Farms a mile south. Clifford's father, who raised a few pigs himself, would always tell him, "That's the smell of money." And that was why Clifford had decided early on that he wanted to make his money in some other way. He didn't care for the stench.

The moist air massaged Clifford's lungs and nasal passages as he breathed in and out. He noticed that he wasn't choking on bugs like he had done earlier in the season. He homed in on the sounds of his surroundings: the hoot of an owl, a crow gargling, Sir Ralph's damp panting and jingling tags. He glanced down and laughed at the big, goofy grin on his running partner's face.

I love this, Clifford told himself—moving through the countryside under his own power, to the steady cadence of his feet landing on and pushing off a gravel surface, his dog beside him. *Addictive. Not football.*

As the pair rounded their first left-hand turn, a red fox scurried off the road in front of them. Sir Ralph feigned chase before the fox ducked into the cover of the hardwood stand to their right, the same grove where Clifford sometimes hunted squirrels with his buddy Andy Johnsson. A hundred yards farther, two white-tailed deer bolted from the cornfield on the left side of the road and into the same long patch of woods. *Pop must've missed some corn in that field at harvest.*

Two miles into their run, Clifford heard a vehicle crunching up from behind. He throttled down to a walk, holding Ralph at heel. He didn't want the occupants to see him running like an elephant. The green pickup truck eased by, its tires kicking a fine dust up off the rain-starved road. After it had gained a couple of hundred yards, the pair resumed running.

At the high point of their loop, Clifford stopped to look out over the undulating farm country. He saw a manipulated patchwork of right angles, the squareness of it an ever-present reminder of the hand of man. A gravel or paved road traced nearly every section line, north to south and east to west, each road one mile distant from the next one running parallel to it. Clifford considered how anyone flying overhead would look down on a checkerboard of mile-by-mile squares, only the river valleys, villages, and occasional lakes or undrained bogs disturbing the geometric perfection.

The runners' standard route encircled the 640-acre block composed of the Gustafsons' 320 acres and the adjacent 320 acres of the Verne Anderson family. They ran the perimeter of one square mile, four miles in all.

As usual, Clifford and Sir Ralph had begun by running north for half a mile, then turned west. This enabled Clifford to spot Red Earth's water tower, six miles distant, silhouetted at this time of day at this time of year against the illumination of the setting sun. After one mile of westbound trotting, they turned south; in another mile, east; and, after a total of three and a half miles, they turned back north to run the final half mile home.

That was the typical routine. Occasionally, however, at the three-and-a-half-mile mark, instead of turning north the boy and his dog would continue running east for a mile to the Bobby Wilson Golf Course. That they did on this sultry evening.

On arriving at the parkland course, Clifford removed his shoes and socks and stashed them beside the tee box for hole number one.

After thumb-punching the start button on his stopwatch he resumed running, intending to cover the nine-hole course in the same hole-to-hole progression golfers followed. Clifford had run it dozens of times, and he knew it made up the two-mile course the high school cross-country team practiced on and competed over for home meets.

Just days before, Clifford had concluded that the Bobby Wilson Golf Course was his favorite place to be, of anywhere he had been. The luxuriant carpet of grass played gentle on his feet and easy on his mind, whether he was running with Ralph or golfing with his dad.

"I have a strange connection to this place, Ralphie," Clifford said as they ran.

I really do love it, he thought. It seemed to him Sir Ralph liked it a lot, too, or at least he found the smells more interesting than out on the gravel roads.

Clifford felt strong and good on this summer-fall evening. He pushed it a bit, picking up the pace. His bare feet landed to the beat of "96 Tears" playing in his head. The tune, recorded by the artists known as Question Mark and the Mysterians, had been stuck there lately, owing to its contagious rhythm, repetitious organ riff, and incessant airing on radio station KDWB out of the Twin Cities. But on this evening the smash-hit song spun around the turntable of Clifford's mind at a clip much faster than forty-five revolutions per minute. It had to in order to keep up with his relentless pace.

Upon reaching the ninth green, Clifford punched the start/stop button on the stopwatch. He geared down to a walk and held the watch face up: eleven minutes and twenty-four seconds. *Not bad for an elephant*, he thought. Clifford realized that he and Ralph had covered the two-mile course fast enough to make him the number-two man on the Red Earth High School cross-country squad, second only to Andy Johnsson, had he opted to stay that route instead of playing football.

On the mile-and-a-half jog back home, Sir Ralph the Wonder Dog and Clifford Gustafson, his shoes and socks back on his feet, shared the cardinal-point gravel roads with an opossum, a skunk, two raccoons, at least four cock pheasants, and several other birds Clifford couldn't identify in the waning light. But no additional vehicles interrupted their quiet outing.

About as peaceful as anything could be, I reckon.

After showering, Clifford lay in bed—Sir Ralph snoring in his own floor-bed on the other side of the room—and played with the dial on his Heathkit radio, a model he'd assembled himself in eighth-grade shop class. Searching for faraway radio stations was one of his favorite pastimes on autumn and winter evenings. He tuned in WEBC, "The Big 56," out of Duluth, and learned it was thirty degrees cooler and thirty humidity points lower at the far north end of Minnesota than in the Red Earth country.

Clifford drifted off to none other than "96 Tears." Through the thickening haze, he wondered: *could Question Mark really be Tiny Tim, like Billy Anderson told me a few days ago?*

5
PARSONS

Bill Parsons stopped in his tracks, pulled a red bandanna out of the rear pocket of his Carhartt coveralls, and wiped his dripping nose. He felt feverish, his cold worsening.

He was searching for a missing "hunter," which is how the man's relatives in Cody had characterized him, but Parsons had long ago pegged Brad Hellerman as a hobby poacher. He was a wily one, who had managed to keep himself free of prosecution, if not from persecution by Parsons himself.

Now the tracker began wondering if Hellerman hadn't received his final comeuppance. Two days overdue, with no word sent and no call home. It was totally out of character, his wife had told the Park County Sheriff. Hellerman had even missed the eleven a.m. Sunday services at the LDS Church in Cody, where he held the position of elders quorum president.

Pausing to blow his nose now and again, Parsons huffed and puffed his way up the steep, deadfall-tangled north flank of Hawk's Rest. The timber-covered knob rose from near the south end of Bridger Lake, a body of water shimmering not far from the confluence of Thorofare Creek and the Yellowstone River, close to where Wyoming's Teton and Park counties and Yellowstone National Park all meet. As Parsons knew, it was about as remote a place as exists in the U.S. outside of Alaska.

Parsons had no real reason to be in this general vicinity, other than he knew the area to be thick with grizzly bears, despite a recent downturn in the animal's overall population in the Yellowstone country. He'd learned from street talk that this fall Hellerman had shown a special interest in *Ursus arctos horribilis*. And, sure enough, some elk hunters camped at the south end of Bridger Lake had told Parsons earlier in the morning that two days previously they'd encountered a man fitting Hellerman's description.

Parsons perked up when he noted the unusually large numbers of magpies and ravens squawking, cawing, and flying about. Not a good sign for Hellerman, perhaps, but one that lent credence to Parsons' intuition that this was the place. Homing in on the epicenter of the avian ruckus, he saw something sticking up from the ground that didn't look quite right. Wandering over to investigate, he found the feathered base end of an arrow, its smooth willow shaft protruding from the back of an apparently dead man lying face down in the duff.

"Brad Hellerman, you're under arrest," Parsons said, mostly to take the edge off the creepy scenario. He checked the body for vital signs and detected none. Thankfully, due to the chilly temperature, there were no flies and there was no stench.

"Where's the guy who shot the arrow?" Parsons wondered aloud. "And why would he leave behind such incriminating evidence?"

The tracker began his return trek to the lake. There he would saddle and mount Jumper, then ride the black mare back to his camp and radio the Forest District Ranger's office. As soon as the smokies arrived, he would guide them back to the incident scene.

"That guy isn't going anywhere," Parsons reassured himself. "Unless ol' Griz finds him and turns him into bear shit."

6
GOLF

"FORE!"

On hearing the warning from behind, Clifford mimicked his father, joining his hands over the top of his head and scrunching low to the ground by bending at the knees and waist. With a loud "THWACK!" a white golf ball made dead-center contact with Gus's forest-green golf bag.

"Wow!" Clifford exclaimed. "That came straight out of the air— no bounce!"

Out of harm's way, he and his dad stood up again and looked toward the foursome playing behind them on hole number four of the Bobby Wilson Golf Course.

"By heck, Pierson!" Gus yelled, hands cupped to his mouth, megaphone-style. "Have some patience, won't you?"

"Gus, I'm so sorry! Got a new driver and didn't know my own strength!"

"Okay, then!" Gus yelled back, then confided to Clifford: "Al Pierson won't let it happen again. But I'll have a heckuva time beating him at men's league on Thursday if he's hitting drives like that."

Clifford knew as well as anyone that golf was Gus's only real hobby, outside of building and fixing things—and those were less hobbies than components of his job as a farmer. He'd never played on another course, but he had golfed thousands of holes at Bobby Wilson. The course, as Gus had told Clifford on more than one occasion, had been excavated, rolled, sodded, and sanded by the Red Earth County Parks Department in 1954 and 1955. It occupied a 160-acre spread of former crop fields resting on a high lip above the valley of the East

Branch of the Red Earth, a river named for the colorful clay bluffs embracing certain stretches of it.

"Clifford, this was the first public course ever built anywhere around here," Gus said, in the incongruously creaky, Andy Devine-like voice that made Clifford wish he could oil it as he would a rusty barn-door hinge. "Probably within a radius of a hundred miles. A guy would've had to go all the way up to Mankato to find a course when I was your age."

"Yeah, I know, you've told me that, Papa." In fact, Clifford couldn't remember an occasion when they'd golfed together that Gus had not told him that. He'd also informed Clifford many times that the course's name honored a popular Red Earth boy killed in Italy during World War II. His family had donated the land in the young man's memory.

"Bobby picked up the game at university in Minneapolis," Gus would say. "And he picked it up real good."

Clifford looked on as his father hit his second shot on the par-four hole, using a fairway wood. "Pop, one thing you never have explained to me is why you hold your clubs that way, cross-handed-like," he lied.

"I haven't? That's strange. I thought I'd told you everything at least once by now. I guess you never asked before. Well, you know I played a lot of baseball as a youngster, including that one season in the Northern League, 1934, with the Brainerd Muskies—I always did everything in life right-handed, except bat. For some reason it just felt proper to swing left-handed, from the moment I picked up the stick as a boy. I tried swinging right-handed often enough, but never could hit the broad side of a cow that way. But, by golly, I was a pretty dangerous southpaw hitter, if I do say so myself.

"So, to make a short story long, if I'd run across a set of lefties when I started golfing back in 1960, I'd probably be golfing left-handed today. But back then, around here anyhow, left-handed clubs were about as common as John F. Kennedy bumper stickers. I honestly didn't know such a thing existed. So, from the very start, I gripped my right-handed clubs like a left-hander, which was the only way I could make the swing feel half normal or comfortable."

"It sure doesn't look normal," Clifford teased.

But it was true. The cross-handed grip produced a strange-looking swing, and what a sight it was to behold: this bulky, Swedish-American farmer in Oshkosh bibs and brown work shirt, trundling about in black-and-white saddle shoes over Argyle socks, topped off with a DeKalb seed-corn cap, with its green, red, and yellow corn-cob logo— swatting cross-handed at the ball, after an abbreviated backswing, harder than you've ever seen anyone swing. And all that in a farm field-turned-golf pasture in southern Minnesota, where an out-of-bounds ball landed either in the thick hardwood forest sloping down toward the East Branch of the Red Earth River or, on the west side of the course, in the lush greenery of a field of corn one summer and soybeans the next (and corn again the summer after that).

Not that Gus ever explored the out-of-bounds areas. He never did hit the ball particularly far; he was a strong man, but his unorthodox grip sapped his power. But it *always* went straight.

"What's your best score, Papa?" Clifford asked as they neared his drive, which lay fifty yards up the fairway from where his father's ball had stopped.

"Now come on, Clifford, I know I've told you this before. You're pullin' my leg. You just makin' conversation?"

"Possibly. But tell me anyway."

"Okay, I don't mind. You know I usually shoot between forty-four and forty-eight. I'm pretty consistent, all right. But there was that one day back in sixty-four, you remember, when I hit my hole-in-one on number seven. That was quite the day. It all came together that round, and I shot a thirty-nine. It's been bringing me back ever since, but I don't know…"

Clifford thought about how his own passion for golf had grown right alongside his father's love of the game. It was the main thing they did together for fun and camaraderie. Gus didn't fish or hunt, so neither did Clifford, except for the occasional squirrel shoot with his friends and their .22s. Now and then, the family went camping up north, but Martha and Clifford enjoyed that more than Gus did. He preferred sticking around home. One of his favorite sayings, which he said often, was: "There's no earth better than Red Earth, yah?"

Unlike his father's modest talent, however, Clifford's capacity for improvement in the game of golf appeared boundless. By the time he turned sixteen, he was consistently driving the ball straight and well over two hundred yards, and doing most everything else right, too.

Gustafson the younger stepped up to the ball. He waggled with his five iron, took a full backswing, then made a smooth forward swing with perfect weight shift. He held his textbook follow-through stance for a full second. The ball carried 165 yards, Clifford estimated, before rolling up and stopping within what appeared to be ten feet of the pin flag.

"Nice shot, Cliff," said Gus.

Is that restraint I hear in his voice? Clifford wondered.

"I've gotta admit," Gus eventually added, "sometimes I get disgusted seeing you hit the ball like that. But it's myself I'm disgusted with, not you. I'm more awestruck and proud of you than anything."

"Thanks, Papa," Clifford said. "You know?" he continued, as they resumed walking, "Coach Hennessey's still trying to get me to go out for track instead of golf. With only a month of my senior year left. Don't you think that's kind of weird, after he talked me out of running cross-country for football? It's ironic; no, it's hypocritical."

"Them's some fifty-cent words you're using there, son," Gus said. "Careful, you might hurt yourself."

Strolling up to the green with putter in hand, Clifford thought back to the autumn of 1966, when Coach Hennessey had done all he could to stifle the young sophomore's desire to run... then, the following spring, he had pulled the big switcheroo and urged him to go out for track and run the hundred-yard dash. "I thought you liked running," Coach Hennessey had implored. But on that occasion, Clifford did not yield or waver. Rather, he looked his elder straight in the eye and said: "I do, Coach, but I don't like anything better than golf. Nope. I run at night so I can play football, I run at night in the snow and cold so I can play hoops, and I'll run at night so I can play golf."

"Okay, Gustafson," the coach finally conceded. "But you'd be better off running track. Golf's a fine game for old football players whose knees are shot, but it's unbefitting a strong young gridironer like yourself. You should be running the sprints."

Now, with the clarity of hindsight, Clifford understood that his resistance to Coach Hennessey's efforts to once again persuade him to switch sports had been a wise choice: In the approaching autumn of 1969, a full-blooded Cheyenne Indian named Clifford Gustafson out of Red Earth, Minnesota, would arrive at the state university in

Minneapolis for freshman orientation, the grateful but deserving recipient of a full-ride, four-year golf scholarship. And his knees were still fine, despite three years of high-school football and basketball, along with hundreds of miles of running.

Equally intact would be his "moral integrity," as Clifford liked to think of it. While it may be true that the impending steamy months were to host another summer of love in hotbeds of hippiedom like San Francisco and the Woodstock Festival in rural New York, for the bashful Clifford—following his nose around southern Minnesota—it was to be another summer of wondering if he would *ever* harvest the storied bounty of the fairer sex.

7
OLD FRIENDS

A redheaded, acne-pocked fireplug of a man, Galen Davies measured five feet eleven inches from the bottom of the tall heels of his black calfskin boots to the crest of his dirty brown 20X-beaver Stetson—cowboy accouterments that made him appear longer at each end than he was. So, among his friends and neighbors, who never saw him when he wasn't wearing one or both, his actual height was a matter of some conjecture.

Early one splendid May morning, Davies moseyed out into his barnyard and jumped aboard his favorite new plaything, a John Deere Model 410 two-wheel-drive loader/backhoe. Oh, how he loved to complain to anyone who would listen how the signature yellow-and-green machine had cost him a bundle, an expenditure he justified—to the bank-loan officer, to his wife, to himself—by vowing to land some earthwork jobs during his winter downtime. But like so many proud, strong-willed men who reside in backland where the spaces are large and the population small, Galen Davies preferred depending on himself for most everything. He knew the Deere would enhance his self-sufficiency, and that was the chief reason he'd gone out on a budgetary limb to purchase it.

Davies planned on this sunny morning to use the backhoe to level ground for a new corral at the base of the Sand Burr Rim, an escarpment of dirty yellow sandstone stretching from the western foothills of Wyoming's Big Horn Mountains west above Sleeping Dog Creek for approximately three miles. Ranging from one hundred to two hundred feet high and about a mile wide, the rim bisected Davies' property and the claims of eight other landowners. Its wall of rock already enclosed the corral-to-be on the northwest side. Davies, who'd added the five acres encompassing the spot to his spread back in 1962, couldn't believe it had taken him this long to think of fencing off the rest of it.

"Damn, I'm dumb," he'd whispered aloud when struck by the revelation, an eye-opener precipitated by his recent backhoe acquisition.

Spring had arrived, yet Galen Davies hadn't emerged from his typical state of winter torpor. He moved groggily through an atmosphere bursting with vernal promise. Songbirds made a joyful racket. A warm up-canyon breeze blowing in from the Big Horn Basin carried a sweet-smelling marriage of cow manure and alfalfa hay. The instant before climbing into the cab, Davies perked up at the resonant, melodic song of a western meadowlark. He spotted the yellow-and-brown bird perched on fencepost. A moment later he saw, out of the corner of his eye, the fleeting flash of a pair of mountain bluebirds swooshing by.

Davies fired up the Deere, let it run for a couple of minutes, then inched the machine toward the rim. Dozens of canyon wrens, those ubiquitous cliff dwellers of the Rocky Mountain West, were busy and about, flitting back and forth, patching their rock-face abodes and shopping the cool morning air for insect hatches. Using the hand controls, Davies maneuvered his backhoe toward the rock face, then lowered the scoop to begin removing sandy soil away from the cliff base.

After just one pass, on which the clawed bucket scraped away a foot of fill, Davies stopped and stared, squinted. He backed the Deere up, jumped down, and ran over to begin brushing rock with bare hands.

"Sohmbitch!" he cried. "SOHMbitch!"

Along the base of the wall, at a level that until a moment earlier had been covered by several inches of soil, Davies made out a line of distinct, dirt-encrusted petroglyphs, shallow etchings carved into the desert-varnish veneer of the sandstone surface; and, to their right, a panel of pictographs painted in dyes of red and blue. He continued brushing the rock with callused palms, wondering almost subconsciously that his fat-fingered hands could still perform work so delicate—especially his right one, bent into a semi-permanent curl, the result of Davies having spent half the waking hours of his life on the back of a horse, gripping the reins.

What Davies' machine and hands had revealed and his eyes now beheld included the likeness of a man holding an atlatl, or spear thrower, loaded with a spear, his arm slung back in a "cocked" position. An etching to the right, in front of the hunter, depicted a full-curl bighorn sheep ram. The next series of drawings, a few inches to the right, looked like four side-by-side dogs, or wolves or coyotes, all curled up and asleep. With ungloved hands Davies dug dirt away at both ends of the panel of petroglyphs and pictographs, trying to determine if they continued farther to the right or left. They appeared to do neither; he seemed to have hit *the* spot on his single pass with the scoop. Then he wondered if they went deeper. But that he would leave for the pros to probe.

Standing back from the wall and looking at it, Davies estimated the entire panel, including man, sheep, and canines, stretched about two-and-a-half feet horizontally and stood at least ten inches high. He knew the artwork he had just uncovered was both ancient and important. He also understood his stock would never be penned here against the rim, for no corral would ever be built there.

"That's fine by me," he muttered.

He also knew he had to get Paul Barlow on the horn, right now. As boys, Davies and Barlow had climbed or crawled over just about every square inch of the Sand Burr Rim manageable without technical climbing apparatus. But never during their explorations had they found anything like this.

Davies turned around and began trotting toward the old yellow farmhouse located nearby on his property, having remembered that he hadn't gotten around to disconnecting the recently departed renters' phone line. He took a shortcut across the corner of the field where he raised barley to sell to Adolph Coors, neglecting even to consider the possibility of stumbling across a spring-riled rattlesnake, typically his biggest fear.

Davies opened the white-trimmed front door of the house, walked in, and picked up the phone in the entryway, picturing his lifelong friend in his mind as he dialed. Barlow was a tall, bear-like man, bulky and awkward-looking, but also strong and fast. He always seemed ruffled, or worse, with his white cowboy shirttail hanging out in back, or one shoe untied. Barlow's degree of dishevelment increased as the day wore on, in proportion to the amount of time that had elapsed since he'd last been with Beth, his wife of thirty-seven years. Beth was the force responsible for preventing Barlow, a virtual genius who hadn't a clue when it came to social graces, from devolving into an altogether unacceptable creature. Just thinking about it made Davies chortle and snort.

***

Paul Barlow picked up the phone ringing on his desk.

"Paul," queried a man's voice on the other end of the line, "you know that Sand Burr Rim out back?"

"Galen? Is that you? It's gotta be. You're the only person I know who gets right down to business without announcing himself. It's been what, two years? Of course I know the rim. You and I were practically born and raised on it. Why?"

"Well, you were right. The Indians used the face."

Barlow jolted up from his customary slouch. "Where are you talking about, exactly?" Holding the phone with his left hand, he rubbed his right paw over his chin and felt a spot of whiskers he and Beth had both missed that morning.

"There at the east end of my place, along the creek in Sleeping Dog Canyon."

"What makes you so sure the natives used it?" Barlow asked.

"I was out digging corral with my new John Deere a few minutes ago, when I uncovered some rock art. Paul, it's so sharp they coulda been carved out and painted yesterday. You gotta see 'em!"

"There's both petroglyphs and pictographs?"

"Yep."

After a brief pause, Barlow nodded to himself. "I'll be there day after tomorrow, Galen. You be watchin' for me. Hey, how's Twinstar and the kids?"

"They're great, Paul, just great, every last one of 'em. Janie's still at home, about to finish her junior year. She'll graduate next year, then it'll be just me and the wife holdin' down the fort. You'll see the two of 'em when you're here this weekend. You are going to stay with us?"

"Sure, Galen, okay. Good deal. Thanks. See you soon."

"You take care, friend. And say howdy to Beth for me."

Barlow banged down the receiver and pulled his chair closer to the desk. He sat up, folding his hands together on the desktop. "I wonder if Twinstar's people could help us out any on this?" he whispered. "Ah, beautiful Twinstar. My saving grace."

"Who was that you were talking to?"

The demand startled Barlow, shaking him from his thoughts. Appearing out of nowhere stood Molly Preston, the University of Nebraska Anthropology Department secretary, her arms crossed and expression stern, in the open doorway of Barlow's first-floor office in Bessey Hall.

"Well, it's none of your goddamn business who I was talking to," Barlow said, smiling. "But I'll tell you anyway. It was Galen Davies. My first-ever and best-ever friend. He's found some rock art on the Sand Burr Formation in north-central Wyoming, where he and I used to explore as kids. I've been convinced for forty years that some important winter campsites would one day be unearthed at the base of that rim, but I've never found adequate evidence to back the theory up. Nor have I found funding to support a decent test excavation, due to the lack of evidence. Sort of a catch-22. Until now, maybe."

"Well, that sounds interesting," Preston quipped, then vanished as quickly as she had materialized.

Paul Barlow and Galen Davies had been close since they were toddlers, and friends for the four decades since graduating from high school. But for a brief few months, during their senior year at Ten Sleep High School, they had been anything but good friends. They had been, in fact, bitter rivals. That was because Beth had been Davies' sweetheart during much of their junior year, until Barlow stole her away the following summer. Thankfully, Davies had eventually conceded that his friend was a better match for Beth than he himself would ever be—a concession far easier to make after graduation, when Davies met Twinstar Morrison, the daughter of a Crow woman and white rancher hailing from the north end of the Big Horn Basin, near the Montana border. Twinstar, then the reigning Miss Cheyenne

Frontier Days, was possibly the most beautiful nineteen-year-old woman in Wyoming. And for some inexplicable reason she had fallen in love with Galen Davies, in those days a cocky bareback rider.

"A human rooster if ever there was one," Barlow said out loud.

Davies had told Barlow time and again that he couldn't believe his luck. His family didn't buy it, either, and at first they worried he would get hurt. Like most area ranch families, Davies' people looked down some on Native Americans. But a young man who looked like Galen—like a pock-marked, red-headed fire hydrant—was so fortunate to have the heart of a woman of Twinstar's beauty, grace, and intelligence that they came to accept her heritage.

Davies, like Paul Barlow, had long possessed a fascination with the prehistory and history of the local indigenous people. With glee, he had told his friend on more than one occasion that his four children could trace their lineage to the legendary Crow chief Arapooish, his wife's maternal great-great-grandfather. To make matters even better, in Davies' view, his entire family rode like Crow Indians.

"Thank you, Twinstar, for saving my friendship," Barlow whispered. He loved Galen Davies like the brother he'd never had, and the hurt he had caused him forty years earlier still stabbed Barlow like a shard of shame he couldn't lose.

"And praise the Lord."

8
COLLEGE

"Hello cowgirl in the sand,
Is this place at your command?"

Clifford sat on the cement landing in the stairwell midway between the third and fourth floors of Ditmer Hall, resting his feet on the first step below the landing. Seated below him, guitar in hand, his dorm buddy Hal Whitworth III was belting out his best Neil Young as Clifford jangled a tambourine, attempting to keep time.

Whitworth's appearance couldn't have been more unlike that of the straggly, former Buffalo Springfield member he was channeling. With his close-cropped and neatly groomed brown hair, pressed slacks, collared shirt, and polished penny loafers, Whitworth was a preview of the lawyer he'd told Clifford he was destined to be.

Clifford, in contrast, looked more like the majority of his and Whitworth's fellow dorm-floor mates, in faded Levi's, black-and-white high-top Pro Keds, and white T-shirt recalling a recent Mason Proffit concert at UM on its back.

"It's the woman in you that makes you want to... play this game."

Whitworth closed it out with a sweet lick on his Martin D-28 acoustic.

"That sounded really good, Hal," Clifford said.

"Thanks, Cliff. But even you singing might sound good here. The acoustics in this stairwell are incredible. Hand me that Ripple, will you?"

Clifford stooped and reached the bottle of Ripple wine down to Whitworth.

"Man, I'm confused," Clifford said, straightening up again.

"What do you mean?"

What he meant, Clifford considered, though he wasn't quite sure how to put it into words, was that he had motored full-throttle into the unfamiliar confusion of college and the cosmopolitan Twin Cities. It had shaken up his values system. Sometimes he felt nauseous with trepidation; at other times, giddy with the promise of possibility.

Clifford shrugged. "Options, opportunities, choices, decisions. They're everywhere I turn. Too many, I think. When I arrived here with my folks last September, I was so cocksure of myself. Like I discussed with them, after four years here at the university I'd have a degree in accounting. To keep from getting drafted, I'd join the National Guard when graduation puts an end to my 2-S deferment. Then I'd study to become a Certified Public Accountant and have a solid future, probably in Red Earth or maybe Mankato.

"But now I don't know what I want to do. Join the Peace Corps? Become a foreign-service agent? A golf pro? I don't know, but I do know I don't want to be a CPA."

"Well, I'm still pre-law," Whitworth said. "But that also could change."

Whitworth resumed playing, taking a stab at his long-running effort to nail Mason Williams' instrumental "Classical Gas." As his friend tickled the strings, Clifford reflected on the four-month whirlwind his first semester of campus life had been. Marijuana, mathematics, golf, Gopher games, beer guzzling, rock concerts, Bach concertos, philosophy, English lit., anti-war demonstrations, troubling questions, compelling ideas, riveting rap sessions…

Not to mention more knockout blonde and brunette girls than Clifford would ever have thought could be gathered at any one location in the world, let alone in a pair of side-by-side cities in his own home state. He'd also finally come to understand that he was a strong and handsome young brave. Having reached his full adult height the previous summer, Clifford stood six-foot-two and weighed two hundred pounds. He found that he did not go unnoticed by the girls on campus, who, to his delight, never tried to kick or hit him.

Clifford began speaking again after Whitworth silenced his guitar.

"What it is, Hal, is that I'm really not looking forward to going home for Christmas. That bothers me. But then again, sometimes I find myself wishing I could go back to living in Red Earth full-time. Things were simpler there, more straightforward."

"You'll get it figured out, Cliff," Whitworth said. "It'll feel right once you get there. I went through some of those same feelings last year after my first semester. Don't fret it, man, you'll get it straight."

"Well, thanks. Maybe it'd help if I cut back on smoking pot. I think I'll do just that... so, are you gonna hand me back that rotgut Ripple or drink it all yourself?"

***

By early evening on Christmas Day the dinner plates and silverware had been cleaned and put away. Aunt Gunde, Uncle Albert, and the three Granrud cousins were on their way home to Beaver Falls. Clifford bundled up and set off on a walk with Sir Ralph the Wonder Dog. A frigid wind battered the pair from behind as they moved along at a good clip, traveling eastward through the dark on snow-packed gravel toward the Bobby Wilson Golf Course.

On arriving, Clifford felt transformed, as he knew he would, even at this cold and snowy time of year. He had been feeling the need to absorb a fresh dose of the magic and power of the place. *Maybe so I can remember it, store it away, and take it with me wherever I go,* he considered.

For old times' sake, Clifford set out to cover the entire nine holes of the course, beginning at the first tee and ending at the ninth green. He jogged beside snowdrifts piled high in the tree lines and sprinted down fairways swept free of snow by the wind. Sir Ralph performed full-speed head dives into the drifts, coming up snow-covered and grinning.

As he trotted alongside his best friend on their favorite ground, a bolt of clarity struck Clifford: *I'm in the process of leaving Red Earth, and Red Earth is leaving me.* For the first time he grasped the truth in the saying "You can't go home again." Now that it had started, he sensed it would happen regardless of what he did or did not do. But he wanted to postpone the divorce. And the golf course, with its healing frozen sod and expansive views over the valley of the East Branch of the Red Earth River, its slopes of dark timber leafless and ghostly late on this Christmas Day, was one part of Red Earth he wanted never to lose.

At the same time, Clifford felt Red Earth would always be "home," regardless of where life took him. He knew it for certain, in fact, and considered it a serendipitous gift he was mighty thankful to receive on this holiest of days.

"Come on, Ralphie," Clifford called. "Let's go home."

The knife-edged wind buffeted Clifford's every step and burnished his cheeks as he walked westward. Behind him, the waning gibbous moon, just one day past full, balanced on the frozen eastern horizon. He felt wonderful, at peace; sad, nostalgic. He thought he heard bells coming from the Catholic church in Red Earth—*his* church in *his* town, more than six miles distant—reassuring the flock that the baby Jesus lay safe in the manger. He felt a pang of guilt for not being there. At university, Clifford had begun questioning his Christian learnings. Tonight he wanted so badly to believe them that he did.

The whirl of thoughts and feelings coalesced to make Clifford teary-eyed, filled with regret and gratitude: for the way things used to be, the way they had become, the way things would never be again… and the way they always would be.

Teardrops blew back across Clifford's cheeks toward the woolen scarf wrapped high on his neck and the plaid stocking cap pulled down over his ears. The wind, relentless, cold, uncaring, robbed his rare and precious tears, recycling their vapor into the ether of the dark and starry night.

As the pair neared the Gustafson farmstead, Sir Ralph looked up at his master with an expression of concern. Or so it seemed to Clifford.

***

Just as Hal Whitworth had predicted, Christmas break in Red Earth turned out to be the potion Clifford needed to get his feet back on solid footing. He returned to college feeling focused.

"I'm myself again, Hal," he remarked to Whitworth when the pair ran into each other in the lobby of Ditmer Hall. "Thanks for what you told me. You were right on."

In fact, as Clifford would soon understand, he had undergone a spurt of growth in maturity. His mind had grown sharp and fertile, prepped for the unexpected sowing of a seed that would grow to become a vital component of his being.

With accounting still his declared major, Clifford signed up for Anthropology 101. He had only a vague notion of what anthropology was, but his course catalog told him what was most important about it to him: Anthropology 101 would help fulfill his social-sciences elective requirements.

But what windows on the world the course opened! Never had Clifford enjoyed time in a classroom like he relished the hours spent in Anthro 101. "It's too much fun to be school," he told his mother during a phone conversation early one January evening. "I actually dread the clanging bell that ends the hour. Can you believe that?"

In Anthro 101, Clifford learned from Dr. William Magnusson, a man he quickly tagged as a genius, how members of certain cultures other than his own, both past and present, thought and behaved. How Clifford's isolated existence in Red Earth, which he had grown up considering the correct way to live, represented one of a hundred ways to think and behave, to carry out the act of being human. Dr. Magnusson, who seemed to Clifford well past the typical age of retirement, told stories about residing with the Hunkpapa Sioux in North Dakota, with the natives of Nuku Hiva in the Marquesas Archipelago of French Polynesia, and with the Bantu-speaking Matabele of Rhodesia. Magnusson's looks and dress reminded Clifford of Mr. Bredal, the proprietor of the haberdashery in Red Earth. Yet this man had witnessed and experienced things Clifford had never dreamt of, things as exciting as the tales told in the greatest adventure stories ever recorded. Clifford was sure of it.

He sat and listened, spellbound, as Magnusson related anecdotes of being captured by guerrillas in Africa; of being stranded in the doldrums at sea in an outboard-motor-driven dugout canoe with two Polynesian men. His companions, Magnusson avowed, had been confident, and wrong, about the adequate supply of gasoline on board when they'd set out for the South American mainland. The trio in the canoe survived only by catching small sailfish with coat hangers, doling out the contents of their lone can of Spam as bait, and by rationing their small supply of fresh water.

"Ultimately," Magnusson told them, "I arrived back in Minneapolis two weeks late for university classes, and found my family planning a funeral. Mine, that is. I should have known better," he admitted, wrapping up the lecture. "Polynesians tend to be overly optimistic. They detest negative thinking, often to a fault. Rest assured, I learned a lesson on that voyage and never repeated the mistake."

Later in the week, Magnusson began another lecture in equally arresting fashion.

"We as cultural detectives must strive to overcome the urge to view the indigenous through the filter of our own upbringing, our Anglo-Saxon Protestant values, despite it being human nature to do so. Yet, even as I say this, when I spent time with a people as magnificent as the Northern Cheyenne, I found it difficult not to admire them for what they were, and still are to an extent, from the perspective of my own culture and background."

Clifford's eyes widened. He sat up. *Whoa*, he thought.

Magnusson continued: "The same way in which we cannot resist admiring trumpeter swans and bald eagles for their traits of lifelong devotion to a single mate. Proud, strong, steadfast, good to one another were the Cheyenne. I could never tell for certain if a Hunkpapa or a Pacific Islander were telling me the truth in any given situation, or simply giving me the answer he thought I wanted to hear. Not so with the Cheyenne. If I asked a question of one of them, he would speak his mind with a straightforward answer. I always knew where he stood, and where I stood in relation."

Magnusson delivered the lecture between one and two p.m. on February 13, 1970, a day Clifford would eventually christen his personal "good-luck Friday the thirteenth."

Clifford knew he had arrived. *I've found my calling.*

That afternoon, after their joint three o'clock algebra class and an early supper in the Ditmer Hall cafeteria, Clifford and Hal Whitworth III drove north from Minneapolis in the latter's beautiful bronze, two-door 1963 Chevrolet Impala Super Sport. A series of suburban streets led the young men out of the city and into the freedom of a winter-whipped spread of farm country.

"A few more birch trees here than around my place in Red Earth," Clifford declared. "Otherwise it looks pretty similar."

"Yep, same with Rochester," Whitworth agreed.

The news coming over the car radio reported that four dozen people had been killed by a man-eating tiger outside New Delhi, in India.

"Jesus," Whitworth said.

Between them, over the span of four hours spent driving around, listening to tunes, and looking at things in the dark, Clifford and his friend downed a six-pack of Grain Belt beer and made a serious dent in a fifth of Bacardi dark rum. Country-rock blared from the speakers serving Whitworth's recently installed eight-track stereo system. Clifford attempted to out-shout the music.

"Count money, help people figure their taxes, taxes that build bombs to burn women and children. That sounds like a helluva way to make a living. Doesn't it, Hal?"

"Yeah, that would be weird stuff."

"This anthropology ..." Clifford slurred. A full minute passed before he resumed speaking, his attention having migrated to the story being told in song about a Glendale Train. "What is this?" he finally blurted out.

"My cousin in San Francisco sent it to me. It's a bootleg tape from a concert there, New Riders of the Purple Sage. Stan told me that's Grateful Dead's Jerry Garcia on pedal steel."

"Wow, it's good! Anyway, this anthro. It's something I think I can sink my teeth into. You know what I mean? Maybe you don't, but... I don't know, it's hard to explain. But it feels right."

"That's groovy, Cliff," Whitworth yelled. "I'm glad for you. I don't really know what anthropology is, but maybe you'll explain it to me. I'm now thinking myself of getting out of pre-law, even though my dad will shit bricks. I'm considering recreation. Cliff, I want to be a national park ranger. Can you imagine it? As soon as the Whitworths of Rochester pick a full name for their newborn son, they tack 'Attorney at Law' onto the end of it. What'll they say when they hear I plan to feed bears and fight fires in Yosemite? I don't know if I'll make it, but I want to try."

"I definitely think you should do your own thing," Clifford said. "Hey—Hal?"

"Yeah?"

"I've also been getting into languages and linguistics lately. You know what English is? It's a hard language full of stiff vowels and rigid consonants. Not as bad as German, though. Now, I've given this a lot of thought. French is arrogant, like a spitting, guttural throat clearing. But Spanish—ah, Spanish. It's beautiful… the language of gods, of the angels, of lovers. I'm gonna get fluent in it."

"Damn, Cliff, that *is* beautiful. But what I want to know is where dirty sayings like 'pissed off' come from."

"Yeah. Good point. What about 'Fuckin' A'?"

Hal laughed. "Shit up the creek."

That got them both giggling.

"Pissant," Clifford offered.

Whitworth roared. "I'm going to write a dictionary!"

"Hey, Hal, not to change the subject, but you'll tell me if I ever have hair growing out of my ears, wontcha? Like Dr. Dodson does?" Clifford asked, referring to the young men's algebra professor.

"Don't worry, Cliff, you're an Indian. You never will. You'll probably never even have to shave."

"Okay, but promise me anyway. Okay?"

"Sure, okay, I promise."

Whitworth began giggling again, and Clifford joined in. They were laughing so hard, at nothing in particular and anything in general, that they couldn't stop.

"Hal, help. I gotta take a leak."

"Me, too. My teeth are swimming."

Whitworth began slowing the car, intending to pull into a farm driveway he'd spotted just ahead to the right. But he misjudged the turn on the gravel road's snow-packed surface and skidded past the driveway. He managed to keep the fishtailing car on the road, but its rear end swung out and the right rear fender made contact with a complex of mailboxes standing just beyond the driveway.

After bringing the Chevy to a standstill, Whitworth backed up and shone the headlights on the wreckage.

"Shit, Cliff."

"Yeah. Shit."

The main wooden mailbox, formerly shaped like a cow's head, had been designed so the mailman would open the bovine's mouth to deposit mail. Now the smashed-in left side of the cow's face made it look more like a cat than a cow. And what previously had hovered high above the mailbox, attached to a tall pole—a wooden duck with "AIRMAIL" painted on its sides—lay horizontal in the snow-filled borrow ditch. The pole had been snapped in half, and the quacker's whirl-a-gig wings had flown some fifteen feet away from their body.

"I remember passing by here last spring, Cliff, on the way to a biology field trip outside Wyoming. Wonderful thing to see. Now we knocked it over."

"What you mean 'we,' white man? And what do you mean 'Wyoming'?"

"You know, the town. Wyoming, Minnesota. Not far from here. Just north of Forest Lake."

"Really? I know it's a state, one I like the sound of."

"Well, duh. Colorado's a state, too. Man, I feel bad about those mailboxes. I bet it was a source of pride for some dairy man. He probably worked on them in the winter. After the cows were milked and before they needed milked again."

"Let's take a leak and figure out what to do," Clifford said. "Or if we should do anything."

It was almost midnight and no lights shone from inside the farmhouse belonging to the destroyed mailboxes. The house sat a good hundred yards away from the snow-whitened road. With the Chevy's motor running, Whitworth cut the headlights and, after Clifford had exited, reached over to lock the passenger-side door. Then he got out, pushed down the lock on his own side, and closed the door.

"Hal?" Clifford said, relieving himself as a glacial north wind blasted his back and burned his bare ears. He could see the lights of the city reflecting off low cloud cover, illuminating the southern distance. To his left, a blanketed horse resting its head on the wooden crosspiece of a section of corral looked in his direction. *What's that horse doing outside the barn on a night like this?*

"What, Cliff?"

"What'd you just do?"

"Locked the car, why?"

"Well it's still runnin'. Why'd you do that? The keys are in it!"

"Shit, Cliff. SHIT! I spaced out. I was thinking... well, I'm not sure what I was thinking."

"Dumfrey! Do you have any other keys?"

"No."

"What're we gonna do?"

"I don't know."

"Break a window?"

"No way!"

A short silence followed. "Well, then, I guess we'd better go face the music before we freeze to death," Clifford decided. "The wind chill must be forty below."

"Call triple A?" Whitworth ventured. "Are you a member?"

"No. Farmers can fix anything. That dairyman will get our car doors open somehow... once he gets over being PO'd at us for getting him out of bed and smashing his mailboxes."

"Fuckin' A, Clifford, you pissant!" Whitworth yelled, and with that took off in his leather penny loafers and neatly pressed attire. Clifford ran to catch up with him, clad only in T-shirt, blue jeans, and tennis shoes.

Side by side, screaming with laughter as the bitter wind flailed at their exposed skin, Clifford and Whitworth sprinted to the dairy farmer's house. They banged on the door for five frigid minutes before lights finally flickered on in the kitchen.

9

THE HUNTER

Pete Patterson stood tall in his trophy room. His chest-out, gut-in, back-straight posture hinted at a military career, though it was already twenty years behind him. So did the brown-and-green camo fatigues he wore. With trained patience, he revisited his strategy, making marks on his mental checklist, while admiring with his eyes and feeling with his left index finger the sharp metal point tipping the arrow shaft he held in his right hand. He thought back over the course of the past twenty-two autumns, when he had gone to great lengths and expense to travel the high mountains and wind-buffeted prairies of Wyoming in pursuit of big game. His fascination with stalking large animals and killing them using only arrows and a recurve bow had over time evolved into obsession. Four years ago, the obsession had finally cost him his marriage.

"Oh, well," he whispered, recalling the tumultuous divorce period.

The results of his efforts were impressive. He smiled as he surveyed the largest of his parlor walls—the one opposite the picture window offering an unobstructed view of the foothills and high forests of the Big Horn Range—and his gaze rested on the head of a bull moose. Its huge antlers boasted a daunting outside spread of fifty-one inches, according to measurements Patterson himself had taken. To the right of that hung the head mounts of two bull elk; next, those of a brace of trophy white-tailed deer and an immense mule deer; and, finally, three pronghorns. Patterson's gaze moved on to inspect the full body mount of a pure white Rocky Mountain goat. The animal stood lifelike on a simulated habitat platform the hunter had constructed of plywood, green indoor/outdoor carpet, and small boulders he'd hefted into the bed of his Chevy pickup truck during summer scouting-and-camping forays in the Big Horns. Next to the goat, which Patterson had bagged in the southern Beartooth Range in the fall of 1968, stood a burly, thick-bodied bighorn sheep, occupying a habitat stand similar to that of the goat's. The sheep he'd killed not far away, as well, in the Absaroka Mountains, a few miles northwest of Cody.

Patterson's favorite display was the grizzly bear, which stood over eight feet tall and wore a fierce snarl. With its horrifyingly long and stout front legs and sinister-looking claws, the bruin reached out and down at a mountain lion, itself measuring nearly nine feet from its nose to the tip of its tail. Frozen in movement, the cat charged the ursine monster. Patterson had killed the two beasts seven years and some four hundred miles apart, yet he'd realized as soon as he shot the cougar how badly he wanted the bear. It hadn't taken him long to envisage what the exhibit would look like once he'd accomplished his mission: just as it looked now.

Patterson had killed the grizzly bear the previous autumn on the Beartooth Plateau, at the base of high barren peaks ranging from domes to serrated sawtooths. He'd held a legitimate Montana license, which he won in a lottery after putting in for it twelve years straight. His home state held no legal hunt for grizzlies, but Patterson didn't let that prevent him from killing the bear on the Wyoming side of the state line. "All of my collection must come, will come, from Wyoming," he whispered often, like a mantra. Caliper measurements he'd taken on the bear's massive head revealed that it might be a Montana state record. Yet he had resisted sending the figures in to the state's fish and wildlife agency or to the Boone and Crockett Club. Not because he, and only he, knew the bear had been killed illegally in Wyoming, but because he didn't want people coming around sniffing, asking a lot of questions.

Finally, Patterson's roving eyes found the body-length mirror hanging on the parlor's north wall. He inspected his reflection, and liked what he saw. Barely an ounce of excess baggage. Two decades of rough-country hunting and thousands of hours spent training and keeping in shape for the hunt had him, easing into his seventh decade, as fit as he'd been at thirty. Okay, his knees weren't quite what they once were, but other than that Patterson noticed few effects of aging.

"All the large mammals but two," he whispered, with satisfied determination. "And I'll get my bison over on the Pritchard Ranch outside Gillette this September. That's a sure bet."

10
DIRECTION

"I'm digging anthropology, Alice," Clifford punned. "*Really digging it.*"

Alice Barton, Clifford's fellow anthro major from Connecticut, strolled beside him as they made their way across the UM campus. A chilly October drizzle dampened their cotton clothing, but not Clifford's spirits. "And I like Dr. Mills. I'm eating it up: Ramapithicus, Zinjanthropus, *Homo habilis*, *Homo erectus*, *Homo sapiens*, Neanderthal man, Cro-Magnon man, the controversies and hoaxes surrounding Louis and Mary Leakey, Thor Heyerdahl, Piltdown Man... I feel like it's giving me direction somehow. Even if it's not the direction my mom and pop would like to see me go in. Physical anthropology is quite a stretch from certified public accounting."

"Yes, I'd say so," the tall blonde said. "Wait a minute." She paused, nearly closing her eyes in concentration. "They do have this in common: P-A—physical anthropology and public accounting."

"That's good, Alice," Clifford said, laughing. "Maybe I'll tell my parents I'm still planning to become a CPA, but 'neglect' to tell them the letters stand for 'crazy physical anthropologist.' What about you? Are you still going on to grad school next year?"

"I think so. I like linguistics a lot, so I may go that path. But I'm also really enjoying Plains Indians 602. Dr. Magnusson is an amazing man. The class is giving us a good taste of what graduate school will be like, with us the only two undergrads in there."

"I totally agree. But when you and I got better scores on last week's essay test than all but two of the grad students, the other six probably wished we weren't there."

"Probably so," Barton said, giggling. "Let's go visit with our fellow students right now."

The pair entered the Social Sciences Building, climbed the stairs to the second floor, and walked into Room 203. They each pulled up a chair at a long wooden table, joining the other eight class members. All were greeted at once by Dr. Magnusson, dressed in jacket and tie as usual. He began the day's lecture by explaining that Minnesota and the upper Great Lakes region had been the Cheyennes' ancestral homeland. Not until the late 1600s or early 1700s, he said, after moving west on foot to the Missouri River country and obtaining horses from other tribes, did the Cheyenne adopt the lifestyle of the Plains Indians and migrate toward their eventual home in the high country east of the Rocky Mountains.

This is so far out, Clifford thought.

"It's like magic," Clifford told Barton after the class had ended. "I myself was brought by coincidence, or by God or the Great Spirit, back to Minnesota from the Great Plains to be raised." He drew a mental picture of his distant ancestors camping on the future grounds of the Bobby Wilson Golf Course. In those prehistoric times the uplands would have been prairie covered in tall grasses, he imagined, and possibly utilized by the indigenous people as an overlook for spotting game moving through the thick timber below in the valley of the East Branch of the Red Earth River.

"I've told you before about the Bobby Wilson Golf Course back home—how much I love the place, the ground there? That course, and even golf itself, is magic for me. If a golf course can be good medicine, that's what Bobby Wilson is for me."

"I don't see why it can't be," Barton said.

As Clifford had begun to understand earlier, and was now learning in greater detail, all of his favorite, larger-than-life historic Native American warriors had been born on the high plains. So, too, had his own biological parents and grandparents, and their parents before them.

"The Great Plains region of southeast Montana was the ultimate homeland of the Northern Cheyenne. It bugs me that I've never spent time there. Other than my first four years, which I have almost no memory of."

"You were born in Montana?"

"Yep, that's what they tell me. Near Lame Deer." Clifford felt himself being drawn, like iron filings to a magnet, in the direction from which he had come. "I have to get back there. I vow that I will. Alice, I also know without question that anthropology and I are a perfect fit. I feel sort of like the medical student who dreams of discovering the cure for an 'incurable' disease. Only in my case, more and more, I find myself wondering how the present may hold clues to the past. And how still-covered prehistoric secrets might reveal ways people could live better lives today. I think I'm getting kind of obsessed," he admitted. "But you know, I don't care much for the stuffy ivory-tower types, like Dr. Franklin and Harold Penfold."

"I know what you mean. Exactly what you mean. They're sort of the opposite of down-to-earth. Up-to-sky, maybe?"

"What I am going to become," Clifford announced, the moment before he and Barton were to part ways in front of Ditmer Hall, "is a blue-collar archaeologist. One who gets his hands dirty on a regular basis. Early in my career, at least."

"How'd you come up with that vision?" Barton asked. "Do you have a role model in mind?"

"Well, yeah, as a matter of fact I do. There's this professor at Nebraska I've heard about by the name of Paul Barlow. Dr. Mills says he's famous for his work on the prehistoric Plains tribes. I read a profile of him a few weeks back in the *Journal of North American Archaeology*. He grew up on a ranch in Wyoming, where he spent much of his boyhood doing amateur archaeology. 'Pot Hunter Turned Pro' was the title of the article. From what I know of him, he's someone I'd like to be like. I need to meet him and talk to him. Pick his brain."

***

"Dr. Mills," Clifford began, "it's May already. I'm graduating this month, you know. And I'm ready to get out West." Sitting in front of the desk in Dr. John Mills' quiet office, Clifford looked his mentor in the eye—his good right eye, the one not covered with a black patch. "It's been great taking classes and learning the subject. I feel like I know so much more about the human condition than I did three or four years ago, like I understand the world better. But I'm not ready to go right to grad school. I haven't done any field work at all. Nada. I want to get my hands dirty, smell the sage, find some stone points."

I'm on a roll, Clifford thought.

"I wanna dig some artifacts, spend time typing them and inspecting chipping scars through a magnifying lens. I want to sweat and swing a rock bar, hump a shovel, earn the good stuff deep down like I've heard and read about. I'm ready. Can you find me something, Dr. Mills? I don't even care if I get paid or not. I just need room and board is all."

"I have no doubt you're ready, Clifford," Mills said. He scratched his bowling-ball-smooth scalp just above the left ear, playing in the same vicinity with the elastic band securing his eye patch. "Let me make a call or two. I knew last year you were ready. In fact, when I first met you three years ago, I could see you had a fire in you. I've fanned the flames some, perhaps, but for the most part I've just stood back and watched your blaze explode."

"Thanks, Dr. Mills. I appreciate anything you can do."

A few minutes after Clifford had exited the office, Mills dialed long-distance and reached the switchboard at Chadron State College.

"Listing, please?" asked the operator.

"Conrad Hillary in Anthropology," Mills said. The man he requested to speak to had become a great friend of Mills during their graduate-school days at the University of Nebraska. Hillary taught archaeology and cultural anthropology at Chadron State, a small college in northwestern Nebraska.

"Hello?"

"Rad," Mills said, on hearing Hillary's voice. "It's Mills. I thought I remembered this was your office hour. How are you?"

"Great, pardner," Hillary wheezed through his sixty-three-year-old lungs.

As Mills knew, the tightening of Hillary's breathing apparatus resulted from some fifty years of cigarette smoking and at least four years of recent marijuana use. Yet Hillary possessed a mule-like endurance that awed Mills. He figured Hillary could walk for a week without sleep, food, or water, and may have done so on occasion. Mills pictured the sexagenarian hippie—the habit he had of pushing his rectangular-framed, wire-rim glasses back up the bridge of his nose when he was excited; his long gray hair tied back in a rubber-banded ponytail; the way he pulled with pursed lips on a Camel straight.

"What's up?" Hillary gurgled.

"I've got a young fellow back here who needs some field training. I think you'd find him interesting. He'd be a good hand. Plus, you'd like him. Have you got anything going?"

"As it happens, I do, Pedro. You called at just the right time. I'm lookin' for some diggers. Got a call last week from Barlow, over in Lincoln." He paused to cough, covering the phone receiver with his hand. Then he resumed speaking and didn't pause again until he'd said what he had to say. "Paul says he finally landed some funds for that Sleeping Dog site, not far south of Shell Canyon on the west slope of the Big Horns. Got seven grand from Wyoming state parks and snatched another five thou' from Nebraska's state historical society. Wants me to supervise. Yeah, I know, I'm s'posed to be retiring here soon, but I'm not gonna kick this chance in the butt. Paul says he's confident we're gonna find Paleo Man there and that he has a gut feeling it could be the most significant site north of Clovis. That's in New-way-vo May-hee-ko, *mi amigo*, and it don't very often get as good as it got down there. Bison, camel, horse, mammoth, you name it. But hell, Jeofredo, you know all that better than I do. If Paul Barlow says this site's gonna be big, it's gonna be big, and you can bet your bottom peso on it."

"Yes, sir," Mills said, "that I can. I'm glad Paul finally got the funding. He was awfully excited about that site's potential last September at Buck Creek."

"Oh, yeah, sorry I missed it. Like I told you, had to be out of town for my niece's wedding. You no-goods all come to my country and I blow the territory. By the way, do you know what else happened in Clovis, Julio?"

"What's that?"

"It's where the god of rock 'n' roll recorded 'Peggy Sue.' And a bunch of other songs. Betcha didn't know that."

"No, Rad, I sure didn't."

But Mills knew full well that Conrad Hillary made no bones about being the world's number one fan of the late, great Buddy Holly.

As he put the phone down, he wondered what Clifford would make of his old friend…

***

"A colleague of mine in Nebraska told me about this place," Mills explained. "Twice. It's a site he calls 'Sleeping Dog.' He told me about it once at the Plains Conference two years ago in Lincoln, and again last fall at Buck Creek Rendezvous."

"What's that?" Clifford inquired.

Mills paused to fork up a big bite of green-chile enchilada and wash it down with an even bigger gulp of margarita. Earlier, he and Clifford had departed the UM campus in Mills' Dodge Monaco station wagon. To Clifford the car looked very odd, with its off-green color and faux wood panels lining the sides. But it rode like a dream and had delivered the pair safely to their destination, Rosa Maria's Fine Mexican American Food and Billiards in Turtle Lake.

"Mmmm, that's good," Mills said. "This *is* a strange place for a great Mexican restaurant, isn't it? But here it is, serving food every bit as hot and tasty and spicy as any I've dined on in Arizona or Texas. Or in Sinaloa or Nayarit, for that matter. I bring friends and family here often."

Clifford nodded in agreement, his mouth too full of chile rellenos to speak.

"Now, what was it you asked me?" Mills continued. "Oh, yeah, Buck Creek. It's an annual fall get-together of no-goods over on the Pine Ridge in northwest Nebraska, outside Chadron. The Plains archaeology world is small, you know, and a big bunch of us convene there every September. It's like a gathering of modern-day mountain men, buffalo butcherers, ladies of ill repute, and other questionable characters, mostly archaeologists. But we do let in a few stratigraphic geologists."

Mills' lame attempt at humor drew a blank stare from Clifford.

"Well," Mills continued after a pause, "after having a look at the petroglyphs and pictographs an old boyhood friend of his had uncovered in the lower canyon of Sleeping Dog Creek—that's over on the west slope of the Big Horn Mountains in north-central Wyoming—my friend, Dr. Paul Barlow, said he was more convinced than ever of something he'd long believed: that wonderful things await discovery below the ground surface in that vicinity. For more than two years after that visit, Barlow said, he'd regarded the Sleeping Dog site as his ace in the hole. Whenever he wasn't lecturing, sleeping, eating, or reading, he was usually working on an angle to obtain funding to do the work that must be done to prove his theory."

Trying to remain calm, Clifford marveled at what sounded like an extraordinary coincidence in the making.

"I've read about Dr. Barlow. He sounds like quite a guy."

"He is. 'Wrangler turned researcher,' they call him. He rarely wears anything other than cowboy boots and western shirts. A lot of my colleagues swear he has X-ray vision; that he can see beneath the surface of unbroken ground and tell you what's down there. I know archaeologists who are agnostics and atheists—men and women so scientifically retentive they believe almost nothing until they see it with their own eyes—who wonder if it isn't true."

Clifford tried hard to concentrate, but this talk about Dr. Paul Barlow had sidetracked him. He felt on the verge of hyperventilating. Barlow was reputed to be a genius, though a modest and unpretentious man who would rather spend an evening BS-ing with a couple of rancher pals or a group of students than speaking to a roomful of academics.

"Okay," Clifford finally confessed, "you might find this interesting, or even amazing. Several weeks ago I told Alice Barton that I was going to pattern myself, professionally speaking, after Paul Barlow. And that I wanted to meet him and talk to him. Now it's starting to sound like it might actually happen."

"It's very possible," Mills said, his eye twinkling. "I've known Paul a long time. He's a good friend and an outstanding archaeologist, but he puts his pants on one leg at a time, just like you and me. And he always drinks too much Jim Beam at Buck Creek. His only binge of the year, he swears. Last September he was going around telling the Sleeping Dog story to anyone who would listen, and even to some who wouldn't, on the outside chance they had some spare research bucks floating around. Or might at least know where some were ready to take flight."

Clifford couldn't sit still. No one, not even Dr. John Mills, could understand how he felt at the prospect of working in Wyoming under Paul Barlow. *I know that's what Dr. Mills is leading up to.*

"So, how would you like to join the crew that'll be breaking ground at Sleeping Dog Creek this summer?" Mills asked. "Early next month is when the skeleton bunch will start work."

"Sign me up, boss," Clifford said, his eyes wide. "I'm your man."
Wish I could leave right now!

Clifford wondered if at least part of the explanation for his strong attraction to the historic Cheyenne country awaited him at the Sleeping Dog site. Perhaps he was needed there to give perspective, or to make sure everything was treated with proper respect, or for other reasons he wouldn't recognize until he arrived.

"Clifford?" Mills queried a bit later on, his voice hoarse from toasting Clifford's future and downing his second tequila hooker.

"Yes, Dr. Mills?" The tequila had come on the heels of two margaritas each, so neither he nor Mills were feeling any pain. The fermented juice of the agave had calmed Clifford's nerves in some respects, but fired him up in others.

"Let's see how you are with a pool cue. Proficiency at pocket billiards is a mandatory skill of a Rocky Mountain field archaeologist, you know."

"Really?" Clifford was just bubbly enough, and Mills looked so serious, that he swallowed it cue stick, eight ball, and leather pockets.

"Naw, but it can't hurt. And Cliff?"

"Yeah?"

"You call me John now. You're graduating. You're not my student anymore. You're an aspiring archaeologist. You are my friend and associate."

Clifford grinned. "Okay, sure, uh... John." He felt proud, shy, and happy all at once.

Mills pulled out his driver's license and gave it to the attendant at the billiards window, and was handed a rack of balls in return. He and Clifford walked over to table number six, where Mills poured the contents of the rack onto the table. The ivory balls clanked loudly as they banged into one another and onto the green-felt-covered slate surface.

"Grab that white container and shake a good pile of talcum powder into the palm of your hand, Clifford," Mills said.

Clifford grabbed the container off the rail as instructed and shook some powder into his open hand. Then Mills bowed, offering Clifford his hairless dome of a head.

"Have at 'er, Cliff. Dust that bub up good for luck. Just don't pull off my eye patch. You'd blow your tacos if you saw what's under it."

Clifford obliged, massaging the fine white powder into his professor-friend's bald scalp. It got him laughing so hard that he doubled over and bumped heads with Mills.

"Is eight ball your game?" Mills asked.

"Yeah, I guess," Clifford said, sounding unsure. Yet he racked the balls with a deftness hinting at more than a casual acquaintance with the pool table. And sure enough, after Mills broke the rack and Clifford took over, the young CPA-to-be ran the table. "Eight ball in the side pocket," he said, then finished the job.

"You sly devil," Mills commented. "I think you've played before."

"Yeah, well, I did grow up with a table in the basement." He stopped to laugh before continuing. "When I was a junior in high school, I actually played my geometry teacher for a grade. He thought, rightly, that I wasn't applying myself in class. Somehow, the topic of billiards came up one day, and I told him I played some. Mr. Fredrickson was his name. He said, 'If you can beat me in a game of call-shot to a hundred, I'll give you an "A" on the final. That'd help your overall grade quite a bit.'

"So, we arranged to meet a couple of evenings later at the Curly Cue Tip in downtown Red Earth. I beat him a hundred to ninety-seven. I imagine if word had gotten out, something like that could've gotten Mr. Fredrickson in trouble. Maybe even fired. But I guess he thought if I knew my angles well enough to shoot pool like that, then I had an intuitive feel for geometry. Or something like that."

"Sounds like a wise man to me," said Mills, who commenced displaying some talent with the cue stick himself.

After the first blowout game that went Clifford's way, Mills and his pool shark of an archaeological protegé partnered up and began shooting eight ball with the angels, not once yielding the table to another team until they chose to, at around ten-thirty. That was when Mills declared he needed to get back to Minneapolis.

"Jenny's gonna be pacing the floor," he said. "The twins graduate from Carlton tomorrow, and we need to leave in the morning by six-thirty."

"You have twins? I didn't know that. Boys or girls?"

"Boys, both of 'em. Identical, or so I'm told. Bill and Bob."

"The Mills Brothers."

"Yep, they've heard that one before."

"One of my mom's favorite groups," Clifford said. "I have to get up early, too. We're hosting the Golden Gopher Big Ten Championships this weekend over at Theodore Wirth. I'm matched in a foursome tomorrow with guys from three other schools—Iowa, Michigan State, and Purdue. We, Minnesota, have a pretty good chance of taking the overall title."

"Best of luck to you," Mills said.

As the pair motored back toward the lights of the city, Clifford turned to the one-eyed Mills sitting at the wheel. "Dr. Mills... uh, John, how the heck do you have the depth perception to shoot pool so good?"

"It's all in the talc rub, Clifford, the talc rub."

11
CALDERARA

He loved this more than anything: flying like a bird, looking down on the desiccated sand-dune country unfolding beneath him. He gazed at a lake, shimmering in the distance, that wasn't there, a high-desert mirage fashioned by waves of stored heat released by the cooling earth.

His legs hadn't worked since the accident. The hardest part of operating the Starhook ultralight trike was getting up to and into it. Once he managed that, the rest came easy—flicking the electric starter, taking off, piloting the craft. In the air, he felt as mobile as an able-bodied person. In fact, he felt even *more* so than those who were grounded and lacked wings to fly.

From his modest spread on the western outskirts of Worland, Sal Calderara would lift off and soar above the dune fields, often close to the ground. By traveling west, over untamed country, he often saw and was seen by no one. This he liked. He enjoyed being alone when flying, just him and pronghorns, coyotes, and wild horses below and, sharing his airspace, red-tailed hawks and golden eagles.

Not yet on the market when Calderara had acquired it in the summer of 1971, the Starhook had become his through sheer luck. The NASA engineer who developed it in the late 1960s, constructing the airframe of aluminum and the landing gear of fiberglass composite, happened to be a good friend of his brother's in the Houston area, where Calderara grew up and much of his family still lived.

A single-cylinder, two-stroke snowmobile engine powered the weight-shift ultralight, delivering nearly twenty horsepower and driving a composite propeller. The craft took off and flew at about twenty-five miles per hour.

"The perfect speed," Calderara whispered to himself. "Just ideal."

This evening he stayed aloft for more than an hour.

PART 2
BACK TO THE WEST

12
THE MENTOR

Conrad Hillary leaned against a pillar in the baggage-claim wing of the Billings airport. High over his head he held a white cardboard sign with "CLIFFORD G." scribbled in big red felt-pen letters. As it turned out, the sign was unnecessary. After disembarking from the plane and walking down to baggage claim, Clifford immediately recognized Hillary, even before the writing on the sign registered in his brain. Mills' description of him nailed it: gray hair pulled back and wrapped with a rubber band into a long ponytail, Ben Franklin-style wire-rim glasses balanced on a hawkish nose, and a cigarette hanging from his lips.

"Where the hell'd you get a name like Gustafson, pardner?" Hillary wheezed, moments after Clifford had introduced himself. Hillary squinted at him through his rectangular wire-rims.

"I was adopted when I was four, after my parents died," Clifford said. "I grew up in Minnesota."

"Ah, so that's how you wound up at university in Minneapolis with that no-good scoundrel Mills? I see. I suppose he 'neglected' to tell me you were an America Indian on purpose. Figured such an oversight would aggravate me no end, which it does. Where were you born?"

"Not too far from here, in Lame Deer, Montana. I'm Northern Cheyenne."

"Well, that sounds about right from the looks of you. Hey, we better get on up the road. Daylight's burnin'. Tell ya' what, though. Let's take the scenic route."

Once Clifford had grabbed his checked duffel bag from the carousel, he and Hillary left the terminal. The latter hacked and spewed phlegm as they walked toward the short-term parking lot.

"Why'd you fly?" Hillary asked. "Don't you own a car?"

"No," Clifford said. "I've never needed one. Never had a problem hitching rides with friends back and forth to college. And I walked or bicycled anywhere I needed to go on campus. But now it's starting to sound pretty good. Maybe I'll buy a new Cadillac with all the money I make this summer."

At that, Hillary gave a snicker that descended into an uncontrollable coughing fit. When it finally subsided, he and Clifford climbed into Hillary's pickup truck, and the driver pulled the bright-red Ford four-by-four with State of Wyoming license plates out of the parking lot.

After finding his way to the outskirts of town and onto the relatively quiet Pryor Road, Hillary pointed at a sign reading "Petroglyph Cave 5 miles."

"That's a state site," he said. "Got trashed by keggers and graffiti back in the sixties, but they're improving it now." He coughed and cleared his throat, then spat out the window. "Archaeological keystone site for this part of the world, really. Your man in Minnesota, Bill Magnusson, was one of the chief investigators."

"Oh, yeah. I remember Dr. Magnusson talking about that."

"Yep, they dialed in the region's diagnostics there at Petroglyph Cave way back in the thirties. WPA project."

"WPA?"

"Works Progress Admin. Part of FDR's make-work strategy during the Great Depression. Plenty of good public works, archaeological and otherwise, got done during those down times," Hillary opined, then launched into another coughing session.

Concerned about all the wheezing and hacking, Clifford hoped his new friend wouldn't expire en route to the Sleeping Dog site.

"Don't know how I'd get there," he inadvertently said out loud.

"Huh?" Hillary grunted.

"Oh, nothing. Sorry, I was just thinking."

"This is the heart of Crow country, son, so keep your Cheyenne head low," Hillary teased, glancing sideways at Clifford.

The prodding went right over Clifford's head. Eyes agape and lips parted, he was too busy absorbing the splendor of the terrain unfolding before him, taking it all in. He could see the road they were following as it twisted ahead of them over a high butte approximately a mile to the southwest. A dust-raising herd of pronghorns raced along parallel to the road, about fifty yards out. Shadow-throwing pine trees hugged the north-facing slopes of the surrounding hills and buttes. The silvery glint of sagebrush, individual leaves dancing in the breeze, softened the landscape's hard, dry edges. With his window rolled down, Clifford inhaled the essence of the high plains, a heady mix of juniper, sage, pine, prickly pear flowers, cow dung, the previous summer's forest fires, sandstone dust, and more.

A gangly coyote sitting on the right-hand shoulder of the road grinned as the pair drove past. To Clifford its expression looked halfway between mad and embarrassed.

"Ko-YO-tay massa'ne," said Hillary, attempting to mix Spanish and the Cheyenne language. "That kyote must be deranged to sit there like that."

After a few moments and several more miles had passed, Clifford pointed out his window. "Is that a wild horse? I've read they live in this part of the country."

"Nope," Hillary replied. "That's someone's Appaloosa. The Nez Perce bred 'em up in Oregon and Idaho. There's a few of them around the other reservations these days. Tough pony, good to ride in rough country."

"It seemed like he was staring at us as we drove by."

"They're a smart horse. Maybe *she* was."

The pair approached the tiny Crow Indian settlement of Pryor, visible in the near distance. Clifford felt a euphoria coming on, not unlike that which embraced him when he ran late in the day on the Bobby Wilson Golf Course, Sir Ralph the Wonder Dog at his side. To his surprise and confusion, tears welled in his eyes and his breathing quickened.

I've just returned home, for the very first time.

"You gotta see this, Pedro," Hillary said, snapping Clifford out of his reverie.

Hillary steered the rig into a parking space next to a small wooden signpost reading "Chief Plenty Coup Memorial." The two got out of the truck, slammed the doors shut, and strolled up to an excavation adjacent to the parking lot. "Visitor center under construction,"

Hillary read aloud as he eyed a hand-written note thumbtacked to the park kiosk's bulletin board. "Projected finish date: June 1974."

"Jesus H. Bartlett, that's a year from now," he muttered. "Those god-damn lazy Indians…" Then he grinned at Clifford. "I'm just kidding, you know. I do that a lot. I try to restrain myself, but I'm a hopeless case. It's the State of Montana, not the Crow Tribe, that's responsible for the slow going here. I remember about a decade ago a group of Crows threatened to sue the state for neglecting its duty to protect this place, which the Indians regard as sacred, sacred, sacred. An acquaintance of mine, Herbert Medicine Crow, told me that back then cattle were treading on Plenty Coups' grave, and pigs were desecrating the Medicine Spring. Disgusting. Absolutely unacceptable."

No other human beings were there to share the memorial grounds with Clifford Gustafson and Conrad Hillary early that fine late-May morning, when a flowering explosion of spring was arriving on the heels of a tough winter and wet, windy April. They ambled about, taking their time, looking across at the high, protective sandstone rim rising a half mile to the north. Turning around, Hillary pointed south at a line of distant hills. "Those, my young friend, are the Castle Buttes of the Pryor Range. Mountains chock-full of evidence left behind by the Crows and their predecessors. A hundred years ago and more they saw plenty of skirmishes between the Crows and your people and the Blackfeet."

Clifford glanced at his companion, who was gazing far, deep into the distance, as if in a trance. Clifford understood that Hillary could see things he himself couldn't. *Not just yet, but soon enough I will.*

A flock of chickadees flitted in and out of a confused clump of box elders. "That bird was Plenty Coups' personal good medicine," Hillary remarked.

"Neat," said Clifford. He studied the sunlight reflecting off Pryor Creek as it danced beneath the shrubs. He listened to the soothing sound of the water, whispering in riffles over rocks and pebbles. After a few seconds, he imagined the feeling of the cold water running through his earthly body.

"It's strange," he finally said. "I feel complete here, or almost complete, in a way I've never known. What do you think it means, Dr. Hillary?"

"I think it means it's good we came here."

Though the structure had been standing for many decades, the corners of the stout, hand-hewn log house in which the great Crow chief had once resided looked square as square can be. Nearby, Plenty Coups' grave, smothered under fresh Memorial Day bouquets and wreaths, lay beneath a large American flag waving atop a tall metal pole. The vision filled Clifford with pride and patriotism, with an appreciation that he was both an American Indian and a native-born U.S. citizen. He liked this spot a great deal, and he liked Hillary for bringing him to see it.

Clifford studied the words etched into a wooden sign fronting the grave. They explained that Plenty Coups was born near present-day Billings in 1848 and died in 1932. They also detailed the story of the time the chief was chosen to represent all Indians of the nation in a 1921 ceremony at the Tomb of the Unknown Soldier in Washington, D.C. "For the Indians of America," Clifford read aloud from the sign, quoting Plenty Coups on that occasion, "I call upon the Great Spirit... that the dead should not have died in vain, the war might end, and peace be purchased by the blood of red men and white." The text went on to reveal that Plenty Coups' brief speech had brought tears to the eyes of more than one tough old Indian-fighting cavalryman in attendance.

"Whew!" Clifford managed to say as he and Hillary strolled back toward the parking area.

"I agree with you wholeheartedly, son," Hillary said, wheezing. "Let's kick that damn Ford square in the butt. Daylight's a-burnin'."

"Yessir," replied Clifford, his spirits high.

"How 'bout a libation, chief?" Hillary asked as they neared the truck.

"Sure, I guess," said Clifford uncertainly.

Hillary opened the red Thermos cooler resting toward the front of the truck's uncovered bed. His large right hand dived in and emerged holding the necks of two dripping bottles of Coors beer.

"Banquet beer," Hillary proclaimed, handing Clifford one of the bottles. "You'll find an opener in the glove box there."

Beer in hand, they jumped into the truck. Hillary fired the engine, navigated out of the parking lot, and sped west on the rust-colored scoria road toward the tiny settlement of Edgar, where he would turn south onto pavement in the direction of Wyoming.

"You got any kids, Dr. Hillary?" Clifford asked, after they'd put a few miles behind them.

"Nope."

"Married?"

"Oh, yeah. To Charlotte, forty-two years now. Can you believe that? Best woman in the universe. Actually, we had a son, but he was killed in a bicycle–car collision. When he was just ten. But that was a long, long time ago." Hillary went silent for a few moments. "Say," he resumed, "did Barlow tell you in the letter that the pay is two-fifty an hour? Plus graduate credits and room 'n' board, of course?"

"Yep, and that all sounds fine to me."

"Great."

On motoring into the town of Greybull, Hillary and Clifford nearly found themselves caught up in the tail end of the town's Memorial Day parade. The festivities had just broken up. Folks of all sizes and ages milled about. Candy wrappers and chocolate-milk cartons littered the sidewalks, and fresh horse manure pancaked the main-street parade route.

Just beyond the heart of downtown, where things appeared relatively deserted, Hillary jerked the truck to the right and pulled into an angled parking spot next to a huge bronze Chevrolet pickup truck with chrome side pipes and running boards.

"I love tampering with these bozos' rigs," he said, "and with their minds. You'll always find those 'Wyoming Native' bumper stickers on the biggest, gnarliest outfits."

"Sir?" Clifford inquired.

"You watch, son. Pay attention. You might learn something. And please drop that 'sir' and 'Dr. Hillary' crap. You call me Rad, cuz that's what I am. Reach in the glove box there and hand me one of those yellow-and-brown bumper stickers, would ya'? I always carry both stacks around whenever I'm traveling Montana or Wyoming, which has been a lot in recent years."

Clifford opened the glove compartment and found two rubber-banded stacks of bumper stickers. The red-white-and-blue stickers read "Montana Native"; the others, "Wyoming Native." He handed Hillary one of the yellow-and-brown Wyoming models.

"Keep watch, Speedy, and let me know if anyone's comin' who looks like they might own that truck. He's probably short, and he'll be wearin' cowboy boots and a big hat. Maybe a neckerchief."

Hillary opened the door and hopped out from behind the steering wheel, hacking and snickering all the while. Door still open, he grabbed a pair of scissors from under his seat. Clifford watched as he cut the bumper sticker in half. Then he cut a small slice off one of the sections. Grimacing, and surveying his surroundings with what Clifford interpreted as phony trepidation, Hillary walked over to the Chevy truck then knelt out of Clifford's line of sight.

A few seconds later, Hillary jumped back into the pickup, grinning. "Yes!" he exclaimed, offering the young man a high five. "Let's get outta here. Daylight's a-burnin' and there's no turnin' back!"

Clifford returned the hand slap, still unsure of what had transpired. Then, as Hillary backed out of his parking spot, Clifford saw the new, improved bumper sticker covering the old one on the back of the bozo's big rig. It read, "Wyoming Naive."

Clifford slapped his knee and looked at Hillary with a mixture of surprise and admiration. Speeding away, Hillary honked the horn and wheezed out his window.

"Yippee yi yo! Wyoming Native, my ass! Hell, Jeofredo, your Cheyenne people were here in the Big Horn country a hundred years, two hundred years, before that bozo's ancestors ever left England or Germany or wherever. And you're from Minnesota! That's precious! I love it! I bet the irony of it would go right over that truck owner's Stetson-covered head."

Clifford had suspected it earlier in the day, and now he knew it for certain: He was going to get along swimmingly with this middle-aged-and-then-some prankster-hippie-yippie anarchist of an archaeologist.

13
ARCHAEOLOGY

Kicked back in his "thinking chair," Paul Barlow scratched his chin. The living room of his big white colonial home on Vine Street in Nebraska's capital city featured a décor not unlike that of other living rooms in this middle-class neighborhood, excepting a few nods to what he called his "occupassion." These included a big bison skull hanging above the fireplace on the west wall and a glass-topped coffee table displaying an array of chipped-stone tools made of obsidian and chert.

Beth Barlow sat nearby on the couch, knitting. It was a common practice of Barlow to use his wife as a sounding board for his ideas.

"I'm convinced the natives wintered in that canyon for at least ten thousand years. Off and on probably, not continuously. But I could be wrong about that part. It's obvious they were still there when the white trappers pushed in. We can see that by the trade beads we've screened out of surface scrapings. But do you know what bothers me most? Not wondering what we're going to find as we excavate—I'm confident that site is artifactually verdant for many vertical feet to come—but why no one I've ever met has been able to tell me why that creek and canyon are called 'Sleeping Dog.'"

Beth looked up from her knitting at her husband and smiled. He could be such a mess. When he went out of town for something relatively formal, like a Plains Archaeology conference, Beth would pack his clothes and prepare detailed notes instructing him what to wear with what, and where and when to wear them. These notes she pinned to the appropriate articles of clothing. Then she prayed for divine guidance for her beloved husband, because she could readily picture him waltzing around at a pre-banquet cocktail function with a big white piece of paper containing small, neat handwriting pinned to the lapel of his sport jacket opposite his name tag:

"Wear with the gray slacks, black socks and shoes, white-and-gray shirt, and orange-amethyst bolo tie. Wear outfit only to the most frml. occsn., like the awards banquet. Before wearing second time check for food stains, esp. on the shirt."

There was something else Beth knew about her husband that Barlow hadn't shared with many others—he was both a devout Christian and a dedicated Darwinist. He didn't talk about it much. She knew he wasn't ashamed of these things, but that he considered them his own private business and no one else's. "My Christian beliefs would be considered a huge aberration by many of the heathens who are colleagues in my chosen field," he had once told her. "And my scientific leanings would come under fire from certain friends of ours at church. You know that's true. They're convinced the teaching of evolution is some kind of satanic plot. They'd press me, asking how I could believe in such a thing."

But he did, and Beth knew that in his own mind her husband had evolution and creationism working just fine together, side by side. Not a simple man. As he'd continued explaining to her during that rare moment of personal exposition, Barlow believed in the persuasive evidence supporting evolution, but also that the universe displayed too much inherent beauty and elegance for it all to be an accident of nature.

"I regard both the narrow-minded atheists and the narrow-minded creationists as full of horse manure," he'd declared, wrapping up his soliloquy.

"Yes, dear," Beth had said at the time, grateful to have had her chronically reticent husband open up and let her peek inside for once.

Barlow resumed speaking after a long silence. "That Sleeping Dog thing really nags at me. I've wondered about it most of my life. Not even old Herman D'Ambrosio could tell me anything. You remember him—told us he fought at the Fetterman battle and claimed to be the only white survivor? Then moved over to ranch on the west slope after resigning his Army commission? Older than Adam when you and I and Galen were kids. Anyhow, Herman told me it was called Sleeping Dog Canyon when he moved there, and that must've been around 1870.

"Now that we have those pictographs of dogs—or coyotes or wolves—that Galen uncovered, I think we're homing in on the answer. It brings up at least two new questions, though. Did a nineteenth-century English speaker run across that rock art, or similar art somewhere close by, then name the creek? Or was Sleeping Dog the name of the canyon prehistorically, in the Cheyenne or Crow tongue? I've asked a couple of old-timer natives up in the Pryor country that very question, but they didn't know. Or so they said." Barlow paused for a moment. "Maybe it's just a coincidence."

Beth knew this wouldn't sit well in her husband's analytical, cause-and-effect-oriented mind, so she preemptively agreed with him: "I don't think so, dear."

"I don't either," Barlow said. "Too many questions. Thinking about 'em is driving me to distraction. It's time to start excavating. Time to expose some long-buried answers to the fresh air. Even if they aren't answers to the questions I have right now. Anyhow, when I think about it rationally, the name thing doesn't much matter. It's probably not important, archaeologically speaking, compared to what we'll find below the ground surface, above where the canyon opens onto the basin. If my name's Paul Barlow, that lower canyon is artifactually verdant," he repeated, looking over at Beth. "Of that we can be sure."

***

"People, you may not know it yet, but you are sitting amidst a bunch of archaeologists," Hillary announced, "who, as a population, possess the highest level of intelligence and caliber of character found in the *Homo sapiens* species."

It was the evening of June 3, the day before the first Monday of field camp. Hillary stood on the unkempt lawn fronting the farmhouse on Galen Davies' satellite property. The old two-story, stick-built house, yellow with flaking white trim, would serve as home for the next three months-plus for the majority of the crew. Hillary faced eight individuals seated at various levels on the four steps climbing to the front porch of the house. They all appeared to be at least forty years younger than he.

"Not all the locals around here will understand us," Hillary continued. "Especially you hippies." He stared at Clifford and then at the similarly longhaired young Asian man sitting next to Clifford on the third-highest step. Then he held up his hands and looked at his palms. "Okay," he added, "*us* hippies. But Dr. Paul Barlow asked me to pass it on to you all that if any rednecks or K-Mart cowboys give you any unwarranted crap, he vows to back you up. And Barlow knows a lot of folks here on the west slope of the Big Horns."

"I'll back you hippies up, too." The words came from a stocky young cowboy seated on the top step. "I've been in a tussle or two in my time, but never lost one yet."

"Well," Hillary said, "thanks for that, Mister... Riley, right?

"Yep. *John* Riley."

"Good enough," Hillary responded. "On the other hand, if any of you get into any kind of dumb-ass trouble that's of your own making, Barlow will not be pleased. And if Paul Barlow is made unhappy, life could get miserable for all of us. I guarantee it."

Hillary paused for a moment to hold his cupped hand to his mouth and cough, then resumed speaking. "Since Mr. Riley has already introduced himself, let's let him finish. Then I'd like to hear from the rest of you. I know several of you have already met one-on-one, but let's make sure everybody knows the basics about everybody else. John Riley, where are you from?"

"Kaycee, Wyoming. I grew up on our family's sheep ranch. Studied anthro and rode bulls under Dr. Barlow at the University of Nebraska. I graduated last month, and I'll be going to grad school in New Mexico come September."

"Swell, thanks for that," Hillary said. "How about you, fair lady?"

"I'm Josie MacDonald," said the young American Indian sitting next to Riley. "Salish, 'on loan' from the Kicking Horse Job Corps Center on the Flathead Reservation in Montana. My official assignment here is to learn archaeological heavy-machinery technique from the master, Dr. Conrad Hillary."

Hillary looked around, up and down, as if searching for the celebrated heavy-equipment operator. "Oh," he finally said. "You mean *me*?"

"Yes, sir," Josie said, smiling. "Up our way rumor has it you can remove the stinger off a honeybee with a backhoe, then reattach it with the front-end loader and watch the bee fly away. Is it true?" she asked, giggling.

"No, that's just the buzz," Hillary said, then winced as the collected throng groaned.

"I don't know, Rad, you can work miracles with a bumper sticker," Clifford Gustafson interjected. "Maybe you can with a honeybee, too."

The others looked at Clifford questioningly, while he and Hillary just grinned at one another.

"I'll fill the rest of you in later," Clifford confided.

Hillary turned back to Josie. Short and stout, Josie MacDonald had short dark hair to match. She wore thick-lensed spectacles with heavy black frames.

"Where'd you get those glasses, Josie?" Hillary asked, out of the blue. "They look like they came from Buddy's estate. I like them. A lot."

"Buddy?"

"Holly. Buddy Holly. The true king of rock 'n' roll. Elvis is an imposter to the throne, you know."

Josie giggled again, and the others joined in.

"What about you, Mr. Ashton, what's your life story?"

Hillary already knew Peter Ashton hailed from North Platte, Nebraska. He and Clifford had watched earlier in the day as Ashton came tearing up to the parking area in a newish, dark-green MGB convertible. Minutes after arriving and familiarizing himself with the lay of the land, the brash young man had insisted on claiming for himself one of the three privacy-rich log cabins nestled along the creek a couple of hundred yards upstream of the excavation area. Galen Davies had built the cabins in the late sixties, intending to get into the business of outfitting big-game hunters—intentions as of yet unfulfilled.

Surly attitude intact, Ashton introduced himself, not failing to drop the name of the Connecticut prep school he attended prior to studying zoology and pre-med at the University of Nebraska.

Next, it was Clifford's turn. "I grew up on a farm in Minnesota," he said. "I was adopted when I was four, almost five. Lost my biological parents in an accident on the Northern Cheyenne

Reservation not far north of here. I went to the state university in Minneapolis on a golf scholarship. Thought I was going to study accounting, but then I stumbled across anthropology and loved it. So, here I am."

Following Clifford's concise introduction, an attractive young woman who identified herself as Bobbi Alder spoke next, explaining that she had been born and raised in the Star Valley of western Wyoming. "I attended Brigham Young University my first year of college," she told them, "but transferred to Utah State after that. I graduated with a degree in anthropology a week ago today!"

"She has promise," Hillary had murmured to Clifford earlier that day, after the pair met and shook hands with Bobbi. "Don't be surprised if she's a member of the church of Mormon reformed by summer's end. That is, if she's not already."

Clifford hadn't understood what Hillary meant, but out of courtesy he'd chuckled all the same.

One of Hillary's own students spoke next, introducing himself as Tom Jefferson. A tall, rangy black kid with a lofty Afro hairdo, Jefferson was perpetually dressed in khaki soldier's pants and black tennis shoes. The only item Hillary ever noticed alternating in his wardrobe from day to day was Jefferson's choice of T-shirts, of which he seemed to have an endless collection. A warm-water bass in cold trout waters if ever there was one, Jefferson had ended up at Chadron State College almost by accident, after filling out a scholarship application he'd found posted on the student-alert bulletin board at his Philadelphia high school.

"I only had a vague notion of where and what *Nebraska* was when I hopped aboard a Greyhound and headed there in September of 1969," he said. "Never mind Chadron. Once I got there, I was drawn to the anthropology department, probably because it was full of people intrigued by others with cultural backgrounds different from their own. And believe me, my background was *way* different than any of my Chadron State classmates." Jefferson laughed at that, and the others chimed in.

Rounding out the advance crew were graduate students Danny Ho and Mary O'Donnell who, by asserting their seniority, had commandeered the two remaining creekside cabins. Ho's doing so evicted the lower-ranking Clifford, who had set up temporary quarters in the westernmost cabin, chasing him into the farmhouse attic.

O'Donnell revealed nothing more to the others than that she was a University of Wyoming grad student from Great Falls, Montana, via Okinawa, Panama, and other foreign places where her Air Force-lifer dad had been stationed.

"Curt and overtly ambitious," Hillary penciled into his mental notebook as she spoke. "But sharp."

Danny Ho, grad student number two, explained that he was a San Francisco native coming out of the University of California at Santa Barbara. "I'm here primarily to serve as Dr. Hillary's assistant," he said, in a voice clearly effeminate in tone and timbre.

Paul Barlow had admitted previously to Hillary that, although he probably should have known better, he had indeed hired Ho to be Hillary's chief assistant, an appointment based on a request from Barlow's sister Florence, a friend of the Ho family in San Francisco.

"We'll see," Hillary whispered.

***

Hillary pulled up to the Sleeping Dog site the following morning at half-past eight. The sun was scratching the tops of the beefy poplars guarding the eastern boundary of the site, sending a few exploratory rays into the western reaches of the soon-to-be excavations. After parking beside the site's utility shed and shutting down the engine, Hillary sat in his truck for a moment, surveying the scene before him and thinking about his plan of attack. As orchestrated by Paul Barlow from afar, the advance crew of eight student archaeologists were all in place, with another four slated to show up and start work in three weeks, on June 25.

Hillary emerged from the truck and walked over to where the crew had gathered. "This is the rough stuff we'll start this morning," he announced. "The methodology we arkies use when we don't know yet whether or not we're into artifactually verdant ground. By the way, that's a phrase I picked up from Paul Barlow. Pretty clever, huh?"

"Dr. Hillary?"

"Yes, Josie?"

"You also used the word 'arky'."

"Uh-huh?"

"Is that spelled with a 'ky' or 'chy'?"

"You know, I've never thought that about that. Let's see… we'll go with 'k'. A-r-c-h-y might get mixed up with a red-headed comic book character. Oh, and Josie?"

"Yes?"

"Please call me Rad."

"Oh, okay," Josie said, giggling.

"Once we get into obvious habitation levels—you know what to watch for: charcoal and stone flakes and small pieces of bone—things will get a lot more precise," Hillary continued. "Even then it's not brain surgery, but it's a lot closer to brain surgery than the ditch digging you'll do for the first few days, at least. You'll lay aside those flat-blade shovels and goon spoons and metal bars, and grab trowels and dental picks, whisk brooms. And water-filled spray bottles, which you'll use to wet down the vertical walls to highlight their stratigraphy for photographs. But I'm getting ahead of myself. The Ho'Donnell team will lead you through it when we get there."

Hillary saw Danny Ho grinning at his name-blending gag, while Mary O'Donnell retained a rather grim expression.

"Okay, string off a square just like this one ten meters due east," Hillary instructed, then paused to cough into his hand. "Then another ten meters east of that, and then another. Get the corners square; be sure all your sides are exactly three meters long and parallel to the ones next to it."

Graduate students Ho and O'Donnell, with three summers and two summers, respectively, of fieldwork under their belts, aided Hillary by demonstrating how to shoot in square excavation test units using a big tripod-mounted compass for orientation.

Paired with Bobbi Alder, a situation for which he made a mental note of giving Hillary huge thanks later, Clifford helped lay out a perfect three-by-three-meter square. After he had pounded a wooden lath into the ground at each of the unit's four corners, Bobbi outlined the square by connecting the four stakes with white cotton twine. Two sides of the square pointed true north–south, as determined by the fresh-out-of-the-box Brunton compass with which John Mills had entrusted Clifford for the field season. "If anything can figure out direction in Wyoming, it's a Brunton," Mills had told him. "They're made there, since last year. Right there in Riverton city."

Just up-canyon to the east of Clifford and Bobbi, John Riley and Tom Jefferson worked to lay out an identically shaped test unit. Hillary watched Riley move.

"Pure cowboy," he mumbled, then chuckled.

Riley wore his blonde hair close-cropped. As far as Hillary could discern, sideburns growing to the level of the bottom of his ears were his only concession to early 1970s fashion. Riley's uniform consisted of scuffed brown calf-leather boots, a light-brown Stetson with a broad brim, Wrangler jeans, and a striped western shirt. His lower lip, stuffed with a wad of Skoal, puffed out like a small balloon. A bulging, faded ring on the right rear pocket of his blue jeans revealed where his can of chew resided. A gaudy, silver-and-gold-and-mother-of-pearl belt buckle shone as proud evidence that he reigned as the "1972 NCAA Great Plains Region Bull Riding Grand Champion."

Hillary watched as Riley and Tom Jefferson worked on Sleeping Dog Site Unit #3. Thinking back four years, he recalled how he had recognized a streetwise intellect in Jefferson when they'd first become acquainted at Chadron State. Since then, the two had grown to be friends. Hillary grinned, watching the two young men working together, side by side. Though they spoke the same language, more or less, Hillary understood that John Riley's and Tom Jefferson's cultural foundations were about as far apart as Micronesia and Manitoba. But early clues and his intuition also told him the pair would become fast friends.

Hillary shifted his gaze back to the west of Riley and Jefferson, where Clifford and Bobbi Alder worked Unit #2. He moved closer, intending to eavesdrop.

"Like I said last night, I transferred from Provo to Utah State after my sophomore year," Bobbi was saying, as she shoveled dirt into a sifting screen manned by Clifford. "It was a real eye-opener. My first roommate at Logan had the same introductory biology textbook we'd used at BYU. I never knew what forbidden secrets pages forty-seven through sixty-two of the book held, because they'd been removed from all of our books at BYU. Well, they were still in Sheila's book in Logan, and what they were all about, I learned, was evolution and genetics, and how humans evolved from lower primates. My church doesn't subscribe to those theories, so they'd torn the pages out of all the textbooks before we students took possession. Can you believe it?"

"No," Clifford said. "Really?"

Hillary noticed Clifford gazing at Bobbi in a curious manner. He surmised that his young friend was staring at his excavation partner while trying to look like he wasn't—a tall order, for Bobbi Alder was attractive. Five-foot-seven lanky, she had smart green eyes and straight, silky brown hair falling to the middle of her back. As Hillary had learned from her resumé, she'd run track and cross-country at BYU and then at Utah State. In person, he saw in her the spark, the positive energy, he'd found to be a common trait among endurance athletes.

"What brought you here to Sleeping Dog?" Clifford inquired.

"A connection between my advisor at Utah State, Dr. Bela Randolph, and Dr. Barlow. I was camp cook for them when they went elk hunting one weekend in the fall of seventy-one up in the Bear River Range. Dr. Barlow and I seemed to hit it off."

Hillary moved on. To the far east, Josie MacDonald and Peter Ashton worked Test Unit #4. Its eastern edge lay thirty meters east of the counterpart edge of baseline Unit #1, established by Mary O'Donnell and Danny Ho. The north edge of the baseline unit, the westernmost of the four test units, was just two meters away from the foot of the Sand Burr Rim. The rim trended east-northeast from this point, so from west to east each unit lay a little farther away from the cliff's base than the previous one. The net result was that about five meters separated the north edge of Unit #4 from the base of the rim.

"Okay, Mary," Ho instructed, "grab the handles of that one-man screen and start rockin' and rollin.'"

"One-woman screen," she said without a smile.

"What?"

"If I'm running it, it's not a one-man screen, it's a one-woman screen."

"Oh, boy," Ho whispered, then turned away to grab a Marlboro out of his shirt pocket and the lighter out of his pants. He lit the cigarette and took a long draw on it before turning back around.

"Okay, then, grab the handles of that one-woman screen, would you, please?"

O'Donnell did so, and Ho, cigarette squeezed between pursed lips, proceeded to drop a shovelful of dirt into it.

"You shouldn't smoke, you know," O'Donnell lectured as she began moving the sifting screen to and fro.

The handles she held were extensions of two sides of a three-foot-square box frame, its bottom covered with quarter-inch wire mesh. Loosely attached wing nuts joined the plywood sides of the frame with the top members of a U-shaped ground support constructed of two-by-four boards. The loose wing nuts permitted the screened box to be moved back and forth, while the base remained stationary on the ground. As the operator rocked the gizmo, dirt filtered through the screen mesh, leaving only rocks and dirt clods, the occasional wriggling worm or beetle, and, or so the aspiring archaeologist hoped, chipped-stone and pottery artifacts and fragments of bone.

***

Two days later, Wednesday afternoon, the eight student archaeologists were all hard at it, shoveling, sweating, rocking their sifting screens. Each of the quartet of test units had been excavated to thirty or thirty-five centimeters below ground-surface level.

"Hey, Gustafson," Tom Jefferson yelled from Unit #3, "you just graduated, like Riley and me. Was your brush with the draft as close as mine? You probably had a 2-S deferment that you lost after graduation. Like I did, right?"

"Right," Clifford said. "I don't know how close your call was, but I made it by the skin of my molars. I drew a three with my birthday, July 25, in the 1970 lottery. Can you believe that? If Nixon hadn't gotten us out of that mess last winter, right now I'd be toting a rifle through rice paddies instead of shoveling dirt in Wyoming. What's your number? Were you born in fifty-one as well?"

"Yep. Thirty-seven," Jefferson said. "But no rice paddies for me, thank you. I'd be in a café in Montreal sipping café lattes."

"Ooh la la!" exclaimed Hillary, who was walking toward the workers and had caught the tail end of the conversation. For whoever could see it, he held his right hand aloft, pinky extended as if holding a teacup in the fashion of a refined blue blood.

"Damn draft dodgers!" chimed in John Riley. "You guys would be making me feel real safe here at home. Like I told Tom, I drew 325 in the lottery."

"Maybe we could've talked Riley into going for both of us, Clifford," Jefferson said. "He'd probably do twice as much damage to the Viet Cong as you and me put together, anyway."

Clifford laughed. "At least."

A few minutes later, shovel in hand, Clifford stopped and stood in the center of the shallow excavation. He turned a circle, looking around admiringly. "Our square looks squarest of all," he said, grinning at Bobbi Alder.

"Do you really think so?"

"Naw, they're all just about perfect. But ours sure looks good."

"Yes, it certainly does." Bobbi caught Clifford's eye and smiled, revealing a fine line of white teeth that glistened against her tanned skin.

My goodness, Clifford thought.

***

"Sure is a diverse bunch you've rounded up, Paul," Hillary said into the telephone receiver.

He was standing, sweating, and talking in Mercerville's lone telephone booth, late on the Saturday morning following the first week of field camp. As he spoke, he scratched his head and gazed across the town's gravel main street at the timeworn façade of the Tired Puppy Tavern. Though the phone booth and bar were new to him, he suspected both were places he and his crew members would become intimately familiar with over the coming weeks.

"These kids range from motley to tidy," he added, then paused to cough and cover his mouth with the hand not holding the phone. "But I'm trying my hardest not to hold the clean-cut ones' appearance against them."

"You geriatric hippie," Barlow replied, laughing. "Hey, the reason I asked you to call me is I need to update you on my schedule. I won't be able to make it there by mid-June, like I told you earlier. Looks like now I have to be in Lincoln until the end of the month. But with you at the helm, I have no worries that things won't be running smoothly when I get there, whenever that is."

"Sure, I can hold down the fort, no problemo. Hey, by the way, where'd you find that wild man John Riley? He's a student of yours?"

"Ah, yes. Mr. Riley. Well, you could say he was the teacher's pet, me being the teacher. But I don't think you, or anyone else, would want to call him that, not to his face anyway. He's a scrapper. And a helluva bull rider. I'm still assistant rodeo coach here at UNL, you know. As always, a job I do for the love of it, not for money. I first got to know Riley in that role. One day early on I found myself thinking, 'He reminds me of me.' That's why I steered him into archaeology. An easy task, really; he came equipped with a keen working knowledge of the subject. He grew up outside Kaycee, a sheep grower's son, surrounded by evidence of prehistorics, a lot like me as a kid in the Ten Sleep country. He'll be goin' to grad school in Albuquerque in September. Did he tell you that?"

"Yes, he did. And I think it's fair to predict that the department at New Mexico will never be the same for it."

"Ha! I believe you're right. I haven't warned our buddy MacIntosh about him. Don't think I will, either. Just let it be a surprise. My little gift to old Mac."

"All in all, if early indications hold steady, I couldn't've hand-picked a better bunch, Paul. There's not a one of 'em I don't get along with and who's not pulling his weight. Mary O'Donnell is a little tense, but I think she's starting to loosen up some. Is she a lesbian? My typically spot-on character-o-meter leads me to suspect that she and Danny Ho are both predisposed toward individuals of their own gender. If I'm right, do you think this could be a double-negative type of situation? I mean, could a pair of homosexuals, one male and one female, go for each other?"

"I don't think so, Conrad. I don't think it works like that."

"No, I don't either."

"And I honestly don't know, or don't care, much about either of their sexual leanings. We social scientists have to be open-minded, right?"

"Right on. You're a cowboy and I'm a hipster, and we get along just fine. Don't we?"

"We do," said Barlow.

"Oh, the one possible exception in an otherwise stellar group is that Peter Ashton. Seems like a bit of an odd duck out of water."

"Sorry," Barlow said. "I should have warned you about him. Peter Ashton, from my observations, is a walking cliché. He's a spoiled doctor's son who has tried a little bit of a lot of things, and whose time is running short. His father's patience and monetary support are running short, that is. He's twenty-five now. Recently decided he'd like to try his hand at archaeology, and because his alumnus father is a major contributor to the university, he had no trouble landing a spot on my crew. Once he convinced his dad to give him another shot, that is, and after President Schwartz had a word with me about it."

"Hmm," Hillary said. "Interesting. Oh, well. But I sure like that Gustafson boy. More and more all the time. And is he ever looking forward to meeting you!"

"Well, Mills did tell me we'd find something special in him. I look forward to meeting him myself. Mills says he's got something bigger than brains—fire, an interest, maybe some intuition. Not that he's a whiz kid, Mills said. In fact, he told me Gustafson fought tooth and nail to cop a B in Comparative Society. But John also said he aced out most of the grad students in Bill Magnusson's 600-level Plains course. We should groom him, Conrad, keep him inspired, make sure he keeps at it. I've lost too many potentially good archaeologists to the oil and coal survey contracts the last couple of years."

"I know what you mean, but he's definitely keen on what's going on here now." Hillary paused again to cough. "And I don't think that's going away any time soon. He shows signs of turning into a heckuva rockeologist. You know, he may even be the one who evolves into my actual assistant, my right-hand man. I know you picked Danny Ho for that role, but he's kind of a clown, really. For the first two or three days of work, he followed me around and sort of tried to emulate my movements. Bit of a pain. He is a good worker, but the others don't take him overly serious, so far anyhow. But Gustafson, I sense he could be a natural leader. Talented, affable, energetic, but modest and easy-going at the same time."

"Sounds ideal to me."

"Got anything else, pardner?" Hillary asked.

"How're the findings coming along?"

"Slow. I've been surprised by the small quantity of surface finds on the canyon floor, and in the first thirty centimeters of fill. But, like you said, it's probably not that they've never been there; more likely they were there, but Sleeping Dog Creek washed 'em away during spring high-water events. Whenever I start getting a little disappointed I think back on those flakes of obsidian and Hartville chert you and your friend Davies sifted out of the dirt from below the rock art. I do think we'll start getting into something bigger and better here before long. After all, the legendary Dr. Paul Barlow guaranteed it."

"That's right, Dr. Hillary, he did. And we shall. I'll talk to you again soon."

"Adios, amigo. Vaya con dios."

***

Eight work days into the summer and sixty centimeters below ground surface, the crew members in all four units encountered solid rock. But it wasn't bedrock.

As they laid bare the expanse of sandstone, Hillary surmised what had happened. He'd seen it before: a rock overhang formerly attached to the cliffs above had crashed and fallen, he estimated, between five hundred and a thousand years ago. Subsequent sedimentation from spring flooding over the course of decades had covered the slab with the sandy loam the crew had to remove to re-expose the rock to the elements.

"This could be the break I've been praying for," Hillary proclaimed from on high, gazing down into the excavation units as the young men and women, kneeling, continued sweeping soil off the continuous slab of sandstone.

"What do you mean, Rad?" Tom Jefferson said. "And I didn't know you prayed."

"I mean this site just hasn't been turning up occupation levels like Dr. Barlow and I expected. I think the creek over the years has periodically risen high enough during spring runoff to run through here and wash away a lot of the evidence prehistoric occupants would have left behind. Erode and redeposit, erode and redeposit.

That's how these flattish canyon-mouth creeks sometimes work. As you all know, we've found nothing *in situ* so far, just a couple of tools and a few chippings scattered about in random fashion. Well, I'm thinking it's possible, or even probable, that this big slab has protected whatever lies beneath it, holding it in place and preventing it from being affected by the water action. Almost like displaced cap rock."

Hillary pointed up at the Sand Burr Rim. "It's like the cap rock of limestone up there, which protects these sandstone walls from eroding. The way streams like this act over time, you know, is they move around laterally. There's a good chance Sleeping Dog flowed farther over there to the south in the past. A thousand, two thousand years ago, it might never have gotten to the cliff base even at its highest. I do believe the floods affecting us here are relatively recent phenomena, over the last few hundred years."

"How do you know these things, Rad?" Clifford asked.

"Part intuition, part book smarts, part experience. But mostly it's the simple fact that I'm a frickin' genius."

Hearty laughter rang out from the test units.

"How will we get through the rock?"

"Well, I hope we don't have to bring out the big guns."

"What are the big guns?" asked Josie MacDonald.

"Dynamite," Hillary said, eliciting more chuckles from the crew. But this time he was not joking. "Eleven summers ago I led an excavation team at a rock-overhang site in south-central Colorado, where we ran into a similar rock slab lain bare. I really did have to resort to blasting it to pieces with dynamite. But first, I'll try to break this one up with the backhoe scoop. I'm hoping that'll do the trick. Dynamite would really bum out the swallows and our other fine feathered friends here in the canyon."

14
SPECULATION

An open-country plainsman prone to mild claustrophobia if his surroundings weren't just so, Conrad Hillary had parked and leveled his eighteen-foot Moonraker trailer at the western edge of Galen Davies' property. From there he could see to the south, north, and west—up, down, and across the open expanse of the Big Horn Basin. To the east, his view comprised the sandstone-protected confines of Sleeping Dog Canyon and, above that, the rocky, timbered fastness and scoured alpine tundra of the massive Big Horn Mountains.

Out where he bedded down each night, the wind gusted often and hard. That suited Hillary fine. It made him feel at home.

He saw and heard Friday, June 22 dawn cool and cloudy, with an occasional soft sprinkling of rain. He hadn't slept much through the night, so his head was fogged. The wind had picked up at around half-past midnight and blown hard for three hours, harder than even he liked, rocking his small trailer arrhythmically. It made him half seasick. He had even begun dreaming of himself back on the deck of the *USS Arizona*, which he had served aboard in the early 1930s in the turbulent waters off the coast of California.

Hillary had finally fallen sound asleep just after three a.m., only to be awakened an hour and a half later by the loud, early summer singing of robins and canyon wrens. "Shut the hell up!" he'd yelled at the birds, producing a rush of adrenaline that woke him up for good. Exasperated, he had risen, brewed a pot of strong coffee, and drunk it. Then he had headed out for a walk to clear his groggy noggin.

Hillary and the crew had been hard at it for three weeks. They were gelling and, now that they'd finished busting through the fallen rock slab with the backhoe and iron bars, getting into some interesting subterranean territory. They'd even sifted out some sherds of Fremont pottery, causing both Barlow and Hillary to scratch their heads. No one ever, to their knowledge, had found evidence of the Fremont culture this far north. The pottery also supported Hillary's estimate that the rock slab had broken away from the cliffside around a thousand years ago. Radiocarbon dating of Fremont artifacts consistently indicated these people were active from approximately 600 to 1300 AD.

The four new crew members were expected to show over the coming weekend, just in time to miss out on the hard labor of heavy digging and just in time to get in on the precise excavating and excitement of extraordinary finds that Hillary sensed they were closing in on. But for today, it was still the original eight, who, in Hillary's view, had solidified into a damn good crew; tight, possibly the best he'd been associated with in his thirty-four years of field camps. Danny Ho had loosened his grip on Hillary, and he'd even caught Mary O'Donnell smiling at Ho's corny jokes a time or two.

Hillary strolled up the canyon, smoking a Camel straight and stopping occasionally to hack and spew. He ambled past the four test units, now expanding horizontally as well as vertically and threatening to overtake one another. He passed Galen Davies' trio of streamside cabins and the sleeping occupants within, then stepped gingerly over the cattleguard gapping the barbed-wire fence. Here the canyon narrowed and the gravel access road deteriorated into a sandy two-track, leaving Davies' property and entering lands administered by the Bureau of Land Management. Sleeping Dog Creek gurgled along to his right.

As he continued walking upstream between the confines of sandstone cliffs, Hillary heard soft footsteps padding up behind him. He turned around to see Bobbi Alder jogging his way, dressed against the cool and damp in cotton sweats. The front of her top read "Utah State Aggies Track." Bobbi slowed to a walk when she reached her site supervisor.

"Good morning, Conrad," she said. "You're an early riser, too?"

"Yeah, well, sometimes. When I can't sleep, I figure I might as well get up. Those damn birds were making so much noise this morning. I do like walking early in the morning and just thinking about things," he added. "This canyon is a beautiful place to do just that. Good for training, too, I reckon?"

"Yes, well, I'm not really in training, but it's hard to break the habit of running. Mind if I walk with you awhile?"

"Not at all. Mind if I bounce some ideas off you?"

"Not at all," Bobbi said, smiling.

"Okay then. I've been thinking about what we've found and where it might be taking us. We found a little bit of historic Crow evidence above that rock slab, along with horse bones, some glass trade beads, and three metal straight-edges. Immediately below the rock, we found Late Prehistoric artifacts. In addition to the Fremont potsherds, we have those small chert corner-notched points, what the amateur arkies often call 'bird points.'"

"Right. They actually mark the switch from atlatl-launched spears and the larger projectile points of earlier times to the bow and arrow, right?"

"You are absolutely correct, madam," Hillary said. "Arrows were a huge advance over the spear because they were more accurate and they traveled at a far higher rate of speed. Those points, almost like a bullet, would've done substantial damage to an animal, even something as large as a bison or a bear.

"Bison, bison, bison," Hillary continued absently. "Now that's what's gnawing at me. Nowhere in the bone-dry Big Horn Basin, or in the relatively verdant foothill canyons above, has anyone ever, as far as we professional archaeologists know, tracked down a large-scale, communal bison-kill site. It's as if this micro-region was an isolated Great Basin island surrounded by plains and mountains. Pishkuns, or buffalo-drive jumps, have been unearthed not far from here in every direction. Yet the Big Horn Basin proper acts more like the Great Basin of Nevada, southeast Oregon. It looks like these people killed a lone bison or two occasionally, but smaller critters were their mainstay. Great Basin, no bison."

"Lots of questions to answer, huh, Boss?"

"Boss. I like that. Bobbi, there sure are. Such as the mystery of the apparent time gap below the Late Prehistoric finds. Barlow and I expected to find corner- and side-notched dart points of the Late Plains Archaic—Pelican Lake, Besant, others—underlying the Late

Prehistoric artifacts. Instead, you all began uncovering grinding stones and McKean lanceolate points, telltale diagnostics of the Middle Plains Archaic period. That's a missing period of at least ten centuries.

"But the biggest surprise of all, at least for me, is that it's starting to look like people persevered here right on through the Altithermal, the Early Plains Archaic. Let me know if I'm telling you something you already know, but that extended dry period ran from roughly five to eight thousand years ago. The natives for the most part deserted the plains and migrated up into the Black Hills and other mountains of the region, where things would have remained relatively verdant."

"Sure, I learned some about the Altithermal in school."

"At Sleeping Dog, as of yet, we've found no break in the continuity during those times. Somehow these foothills and valleys must have remained good places to make a living during that long drought period. Was this country that's drier than any of the surrounding areas today wetter than the rest of the plains back then?"

"We do have our work cut out for us, don't we, Boss?"

"That we do. We surely do."

The pair walked in silence for a few moments, Hillary consumed in thought and feeling energized about the Paleoindian evidence he sensed they would be uncarthing soon as the crew probed deeper into the ground and the past. They strolled past several cliff-base flats, which, Hillary knew, could give up artifacts as abundantly as the current dig site.

"God, this is a rich canyon," he said, his reverence obvious. "We've got the canyon, with plenty of rock shelters and overhangs; and the riparian areas along the creek, with willow, box elder, chokecherry, buffalo berry. We have the rocky foothills, and the meadows and spruce-fir stands in the mountains above... well, we've just about got it all, making it a perfect setting for exploitation by archaic cultures. Then, to boot, we have what's looking like centuries of deposition at the main site, once we got beneath the fallen sandstone slab. Most of the rest of this region is eroding. All in all, a rare and beautiful situation."

"It all feels sacred somehow," Bobbi said.

The young archaeologist and her supervisor reached the point where, as they faced back downstream, Sleeping Dog Creek made a forty-five-degree, left-hand turn to the southwest. Here the creek had undercut the north bank, carving a big, deep hole. Hillary lay down and hung his head over the side of the bank, and Bobbi sat down on a big sandstone boulder several yards away. Two fat brown trout, sixteen inches long, Hillary guessed, sensed him and darted toward shallower, faster water.

"I need to remember to buy my fishing license next time I'm in Worland," Hillary yelled, loud enough for Bobbi to hear. "And to have Charlotte send out my fly rod and gear from Chadron. I can't believe I forgot to pack the stuff into the trailer."

Hillary thought about seducing trout with artificial flies he had tied by hand almost as much as he ruminated on the prehistoric Great Plains. In fact, inexplicably, thinking about one of them often triggered suspicions or conclusions about the other. Four years earlier, almost to the day, Hillary had sat at the vice tying a size twelve Yellow Humpy, bifocals balanced on the far end of his big nose, when it struck him that almost certainly a stratified Paleoindian site existed in the vicinity of an arroyo he had explored in the chop hills east of Alliance, Nebraska. Later that summer, Hillary had organized a Chadron State field crew that proved out his hunch. He couldn't explain why it happened, this juxtaposing of fly fishing and archaeology; he simply accepted it as a gift and sure as heck didn't argue with it.

"Maybe if I come up here and cast a few flies I'll figure out the whole convoluted quagmire of Sleeping Dog Canyon," Hillary speculated. "Although I really don't consider it a quagmire. I know as well as anyone that an archaeological excavation rarely, if ever, behaves exactly as one hopes or expects it to."

Still hanging out over the bank, Hillary removed his wire-rim glasses and laid them aside, then pulled off the rubber band holding his ponytail in place. He lowered his forehead and all his loosened hair into the cold stream, whose waters not long ago had been frozen up in mountain snowpack. He instantly earned an intense headache, of the sort caused by eating too much ice cream too fast. He jumped back to his feet and pressed his warm palms against his temples, then wrung out and pulled back his hair and re-rubber-banded it. He picked up his spectacles and rebalanced them on his nose and ears.

"You're brave," Bobbi said. "That water is cold."

"It woke me up, all right. I hoped it would shake me into some sort of revelation. Like, how many people might have lived here at once? And how did they survive? We know by the faunal remains that the prehistorics were eating rodents, birds, rabbits, pronghorn, deer, fish. Occasionally bison. But what plants were they gathering? Might the later folks have run rabbit and cricket drives like the Paiute and Washo in the actual Great Basin? Forgive me, Bobbi. I never seem able to begin processing data into hypotheses or conclusions until I confront myself with questions like these."

"No problem, Boss. I'm enjoying the show."

"Okay, then. Were these people half Great Basin and half Great Plains, or what? Shoshone–Blackfeet forerunners? And when were they here? Only in winter, or year-round? If the latter, did they at any time practice rudimentary agriculture? The results of most field studies in this region would lead you to believe they'd have lived in the canyon only in winter, when the south-facing rock walls absorbed the warming rays of the low-slung sun and acted as a barrier to cold northerlies. In summer, they might have ventured upstream along the valley of the Wind River, or the Tongue, the Powder. Or even high up the Yellowstone. Places where they would have found bigger bison herds. This would've been true especially after the Crows and Cheyenne and Sioux arrived with the horse. But it could have been so even before that, when the Shoshone and others lived in smaller bands and hunted bison on foot."

Hillary shifted gear and reconsidered the pair of fat trout in the creek's deep hole. He thought about which fly and what casting strategy he would use to hook them, where he would stand and how he would get there with soft-footed stealth to avoid spooking the fish. Something in his brain clicked. He didn't know why, but he knew it to be.

"Bobbi, that site where we're digging, and this upper canyon as well—the aboriginals resided here the year around. And not just for a year here and a year there, but continuously through a substantial span of prehistory. Among other things, this could help explain the lack of evidence of large-scale bison butcherings. Maybe the canyon's residents had enemies they feared confronting on the outside, and the canyon served as a refuge. Or perhaps the outlying landscape itself had turned too inhospitable, especially during the Altithermal. And this is a good thing, because we'll learn more at a long-term campsite than we ever could at a seasonal bison-kill site." He broke off and coughed. "Well, daylight's burnin.'"

"You're right, Boss. I'll run back to the farmhouse and get dressed for work. See you in a while?"

"Okay, Bobbi, see you later."

Hillary lit a cigarette and set off at a brisk pace, following the water coursing downstream toward the Sleeping Dog site.

***

Hillary returned to the site at nine o'clock sharp, feeling awake and mentally honed, invigorated by newly realized possibilities and certainties. As the other trio of two-person teams dug and scraped away in their units, Peter Ashton and Josie MacDonald bent over the stationary water-screening structure located midway between the excavations and the equipment shed.

"A beautiful sight to behold!" Hillary proclaimed.

"Hey, Rad, come 'ere man, quick!"

The directive came from Unit #3, where a standing Tom Jefferson waved his arms in a beckoning gesture.

"What is it?" Hillary yelled, then jogged the remaining thirty yards.

Below Jefferson knelt John Riley, huddled with his head down, on the floor of the excavation, which was now four meters square and a meter and a half deep. The buffed, smooth walls revealed subterranean strata composed of sand and loam deposits of varying thicknesses. The layers of the east and west walls slanted up toward the Sand Burr Rim, according to measurements Riley and Jefferson had recorded, at between five and ten degrees.

"What is it?" Hillary repeated, hovering above.

Riley slid to his left, making space for Jefferson and Hillary to join him on their knees on the floor of the unit.

"Holy spit," Hillary exclaimed in an intense monotone. "Unbelievable!"

He watched Jefferson as the steady-handed young man scraped with a blunt-ended Marshalltown trowel around the bottom of an object embedded in the dirt floor. He then dusted away loose dirt using a small whisk broom.

"Hold up just a second, Tom."

Hillary ran his right palm over the smooth globe of dark-brown bone, then felt under his fingertips the sagittal suture, where the right and left parietal bones met.

"An adult male," Hillary announced. "See how pronounced the brow ridge is? I'd say this individual died more than six thousand years ago, considering that Lookingbill point base protruding from his temple. Here he lived until he died, during the Altithermal, a time when we thought no one could have survived in this country. But it's truly odd to find just a skull, no skeleton. It's not a burial, nor would I expect to find a burial here."

"Then what is it?" Riley queried.

"Boys, I think you may have uncovered some long-dead American Indian's rather ghoulish trophy head. I wonder if it hung on a wall?"

Jefferson and Riley emitted nervous chuckles.

"This is extraordinary." Hillary stood to brush off the knees of his khakis, then called over to Clifford Gustafson: "Chief, grab the camera and a clipboard and some graph paper from the shed, will you?"

"Sure thing, Rad. What do you think of what the cowboy and soul man have dug up over there?"

Hillary cleared his throat, then spoke up so that everyone could hear. "I feel strongly that Misters Riley and Jefferson have uncovered a fellow who was a head of his time."

Groans emanated from all corners of the excavation.

15
CAUSE

"Look, maybe the only way to get 'em out of there is to put a little scare into 'em."

Proposing this sinister-sounding course of action was Dan Oberlin, thirty-five years old, bald, wearing a blue-neckerchief head-band and a gold ring in his right earlobe. Oberlin was presiding over the second-ever meeting of the northern Wyoming/southern Montana chapter of Citizens Against Unfair Stockgrower Entitlements. Like grassroots CAUSE chapters popping up throughout the West, this one met under clandestine conditions, today in the bath-room-sized living room of member Helen Richardson's tiny rental apartment in downtown Worland.

The CAUSE chapter had avoided listing its upcoming meeting in the "Happenings" section of the weekly *Big Horn Basin Bugle* newspaper. If a local rancher or businessman found out an individual belonged to the group, the chances were that it would not be good for that person's health or well-being. CAUSE's mission statement, "To rid our public lands of freeloading cattle and sheep," was not a popular sentiment in the Big Horn country, nor anywhere else the underground entity operated.

"Why do they think they have to dig up the past, anyway?" Oberlin asked. "Why not just let it be?" He cast an individual glance at each of the others in the room.

"But think about it this way," said Alan Alvarez, a recent arrival in Wyoming. He had come north after hearing through the grape-vine that the law in northern New Mexico wanted to question him regarding a recent gas-tank sugaring of a trio of logging trucks high in Cisneros Park. "If what they find is important enough, the canyon might become a state park, or even a national monument. That'd get the cattle out."

"Where have you been and what have you been smoking?" Oberlin growled. "We're talking Wyoming here. Grand Teton National Park—not national monument, but national *park*, that's supposed to enjoy the ultimate protection—permits those four-legged locusts of U.S. Senator Cary Higgins to trample the sagebrush and crap in the Snake River. You think the government will stop allowing cattle to hammer Sleeping Dog Canyon just because it's a national monument? Hell, they'd probably decrease the grazing fees and increase the head allowances for Galen Davies and those other bastards just to be sure visitors can get a taste of the Old West. No, I don't go for that. That's the worst thing that could happen. It's my biggest fear, in fact."

"Why is that canyon so important to you?" asked Jimmy Fanslow. "That particular canyon, out of all the canyons and mountains there are to worry about?"

Fanslow, a recent biology grad from Jacksonville, Florida, had landed in Wyoming the previous summer after securing a summer job as a service-station attendant at Fishing Bridge in Yellowstone National Park. His time spent in and around the park with other young people had awakened in him a keen concern for western environmental issues.

"I have my reasons," Oberlin snapped. "For one thing, it's the closest thing there is to a pristine foothills canyon remaining on the west slope of the Big Horns. And for another… well, like I say, I have my reasons."

"Suppose we agree," said Richardson. She was a U.S. Forest Service seasonal firefighter obliged to bide her time while waiting for the forests to dry out after a snowy winter and damp spring—she and a co-worker had even discussed the possibility of setting a make-work fire or two themselves. "They're probably super-committed to getting the job done, you know. We've all read about Dr. Paul Barlow in the paper: local boy makes good, gets big-time funding for excavation he's wanted to do for years… what do you propose we do to give them a scare? Go in and say 'boo'?"

"Come on, Helen," said Oberlin. "We have to get more serious than that. *You* have to get more serious. Let me think on it some. I want to have a plan in place by next week."

The fifth individual in the room nodded in agreement, but said nothing.

16
LOVE

"This cool evening air reminds me so much of running back home after supper in the fall," Clifford said. "Only here it's summer."

He and his excavation partner were jogging along at a relaxed pace, side-by-side, on the sandy two-track penetrating the BLM lands east of the Sleeping Dog site.

"Did you run in high school?" Bobbi asked. "Or college? You're big, but you have a nice smooth stride. Probably not in college, I guess, since you said you had a golf scholarship?"

"That's right. I didn't run competitively in college, or high school either. I was recruited, or kidnapped I should say, early on by the football coach at Red Earth High. But I've always liked running. I especially like running barefoot on the Bobby Wilson Golf Course near our farm with my dog."

"What's her name?"

"His. It's a he. He's a yellow Lab. Sir Ralph the Wonder Dog."

"Really?" Bobbi said, laughing. "What a great name!"

"Ralph, or Ralphie for short. Do you play golf?"

"No, but I'd like to learn."

"Well, maybe we'll get a chance to remedy that unfortunate situation sometime soon. There's a public course in Worland. One in Lovell, too."

"I hope so!"

Oddly, Clifford felt himself turning twitterpated, nervous, not his typical state of being at all. He tried concentrating on the sound of his and Bobbi's feet simultaneously hitting the soft, sandy ground; on that of their syncopated breathing, which corresponded to their footfalls, merging as though they were one. Three breaths in and two out: one-two-three, four-five; one-two-three, four-five... Now and then a cowpie interrupted the rhythm, when one runner or the other had to alter stride length to avoid splashing through fresh evidence of Galen Davies' cattle.

"Do you have any brothers or sisters?" Clifford asked.

"Yep, one of each. Billie, she's a year younger than me. And Buddy will be a senior in high school this fall. How about you?"

Clifford paused. "Uh, yeah. A sister. Mary. She's a little older than me."

"Where is she? What's she doing?"

"I don't know."

"What? Why?"

"I haven't seen her since I was four. Since the house fire. When I got sent to Minnesota, they shipped her off somewhere else. I don't know where."

"Well, Clifford, you have to track her down! You must."

"How come?"

"You just do. She's the closest relative you could possibly have. I'll help you find her."

"You will? Why?"

"Because you're a nice guy. And I like you."

"Oh... thanks." *Brilliant response, Einstein.*

A hollow whooshing sound coming from above caused both Bobbi and Clifford to look up.

"What was that?" Clifford asked.

"A diving nighthawk," Bobbi answered. "Strange sound, huh? What's the farthest you've been up the canyon? Does this track fade out, or does it continue up into the mountains? Do you know?"

"I've gone probably four miles up. It starts getting really steep at that point, but it did seem to keep going."

"Maybe Dr. Hillary would let us use a state truck to go exploring up there one of these weekends. Would you want to do that?"

"Yes," Clifford said. "I'd be way into it. Hillary prefers to be called 'Rad,' you know."

Clifford glanced at his running partner and she looked back at him, her emerald eyes smiling. It sent a quiver down his back.

He couldn't help noticing Bobbi's bare neck glowing in the twilight under a sheen of perspiration.

"He also likes being called 'Boss,'" she told him.

"Does he? Well, he's a boss boss, I'll say that for him."

They ran on in silence for a few seconds.

"What did you run in track?" Clifford asked. "Rad told me you ran cross-country, so probably the distance events, or middle distance?" He already knew the answer, but he also knew he wasn't the best of conversationalists, and he wanted to make small talk.

"Yep. The mile and two-mile."

"Were you good?" *Geez, give yourself a swift kick in the butt later for asking such a stupid question.*

"I did all right, yes."

The fact was Hillary had already told Clifford that Bobbi had set a new Utah State University record for the women's mile run just two months earlier.

"Well, I sure am glad you like running up this canyon like I do. Wanna do it again?"

"Sure. How about tomorrow evening? And the one after that?"

"Count me in," Clifford said, trying to appear cool while banging about on the inside like a Mexican jumping bean. "That big old juniper tree there is the mile-and-a-half mark. I measured it last weekend with the truck. Turn around here and we'll have three miles in. Sound good?"

"Sounds perfect, Clifford."

Their canyon-enclosed surroundings growing ever darker, Clifford Gustafson and Bobbi Alder turned around and padded downstream at an accelerated pace, regaining the Sleeping Dog site in ten minutes' time.

***

Paul Barlow pulled up late in the afternoon of July 1, which also happened to be the first day of the summer to top a hundred degrees at the Sleeping Dog site. A displaced mountain man who resided on the plains of eastern Nebraska, Barlow preferred the woods over open country. Pulling his travel trailer behind his pickup truck, he rattled across the cattle guard at the east end of the site, driving onto BLM land, and then parked and leveled the trailer about a half-mile up the canyon, next to the track and Sleeping Dog Creek in the shade of a tall cottonwood tree.

Barlow planned to be on site about halftime now, and that made Hillary happy. Most of the remainder of the days he would spend brainstorming with local amateur archaeologists and with colleagues, making whirlwind trips to the surrounding state universities in Bozeman, Laramie, and Boulder.

In the morning, on the first of what would become their regular up-canyon, down-canyon walks together, Hillary updated Barlow on the status of the crew and their work.

"Now, with twelve on, things are humming along," Hillary reported. "Although maybe a few degrees less harmoniously than before. I expected that with the addition of the four newcomers, because the original crew grew so tight so fast. Except for Peter Ashton. Just yesterday he got into a brief scuffle with that new young man, Harry Old-comb. He seems like a strange one, too. Doesn't seem to have much interest in archaeology. He hasn't told us much about himself."

On hearing this, Barlow sighed. "Yep, he's a smart-ass nineteen-going-on-sixteen-year-old. I haven't let you in on this, or anybody else, but now I will. He's out of the University of New York at Buffalo, as you probably do know, where he has yet to declare a major. Here's the part you don't know, or at least I don't think you do—Harry Oldcomb's stepfather is Dr. Albert Q. Bartlett, the ethnologist who specializes in South American tribes and lectures at Harvard and Cambridge. Bartlett implored me to hire his stepson for the season to see if a summer out West might spark some motivation in the boy. I obliged, because I really couldn't say no. I owe that generous man more than one favor."

"What about Ben Reed?" Hillary asked. "How'd you find him?"

Redheaded, wild-eyed, and fresh out of nearby Manderson/Mercerville High, Reed had informed Hillary that come October he'd be joining the Marines.

"He's balls-to-the-wall gung-ho about everything he does," Hillary observed. "I'd say he exudes the rawness of this wild country that nurtured him. If I wanted to get fancy with my words, that is."

Barlow chuckled. "That he does. I love that kid. He may not know what we're doing or why we're doing it, but mark my words, he'll be one of the best at it within a couple of weeks. Shoveling, sifting, scraping, whatever. And he'll have a lot of fun doing it. You do know he's Galen Davies' nephew, his sister's son? Up in the foothills, he'll be the one who shows the other young 'professionals' where to find arrowheads, edible wild onions, that sort of thing."

"Marge Paavno sure is the likable sort," Hillary said. "She told me she went back to school at Kent State just last year, at age forty-six."

"Did she tell you the rest of her story?"

"Not that I know of. How's it go?"

"Well, last year the youngest of her three daughters also went off to college. Not long after that, her doctor husband of twenty-four years left home, too, but not for college. He left Marge for a nurse the same age as their oldest daughter. After recovering from the initial shock and heartbreak, Marge told me, she realized she was footloose to a degree she had never known. Those loose feet jumped at the opportunity to apply to work for the summer on a dig in Wyoming. Becoming an archaeologist is a dream she's harbored for a long time, she said, and she saw a job notice about our little excavation here posted on the announcement board in the Anthropology Department at Kent State. Providential, she believed."

"Hmm, I think so, too," Hillary replied. "It looks to me like Dr. Paavno's loss is our gain. What about Jesus Padilla? Chuy? Says he's from down near the New Mexico–Chihuahua border and goes to school in Albuquerque, where John Riley's headed in the fall. Seems like a good kid."

"He comes highly recommended by MacIntosh. He'll be a senior next year, and probably go on to grad school at New Mexico, too."

***

That day, after work and a light dinner, Clifford and Bobbi went for a run, as they'd done every weekday evening since their first canyon outing a week earlier. It was unmistakable, to Clifford at least, that in this short time—only a month of knowing each other—their relationship had grown into something deeper than friendship.

"Bobbi?" Clifford began as they neared their regular turnaround point. *I have to be brave.*

"Yes?" Bobbi glanced over at Clifford and the two made eye contact.

"Are you feeling what I'm feeling? I mean, what I'm feeling about you?"

"Stop for second."

Clifford did as told, and Bobbi turned toward him. She reached behind his head with both hands, pulled his face down to hers, and gave him the longest, most genuine kiss he'd ever experienced. Both were winded from jogging, so they after a second or two they had to pull apart, laughing, to get their breath back. Then they resumed the smooch, ratcheting up the intensity of their embrace by a few degrees.

"Does that answer your question?" Bobbi finally asked.

"That would be an affirmative?"

"Yes."

"Well, okay then, let's head for home."

As they resumed their run, Clifford felt like he was running on a cloud of joy. "Hi-ho Silver! Away!" he shouted. Then he paused. "Wait a minute. It's the Lone Ranger who says that. I guess I'd make a better Tonto, huh?"

"Well, one way or the other, you're my Kemosabe," Bobbi said.

***

"Archaeology and prehistory get all mired up with a lot of romantic notions," Barlow began.

It was two days after his arrival at the site, and the night before the big Independence Day Oldtimers' Picnic and Rodeo in Mercerville. Hillary and all but two of the twelve crew members had joined Barlow after supper, everyone sitting on stumps or on the ground around a campfire beside Barlow's trailer upstream from the site. It was the first of several such gatherings he would preside over during the coming weeks, either here or on the farmhouse porch. For the student archaeologists, these impromptu evening lectures and back-and-forth sessions with the preeminent Paul Barlow would be one of the real treats of the summer.

"Some of it's spewed by white liberal revisionists," Barlow went on, "but a fair share comes from certain Indians themselves. They want us to believe that the noble and untainted red man was in total harmony with nature before the white man arrived, in tune with the universe. None of these guys likes hearing me say things like this, but the Paleoindians helped push the woolly mammoth over the brink of extinction. I'm convinced it's the case. Some say it came about to due to changes in climatic conditions, but I just don't believe environmental change happens that fast, in as short a time span as it seems to have taken the mammoth to disappear—unless something catastrophic happened, like volcanic ash blocking out the sun for weeks, months, years. But the geologic record doesn't support such a theory. It looks to me like the Paleos were killing the young, pre-adolescent male mammoths, eliminating the future breeding stock. Can't blame 'em, either, because an old bull pachyderm would taste like crap warmed over. Not to mention that a younger, smaller animal would've been easier to kill and butcher.

"The fact is, American Indians simply weren't as organized or as technologically advanced as the Anglos, although some were heading toward it. Give 'em another hundred years undisturbed and they might've gotten there. Savvy enough and large enough in population to screw up the western environment almost as badly as the nineteenth century Euro-Americans did. Anyway, that's what I believe. But none of these guys wants to hear me say it."

***

"I could not *believe* it when you guys got up there on stage last night," said Josie MacDonald, toiling beside the others in the excavation units mid-morning on the day after the big Fourth of July bash in town. Most everyone was suffering a headache. "Where'd you get the nerve?"

"Bottled bravery," John Riley said. "Nerves of Coors."

"Not me," chimed in Tom Jefferson. "I only had two beers. I'm a natural. Cool and calm, as always. And I've got *soul*."

"Well, it may have been the beer for you, John, but you're still a darn good guitar player," said Josie. "Sure was nice of the band to let you and Tom take over their instruments."

"I have never laughed so hard in my life," said Conrad Hillary, standing at his regular perch above the excavations. "I thought you were all going to have to take me to the hospital. I didn't think Riley could possibly top Jefferson's rendition of 'Your Cheatin' Heart,' but he did it with his James Brown act. Hey," he added, "you guys know any Buddy Holly tunes?"

"Owww!" said Riley, screeching like the Godfather of Soul.

"That would be a yes," Jefferson said. "We'll practice and then play them for you sometime, Rad."

"Boys, I'd be honored."

17
A SIGN

Barlow and Hillary strode side by side up the canyon of Sleeping Dog Creek on a warm morning in mid-July. Barlow's low-slung, plumber's-butt Wranglers secured the front of his white cowboy shirt, but the rear tail hung out, loose and flapping. His salt-and-pepper hair, neither particularly long nor short, badly needed a good brushing.

As they went along, the two professional archaeologists discussed what the crew had discovered so far at the Sleeping Dog site, speculating on what it all meant. It was a fruitful site, of that they were certain, thus far yielding a nearly continuous record of Great Plains aboriginal life. From the top down, the occupations extended from historic times to at least nine thousand years before the present. The only piece missing in the continuum was evidence of the Late Plains Archaic. Sleeping Dog promised to be the sort of site every Plains archaeologist dreams of discovering, excavating, and publishing the findings from. Barlow and Hillary understood the magnitude of their great fortune and the responsibility that came with it. They also agreed that this site would likely become what they would both be best remembered for in their chosen professional field.

The pair of veteran field archaeologists spoke of things second nature to them, but good to air all the same. It helped each stay fresh and on top of his game.

"In the western U.S., evidence of sustained permanent occupation is generally restricted to certain coastal areas," Barlow ruminated, "and to the great Southwest, where moderate weather, coupled with abundant streams for irrigation, permitted husbandry to develop. That led to enduring villages of cliff dwellings and stand-alone, adobe-brick structures. I don't need to tell you this, Rad… I'm just thinking out loud. There's nothing like it known in the northern Plains or northern Rockies. Here early man hunted and gathered in mobile bands. Permanence, or continuity of place, would've been the rare exception."

"Yep," Hillary agreed. "This region was no doubt an extremely tough place to make a living for a hunter-gatherer. It demanded a nomadic lifestyle based on the whims of the bison herds and the seasonal explosions of edible plants. Obtaining enough food to get a family through a cold, barren winter would have been a tough job."

"Survival would have hinged largely on how successful the summer and autumn hunts were," Barlow said. "Or, alternatively, on following the herds to their wintering grounds. Around here that would have been places like the dune desert west of Worland, which, today anyway, gets very little snow in winter."

"Uh-huh. Yep, the seasonal travel and transitory settlements of the prehistorics make for some pretty spotty archaeology here where we work."

"But it's also where it's at," Barlow said, "if what you're most interested in is the Paleoindian. We've got the kill sites—pronghorn, bison, bighorn sheep. Not many elk, though, and that fact still confounds me. The wapiti was more of a plains animal than a mountain dweller back then. That obviously begs the question, why aren't they more common in the archaeological record? Maybe we'll find 'em here. Maybe we'll also learn why the prehistoric people moved on from the Agate Basin to the Hell Gap point. That's always mystified me, too. That Agate Basin projectile sure looks to me like it would've been a superior bison-killer."

"I'm not sure I agree with you on that, Paul. But I do hope we get into both of them as we probe deeper."

Barlow changed the subject. "What do you think of Bobbi Alder?"

"I think she's wonderful," Hillary said, coughing. "Why?"

"When I met her at hunting camp in the Bear Rivers down in Utah, she immediately struck me as one of the most appealing women I'd ever met. Serving as camp cook, I learned, was one of a great many things she does outstandingly well. And an anthro major! Rad, on that trip it occurred to me that, were I thirty years younger and not married to the love of my life, I'd go after Bobbi Alder like a hungry cutthroat trout going for a fat grasshopper on a late summer day." He smiled at his simile and looked over at Hillary, only slightly embarrassed.

"Why, Dr. Paul Barlow, I think you have a crush going there."

"Nah, just a dream. An old man's gotta have a dream, right?"

"I suppose so. But for a young man like, say, Clifford Gustafson, I think it's more than a dream. Or maybe a dream that's coming true."

***

The brutal force of the sun came down hard on Clifford, like a hammer of heat. His watch was back in his quarters in the farmhouse attic, but he could tell by the angle and intensity of the sun, and by the growling in his stomach, that break time was near. The natural, solar-heated amphitheater he toiled in had no doubt kept Crow Indians and a parade of predecessors relatively comfortable through the Big Horn Basin's bitter winters. But the same rock walls made working under the midday summer sun unbearable. Since early July, when it started getting truly hot, the crew members had been dividing their requisite eight-hour workday into two shifts. The first ran from seven to eleven in the morning; then, after knocking off for three hours, they'd work again from two until six. Thus they took advantage of both the chill of morning and the afternoon shade provided by the sandstone rim, while avoiding the searing midday sun.

After their early lunch, several of the budding social scientists sat or reclined on the porch floor of the old farmhouse, reading, dozing, or talking. They chatted about this and that, about what they'd uncovered in the test pits that morning.

Danny Ho, Tom Jefferson, John Riley, and Josie MacDonald had strolled down-canyon a half mile on the gravel road to cool off and clean up in a favorite deep pool in Sleeping Dog Creek. It sat in the shade of some sturdy poplars just below a short stretch of gentle rapids, immediately across the road from Galen Davies' main residence. Prior to hitting the water, Riley—dirty with dust sweat-caked onto his face and torso—looked only a shade or two lighter than his friend and workmate Jefferson.

Ho had hauled along his compact, battery-powered transistor radio and placed it on a low boulder above the creek. It blared KWOR-AM out of Worland. At high noon, the weather report—squeezed in by the deejay on duty between the Beatles and Barbara Mandrell—informed the foursome of an air temperature of a hundred and three degrees.

"That means it's at least a hundred here," Riley said to the others.

Nevertheless, the creek's water proved to be numbingly cold. Forty seconds of submersion was the longest any of the skinny young men could endure. Josie MacDonald, thanks to her greater surplus of body fat, managed a full minute in a friendly freeze-out competition.

Despite the heat, Clifford hadn't been in the mood for jumping into the creek. Nor had he felt much like talking or reading. He gobbled down a huge lunch of two peanut-butter sandwiches on rye bread, half of a big bag of crinkle potato chips, and a quart of orange juice. Then he walked onto the porch, stretched out on his foam pad, and tried to fall asleep. But each time he began drifting off, the noise of another crew member or the tickle of a fly on his nose brought him back around.

"I'm gonna take a walk up-canyon," he said to Bobbi.

Bobbi sat on the porch, leaning against a pair of cushions propped against the side of the house and reading a James Michener novel. She smiled up at him.

"Okay, Clifford, I'll see you at two. If not sooner. I'm looking forward to our run tonight when it cools down."

Her sparkling green eyes held Clifford's captive in their gaze for a moment, yet he lowered his glance before turning around. Earlier in the day he'd noticed Bobbi, for the first time to his knowledge, had adopted the bra-free style followed by the other young women on the crew. *I approve of the change*, he said to himself.

"Oh, do I approve," he whispered as he walked away from the porch.

"What's that?" Bobbi asked.

"Oh, nothing. Sorry."

"Wait a second," she said. "Come here."

Clifford turned around and walked back up the stairs onto the porch.

"Here," Bobbi said, pointing to her mouth.

He knelt and kissed her.

Although bashful by nature, Clifford hadn't a shred of embarrassment or self-consciousness. He didn't care who saw them smooching. Obviously, Bobbi didn't either. The fact was, Clifford had half a mind to commandeer one of the state rigs and drive down to Casper, find the studios of 50,000-watt clear channel KTWO radio, grab a microphone, and broadcast his declaration of love for Bobbi Alder for half the western United States to hear.

Clifford liked, loved, everything he knew about this beautiful young woman. She had long, silky, dark-brown hair and the curves of a figure skater. But despite her knockout looks, she didn't act coy or snobbish when someone looked at her or tried to strike up a conversation. Forthright, she always looked Clifford in the eye and had a welcoming smile.

The crowning event of the previous evening had only magnified his feelings.

After work, Clifford and Bobbi had jumped into one of the state pickup trucks and driven to Worland to shop for groceries. After that, they had slipped over to the Cowboy Bijou to see *The Getaway*. Both had enjoyed it a great deal, Clifford's appreciation coming in large part from the fact that he was sitting next to a girl he considered more beautiful than Ali McGraw's character in the movie.

On their way home, as they motored along the deserted byway separating Manderson and Mercerville, Bobbi had said, "Pull left onto that road, Clifford."

He had pointed out the dirt spur road as they drove in the daylight toward Worland earlier in the evening. The rough-looking BLM track appeared to penetrate a protected canyon, possibly a good place to scout for artifacts.

Clifford did as told, navigating the truck off the pavement and a quarter mile into the dark canyon.

"Stop here."

Clifford applied the brakes and shut down the engine.

"There's something I want to tell you, Clifford Gustafson," Bobbi said, her soft, warm voice like September sun on sandstone.

"What is it?" Clifford queried, his interest piqued.

"To propose this is against my religion, but not against my heart. I believe it's the right thing to do. If the time is right for you, too, that is. I *love* you, Clifford. It's crazy how fast this has all happened. I can't quite explain it, but it's happened all the same. I've never felt anything close to it. And now, right this minute, I want to get as close to you as possible."

"You mean..."

"Yes. I mean."

Now, massaging thoughts of that discourse and of what unfolded immediately afterward, Clifford stood beneath the blazing, twelve-thirty sun above his and Bobbi's excavation unit. He told himself the next time he traveled to Worland he needed to stock up on replacements for the condom that had come in so handy on the previous, magical evening. He'd had it in his thin leather wallet so long it had made a tale-tell, permanent ringed impression. *Yup, finally found a use for my emergency rubber*, he joked to himself, meaning no disrespect to Bobbi whatsoever.

Looking down into the unit, Clifford saw shade spilling into its far west side, creating a spot that appeared large enough for him to squeeze into. Rather than continuing up the canyon as planned, he succumbed to his post-meal drowsiness and sat, legs dangling, at the edge of the excavation. Then he dropped in. *We've made a lot of progress here*, he thought. *Ground level is up to my eyes when I stand on the floor.* He squatted and nestled in, back against the north wall and right shoulder touching the west wall. He barely fitted into the available shade.

Cool and comfy, even at the hottest part of the day. Clifford meditated for a moment on the glare of the east and south walls, and on the flat floor of the unit. All appeared flawless in their smoothness, ninety-degree angularity, and vertical or horizontal aspect. *This hole is a work of art, and I helped create it.* Better yet, he and Bobbi Alder, his first true love—his only love, he hoped—had fashioned it together, as the team they were.

Like the beautiful sculpture revealed by an artist's chiseling away at a slab of marble, this well-proportioned hole had always been there— it had simply been filled with sand and loam. The layers of strata lying above the fallen sandstone slab, still visible in all four walls, resulted from sediment deposited during periodic flooding of the flats; when spring and summer snowmelt caused Sleeping Dog Creek to overflow its banks countless times over the decades. The strata lay not quite parallel to the top and bottom of the unit, but slanted upward toward the rim.

The whisk-broomed, baby-bottom-smooth walls read like a north-central Wyoming prehistory book. On the south wall, midway between top and bottom, Clifford could see dark charcoal marking the food-preparation pit he had excavated a couple of weeks earlier. It happened that the plane of the south wall ran dead center through the pit, which measured about sixty centimeters in width. He and Bobbi had screened out a lot of animal-bone fragments and fire-cracked rock remaining from prehistoric cooking fires. The bones they dropped into plastic bags, along with small pieces of paper bearing Clifford's pencil scribble. The writing identified the coordinates of depth, distance, and direction from the primary point of reference, that being the original southwest corner of the excavation unit. Clifford recalled Bobbi, in her neat and steady hand, drawing a representation of the scene on graph paper. According to Hillary, fires in the circular, thirty-centimeter-deep pit had blazed some four thousand years ago, as he believed the basin-shaped food-preparation pit to be McKean in age. Clifford and Bobbi added fodder to Hillary's hunch when they uncovered, on the same occupation level, several lengths of cordage made from twisted strands of milkweed fiber, along with a large, base-indented lanceolate spear point of a dark-purple chert.

Granted, Clifford considered, they might not do much for the man on the street. But for an aspiring field archaeologist like himself, the polished stratigraphy and food-pit cross-section were beautiful things to behold.

Far out, he thought as he drifted off. *Ex-treme-ly far out.* Soon he dozed, dreaming of Bobbi Alder. Of him and Bobbi together unearthing the ancient burial of a Paleoindian. Of a house fire long ago.

As Clifford napped, the shade in the unit inched eastward. Several feet away, near the base of the rim, a fat old prairie rattlesnake trailing seven rattles became irritated, or perhaps sensed imminent doom. A ray of sun had squeezed down through a gap in the rocks and hit the snake's side full-force. In an instinctive quest to avoid boiling in its own blood, it slithered away, seeking shade. Perceiving some, it lowered itself over the edge of the excavation, fell onto the floor, and coiled into the southwest corner of the unit opposite the dozing Clifford. Once the rattler got settled, less than two feet separated its head from Clifford's bare feet. The snake's tongue, sampling the surroundings, darted in and out of the reptile's mouth at irregular intervals.

A few minutes later, Clifford stirred, awoke, and opened his eyes.

"Shit!" he screamed.

His feet and legs propelled him up and out of the excavation unit. If he'd had time to think about it, he would have stayed put and sat still, knowing that sudden movement could trigger a strike from the coiled snake. But he thanked God he hadn't had time to think about it, because then he'd be in one heck of a jam.

Angry, scared, and juiced with adrenaline, Clifford grabbed one of the long-handled shovels protruding from the large pile of backfill beside the unit. Lying down and reaching over the edge, he stabbed at the rattlesnake with the digging tool's blade.

"Scum-sucking–dung-head–reptilian–bastard–snake!" he yelled, keeping time with his shovel thrusts. "Ruin *my* nap!"

The snake, mad as a pack of hornets but headless now and dying, rattled its last rattle. The buzz continued for several moments before fading to silence.

Clifford had never before killed anything out of anger or fear. He just stood there trembling, hands to knees, feeling nauseous. The hot sun bore down on him. It all brought him to the precipice of giving back his big lunch. He decided to take a swim after all, and try to wash himself of the terrifying experience.

18
RESENTMENT

Dan Oberlin stopped to mop his sweaty bald head with his neckerchief. He'd known that even in the dark of night he would be
unable to move undetected into the upper reaches of Sleeping Dog
Canyon via the easy route. Not with all those damn archaeologists
congregated around the mouth of the canyon, where the creek flowed
from BLM lands onto Galen Davies' property. So, he had chosen
to follow this longer and hillier route, one made no easier by the
seventy-pound pack full of provisions he carried on his back.

When planning his trek, Oberlin had considered the possibility of
coming in from the north. That would have made it a shorter hike from
the point to which he could drive and park. But, despite the love he pro-
fessed for the canyon to his fellow CAUSE members, he remained too
unfamiliar with its nooks and notches to know if an easy hiking route
existed from the Sand Burr Rim down to the level of Sleeping Dog Creek.
If it did, he hadn't been able to identify it on the USGS quadrangle map
covering the canyon. Conversely, on the map it looked as if dropping in
from the south would make for a doable, though longer, hike.

Oberlin had driven his old two-toned green Ford pickup truck,
lights off and navigating by the light of the full moon, on the dirt track
that inched upward from the toe of the long, gentle ridge separating
the watersheds of Sleeping Dog and Bear creeks. Where the track ter-
minated, at a point marked by a six-foot-high cairn of flat rocks, he
shut down the engine, got out, and hefted the heavy backpack out of
the truck's bed and up onto his shoulders.

Having memorized the portion of topography relevant to his
journey, Oberlin knew his exact location. He would have to continue
up the steepening ridgeline for exactly a mile and a half. With his

heavy load, he guesstimated that would take forty-five minutes. He snapped on his flashlight, pointed it at the ground in front of him, and commenced walking, shining the beam on his wristwatch now and then to monitor the time elapsed.

"God-damn cows," he complained out loud fifteen minutes into his hike, as his flashlight's beam spotlighted a minefield of crap piles. He despised the fact that Galen Davies could graze his cattle on, and make money off, these lands owned in common by the American people. At the same time, Oberlin wanted to overcome some of those feelings and get friendlier with Davies. He had become smitten with Davies' daughter, Janie, home from college for the summer. He'd met her at a street dance in Worland a couple of weeks earlier. "Damn," he'd said to Alan Alvarez, "she is about the most *beautiful* thing I've ever seen... I still can't believe that ugly red-haired son-of-a-bitch land-trasher is her old man."

After hoofing it uphill for forty-four minutes, Oberlin stopped and squatted, back first, against a low, table-like boulder. He set the backpack down on the rock, unbuckled the waist strap, and extricated himself from the shoulder straps. He had done a fair amount of day hiking over the summer, but nothing with a seventy-pound load. This involved heavy sweating, hard breathing, and screaming quadriceps. He knew that from here it would be an easy downhill hike of just over a mile to reach the junction of the wet and dry forks of Sleeping Dog Creek; and, from there, a gentle upstream mile followed by a final steep quarter-mile push to his destination. Afterward, walking down and up and back down to his truck would be a relative piece of cake. Though he'd still be hiking in the dark, his backpack by then would be emptied of most of its contents.

Oberlin caught his breath and took a big drink of water. He reattached himself to the heavy backpack and proceeded downhill in a northerly direction.

***

"Hey, did you hear what happened at the British Open?" Clifford asked.

He paused, partly for effect but mostly to take a big swig out of his cold can of Coors. Balanced on the bar stool beside him in the Tired Puppy Tavern sat Peter Ashton, the only other golfer on the crew. Interest in the game seemed to be the only thing Clifford and Ashton had in common. Through the bar's open front door, Clifford could see that a curtain of darkness had descended on the day.

"No, who won it?" Ashton asked.

"Tom Weiskopf," Clifford answered, "at Royal Troon. That's over on the southwest coast of Scotland. Which is great—but the really cool thing is Gene Sarazen got a hole-in-one on a short par-three they call the 'Postage Stamp' hole. Seventy-one years old. Pretty amazing."

"He's a sawed-off son of a bitch," Ashton said. "Bet he's not five-foot-six. Came up to here on me." He held his flat hand open, palm down, parallel to the ground and against his lower neck.

"You mean you've met Gene Sarazen?" Clifford asked.

"Oh, hell, yeah. My dad and I played a round with him at Pebble Beach two summers back. He told me some really interesting stuff."

"Man, you run in different circles than I do. Like, what did he tell you?"

"Well, he was born with a different last name. Saraconi or something like that. He's the son of an immigrant carpenter from Italy. Changed it to Sarazen because he liked the sound of it better. Stuff like that. And that he almost died from the flu as a kid. And Howard Hughes taught him to fly airplanes. Said watching the plane's tail move around somehow gave him the idea for making a sand wedge, which Sarazen more or less invented."

"That's crazy," Clifford managed to muster in response. He believed everything Ashton had said, but couldn't quite wrap his mind around it.

"That Royal Troon's a nice course," Ashton added. "But man, hold on to your hat. It's windy as hell."

Lips parted, Clifford just stared at his bar companion.

"Dad and I went a round there with Gary Player back in sixty-nine. That trip was my fourth time across the pond, a college graduation present."

***

Sal Calderara sat at his desk in an alcove of the BLM's Worland District Office, sorting through paperwork. The sun came hard through the window, making him squint. The worried furrow between his eyes was more the result of years of pain, than of heredity. A large nose, pitted, plump, and purple, hinted at his yen for the clear-colored poisons of gin and vodka.

Calderara felt even more miserable than usual; pushing papers, sorry for himself. He'd read in the newspaper that morning of the latest finds at the Sleeping Dog site: two Hell Gap points, recovered at nine feet below the ground surface, in direct association with the immense skeleton of a *Bison antiquus*. The Pleistocene forerunner of the modern bison, the animal had been extinct for at least nine thousand years.

"Unbelievable," Calderara hissed. "I should be the one recovering that stuff. That Barlow is so lucky."

He had tried to strike a balance between the envy he felt for Dr. Paul Barlow and the respect he had for him as a professional. Or at least he thought he had tried, but his covetous side had prevailed. He also knew he should be paying regular visits to the site, but he always wound up telling his supervisor he had more important things to do. Sure, he would then tell himself, important things like filling out these forms so Shell Oil can poke more of their damn exploratory holes into the basin.

In truth, Calderara didn't want to let Barlow and his sidekick, Dr. Conrad Hillary, know he had any interest in what they were doing out there. Calderara knew himself well enough to know he was smart and capable. After all, he held master's degrees in both anthropology and geology to prove it. But he was a frustrated academic. Rather than going the full Ph.D. route, he'd settled for this decent-paying position as a government archaeologist. Pushing forty, he felt comfortable but unfulfilled; content but not satisfied.

Propelling himself with his strong arms and hands, Calderara backed himself in his wheelchair away from his desk, then moved forward toward the reception area.

19
TRAGEDY

For Hillary, for Clifford and Bobbi, for everyone, time had begun to blur. Weeks passed, with every day dawning and ending much like the previous one. So, too, did this mid-August day start out like just another repeat of the previous month of days: clear and warm, headed for hot. Such would be the shattering, soul-searing nature of the morning's incident, however, that Clifford Gustafson henceforth and forever would divide his existence into two chapters—the things he experienced prior to Wednesday, August 15, 1973, and everything else that happened, or would happen, to him after the horrific day.

At eight a.m. the sun had yet to reach the canyon floor, but the basin beyond blushed in a terracotta dawning glow. Darlow was away, having driven northwest to Bozeman to spend a couple of days consulting with his colleague Dr. Janet Perkins at Montana State University. Hillary had hit the water early, trying out an assortment of dry flies on the finicky brown trout of Sleeping Dog Creek. It was warming fast where he stood, a mile east of the dig, above the promising hole where the creek took a big forty-five degree turn. The canyon widened here, allowing the desiccating sun of spring and summer to create a semi-desert ecotone on the south-facing slope to the north of the creek. Conversely, brush grew thick on the south side.

Noticing the time, Hillary gathered up his gear and began hustling back toward the site. By the time he got there, he figured, the crew would have been hard at it for an hour and a half. He didn't want them thinking he'd turned into a slacker.

On returning, no longer did Hillary see four distinct test units; they had grown together into one huge excavation, the various quadrants excavated to different depths. Seven crew members stood, sat, or knelt, working at assorted levels within the complex, while the other four operated, or leaned against, dirt-shifting screens above. The sight struck Hillary as slightly surreal, like workers in a quarry or a chain gang toiling atop a mass of buried skyscrapers.

"This is what you all went to college for?" he teased. "Ditch-diggers get paid about four times what you're getting, you know."

Then he climbed in to take a turn at helping Chuy Padilla and Marge Paavno dig around some post-hole remains at the far western edge of the excavation.

"Damn!" Hillary growled, coughing, just as he got down to business.

"What's wrong, Conrad?" asked Paavno, looking up. The heavy-set woman tossed her head sideways to sweep her brunette bangs away from her eyes.

"I just remembered the cotter pin. I took that dang trailer-hitch cotter pin out of my back pocket where I was fishing, 'cause it was stabbing me in the butt. I'm planning to trailer the backhoe into Worland at lunchtime to get it worked on. It's getting harder and harder to shift into reverse. Must be a problem in the linkage." Hillary straightened up and barked over at Clifford. "Hey, Gustafson! You hear what I'm saying, my favorite U-Minnie Golden Go-fer?"

"Yeah, Rad."

"How about running up and grabbing that cotter pin for me?"

"Okay, sure." Clifford sounded less than enthusiastic.

"Lemme do it, Boss," said Bobbi Alder, who was manning the sifting screen into which Clifford tossed the occasional shovelful of dirt. "I'd like to take a walk and check it out, anyway. I've never been up there this time of day."

Clifford had been suffering from an intestinal upset all morning. He'd told Bobbi as much and she'd watched as he rushed over to the outhouse at least four times. But she knew nothing would stop him from doing anything Conrad Hillary asked, regardless of how he felt.

"Yeah, okay, sure," Hillary said.

"Where is it, exactly?"

"You know where the canyon widens and the creek takes a turn about a mile up?"

"Sure, uh-huh. I know exactly where you're talking about."

"There's a huge sandstone boulder about twenty yards due north of the turn, right up against the rim. Below that big overhang, you know."

"Sure. The rock I sat on after you and I walked up the canyon together back in June. While you dipped your head in the creek."

"Oh, yeah, of course."

"Okay. I'm gone. Outta here."

Stepping away from her post at the sifting screen, Bobbi tossed her head back and moved her hands through her long brown hair. Revealing sunrays backlit her profile and Clifford could see the outline of her breasts beneath her threadbare, white-on-blue Utah State Aggies T-shirt. He peered over the edge of the excavation to follow her movements as she jogged away upstream.

"Dang," he said aloud.

"What's that?" asked Josie MacDonald, looking up. She was on her knees, whisk-brooming the ground around a long stone Agate Basin projectile point. There it had lain, right where she'd found it, for perhaps ten millennia.

"Oh, a mosquito bit me," Clifford lied.

"Huh, that's strange. I haven't noticed any mosquitoes all morning," Josie replied, with a smile.

Clifford knew that Bobbi often confided in Josie, yet he didn't know what or how much she told her. He felt it would be impossible to explain to her how it made him feel, watching Bobbi move, her long legs and petite rear end fitting so well into her Levi's, her long hair trailing behind. Watching her, he felt it in his groin and in his stomach, where on this particular morning it got all churned up with his diarrheal upset. He simultaneously felt sick, excited, and terrified. It all combined to confuse him, but in a good way.

Fifteen minutes went by. Then a half hour. A full hour passed and Bobbi still hadn't returned.

"Conrad, that should've taken Bobbi a half hour at most," said Mary O'Donnell, scratching her head through her thin, white-blonde hair. "She's not one to dawdle."

Clifford, a bit surprised by O'Donnell's concern, piped in. "I'll hoof it up and see what's going on." His intestines had settled down some, and lunch, just twenty minutes away, was sounding good.

"Okay, Pedro," said Hillary.

Clifford climbed out of the unit, dusted off the knees of his jeans, and started jogging up-canyon.

He reached his destination ten minutes later. *No Bobbi*, he thought. "Bobbi?"

No answer.

"Bobbi?" he said louder, with mounting unease.

Still nothing.

Then, glancing around, Clifford saw something on the ground to his north, protruding into the sunlight from the shadows cast by the rock rim. He walked over to investigate. What he found was the lower left arm and long-fingered, tanned hand of Bobbi Alder. The ring of emeralds and two-toned Black Hills gold adorning her little finger glimmered in the late-morning sun.

"Oh Jesus, Bobbi, what happened?"

Clifford fell to his knees. Bobbi lay face down, unmoving. From her back, opposite her generous and loving heart, protruded the feathered end of a primitive-looking arrow. Clifford pinched her wrist for a pulse. Nothing.

"Oh, God. No!"

Clifford wanted to lie down beside Bobbi and never get up. Instead, he forced himself to stand and start running, faster than he had run in years, flowing like a quickening breeze storming down-canyon off the high Big Horn peaks.

***

"Josie, Riley, Jefferson, Ho!" Hillary shouted, and then paused to hack into his palm. "Grab a couple of those lodgepoles behind the shed. Marge, you run into the house and get a blanket. We need to make a stretcher. Oldcomb, you get over to Galen Davies' place and call the sheriff. Tell him exactly what we know and where we need the ambulance."

"Got it, Conrad," said Harry Oldcomb.

"Okay," Hillary said. "Clifford? A few of us will head up in the Jeep. You go down to the road head and help get those ambulance people up there as fast as possible."

Reeling, Clifford did as ordered. In a moment of lucidity, he marveled at how cool and in control Hillary seemed. He understood his friend and mentor knew how he felt about Bobbi Alder, and that Hillary wanted to give Clifford other things to think about; to take his mind away from the horrible situation at hand.

All was in vain, as Hillary verified on reaching Bobbi's limp body. The arrow had pierced her heart.

"Ho, Josie, take the Jeep down and intercept Gustafson. Please. Then call the coroner in Worland from Galen's house. The ambulance people will want to come up, too, but they won't be able to get all the way here. Not with that big rig. And Josie?"

"Yes?" she said through tears, her shoulders shaking.

"Stay with Clifford. Don't let him come back here."

"Okay. I'll do what I can. This is awful, Conrad."

"Hey," he said, wishing to comfort the young woman. "I know it is terrible, awful. But we will persevere. And we will find whoever did this."

✳ ✳ ✳

"I got here quick as I could, Conrad."

On receiving the heartbreaking news, Paul Barlow had jumped into his truck and retraced the three hundred miles from Bozeman faster than was prudent or legal. He arrived in time for the impromptu memorial service and wake the crew had arranged for Bobbi at the Tired Puppy Tavern on the morning following the tragic event. Bobbi had enjoyed her first ever, and last ever, beers and shots of tequila at "the Puppy," as she and the others had come to call their favorite watering hole. Not that they had much choice; the Puppy operated as one of just two business establishments in Mercerville. Barlow and Hillary stood in front of the other, the Big Horn Mercantile and service station, which in a small alcove also housed the U.S. Post Office. As they talked, the two men gazed eastward up the gravel street leading past the scattering of small houses and dilapidated outbuildings rounding out the town's facilities.

"I know you did, Paul," Hillary grunted. "I just wish none of this had happened. It's terrible. Devastating."

Bobbi's remains were on their way back to Star Valley, where her family was organizing a full-fledged LDS funeral service. Whether that would have been among her final wishes was anyone's guess, in view of what she had learned and experienced that summer. Today's service was for her archaeology buddies, who, over the course of the previous two and a half months—working and living together day in and day out—had become some of her best friends ever. They knew it, too. Bobbi had declared as much on more than one occasion to both Josie MacDonald and Clifford Gustafson.

The entire bunch showed up for the service, even Peter Ashton, the only crew member absent on the morning of Bobbi's death. He'd taken that day off without pay, as well as the previous Monday and Tuesday, to do a solo hike into the high Cloud Peak Wilderness of the Big Horn Range.

Several locals appeared at the bar that Thursday morning as well, Pete Patterson among them.

"Hi, Paul," Patterson said, on encountering Barlow. The former high-school classmates hadn't seen one another in at least thirty years.

"Pete? Long time," said Barlow. The pair shook hands. "You sure look fit. I'd better start getting some exercise myself." Barlow patted his substantial belly to underscore the fact. "How's Abigail?"

"She passed on two years ago," Patterson said. He didn't mention that Abigail had left him two years prior to that.

"Oh, I'm really sorry to hear it. Did you know Bobbi Alder? I'm sort of surprised to see you here." Barlow's left hand found a spot on his chin where he'd missed some whiskers that morning.

"No, I didn't, but I read in the paper where she was working for you out here when she died. I came out of respect for you."

"Well, I appreciate that, Pete. Thanks for coming. I hear you've become quite the bow hunter."

"Yep, that's right. It's a great hobby for a retired military man."

"I'll bet it is."

Turning away, Barlow gritted his teeth and squinted. He wandered over and took Hillary by the arm, leading him away from the crowd.

"That's Pete Patterson over there, an old classmate of mine," Barlow muttered. "Says he came today out of respect for me. Why in the hell would he do that? We've never gotten along, and neither did our dads. Our families have barely been on speaking terms for as far back as I remember. Something to do with a cattle transaction gone bad that happened when he and I were toddlers, and which I've never fully understood. Galen's never liked him either."

"I can't tell you why he would say that, Paul," said Hillary.

The service began at eleven a.m. Several crew members eulogized Bobbi, a couple of them beautifully, as did Hillary and Barlow. The latter spoke about the first time he'd met her at hunting camp in Utah. "I knew right off the bat there was something special about Bobbi Alder," Barlow declared. "It was an impression that only grew stronger the better I came to know her. She was on her way to becoming an outstanding field archaeologist. She was already a first-class person. I believe she was born that way."

Hillary noticed Clifford remaining close-lipped. He felt so badly for his young friend.

After the service, Barlow took Hillary aside once again. "I don't know, Conrad. Have you thought any more about who would do such a thing?"

"Of course I have," Hillary said, slightly irritated by a question with such an obvious answer. "But I haven't come to any conclusions. Other than I don't believe it could be someone who was after Bobbi personally. She had no enemies. She couldn't have, you know that. It had to be someone who's either just plain stark raving mad, or someone that doesn't want us fooling around in that canyon. Or both."

"Who could that be?"

"I have no idea," Hillary said. He paused to cough and spit. "But I'd say we're in a better position to find out than Hendrickson is. For one thing, we have more manpower than the sheriff does. For another, we care about Bobbi. We also have to realize that you and I and the others on the crew are potentially in harm's way. We need to watch each others' backs."

Barlow and Hillary temporarily parted company, each moving through the small congregation to shake hands and chat with locals.

"Hello, Dr. Hillary." The words came from the man Hillary had noticed sitting outside the Tired Puppy in a wheelchair during the service, apparently unable to get up the stairs and into the tavern. "I'm Sal Calderara, BLM."

"Mr. Calderara. I'm pleased to finally meet you, after the phone conversations we've had." Hillary had no patronizing intentions by referring to him as "mister," yet he thought he noticed Calderara wincing at his use of the title.

"Hello, Calderara. I'm Paul Barlow," the bearlike Barlow chimed in, having overheard the exchange. "Out of the University of Nebraska."

"Of course, Dr. Barlow. I know of you and your work. Dr. Hillary here told me you'd be at the Sleeping Dog site off and on this summer."

"Yes, and a wonderful experience it has been. Other than the present situation we're dealing with, of course. You need to come out and see what we've accomplished, and what we're still up to."

"Well, thanks for the invite. And you're right, I should." With that, Calderara wheeled his way across the gravel street to his handicap-accessible van.

Other than breaking for the memorial service, Bobbi's archaeological buddies devoted every daylight hour of the two days following her death to combing the floor and the south rim of Sleeping Dog Canyon. Also helping out in fits and starts were Big Horn County Sheriff George Hendrickson and several deputies and community volunteers. Neither in the canyon proper nor on the slopes above, from where a skilled archer could conceivably have made a successful shot, did they find any clues. No tire tracks, no footprints, no disturbed vegetation. Nothing.

Though distraught and in more distress than he'd ever experienced, Clifford knew in his heart he had to keep his wits about him. He needed to decipher what had happened, and why. *I have to be the one to do it, and I will be*, he thought. *There's too much at stake.* He owed it to himself and to Bobbi Alder, whom he swore forever would remain the love of his life.

Think I'll go on a little scouting mission.

In the morning, Clifford had vanished. Gone, too, from his attic quarters were his duffel bag and most of his clothes and gear. When the other occupants of the old farmhouse questioned one another about his disappearance, it emerged that no one had seen or heard him leave.

PART 3
THE QUEST

20
RECONNECTING

Clifford walked along the gravel road toward Mercerville, brimming with purpose but lacking direction. The first rays of the sun poking through the deep troughs between the high Big Horn crags illuminated a thin, low-lying fog that filled the basin's bottom. The sweet smell of fresh-cut alfalfa, damp under the morning dew, permeated the chilly air. To Clifford's right several mule deer wandered about, browsing in a hayfield as if they owned it. A V-shaped formation of Canada geese honked overhead, aiming south. Lights blinked on in ranch houses and shelterbelt-protected outbuildings as the working day began.

Everything seems so normal, but nothing's the same. Bobbi's gone.

Clifford began sobbing. He stopped, knelt on the ground, and dabbed at his eyes with a sleeve of his blue cotton work shirt.

"God," he said out loud, looking up at the sky. "Damp in the attic, that's what I am." Regaining a grip, he stood and resumed walking.

By the time Clifford had covered the five miles between camp and town, the sun had lifted over Cloud Peak and the day was in full bloom. He continued to the county highway that dead-ended at the north edge of Mercerville and stuck out his thumb after hearing, then seeing, a late-model Dodge pickup approaching him from behind. The rancher-type driving the truck stopped and signaled to Clifford to throw his duffel into the bed and waited for him to climb into the cab.

"Where ya' going, son?"

"Greybull, I guess. Then north from there."

"You're one of them youngsters working out there at the archaeology dig, aren't you? The wife and I was on that tour Paul Barlow gave for locals a couple weeks ago. Barlow's a few years older 'n me, but I watched him play six-man football for Ten Sleep when I was in fifth and sixth grade."

"Six-man?"

"Yep."

"Sounds like a lot of running."

"It's fun to watch, all right. There's a league in Wyoming for some of the really small schools like that. Meeteetse, Dubois, a few others. Barlow was big back in those days, but fast. Not as big as he is now, 'course. Back then he could see his feet." The man grinned and looked over at Clifford, who had re-entered a world of his own. "Say, that's really too bad about that young girl. What a terrible deal that was. I was awful sorry to hear it. I don't know who would of done somethin' like that in this country. Who would have thought it? I mean, what are the chances of getting killed by an arrow in Sleeping Dog Canyon?"

Clifford grimaced. He didn't tell the man that his own chances might have been quite good if he hadn't had diarrhea on that fateful morning. And if Bobbi—beautiful, gracious, classy Bobbi Alder—hadn't felt sorry for him and gone to retrieve that cursed cotter pin in his stead.

Clifford turned and looked through the cab's rear window to inspect the golden retriever standing in the truck bed.

Beautiful dog. The kind that makes a man look twice.

The canine was sticking his head over the edge of the bed on the driver's side, and Clifford watched him as he pointed his snout into the wind, his ears flapping.

"Nice dog you have there," Clifford said.

"Thanks. Name's Ralph."

"You're kidding me! That's my dog's name."

"Really? What is he?"

"A yellow Lab. He's back on the farm in Minnesota."

"Well, well…"

When the pair pulled into downtown Greybull, Clifford thanked the man, hopped out, and then grabbed his bag. As he resumed walking he thought back to Hillary's bumper-sticker shenanigans in this same downtown area weeks ago; he kept an eye out for the bozo's big rig, but he didn't see it. He glanced eastward up at the distant, scooped-out beaver-slide profile of Beaver Butte. The isolated mountain had become a favorite weekend haunt of his over the summer. Only two weekends ago he and Bobbi had hiked to the table-flat summit...

Clifford stuck out his thumb at the east edge of town. Again, the first pickup to approach pulled over, its driver welcoming him into the cab. This truck carried a pair of cow dogs in the bed and pulled a trailer containing two horses.

"Where to, chief?"

"I'm going up to Montana," Clifford said. "Lame Deer."

"Got relatives there?"

"I might. I plan to try and find out. That's why I'm going. Among other reasons."

"Thought maybe you were headed there. Crow Fair's going on up near Custer's battlefield. Lots of tipis. And friendly squaws, I've been told." The young cowpoke shot Clifford a sly look. His blond mustache was so long and bushy that Clifford could hardly see his mouth move when he spoke. "Say, you weren't involved in that standoff over there in South Dakota last winter, were you?"

"What, at Wounded Knee? No, that was AIM, the American Indian Movement. I guess those guys might be accomplishing something, but they're also creating a lot of ill will."

"They sure are," the driver agreed.

The truck and trailer continued up the winding road through Shell Canyon, with its many curves and switchbacks. The motion lulled Clifford to sleep, long enough for him to start dreaming he was immersed in a sea of tipis.

He jumped awake. "You know what?" he said, turning to the driver. "I think I may go to this Crow Fair, now that I'm here. I don't know what it is, exactly, but I've heard it mentioned a few times. Drop me off the closest you come, will you?"

"Sure thing."

At the high elevations they were driving through, long lengths of drift fence paralleled the highway to the south, reminding Clifford of the wind and snow that winter would bring. After cresting Granite Pass, the driver continued downhill and into the small town of Ranchester, where he deposited Clifford before turning right toward Sheridan.

An hour later, Clifford sat perched high in the cab of an eighteen-wheeler. He and the truck's heavy-set, stoved-up driver crossed the state line on U.S. Route 87, entering Montana. On arriving at the U.S. Highway 212 junction, the driver turned east toward Lame Deer, Broadus-bound, then pulled over to the side of the road.

"Thanks for the ride, mister," Clifford said as he opened the door and tossed his duffel bag to the ground, where it landed with a soft thud.

"No problem, son. It's been nice talking to you. Like I said, it's only a hop, skip, and a jump into Crow Agency from here. You be safe now, and best of luck to you."

Clifford slammed the truck's door shut and started off, shouldering his heavy duffel bag first over his right shoulder and then over his left. After twenty minutes of walking, he rounded a tight bend and found himself gazing down on Crow Agency in the valley of the Little Bighorn River. The sight stopped him in his tracks.

"Holy cow!"

An ocean of tipis, hundreds of them, flooded the flats between the cottonwood-shrouded riverbank to the west and the row of low bluffs to the east. In the bright light and still air of late morning, smoke lifted straight into the sky from dozens of canvas-covered lodges.

Beautiful, Clifford thought. He hurried ahead, anxious to learn all about it.

Clifford took an audible bearing on the noisy rodeo arena lying between him and the tipi flats. As he continued toward it, he inhaled the sweet aroma of smoldering cottonwood embers and smoking meat.

I'll bet it's venison, or bison.

When he got to the grounds, it seemed to Clifford that everyone involved in the Crow Fair must be at the rodeo. Sporadic cheering, clapping, and screaming erupted from the grandstand. A man's voice resounded through loudspeakers.

"Say 'hey hey' for that cowboy!" boomed the rich Oklahoma or Texas baritone at the microphone. "That there is a buckin' horse and he stuck to 'im for the full eight-second main course and gave us an extra two for dessert. Looked like he coulda stayed aboard for an hour; could of ridden that bronc all the way back home to Air-i-zo-neeee. Come on, folks, give the boy a good hand. That's eighteen-year-old Ronny BE-gay, out of Window Rock, Navajo Nation."

Finding the bleachers somewhere between full and overflowing, Clifford sat on the ground at the north end of the stands lining the east side of the arena, using his duffel bag as a backrest. The hot prairie August sun glared down from overhead. Indians of every shape and size and mode of dress, and dozens of whites as well, sat in the bleachers, stood around, or milled about. The clay dust kicked up by the animals' hooves pounding the sand scattered over the arena grounds was fine, light brown, and everywhere.

"Ladies and gents we have a real treat comin' up next. Let's hear a big southeast Montana 'Howdy-do' for the Crow Country Riders. These young men are from nearby, from Lodge Grass, Montana, and they ride bareback better than you or I ride with saddle and stirrups. With them is the beautiful young Virginia Mae Real Bird, Miss Crow Nation 1973."

Miss Crow Nation, astride a gelding, cantered into the arena in the middle of a formation of twelve young men also on horseback, each of them kaleidoscopically outfitted in unique combinations of rawhide, beads, elk ivories, bear-claw necklaces, and eagle feathers. Their horses, kicking up a storm of dust, were likewise bedecked in silver spangles, hawk feathers, and porcupine quills... every color in the rainbow, and then some. After looping around the arena twice and then escorting Miss Real Bird to the exit, the riders turned and raced ahead as one, before splitting into two groups of six to feign battle and perform acrobatic maneuvers of horsemanship more fantastic than Clifford would have thought possible. Enraptured, he held his breath with anxiety for the riders' safety. The horses and horsemen all appeared so carefree and wild. Certain catastrophe seemed ever at hand, yet no horse went down and no two horsemen collided. For fifteen minutes the shrill cries of the riders and the reverberations of the animals' pounding hooves filled the arena. Then, as suddenly as they had appeared, all were gone, settling dust the only clue that they had been there.

The spectators remained speechless for a moment. Then a low murmur ensued, and after rapturous applause the rodeo momentum picked up again.

Engrossed in watching the action and in surveying others taking it in, Clifford had forgotten all about the time. He glanced at his Timex: four-thirty.

Dang, I haven't eaten a thing all day.

To remedy the situation, Clifford strolled over to the concession area and purchased three Navajo tacos and a can of Coke, and slammed it all down.

"Folks, thanks for droppin' by to watch this top-notch rodeoin'!" said the announcer at around five o'clock. "Whoooo-eee! We had some fun today, didn't we? Tonight's powwow starts up in about an hour, down at the Sioux encampment arbor off Brushy Fork Road. Don't miss it. And we'll see you tomorrow, same time, same place, for some of the best get-down-and-get-dirty Indian COW-boyin' you'll ever have the pleasure of watchin'!"

Clifford drifted away from the rodeo complex with the rest of the crowd, falling in with what seemed the biggest group of Indians headed in a northwesterly direction.

"Is this the way to the powwow?" he asked a teenage girl wearing beads, leather, and fabrics of vibrant greens and reds.

"Yes," she said, staring straight ahead at the ground.

"Are you dancing?" Clifford queried.

"Yes."

She glanced up at Clifford, smiling, and they made brief eye contact.

The sun hovered below the tops of the tall cottonwood trees lining the Little Bighorn River flowing beside the moving crowd. A gentle breeze drifted up the broad valley, cooling Clifford some. The closer he came to the Sioux encampment, the stronger the aroma of wood smoke and the boom-boom of drum-pounding became. He could hear high-pitched, wavering wails that sounded human, sort of, yet to his ears as eerie and wild as the pre-dawn yammering of the lower Sleeping Dog Canyon's resident coyote pack.

I'm not in Minnesota any more, Ralphie, Clifford relayed telepathically to his dog back on the farm.

As he neared the powwow site, the singing and drumming intensified in power and volume. Soon, Clifford stood just ten feet from a circle of men with a drummer at its core. The sound of their singing or wailing was loud and all-consuming. It pierced Clifford's skull and reached deep into his cranium, stirring his genetic memory. He sensed indescribable things he'd always had inside but had never known, and even now couldn't have verbalized if he tried. He felt the rhythmic pounding of the drum in his face and chest as much as hearing it with his ears. Two dozen dancers of both sexes and a variety of ages, driven by the drummer and absorbed in the singers' sacred chanting, turned circles around the circle. The overriding aroma came from a huge pine- and cottonwood-log bonfire.

"Unbelievable," Clifford whispered, barely moving his lips.

With tears welling up again, he backed away from the crowd. Finding a tall, fat poplar, he put his duffel bag on the ground and sat himself down against the trunk of the tree. Sequestered in the shadows away from the fire, no one paid him any mind. He buried his face against his folded knees. The singing and drumming, the dancing, the fire; it all melded into a single living organism that reached inside him and made his heart tremble. It plucked out of him a terrible sadness, casting it to the evening breeze.

A sudden understanding struck Clifford's brain like a bone-chipping tool striking an obsidian core: Bobbi Alder's spirit and soul thrived, and were in good hands.

Maybe they're with me now, part of my own heart.

Clifford felt ancient, yet like a baby. Connected. He became nothing but a low-growing limb jutting out from the gnarled old tree trunk supporting him. Here he remained, alive and composed of growing wood, alternately weeping with grief and laughing with joy, as the drumming, dancing, and singing of a procession of groups continued far into the night. The sounds, the wood smoke, the lion's share of Clifford's distress soared together high into the void of the night sky, the spirit of the people driving it all upward. There it dissipated to mingle with the stars.

Things began breaking up a little before one a.m. Clifford pulled his sleeping bag from his pack, rolled it out, and crawled inside, lying face up. Using the duffel as a lumpy pillow, he contemplated the sky above. In the gap between two cottonwood branches he found his old friend, the man in the moon, smiling down on him.

For the first time in days, Clifford felt at peace. He felt exhilarated. And exhausted. He slept, soundly.

21

DSR

"Hey, dude, what are you doin'?"

Clifford stirred and opened his eyes. A man-boy stood over him, looking down, sizing Clifford up.

Seems about my age, Clifford thought.

Like Clifford he had long hair, but oddly gray-streaked. A small ruby-colored stud shone in the lobe of his left ear. Above cowboy boots, blue jeans, and a brown cotton-weave belt he wore a silver-buttoned black leather vest, open in front and with nothing under it, exposing a hairless chest. His upper left arm displayed a tattoo containing the letters "DSR." The top half of each inch-high letter was red; the lower half blue. The likeness of a black arrow, with feathers at one end and a traditional chipped-stone arrowhead at the other, underscored the red-and-blue letters. The young man wore a red bandana as a headband.

Looks like a cross between a warrior and a Hell's Angel, Clifford thought. *He must be cold, with just that vest on.*

During the clear night the mercury had plummeted. Clifford guesstimated the temperature to be fifty degrees cooler than the high of ninety-six the rodeo announcer had declared on the previous afternoon.

"Oh, hi. I'm just waking up. What time is it, anyway?"

"About seven. You a Sioux?"

Clifford had to think for a second what the question meant. "Oh, uh, no. I'm Cheyenne."

"Oh, good deal. Justin told me he saw you stretched out over here last night at the powwow. Gather up your stuff there and follow me."

Clifford sat up, rubbed his eyes, and pulled himself out of his sleeping bag fully clothed, except for his stockinged feet. Onto those he pulled his high-top tennis shoes, their canvas tops damp with dew. Then he stood, stuffed away his sleeping bag, and lifted the duffel.

"Where're we goin'?" he asked.

"DSR camp. You'll see. Just follow me." He held out his hand. "Jamie Newhouse."

"Good to know you, Jamie," Clifford said, extending his own right hand. "Clifford. Clifford Gustafson."

Jamie looked startled, but said nothing.

"Oh, lemme brush my teeth first, okay?" Clifford requested.

"Sure, no problem."

Clifford retrieved his Dopp kit and a half-full water bottle from his red-and-green Red Earth High School duffel bag and proceeded to freshen up. He and his new acquaintance then sauntered a half mile downstream along the Brushy Fork to its confluence with the Little Bighorn, where they turned south to walk upstream along the river.

After passing through Crow Agency, the pair crossed the river by a bridge and continued for another ten minutes before veering west up Crows Comb Wash. Here Clifford noticed vegetation more abundant and lush than what he'd seen in the Brushy Fork drainage.

This narrow valley must let in less sunshine and retain more moisture than Brushy Fork.

Such a thought wouldn't have occurred to him earlier in the summer, before spending time outdoors on Beaver Butte and in the Big Horn foothills in the company of Hillary, Bobbi, Ben Reed, and the others.

"What's this DSR stuff, Jamie?"

"It's not stuff, Clifford. It's for real. It's important. Stands for 'Dog Soldiers Resurrected,' and we're gonna bring about change in this old world. What's your last name again?"

"Gustafson."

"Gustafson. That's what I thought you said. Where the hell d'you get a name like that?"

"Minnesota," Clifford said, matter-of-factly. "What's the DSR do? How are you going to change the world?"

Clifford found himself thinking back to his favorite college class, the graduate-level Plains Indians 602, formally "Plains Indians: Cultural Trends and Divergencies of the 18th and 19th Centuries." He recalled Dr. Magnusson telling the story of how the Cheyenne Dog Soldiers, as self-proclaimed protectors of the tribe, had become legendary for their fighting fury during the Indian wars. At some undetermined point in time they had transitioned from a simple military society into a band. Until then, each Cheyenne band—the Burnt Aortas, Prognathous Jaws, others—had consisted of extended-family members. In turn, the members of different bands, or families, had composed the various military societies. The Dogs, defying the traditional Cheyenne way by being a familial-based fighting entity, had grown powerful in both military and social matters.

"You just hang around here for a while, Gustafson, and you'll find out about DSR. We're gonna bring back the buffalo for one thing. We're ghost dancing, calling on the spirit of Wovoka."

After they'd walked another mile or so, Clifford's nose told him they were getting close to a camp. He breathed in some of the same rich aromas he'd enjoyed the day before—wood smoke, frying bacon, roasting venison or buffalo. But this downslope breeze also carried on it the scent of burning marijuana. No doubt about it.

Clifford and Jamie rounded a right-hand bend and entered the camp. It looked similar to the others Clifford had walked past, but high atop a straight, limbless pine pole flapped a large, white flag emblazoned with the "DSR" symbol in bold red, blue, and black. It was the same icon Jamie had tattooed on his arm.

"Hey, everybody," announced Jamie. "This is Clifford. Clifford for God's sake *Gustafson*." He laughed. "He's a Cheyenne, despite his last name."

A round of "Hey, Cliffords" and "Hi, Cliffords" came from the fireside throng. It looked to Clifford like no one in this party would change things much at all, at least not on this day. It wasn't yet eight-thirty in the morning and the nine young men and women sitting around the fire all looked wasted. When a girl offered Clifford one of a pair of reefers making its way around the circle, he accepted it and took a hit, holding the smoke in his lungs until he coughed and laughed it out, assuming a sheepish grin. Clifford had never been real big on marijuana—he'd never purchased any himself—but when available, as it generally had been in the dorm and at parties at UM, he often partook, and enjoyed it. One of his more serious pot-head dorm mates had once asked him why he never forked out the bucks to pay for some. "Why should I?" Clifford had responded. "You guys never run out." He smiled at the memory.

On each of the bare upper left arms visible, both male and female, Clifford saw the red, blue, and black DSR tattoo. Those with arms un-exposed included a tall and attractive young woman with pronounced cheekbones and deep brown bloodshot eyes. Wearing a long-sleeved cotton pullover, she stood and moved over to the campfire, where she dished into a big ceramic bowl a ladleful of whatever simmered in the iron kettle hanging over the flames. She slipped a large spoon into the bowl and handed it to the newcomer.

"Eat well of the bison, brother Clifford," she said.

"Thanks," Clifford said, smiling and kneeling on the ground. He sampled a bite of the stew but it burned his tongue, so he set the bowl down for a couple of minutes to let the contents cool.

After two more tokes of the joint, Clifford was floating and feeling in sync with his new friends, though he knew none of their names other than Jamie's. He figured one of them must be Justin, whom Jamie had mentioned when waking Clifford up, but he didn't know yet which one he was. This he did know: the buffalo stew hit the spot.

Suddenly, the jovial and trivial nature of what little conversation was rattling around took a nosedive, grabbing Clifford's drug-induced euphoria by the neck and strangling it.

"Hey, Justin, Jonesy drove in from Wyoming late last night," Jamie Newhouse said. "He says those archaeologists are still digging down there in the canyon. What if they find it?"

Clifford almost choked on his stew.

"Maybe Jonesy needs to go back and give them a warning," said Justin, who turned out to be a short, heavy-set young man sitting immediately to Clifford's left.

Clifford guessed Justin's age to be around twenty-eight. His most distinguishing characteristic was something he didn't have: his two upper front teeth. Their absence made his speech somewhat comical, which felt incongruous to Clifford in the context of what he had just said.

Clifford continued eating as he listened, trying to appear indifferent to the dialogue.

"I don't know," Jamie said. "We're really taking our chances. We might want to let sleeping dogs lie."

What? Clifford struggled to retain his façade of nonchalance as his marijuana high plunged even lower. *Was the cliché coincidental or were they really talking about the site? Could the person who killed Bobbi be in this group? And who's Jonesy?*

It blew his mind to think he might've stumbled like this into a situation relevant to Bobbi's death. Or perhaps it was the dream he'd had in the pickup truck, the vision of tipis, that had brought him to the Crow Fair for this reason.

Pay more attention to your dreams from now on, Pedro!

Clifford didn't know what to do, but he did know what not to do: ask questions. Or tell anyone here about his involvement at the Sleeping Dog excavations. Fortunately for him, the girl who had dished out the stew changed the subject.

"I'm sorry, Clifford, what's your last name again?" she asked, looking over at him.

"Gustafson."

"Clifford *Gustafson*," interjected Jamie. "Do you believe that shit? A gol-danged Cheyenne Scandinavian? A Cheyenndahoovian!"

Justin laughed and a few of the others joined in. The young woman, Clifford noticed, was not among them. Instead she was still looking at him.

"Mine's Amy Looksbehind," she said. "What brings you to Crow Fair, Clifford? Are you alone?"

Clifford had to think fast, which he found challenging in view of the paranoia brought on by the combination of pot smoking and the recent topic of discussion.

"Yes, I did come alone," he said. "I'm from Minnesota, a farm. I was adopted." All true so far, but then he felt he needed to elaborate.

"I've heard about the Crow Fair for years, so I decided to hitchhike on out. I grew up around white folks, so I thought it was about time to come out and look into my biological heritage. My dad's retiring after this summer, and I'll be taking over the farm next year. Thought this might be my last chance for a long time to get away in the summer."

"Well, that's neat, Clifford," said Amy, smiling.

Clifford smiled back. Amy seemed a little less rough around the edges than her companions.

"What about you, Amy? What's your background?"

"I ran into these guys just last night. Haven't seen 'em in seven years. How time does fly. I grew up on the Northern Cheyenne rez with Jamie and Justin and Finneas over there." She tipped her head in the direction of a young man flat on his back, asleep next to a big fir tree. "I went away to college in Denver and now I'm a nurse in Seattle. Haven't been to Crow Fair since I was a teenager. I finally accumulated two weeks of vacation, so it seemed like a good time to come home. This is just like a big family reunion, you know."

Clifford knew he had to stick with this group. He wondered if it would be safe to confide in Amy.

Eventually, maybe, but first I need to learn more.

"So… Jamie, Justin, tell me more about the DSR," he suggested.

"Naaawwww," drawled Justin, getting up. "It's time to PARTY!"

He entered the canvas lodge nearest the fire and emerged with two half-gallon bottles of cheap Spinada wine. He started one of them off around the circle and screwed the lid off the other one before lifting it to his mouth and guzzling.

"Wooooheeeewwwww! Mmm, that's good." He gave a toothless grin, his mouth encircled by purple.

He looks about as silly as anything I've ever seen.

"What time does the rodeo start?" Jamie asked.

"Noon, I think," Clifford replied. "Right after the parade, which I read on a poster starts at ten-thirty."

Jamie nodded. "Okay. Justin's right. We gotta get jacked up. I'll tell you more about DSR this afternoon, Gus. Maybe you'll wanna join up?"

"Maybe, I don't know," Clifford said casually.

Most everyone called Clifford's dad Gus, but no one had ever called Clifford that. It sounded strange to his ear, yet he rather liked it.

After smoking a couple more reefers and downing the remaining contents of the wine bottles, the four women and seven men—including a now half-awake Finneas "Jonesy" Jones—headed as a group down the creek to make their riotous way to the rodeo grounds.

22
DIVERSION

"Bonnie Anderson at the Tired Puppy flagged me down when I was driving through Mercerville this afternoon," Paul Barlow announced.

He stood facing Conrad Hillary and the ten remaining crew members, whom he'd asked to assemble after dinner in front of the old farmhouse.

"She gave me a message that Jim Wolanski, chief ranger at Yellowstone, wanted me to give him a call ASAP." He paused to run a hand over his chin and scratch his earlobe. "So I went over to the phone booth and called him right away. Wolanski inquired if the park archaeologist—her name's Barbara Sullivan—could 'borrow' us all for a day's work. There's a proposed new sewer line up at Norris that needs to be surveyed and cleared by archaeologists. It's just a couple of hundred feet long, and we only need to survey fifty feet on each side, so it won't take long. But heck, it'll be a paid vacation and we'll get to camp out for a night in the park. Obsidian Cliff's not far from there, so we can make time for a field trip. As you all know, that's where most of the obsidian tools found in this region got their start.

"So," he continued, "be ready to take off bright and early in the morning, say six o'clock. Bring your sleeping bags and some rain gear, just in case. Wolanski said the Park Service would set up wall tents for us at the Norris campground. He also said they'll have some canned MCIs for us for dinner and breakfast."

"MCIs?" asked Marge Paavno.

"It's a military thing. Meal, Combat, Individual rations. Firefighters carry 'em, too. That's why the Park Service has them."

"Sounds delicious," Tom Jefferson said. "I wonder if they have any with fried chitlins and hog maw?"

"Ha! Not likely," Barlow responded. "More apt to be ham and beans, crackers and cheese, maybe some apple sauce, that sort of thing. We'll stop at a grocery store in Cody and stock up on provisions, just in case the MCIs don't do the trick. Which I can pretty much guarantee they won't."

"Tom, I don't think you'll find much soul food in Cody, either," Hillary chimed in. "But we *will* find banquet beer at the liquor store, and we *shall* stock up on it. We're bound to work up a terrible thirst out there surveying."

"Ten-four," Barlow said. "It's around two hundred miles. I figure, with a stop in Cody and with the slow-going we're bound to have through the park, we'll get to Norris around noon. Now, vehicles... Conrad and I will drive one of the state trucks. Danny, why don't you and Tom go in the other one? That leaves eight needing lifts in personal vehicles, probably three of them. Or would you rather squeeze into two? The government will pay the standard mileage rate, so you'll make a little cash by driving. Those of you who have cars here, who wants to drive?"

Four hands shot up.

"Josie, Marge, Chuy, let's take yours. They all look in good enough shape to make it to Wonderland and back in one piece. We can gas up at the Big Horn Merc on our way through Mercerville. Okay? Great. See you all in the morning."

***

"I was grateful for that call from Ranger Wolanski," said Barlow, sitting at the wheel of the state truck with Hillary beside him.

They were leading the motorcade of four other vehicles rolling through Yellowstone National Park. Behind their truck followed the second red Ford state truck, Chuy Padilla's white Dodge Dart, Josie MacDonald's pale-blue Ford Falcon, and Marge Paavno's sea-blue 1972 Chrysler New Yorker four-door hardtop, by far the newest and most luxurious vehicle in the lineup. They'd traveled at a snail's pace through Hayden Valley, stalled by several bear and bison jams.

"Why's that?" Hillary queried.

"Well, it gets the guys and girls away from the site for a while. They're still reeling from Bobbi's murder. I know I am."

"Yep, me too," Hillary agreed.

"And it also gets our minds off Clifford Gustafson, our missing person. Bonnie and Galen have both agreed to keep an eye out for him while we're gone. I'll call them both a couple of times today and tomorrow, just in case."

"Fine," said Hillary. "And, despite the negatives we're dealing with, this trip should be a fun cap to the season for the crew, what with most everyone heading their separate ways soon. I hope Clifford comes back pronto. We'll need him around, with me leaving and just Marge, Josie, and Jefferson hanging on through September. You'll be here quite a bit of the time, of course, but still…"

"It's been an amazing summer, Conrad. Talk about a mixed bag. From excavating one of the most complete records of early man in the northern plains, to losing one of our favorite crew members to, to… I don't know *what* we lost her to."

"I'm sure Clifford's out there trying to get to the bottom of just that, Paul. You'd think he'd have a better chance by sticking around, but that young fellow has some intuition. And a *lot* of imagination."

Barlow applied the truck's brakes on reaching the four-way-stop at Norris Junction. As promised, Jim Wolanski and Barbara Sullivan were there, leaning against the rear end of a light-green Park Service sedan parked at the side of the road immediately north of the junction. Wolanski waved and gave a big "follow me" gesture. The two rangers got into their car and headed north.

"Did you fart?" Hillary asked.

"No," said Barlow, laughing. "That's the geyser basin."

"Could of fooled me."

Barlow followed as Wolanski turned east off the highway and parked near a little log cabin. The four vehicles behind them followed suit. Wolanski and Sullivan got out of their vehicle, and the others did likewise, gathering around the rangers.

"Hi folks," the male ranger said. "I'm Jim Wolanski. This is Barbara Sullivan." He held his hand out toward the park archaeologist. "I know you're wondering why I've asked you all here. Well, actually, you know why I asked you here. What you don't know is why I stopped at this location. You being archaeologists, interested in history and all, I thought you might enjoy learning something about this cabin. It's the Norris Soldier Station, first built in 1886, then replaced after a fire in 1897. It served as an outpost for soldiers when the Army patrolled the park. It was badly damaged in the earthquake at Hebgen Lake fourteen years ago. Closed up now, unsafe, but I wouldn't be surprised if we renovate it one of these days."

"When did the Army stop patrolling?" Josie MacDonald asked.

"1916, if I remember right," Wolanski answered. "That's when the civilian ranger corps—that would be us, now the National Park Service—took over park administration. Private cars were first permitted into the park in 1915, and with more people and more money coming in, the concept of civilian administration became feasible, financially speaking.

"Well, let's get on up the road, folks, and put you all to work. The survey area is only a couple hundred yards east of here, adjacent to the campground. I'll point your tents out as we drive past."

"Daylight's a burnin'," Hillary confirmed.

***

The careful search for artifacts on the ground along the path of the future sewer line took the crew only a couple of hours to complete. The survey turned up nothing of significance, nor did any of the trio of meter-deep test pits they sunk at random intervals along the proposed route. At four o'clock, Barlow regrouped everyone back at the vehicles.

"Let's drop our stuff off at the tents and motor on up to Obsidian Cliff," he said. "We can leave the cars at the campground, too. The weather's nice enough, so let's just pile into the pickups. Ranger Sullivan will meet us at the cliff."

At the campground, the group dispersed into the beds and cabs of the pickup trucks. The drivers, Barlow and Danny Ho, pulled the two trucks out onto the main road, heading north.

"Gosh, this is pretty," said Marge Paavno, riding with Chuy Padilla and Ben Reed in the back of the pickup driven by Ho. "I've never been to Yellowstone."

"I was here when I was ten, but that's it," Padilla said, combing his thick black mustache with an index finger.

"I've come here at least once every summer for as long as I can remember," said Reed. "My dad likes to go fishing on the upper Yellowstone. But I haven't been over in this part of the park much at all."

The pickups pulled over and parked in a wide clearing next to a rustic, rock-and-timber kiosk sitting across the road from a tall, timber-capped outcrop of vertically aligned rock columns. An accumulation of big boulders rested at the base of the columnar-basalt formation. Barbara Sullivan was already there, and she signaled for the others to come over to her side.

"Here we are, at the archaeologically important, and intriguing, Obsidian Cliff," she announced.

She looked smart in her Park Service uniform, including the iconic, broad-brimmed summer dress hat, with its tall crown and Montana Peak, perched on her head.

"For centuries, this was the most abundant known source of obsidian in North America," she said. "It was not unlike a prehistoric arsenal. As you've no doubt read or been told, volcanic-glass tools made from pieces of this old lava flow have been found as far away as Ohio and Michigan, southern Canada, Washington state. It's a rhyolite flow, about two hundred thousand years old. The vertical columns are cooling fractures. The obsidian component is extruded lava that cooled extremely fast; for instance, it may have flowed into cold water. That prevented crystals from forming and lent the rock its glass-like structure. Let's walk around the base a bit. Be careful crossing the road. And please don't take any samples home. That's not allowed, unless you have a special collecting permit."

"Imagine what's taken place here over the centuries," said Danny Ho, hiking alongside John Riley. "How many people in prehistoric times do you think stood on this very spot where we're standing?"

"Boy, that's a good question," said Riley. "Makes you wish you had a time machine."

"What's Ashton doing over there?" Ho asked.

They watched as Peter Ashton, who had wandered away from the core group, bent over, picked something up, and put it in his pocket.

"He goes by his own rules," Riley murmured. "He doesn't give a rat's ass that Ranger Sullivan asked us not to take any obsidian samples. I'll bet he found some chippings, or even a core or a tool. And just between you and me, it wouldn't be the first artifact he's poached this summer."

23
TEMPORARY INSANITY

"Okay, Gus, here's the program," said Jamie Newhouse.

They were all sitting at a small, rickety table in the dingy kitchen of Justin Willits' tiny shack on the western outskirts of Lame Deer. Jamie was sitting between Clifford and Justin. Also at the table were Finneas Jones and Amy Looksbehind. The five of them had driven there together two days earlier, after the Crow Fair disbanded, in Jamie's Plymouth Road Runner.

As he listened, Clifford gazed out through grimy windows at the wending line of willows marking the course of Tobacco Creek. On the windowsill lay a dozen curing peyote buttons. Just looking at them turned Clifford's stomach. He'd been drinking a foul-tasting tea brewed from the buttons off and on over the past three days. He had done so against his better judgment, but in the hope that imbibing with the others might help him get inside their circle. The build-up of hallucinogens had him thinking and behaving quite unlike himself, and he knew it. He couldn't wait to get the residue out of his system.

"All right, Gus," said Jamie. "Amy and I will drive you into the Black Hills, to the canyon near Sylvan Lake where I saw a pair of bald eagles and two eaglets late last spring. They're probably still there, though the young will probably have fledged by now. I'll drop you off at the trailhead, and you're on your own after that, pardner. We'll swing by Bear Mountain on the way," he added, "to get you some good medicine. After we let you off, I'll drive Amy up to the Billings airport. Then I'll come back to the hills for you early on Friday."

"I wish I didn't have to fly back to Seattle tomorrow," Amy said. "But that's the way it is."

"You get back here with the feathers and you'll get your tattoo, Gus," Justin interjected, grinning his toothless grin. His raspy smoker's voice sounded like iron on gravel.

Clifford almost asked, as he had come close to inquiring on a couple of previous occasions, if his companions knew of any Whitetails living in the Lame Deer area. As before, he decided the timing wasn't right.

Maybe I'm not ready to hear the answer.

"What're we waitin' for?" Clifford asked. "Daylight's a burnin'."

He thought about Conrad Hillary as he quoted his pet phrase, and wondered what his friend and mentor would think of the stunt Clifford was about to pull.

"Okay, let's do it, Gus," Jamie said. "But first let's get you another half hour's target practice with the pistol."

***

Amy Looksbehind, Clifford Gustafson, and Jamie Newhouse motored into Sturgis at a few minutes after noon, all three of them sitting on the front bench seat of Jamie's Road Runner. The thirty-third annual Black Hills Rally had ended just a few days earlier, and there were still plenty of biker hangers-on lingering in the community's main street. They milled about, strolling from one of Sturgis's many bars to the next, their chromed Harleys glistening in the sun.

When the trio of young Native Americans reached the northeastern outskirts of town, Jamie took a hand off the steering wheel and pointed at Bear Mountain.

"The Lakotas call it *Mato Paha*," he said. "We call it Bear Mountain."

"Bear Butte is what I call it," said Clifford.

He had learned about the feature in geomorphology class during his final semester at UM, so in some regards he knew more about it than Jamie did. From a few miles away, the butte looked to Clifford like an entire, isolated mini-mountain range boasting three sub-peaks. Its barren, scree-covered south face resembled a clear glass bottle filled with colorful layers of sand.

"It's an igneous intrusion," Clifford lectured, "composed of rhyolite. Erosion removed overlying layers of shale."

"Gus, you gotta lose this scientific mindset and start thinking like a Dog Soldier," Jamie said, eliciting a giggle from Amy. "Next thing you're gonna be tellin' me is us Injuns came to North America from Asia over the land bridge to Alaska. We were created here on this continent, of the land and water, and don't you forget it."

"I agree," Clifford said, only half lying.

Jamie steered his noisy Road Runner up to the trailhead at the base of the small mountain and parked, shutting down the rumbling engine. "Let's go for a walk."

The three climbed out of the automobile and stretched.

"What have you done to this car, anyway?" Clifford asked. "It can't be more than five years old."

His mind had cleared some, and for the first time he noticed what a mess had been made of the Road Runner. Spartan by design, the muscle car's interior featured front and back black-vinyl bench seats and a Hurst floor shifter, with just a rubber boot at its base. No console, no floor carpeting. But that didn't explain the shredded backrest of the rear seat, the windshield's multiple cracks, or the exterior's chipped and faded orange paint and missing front bumper.

"Yeah, you're right, Gus. It's a sixty-eight," Jamie said, laughing. "That was the first year Plymouth made Road Runners, which I guess you already know. You gotta understand, this isn't just my car. It's my jeep, my pickup truck, my moving van, and my dragster. It's even been my bedroom and my kitchen, on plenty of occasions. It already had forty-seven thousand miles on it when I bought it two years ago, and I've put on another thirty-five K. A car like this isn't supposed to run for that many miles. It doesn't get squat for gas mileage, but it gets me where I want to go. Real fast sometimes."

"What's all that cloth hanging from the trees and shrubs?" Clifford asked, looking around.

"Offerings," Jamie explained.

"It's beautiful," Amy said. "So colorful."

After about a mile of steep uphill hiking, the threesome reached Bear Butte's summit. En route, they'd encountered a couple of fat scampering marmots, and Clifford almost stumbled over a panicked badger. Endless plains stretched in every direction except to the south, where the dark, doghair-pine-strangled slopes and naked hogbacks of the Black Hills rippled ever higher before fading into a hazy infinity.

Standing between his two companions, Jamie took Clifford's right hand in his left hand, and Amy's left in his right, then lifted their arms together skyward. He had to yell to make himself heard over the howling wind.

"Oh, Great Spirit," Jamie called, gazing toward the Black Hills, "and brother bear, you who live here, watch over and protect Clifford Gustafson on his quest! It is for you and for the people that he sets out on his hazardous mission."

Clifford thought Jamie's little soliloquy sounded like it belonged in a B western, but he understood the words were heartfelt.

"I'm going to pray now," Jamie said, lowering everyone's arms. "Why don't you two start on down, and I'll catch up in a few minutes."

"Okay," said Clifford, pleased to have Amy Looksbehind to himself for the first time.

"I noticed you don't have the DSR tattoo, Amy," he started, as the pair descended the big hill.

"No. I think those guys—and gals—are getting into some things they'll wish they hadn't. I'm trying to keep my nose clean. I've worked too hard to get where I am to screw it up."

"Do you know what they were talking about the morning I came to your camp? That thing about Jonesy driving in from Wyoming, where some archaeologists are still digging something?"

"I heard something about that earlier. There's a rumor of a Cheyenne burial—or maybe not a burial, but just a happenstance Cheyenne skeleton—located in some foothills canyon of the Big Horn Mountains down there in northern Wyoming. A BLM archaeologist was poking around there three or four summers ago with some Cheyenne elders. Jamie learned about it from one of them, his uncle. Now apparently there's an archaeological dig going on in that very canyon. I think Jamie and his friends are afraid they'll find that skeleton and remove it or otherwise desecrate it somehow."

"Calderara?"

"Huh?"

"Was the BLM guy's last name Calderara?"

"Oh, could be. I don't think I ever heard his name. He's in a wheel-chair, Jamie's uncle told him. Injured in Vietnam or somewhere over there during the war."

"That's Sal Calderara, all right."

"Do you know him, Clifford?"

"Well, I've never met him, but I've seen him. He works out of the Worland Field Office."

"Where would you have seen him?"

"At my, uh, girlfriend's memorial service."

"What? Where? I thought you were off the farm in Minnesota."

"Well, I am. But I've been spending this summer working at the archaeological dig in question. Please, please don't tell Jamie or anyone else that. Okay?"

"I won't, Clifford. I sense your intentions are good."

"They are. Thanks, Amy."

"How did your girlfriend die?"

"Killed with an arrow."

"My God!"

"Yeah. Can you tell me more about the skeleton?"

"I can tell you what I know. It relates to a story the elders tell about a half-human, half-deer being, which, odd as it sounds, in mythology gave rise to the Dog band. It's kind of silly, or at least I think it is. It's considered a sacred site, but Jamie's not sure anyone knows where it is, or if it even exists. He said they didn't locate it the day the archaeologist and the elders were up there, and as far as he knows it still hasn't been found."

"Thanks for telling me this, Amy. It's very interesting. And, like you, I don't think I'll be getting my DSR tattoo. But please don't tell Jamie that, either."

"I won't, Clifford," Amy said. She smiled and locked eyes with him, igniting in Clifford an unexpected flicker of distant recognition. "But if you're not interested in joining DSR, I don't understand why you're taking on this eagle job. You do know you could get in a boatload of trouble?"

"Yep, I know that. I'm trying to get to the bottom of why Bobbi—that was her name, Bobbi Alder—was murdered, and who did it. Someday I'll tell you more, I promise, Amy. Let's stay in touch."

"Okay, Clifford, let's do that. But if you're suspecting Jamie or any of the other boys, I think you're on the wrong track. Deep down, they're goodhearted people."

"Thanks for tell me that, too."

***

Less than three hours later, Clifford was hiking solo along the single-track trail he'd accessed at a trailhead on the north shore of Sylvan Lake. Prior to heading out, he had erected Jamie's little pup tent at the nearby Forest Service campground and stashed his duffel inside it. The steep trail had taken Clifford down into a dissected ravine known as Sunday Gulch. To find that the Black Hills, which appeared so mellow from afar, held anything so rugged both surprised and impressed him. He wondered who'd come up with the idea of building a trail through such an impossible maze of root wads, boulders, and flowing water.

After about twenty minutes of hiking, Clifford paused to watch a handful of aspen leaves twirling earthward, shaken loose by a breeze. The mid-afternoon sun threw its spotlight on the colorful leaves as they performed an acrobatic air dance against a backdrop of blue sky and green foliage.

In another mile or so, Clifford entered the forest of big ponderosa pines where Jamie said he would immediately see the eagles' nest perched high to the right of the trail, in a tree with a big "X" carved into the lower trunk. He found the tree, and looked up to see the nest. It would have been tough to miss: an immense tangle of twigs and branches and other building materials, the nest appeared to be eight or nine feet in diameter.

Clifford sat down to wait on a big granite boulder that afforded him a clear view of the nest. He was relieved to see no young eagle heads; the season's brood had apparently already flown off.

Maybe the adult eagles have abandoned the nest, too, he thought, somewhat hopefully.

Not so. Forty minutes into his silent vigil, Clifford heard broad wings slicing through thin air even before seeing the eagle. Landing, it stood on the rim of the nest. Clifford was startled to see that the eagle's face reminded him of his Aunt Gunde—an after-effect of the peyote tea, he surmised. He reached for Jamie's .22-caliber pistol lying beside him on the cool rock. Sitting, feet and butt on the same plane on the boulder, he rested his elbows on bent knees, steadied his lower right arm with his left hand, and took aim, holding his breath.

A lot of people aren't gonna like this. Including me.

But he curled his right index finger around the cold gun metal and squeezed the trigger. The pistol sounded and the bullet hit the large bird in the neck. She appeared to die instantly, falling at least fifty feet to the ground, ricocheting off several branches on the way down.

Clifford walked over to the bird, taken aback by how immense it appeared up close, and by how little it weighed when he picked it up. He grabbed his Buck knife from its belt-mounted sheath, unfolded it, and began cutting, laying the bird's feathers out on a towel in front of him.

"Son, what *do* you think you're doing?"

Startled, Clifford looked up. His heart sank. The tall man standing above him wore a Forest Service uniform. His right hand rested on the butt of a pistol, still in its holster.

A law-enforcement smoky. Damn!

Clifford realized he had been caught literally red-handed, his fingers covered in eagle blood.

"Uh, well, I guess you can see what I'm doing," Clifford said, trying not to sound smart-ass about it.

"Yes, I can. Leave those feathers where they are and come with me. Do I need to get my gun out?"

"No. I'm not dumb enough to try anything. I'm in enough trouble already."

"Yes, you are."

The ranger—Gary Atwater, according to his nametag—removed his backpack and pulled out a walkie-talkie. "Atwater here. Do you read? Over."

"Ten-four," came a woman's voice through the speaker. "What's up, Gary? Over."

"Melissa, get me a backup to the Sylvan Lake parking lot," he instructed. "I've found a young man out here butchering one of the bald eagle pair in lower Sunday Gulch. I don't think he's going to give me trouble, but just in case. Over."

"Ten-four. I'll send Sheila. She's close by, at Harney Peak trailhead. Why on earth would anyone–"

"Thanks, Melissa," Atwater interrupted. "Over and out."

24
TOUCHING HOME

"Things have been going as well as you could expect, Paul," said Conrad Hillary, straddling a frail wooden chair opposite Paul Barlow at a small round table in the Tired Puppy Tavern.

Each man had an open bottle of Coors sitting in front of him. Barlow's hair looked even more ruffled than usual.

"Or better than you'd expect, what with all that's happened," Hillary corrected himself. "But I still haven't heard from Gustafson. He's heartbroken, no doubt, devastated. But still, it's not like him to not at least make contact." Hillary stopped talking and coughed into a cupped hand.

Deep down, Hillary wasn't too worried. He sensed that Clifford was fine, so he'd avoided contacting any authorities about his disappearance. For one thing, he didn't want to alarm Clifford's parents in case he hadn't called them, either.

Right on cue, the Tired Puppy's co-owner, Bonnie Anderson, came trotting down the stairs from her family's quarters above the bar, where they were having dinner. By now, the shockingly red-headed proprietor wasn't particularly needed downstairs when the archaeological crew was in residence. They were entrusted to tend bar and to retrieve their own beers from the cooler, as well as beers for anyone else who wandered in off the baked basin or out of the high mountains. The customers simply left payment for each beer next to the cash register—an amount that not long after the crew's arrival in June had escalated from thirty-five cents to fifty cents per bottle or can. A standing joke among the crew members was that by field season's end, the additional fifteen cents profit per beer would add up to enough to finance a nice Hawaiian vacation for the Andersons.

"Oh, good, you're still here, Conrad," Bonnie said, handing him a small scrap of paper. On it Hillary found written a phone number and a brief message, asking him to call Clifford.

"It's from Gustafson," Hillary told Barlow. "Area code 605. Where's that, South Dakota?"

"That's right," Barlow said.

Hillary shot out the door and over to the phone booth on the opposite side of the gravel street from the tavern. He dropped in a dime and repeated the number to the operator. Hillary listened as the phone rang. Then a husky female voice answered.

"Pennington County Sheriff's Department."

"What?"

"This is the Pennington County Sheriff's Department, sir. What can I do for you?"

"Uh… is Clifford Gustafson there?"

"Let me check my list here. Yes, sir, he is in one of our cells, if that's what you mean. But he can't come to the phone right now."

"Well—hell—what did he do? And where's Pennington County? Is this Rapid City?"

"That's right, sir. I'm not authorized to discuss the matter over the phone. If you'd like me to have one of the deputies return your call—"

"No," Hillary interrupted, "forget it. Thanks. I'll be there as soon as I can. Please tell Gustafson that Hillary is on his way. Got that?"

"Hillary?"

"Yep, H-i-l-l-a-r-y." He slammed down the receiver and hurried back to the tavern.

"Paul, I'm outta here," Hillary wheezed. "Gustafson's in jail over in Rapid City. I don't know why, but I better get there lickety-split. You're around for a couple more days, so there shouldn't be a problem, right?"

"Yeah, no problem, Conrad. You hit the road. Good luck."

Hillary jogged out the door and jumped into one of the two red State of Wyoming pickup trucks parked in front of the bar. After firing up the engine, he backed out of the parking spot and sped away.

"How the hell far is it to Rapid City?" he muttered to himself. Then he hacked up a wad of mucus and spat out the truck's open window.

***

"Hi, Rad."

Clifford looked beat, and embarrassed.

"Hey there, Jeofredo," Hillary said. "How's the food in this joint?"

Clifford smiled, appreciating the levity. "I've had better. You're probably wondering what I'm doing here, huh?"

"Well, the question had crossed my mind."

"Seemed like the sheriff didn't really want to put me in the clinker. But I didn't have much money, so he had to. Thanks for coming, by the way."

"You're welcome. But first things first. Let's get you out of here. What's your bail? I'll take care of it."

Hillary squared things with the officer on duty and soon they were back on the road aiming west from Rapid City, heading for Wyoming.

"It's like this," Clifford began. He proceeded to relate the whole sordid tale of the Crow Fair, how he'd fallen in with a group calling themselves Dog Soldiers Resurrected and, at their urging, had consented to pulling an eagle-killing stunt in hopes of gaining their confidence and breaking into their ranks.

"I think the peyote caused me to go temporarily bonkers," he confessed. "I can hardly believe I shot and killed an eagle."

Hillary remained silent for several moments after Clifford had finished speaking.

"Leave it alone, chief," he said at last. "It's dangerous and it's dumb. It's not you. Look at how much trouble you're already in. And you're probably right about the peyote. Never touch the stuff myself."

"Yeah, but Jamie and those guys will be looking for me, wondering where the heck I've gotten off to."

"Good point. Let me think on it. Killing that eagle is a federal offense, you know."

Clifford groaned. "Yes, I know."

They drove on in brooding silence for a spell.

"Rad?" Clifford said at last. "I don't know what's going on. I don't know who I am. Am I a white Indian or an Indian white man? People say I have a Minnesota accent, for Christ's sake. You can't go home if you've never had one."

"But Clifford, you *have* a home. You came from somewhere. And I think before you return to Sleeping Dog you should go there for a few days. Visit your mom and dad. Get your bearings back. See your dog, Sir... what's his name?"

"Ralph. Sir Ralph the Wonder Dog. He's a kick. Do you think Dr. Barlow would mind if I brought him back? If I do go to Minnesota, I mean?"

"Better not. Paul loves dogs, but rules are rules. Oh, and by the way, you do have a Minnesota accent."

Though he'd been gone from Red Earth for most of the past four years, and despite not even arriving there until he was almost five, Clifford suspected Hillary had a point about it being his home.

"I've changed a lot since going to college," he said slowly, "but I suppose you're right. Most of my character does come from there. My dad likes to say, 'You can take the boy out of Red Earth, but you can't take Red Earth out of the boy.' That place is pretty much responsible for the way I look at things, isn't it? And really, Rad, it's not such a bad view. It was a fun place to grow up. Everyone should be so lucky."

Hillary turned the rig around and pointed it back toward Rapid City. "There's that old friend of mine I've told you about in northwest Iowa, outside Shanton. I think you should visit him while you're back there. That wouldn't be far from your folks' place, right?"

"I guess not. I'm not exactly sure where Shanton is, but I know I've heard the name. Your friend, he's the tracker?"

"Right. Bill Parsons. Raises hogs with his brother on the family's century farm for a bunch of the year. Then, come late fall, he switches gears and motors on out to northwest Wyoming to track poachers for the feds. He's got a God-given talent for it, they say. He once tracked a poacher from outside Meeteetse to Sheridan with nothing to go on but a gut pile and a couple patches of elk hair. Then, after hunting season's over, he travels for a few months before going back to the farm in spring."

"So, you think he can figure out who killed Bobbi?"

"Well, no, I'm not saying that. But I think you should visit him all the same. I'll call him and tell him you're coming. Okay?"

"Okay, sure."

After putting up for the night at a downtown Motel 6, in the morning Hillary and Clifford walked four blocks to the Avis Rent-a-Car headquarters on Jackson Boulevard. There Hillary rented a Volkswagen Beetle under his name and with his check, as Clifford hadn't attained the minimum age required to rent a vehicle. From there they drove back to the motel, where Hillary handed over the car keys. Then he wrote Bill Parsons' phone number on a scrap of paper and gave it to Clifford.

"I slept on it," Hillary said.

"Slept on what?"

"Your point about how Jamie and the DSR boys will be looking for you."

"Yeah?"

"Do you have Jamie's mailing address?"

"No, but I have Finneas's."

"Finneas? Who would name a baby that?"

"Maybe that's why he goes by 'Jonesy.' Finneas Jones is his full name."

"Maybe it's like Johnny Cash's 'A Boy Named Sue.' His parents named him that knowing it was bound to toughen him up."

"He does strike me as a scrapper."

"Okay, well, you write Jamie a letter in care of Finneas, telling him the truth: you got arrested for killing the eagle, so you're headed back to the farm in Minnesota, and the sheriff in Rapid City has Jamie's pistol, in case he's interested in trying to get it back."

"Brilliant, Rad!"

"Of course. What else would you expect? Now you drive carefully, Jeofredo, and take your time. My own ass'll be cast bass if you get caught driving this thing, especially since you're out on bail. I got you a slow car on purpose. The rest of the crew'll be glad to see you back, but you take your time."

"Okay, Rad. Thanks." Clifford looked Hillary in the eyes. "Thanks a *lot*. Do you want to meet me back here, or shall I drive to the site?"

"Come back to Mercerville and we'll drop the Bug off in Sheridan. It'll cost me half my retirement fund, but what's money to a wealthy rockeologist like me?" Hillary pulled a silly face to underscore the absurdity of what he'd just said.

***

After battling a brutal side wind through eastern South Dakota, Clifford banged the cobalt-blue VW over an ancient steel bridge into Iowa not far north of Sioux City. Looking down on the Big Sioux River, he considered how these waters—along with those of Sleeping Dog Creek and a thousand other streams draining millions of acres—would soon became part of the braided collection known as the Missouri River. And, ultimately, the mighty Mississippi.

Clifford steered the VW up, over, and down the steep catsteps of the Loess Hills, tall deposits of windborne rock flour deposited thousands of years ago as the Pleistocene glaciers retreated. They stood like an arid, earthen windbreak sheltering the verdant state of Iowa from the searing prairie westerlies.

Using his right hand, Clifford flapped open a road map and glanced at it, then negotiated his way to Shanton. On arriving in the pint-sized town, he pulled up to a Standard service station and called Bill Parsons from a pay phone, garnering precise directions to his farm. From there he commenced driving south on gravel.

On a whim, Clifford wound the car radio dial to the far right, to AM-1590. Sure enough, loud and clear came WREG, "Watching Red Earth Grow."

The good reception makes sense, I guess. Red Earth can't be more than forty miles away.

As had been the case ever since Clifford first heard the station, nearly two decades earlier, it was spinning discs seemingly designed to lull listeners to sleep on warm afternoons: Ed Ames, 1,000 Strings, the Ray Coniff Singers… your basic grain-elevator music.

When Clifford figured he was about a half mile from Parsons' place, a salt-and-pepper-colored cat with a long, bushy tail materialized from thick roadside grass on the right and sprinted in front of the VW. Clifford banged on the brakes, skidding to a stop on the gravel surface.

The cat never did slow down, but as it fled Clifford noticed the scared and unfortunate beast now lacked its prominent tail.

"Hell!" he exclaimed.

Clifford shut the engine down, got out, and investigated the road surface behind the car. He located the cat's severed tail and picked it up. Gingerly holding it between his thumb and forefinger, he walked over to the farmhouse the cat had run to and set it on the porch. He could see the feline in the bushes, licking the bleeding gash on its posterior.

"Poor kitty," Clifford lamented. "I'm so sorry."

I really do feel bad.

Knocking on the front door brought no response, so Clifford returned to the car and scribbled a message on a piece of notebook paper. Then he trotted back to the house and slipped the note between the screen door and the door frame.

Weird things do happen sometimes.

Back on the road, radio still tuned to WREG, Clifford hummed along as Wayne Newton reached lofty notes, crooning about red roses for a blue lady. But not even Wayne Newton could anesthetize Clifford on a brilliant August day such as this—there was an early-autumn crispness all around him, aromatic as the earth itself, achingly beautiful.

Motoring down a quiet country road, so reminiscent of the byways of the rural landscape in which he had grown up, Clifford thought back to his Wonder Bread years. He considered how much he loved this place, even though he was still across the border in the land of Iowegians and not yet in Minnesota.

You can take the boy out of Red Earth...

"There's no earth better than Red Earth, yah?" he said aloud.

***

"Hey there, Clifford Gustafson. Welcome," said Bill Parsons.

"Thanks. Good to meet you." Clifford stuck out his arm to shake hands.

"Hillary said you got yourself into some trouble over in the Black Hills?"

"Yeah," Clifford said, hoping he wouldn't have to elaborate anytime soon.

Hillary had warned Clifford that Parsons was a large and potentially intimidating man. But, he'd added, rough and tumble though Parsons may appear—and in spite of his penchant for killing large mammals, both domestically and in far-flung places—he was a gentle man who loved his parents and family. To be close to them was why he still lived in Shanton, Iowa, and not in the Yellowstone country he so loved, the place to which every fall he made his "hunting-and-gathering missions," as he called them. Hunting poachers, that is, and gathering them up for delivery to the authorities.

Hillary could have told Clifford something else about Bill Parsons, as well, but he'd decided to let him learn it for himself—that when the big man related one of his countless spellbinding tales it was an experience you didn't quickly forget. He started quiet, almost whispering, but as the story built, so did the intensity of his voice. At mid-tale the listener would start thinking, "This guy's pretty loud." But he hadn't heard anything yet. By the story's climax, Parsons' rich baritone, booming from lungs bigger than small watermelons, could blast a man twice Clifford's size off his bar stool.

Parsons lived to visit far-off places, he told Clifford, to hunt and to see the things he'd read about since boyhood in his ever-growing library of travel and adventure books. Hemingway and Byrd were his gurus; Lowell Thomas, his tour guide. But despite his addiction to visiting exotic places, the forty-nine-year-old's residence had always been here on the farm outside Shanton, except for four years at Iowa State University in Ames and a yearlong stab at the teaching profession in the capital city of Des Moines. Not being close to family? Unthinkable for Parsons.

"Besides," Parsons said, "years back I came to the conclusion that Iowa is the last frontier. It's a place so plain I knew it would never be discovered to the point of overcrowding. I savored the peace and quiet of living here, an anonymous spot to which few without blood ties ever ventured. Shanton, I felt, was the opposite of a tourist attraction. It was a tourist *non*-attraction. A tourist repellent. I sincerely believed that... until a few months ago."

"What happened?" Clifford asked, taking the bait.

"Red Earth, where you're from, that's a nice place," Parsons whispered, seeming to change the subject. "Just like this place used to be." His voice changed tone, transforming into a low growl. "But they're turning Shanton into a tourist trap. Can you believe that?"

Parsons stood a couple of inches taller than Clifford, who could almost see disgust dripping from his host's graying blond beard.

"Who's 'they'?"

"Backers of the Possum Valley Scenic Railway."

"What's that? And, like you say, why would anyone come to Shanton on purpose? From what little I've seen, the place seems about as unremarkable as Red Earth."

"Exactly what I thought. Precisely. But, like a lot of small Midwestern towns, Shanton's been hurting recently. Farmers in the county have been going belly-up right and left. And, of course, the stores in town have been suffering, too, because the farmers are. Well, a couple of years ago, the word 'tourism' began bouncing off the tongues of Shanton-boosters like popcorn in a kettle. A local lawyer, classmate of mine, Cary Anson, is guiltier than anyone. He must be half pit-bull, that guy. He just wouldn't let go of it. He made this fiery speech at a public meeting organized by the chamber of commerce. He spread it on thick, talking about the proud, the industrious, the undaunted character of Shantonians. 'Shanton's not just another farm town!' Anson cried. 'It's a RAILROAD town!'"

Parsons shook his head in dismay.

"Well, that got the crowd going. I was there to see it. Anson went on and on about how in recent years excursion trains had proven to be viable tourist magnets in Colorado, California, other states. Why not northwest Iowa? 'So what if the spine of the Rockies doesn't bisect the local countryside, or no volcanic peaks loom?' he asked the crowd, closing in on the sale. 'We have the valley of the Possum River!' Anson practically had these folks panting, looking around for the wheelbarrows they'd need to carry all their new money to the bank. He convinced my friends and fellow citizens that here we have, by upper-Midwest standards, the meeting place of the Grand Canyon and the Great Divide. And, dammit, maybe we do."

Clifford inspected the surrounding landscape. The western half of Parsons' property comprised a feral piece of semi-native tall-grass prairie on a high bluff overlooking the timbered valley of the Opossum River. It was a setting not unlike the valley of the East Branch of the Red Earth River, above which perched Clifford's spiritual, medicinal place, the Bobby Wilson Golf Course.

"Bill, you could squeeze nine holes in here," Clifford said, only half-joking. "Nine par-threes, anyway. It would make a beautiful executive golf course."

"I don't think so, Clifford. But I'll keep it in mind."

Parsons' country bachelor pad, a rustic frame job he'd built himself, sat in a grove of respectable-sized oaks and maples. Having just arrived from the arid Rocky Mountain West, Clifford found the interior damp and musty when they popped inside to grab a drink.

"Don't like air-conditioning," Parsons said, unprompted. "And I keep forgetting to buy a dehumidifier. But I don't spend that much time inside, anyhow." He handed Clifford a bottle of Coke.

"I bought these forty acres in 1952. I figured there wasn't a spot on Earth less likely to get infected with the development and commercialism I'd seen invading and spoiling so many places around the world I have visited. Now the Possum Valley Scenic Railway enters my domain not a mile upstream from here. I hear its whistle blow five or six times a day in the summer. And a lot of curious or lost pilgrims come by here on their way down to the river and back up to the highlands. Each passing vehicle grinds the road gravel a little finer," he said, gritting his teeth, "dusting my yard, my house, my car... everything. I mean, talk about adding insult to injury. But what can a guy do? You can't stop progress—if you call going back to a dirty, coal-smoke-belching locomotive 'progress.' Of course, it's a new locomotive—they found it in *China*, of all places! Two hundred thousand smackers. The very last steam locomotive to roll off the assembly line at the only steam locomotive factory still operating in the world. Can you believe that? They called it the *Hawkeye Express*. It pulls open-air cars and a closed dining car from the old depot on the northwest side of Shanton, hauling paying passengers twelve miles north up the Possum Valley and back. It's been successful beyond anyone's wildest dreams. Even Cary Anson's, dammit!"

This guy's pretty loud, thought Clifford.

"But I shouldn't be going on like this," Parsons added hastily. "I apologize. What are you doing here, anyway, Clifford? Conrad told me he thought you'd get here yesterday."

Clifford shrugged. "I don't know what I'm doing here. Rad just said he thought I should come and meet you. Did he tell you what happened at our site? I spent an extra night camped out near Chamberlain. That's why I wasn't here yesterday. I wanted to look around that Missouri River area some."

"Nice country. Lots of pheasants. Conrad told me something about what happened, about a beautiful young girl being killed by an arrow. What a strange and awful thing to have happen... I heard a bald eagle got killed, too."

Clifford winced.

In his brief experience as an adult, Clifford had met only one man whom he instantly knew would become a good friend: Conrad Hillary. Now he sensed the same thing in Bill Parsons. So much so that he proceeded to confide in Parsons, in more detail than he'd told anyone, the feelings he'd had for Bobbi Alder. He also told Parsons about his experiences of running into the DSR bunch at the Crow Fair, and all about the trouble he'd gotten himself into in the Black Hills.

Parsons nodded. "Hillary briefed me on most of that, Clifford. You know, I'll be heading out to Yellowstone come mid-October. I'd like to visit your site, if you're still working. I did a little fieldwork with Conrad in Yellowstone four years ago. It'd be good to get my hands dirty again. God, I love that old fart.

"Oh, you know what?" he added. "I've also done some poacher sleuthing over in the Black Hills. Worked some with that Pennington County sheriff, Ollie Sherman. Not a bad guy, really. And with the Black Hills National Forest folks. I'm sort of a fed myself, you know, part of the year, anyway. If you don't mind, I'll give my friends over there a call and try to explain to them why you did what you did. It might help if they hear it from me, get my perspective on it."

"Oh, man, Bill, I'd appreciate that. A lot."

"When's the last time you visited your folks in the borderland here?" Parsons asked.

"About four months ago," Clifford said. "Early May."

"Whoo-wee! I love that time of year," Parsons said, beaming. "Don't you? Before the air turns summer soggy and buggy? I just love watching the corn and beans sprout in these undulating oceans of loam." He spread his arms and hands in front of him, as if painting the fields that composed his farm and nature preserve. "And listening for the honking of geese, signaling their return to the north country. Northern Iowa might be the prettiest place on Earth at that time of year. As gorgeous as the north of Yellowstone in autumn when the aspens turn and the elk bugle. Southern Minnesota in spring is probably not far behind," he added with a wink.

But today both men had detected a tinge of autumn in the air, early for the area. They strolled out to inspect Parsons' habitat-improvement project, a wide strip of trees and reintroduced native grasses lining the southern border of his big crop field. He whispered as he described to Clifford the varieties of grasses he planted for the sake of wildlife in need of cover and browse. He told him what species of trees he had removed and which he'd left, and why. How he had sweated and toiled to control the intermittent stream running through it all, utilizing native rock gathered in the river valley below. His voice grew louder; his demeanor more animated.

"I expect to see an increase in the numbers of rabbits, pheasants, whitetails..."

As he spoke, Clifford could almost picture the animals among the trees and grasses around them.

"...then I can shoot 'em!" Parsons bellowed.

The words "shoot 'em" blasted like a rifle shot far out across the domesticated prairie and into the river void below. An echo bounced back a second later. Finally, the words were absorbed and muffled by the verdant vegetation filling the river's cleft.

Clifford gave Parsons a startled glance, then looked away. This Hillary *had* warned him about: "You'll like Parsons, but he may surprise you. When he begins a story, you never know where he'll go with it."

The men continued walking toward Hewlett Bridge, sharing some tongue-burning liquor with Spanish writing on the bottle.

"This stuff is highly regarded in parts of the Andes," Parsons informed him. "I got it when I went trekking there three years ago."

They reached the rail bridge and looked out over its span across the broad, deep valley carved by the Opossum River.

"When this bridge was built in 1917 it was the highest doubletrack train trestle in the world," Parsons declared. "Who'd a thunk it, in northwest Iowa?"

The men tip-toed from tie to tie, with only air separating one from the next, looking down the entire time so as not to catch a foot. Peering through the open spaces, Clifford could see driftwood branches and full-sized logs bobbing downstream to the southwest. The summer-becoming-autumn breeze lifted the delicious scent of maturing nature. It also occasionally delivered, depending on the directional whims of the wind, the whiff of a pig farm, still ripe from a humid summer.

"Is that your farm I smell?" Clifford inquired.

"Yes, and a lovely aroma it is, wouldn't you agree?"

"Not really," Clifford said. "I never could get used to it."

Parsons laughed.

By the time they reached the middle of the bridge, the two men were an equal and, for Clifford, uncomfortably long distance from either end. He found himself hoping not to see a Chicago & Duluth freight train come pulsing off the prairie into their quiet preserve. Apparently reading Clifford's mind, Parsons looked at his watch.

"Eastbound's due in an hour-ten."

Clifford stopped worrying, figuring Parsons knew these things. Then another thought struck him.

"What about the westbound?"

Parsons smiled. "Hours away."

The valley they gazed upon encompassed a forgotten swath of wilderness surrounded by thousands of acres of tamed, tilled prairie.

"My refuge has been spared," Parsons philosophized, "only by virtue of its verticality and dearth of topsoil."

It sounded to Clifford like something Parsons had said before, perhaps even written down and memorized.

An explosion of hardwoods—maple, elm, box elder, hawthorn, oak, horse chestnut—made it an uncommonly beautiful place to be, Parsons assured Clifford, "in any season, by anyone's measure."

***

Back at the house, the two men shook hands and said their see-you-laters. After squeezing himself into the Volkswagen and firing up the air-cooled engine, Clifford cranked down the window and began rolling away. Then he stopped.

"Oh, hey, Bill!" he yelled out the Beetle's window. "I forget to mention: I ripped your neighbor's cat a new asshole."

"What?" Parsons demanded.

But Clifford drove off, waving his hand out the window, leaving his new friend confounded.

Going north, Clifford decided to challenge his navigational skills by finding his way home without the benefit of a map. And he would go via gravel roads, those unsigned byways that to him looked like what they were, and still should be: magical paths to mystical places.

Despite the growing shroud of darkness, Clifford soon recognized some of the very roads he and other Red Earth boys and girls had taken on voyages of discovery: to their first keg parties, their first make-out sessions.

Ah, Janey Ellsworth, what might've been!

They were places to which Clifford and his friends had come as kids to do the things they knew in their hearts they shouldn't, because it would have shocked their parents. And they were the places their parents had come two or three decades earlier to do, with a few variations, exactly the same things.

Clifford zipped past the dirt road he and his friend "Buddy" Balster had followed down to the East Branch of the Red Earth one particularly warm day in May during their junior year. Spring fever had raised their temperatures so high that they could not bear another sleep-inducing, post-lunch history lecture from Mr. Cashart. Before the school-skipping afternoon had ended, far from drowsy, they had got themselves screaming-banshee drunk on cheap Old Milwaukee beer—purchased for them, at his one-dollar-per-six-pack profit, by their smelly, old-school hobo acquaintance Bart. A living cliché, Bart the Bum resided in a land-stranded boxcar set on concrete blocks down by the roundhouse in Red Earth.

Never did learn Bart's last name.

That afternoon Clifford managed to shred the flesh of both palms after losing his grip on a long vine he'd been utilizing to swing far, high out over the river before letting go and splashing in. Come evening, after repeated dunkings in the chilly river and trying other half-successful means to make himself sober, the mighty Tarzan had suffered through a most uneasy meal at home with his folks. Only by holding his fork in an altogether unnatural manner had he managed, he believed to this day, to hide the painful, bloodied mess his palms had become.

His mother may have thought otherwise. But if so, she never let on.

To this river valley, rebelling against the conservative constraints of late 1960s Minnesota, Clifford and his peers had come to let down their hair.

***

"So, Clifford, you're sort of bein' forced to grow up this summer, aren't you?"

"I guess so, Papa," Clifford said, sitting at the breakfast table with his father. Both were drinking coffee, while his mother hovered over the stove fixing breakfast.

"I wish it could of held off for a couple more years, at least, son. There's enough time to be an adult, and you're only young once. It's just not fair, you losing that friend of yours that way. What was her name—Billie?"

"No, it was Bobbi," Clifford said. "And Papa?"

"Yes, son?"

"We were more than just friends. I guess you'd say we were boyfriend and girlfriend. To tell you the truth, I was crazy about her. And I think it's safe to say the feeling was mutual."

"I gathered as much."

"How?"

"Well, the day you called from Rapid City, saying you were headed home? Later that same day your friend, or instructor, or whatever he is, Dr. Hillary, called us. Real nice fellow. I had quite a talk with him. He gave me a better idea of the whole situation you have all been dealing with."

"Did he tell you about me getting arrested?"

"Yep, he told me that, too, and how he had rented that Volkswagen for you. But he assured me we don't need to worry about you turning into a hardened felon. Not that he needed to tell me that." Gus chuckled.

"No, that's right. Those two nights in jail were enough for one lifetime, I do believe."

"Clifford?"

"Yeah, Papa?"

"I don't know what you have planned after this summer, now that you've graduated, but your mother and I want you to know you're always welcome back here at home. And you have paid work waiting if you do want to come back. Even if it's just for a few months, or a year or two, before you go on to graduate school, if that's your intention."

"Thanks, Gus," Clifford said. He had never called his father by his nickname, but it seemed the right thing to do at the moment. "I do know that. But I appreciate you telling me again all the same."

"Boys, are your hands clean?" interrupted Martha. "French toast, bacon, and hash browns are on their way."

"We're all set, Mama," said Gus. "And hungry as a herd of hippos."

***

After a week in the Red Earth country—with his parents at the farm, on the Bobby Wilson Golf Course with his father, and alongside Sir Ralph the Wonder Dog in the cool evenings—Clifford felt grounded. A trip to his boyhood home had straightened him out again, just like the Christmas-break visit during his freshman year in college.

On Tuesday morning, after an early breakfast, Clifford bid his parents farewell. He jumped into the Volkswagen and hightailed it back in the direction from which he had come, taking aim at the mighty Big Horn Mountains. A rare easterly tried pushing him faster than the VW Bug was designed to go, but not until he reached the vast, looking-glass prairies of central South Dakota did he let it rip. He was wary of being pulled over in the rental car and getting himself into water even hotter than that in which he was already submerged with the authorities in Rapid City.

"And getting the kind and elderly Dr. Hillary into it with me," Clifford said aloud, chuckling, fifty miles west of Mitchell and The World's Only Corn Palace.

25
THE POINT

The shrill noon whistle sounded in Clifford's ears as he rolled into downtown Worland on September 6. Following an impulse that had struck him a few miles back as he'd motored through the phantasmagoric, hoodoo-inhabited painted desert between Ten Sleep and Worland, he continued straight west instead of turning right toward Basin and the Sleeping Dog site. After clanking across an old bridge spanning the Big Horn River, he left the pavement and continued onto gravel, driving past an ever-dwindling series of farmsteads. His goal was to have a look at the Blackburn Draw dune field Hillary had told him about a few weeks earlier. His mentor had raved about the place, saying he'd seen tons of evidence of prehistoric winter campsites spread about the hardpan separating the area's sand dunes. "Sites thicker'n Tricky Dick Nixon's eyebrows" had been Hillary's exact words.

Sweeps of hay bent with the breeze and filled the air with a delicious fragrance that poured in from the flats through the open window of the Volkswagen. Clifford glanced in the rear-view mirror, which framed an image of the Chugwater Formation, devoid of vegetation and erupting in coral-red contrast to the sea of brown barley stubble lapping at its base. Behind and above the Chugwater, red and yellow sculpted sandstone foothills rose skyward to meet the fingers of pine and fir that pointed toward the Big Horn summits protruding high above timberline.

After putting seven miles of teeth-jarring washboard road between Worland and himself, Clifford came upon a small, ragged, dog-like critter stumbling down the side of the road. As he passed it, the animal looked up and grinned a coyote greeting.

"Que pasa, mi amigo?" Clifford inquired, waving at the animal.

Reminds me of the coyote Hillary and I drove past that day in May when I first met the old hippie...

Eight and a half miles from the bridge in town, Clifford came to a halt before a gate in a barbed-wire fence where a sign read "South Fork Blackburn Draw." He got out of the Beetle and levered open the rickety gate, dragging the collapsed wood-and-wire affair far enough aside to squeeze the car through. Having closed the gate behind him, he drove another mile and a half up a rutted track and parked just before a dry creek bed crossing, exactly as detailed in the written instructions he'd had in his wallet since Hillary handed them over in early August.

Clifford could see through the windshield that the sand formations began immediately on the other side of the arroyo. They stretched northeastward, first as simple ripples and finger drifts, then growing to become high barchan dunes, crescent-shaped mountains in miniature.

"This is so cool!" Clifford whispered.

He grabbed his daypack and got out, slamming the car door shut, then started walking in the direction of the big dunes. Right off the bat he gained an understanding of Hillary's enthusiasm for the place. A cursory glance at the sandy ground revealed flakes of obsidian and chert, definitely chipped by human hands, scattered everywhere.

After exploring in various directions for half an hour, his eyes glued to the sandy floor, Clifford began getting into dunes of approximately his own height.

"A cordillera of quartz grains," he whispered. *Papa would give me grief for using fifty-cent words like that.*

Along with the noise of the wind, Clifford detected a sound reminiscent of soft singing. It came from loose sand tumbling over the crest of dunes and onto the leeward slip face, as the formations continued their imperceptible but relentless march toward the northeast. So intently was he gazing at the ground that he failed to notice a big pronghorn buck standing just twenty feet in front of him until it "barked"—or at least that was what the noise it made sounded like to Clifford. The instant he looked up, the pronghorn took off in the opposite direction. It was going, Clifford estimated, at the speed he had driven the VW in South Dakota when adhering to the speed limit.

"Zero to sixty in four seconds flat," he said aloud, marveling.

Jamie's souped-up Plymouth Road Runner has nothing on the stock Pontiac Pronghorn.

The next moment, to Clifford's surprise, an Appaloosa mare displaced the antelope, materializing apparently out of thin air. Brown in color as far back as the withers and white with dark spots on her barrel and hindquarters, she trailed a thick, dark tail. Like the coyote Clifford had encountered a while earlier, it reminded him of the first drive he'd taken with Hillary, after his mentor-to-be picked him up at the Billings airport.

The mare nickered and whinnied, shaking her big head up and down and side to side. Then she turned around and stormed away toward the north. Due to the height of the dunes, Clifford immediately lost sight of her. He clambered up the windward side of a tall dune to his right for a better look. Still, even from the summit, he couldn't see the Appaloosa.

"Huh," he murmured. "Strange."

Out of curiosity, or premonition, or a mixture of the two, Clifford strolled over to where the two animals, first the pronghorn and then the horse, had stood. There, on the desert floor, sat a textbook-perfect mano and metate of yellow sandstone. The hand-held grinding stone rested in the center of the much larger flat rock that had served as the grinding surface. To Clifford's moderately trained but ever-improving eye, the gritty rock looked like the sandstone composing the Sand Burr Formation that formed the northern walls of Sleeping Dog Canyon.

The past really is the present. It's a continuum. The person who used these tools is long dead, sure, but here's something they made. Perhaps untouched for decades, or centuries, just as they left it.

He wondered if the owner of these tools had died leaving them here, or had perhaps forgotten about them at some point in time.

Then he shook his head. "Not bloody likely," he muttered.

The metate featured a smooth depression of about an inch worn into its surface, resulting from, Clifford guessed, several years or even decades of service. These dune field sites would likely have been seasonally occupied, only in the winter and early spring. No sandstone outcrops rose anywhere in the vicinity, as far as Clifford could see. A person would have had to carry the food-preparation tools some distance to get them there. Curiosity overpowering him, Clifford lifted the entire affair. He estimated the two rocks together weighed twenty-five to thirty pounds. The ground on which they had reposed, now exposed, wriggled to life with the manic movement of hundreds of black ants. He set the artifacts carefully back down.

He felt he should leave the grinding stone otherwise untouched. Yet he couldn't resist the temptation to heft the hand tool just once, to feel it, to sense the present commingling with the past.

Maybe it'll give me a mental image of what the last person to hold the tool looked like, or insight into what he or she was thinking.

He knelt, picked the mano up with both hands, then gasped. On the surface of the metate, hidden until now by the hand stone, rested a small Plains side-notched projectile point of shiny black obsidian. It was beautiful, and apparently perfect in its proportions. Placing the mano on the ground next to the metate, Clifford crouched down for a closer look. The edges appeared razor sharp, with chipping scars so fine they could have been made that morning. Late Prehistoric in age, Clifford calculated, and most likely chipped from a core obtained at Obsidian Cliff in Yellowstone, the most prolific source of volcanic glass in the region.

A special point, no doubt, but why put it here? For safekeeping? As an offering?

Clifford took the 35-millimeter Nikon from his daypack and snapped several shots from various angles and distances. He avoided touching the point. After gently placing the mano back just as he'd found it, he started back toward the car. He couldn't say how or why, but he was struck by an instant certainty.

Not only do the past and the present meld, but this dune field is somehow tied to the canyon of Sleeping Dog Creek. Did Conrad come to a similar conclusion earlier in the summer?

"Hope I can find my way back," Clifford whispered to himself. He hadn't paid attention to his exact whereabouts while investigating the ground surface, and he found himself disoriented amid the towering dunes. He discovered, however, that he could track himself from the occasional foot impressions he'd left in some of the looser spreads of drift sand. He finally returned to where he could see the Volkswagen a couple of hundred yards away.

As he recrossed the dry wash, Clifford yelped and jumped after almost stepping on what he interpreted as an expression of Mother Nature's warped sense of humor—a massive gopher snake lying stretched out on the sand with the back half of a huge bullfrog protruding from its mouth. The frog was kicking its legs in a dying, half-hearted effort. The bulk of the frog's front end caused the snake's neck, at a point just below its head, to bulge freakishly to at least twice its natural circumference. Collecting himself, Clifford wondered how long the snake would have to lie there, vulnerable to predators itself, while processing the oversized meal.

"Crazy," Clifford said.

He removed his daypack and grabbed the Nikon to record the bizarre vision on film.

I'll have to send a copy of this shot to Marlin Perkins.

When he got to the car, his watch, which he'd left sitting on the passenger seat, told him it was seven-thirty.

Wow, I must've fallen into a time warp! Seems like only two or three hours ago I heard the noon whistle in Worland...

26
FRICTION

Steering the VW into Mercerville at five minutes past nine, Clifford spotted several familiar rigs parked in front of the Tired Puppy Tavern. He pulled up and parked in front. After climbing the creaky wooden steps and entering the smoky bar, he found the entire crew inside, enjoying the twin-purpose celebration Hillary had warned him of during a brief phone conversation the day before—Hillary's own sixty-fourth birthday bash and a farewell party for eight of the twelve crew members. Come Saturday, those eight would filter away, John Riley to graduate school in New Mexico, Harry Oldcomb back to the University of New York at Buffalo, Ben Reed to Marine Corps boot camp in Southern California, the rest to various other places.

"Hey, chief!" the birthday boy yelled on seeing Clifford appear in the doorway. "How'd that VW run?"

"Fine, Rad," Clifford said, with a sly smile. "Do you believe that little bugger can do a hundred with a good tailwind? I packed the speedometer at eighty, then kept going."

Hillary glared at Clifford for a moment, feigning severe disapproval, then gave him a huge grin and a big handshake. "Good to have you back, Jeofredo. Pull up a chair and pop open a Coors."

"Don't mind if I do."

After making the rounds to say his hellos, Clifford joined Hillary and several of the younger archaeologists at a bar table. He quickly surmised that various stages of inebriation had been reached depending upon whether the individual had been drinking straight beer or beer as a chaser for tequila hookers. Hillary had been sticking to the suds.

"Guess I'm slowing down in my old age," he gurgled to Clifford, then cleared his throat. "Even at my own birthday party I'm not touching that ta-kill-yuh with a ten-foot person of the Polish persuasion."

"What?"

"You know—a ten-foot Pole."

Clifford grunted and shook his head at the worst pun he'd heard coming from a man full of them, then scooted his chair in closer to facilitate confidential conversation. "Hey, thanks for sending me by Bill Parsons' place. What a neat guy. Says he'd like to swing by here in October if we're still around. We will be, won't we?"

"Some of you will. Jefferson, Josie, Marge. You, if you're game. Which it sounds like you are. I've gotta be back in Chadron early next week to begin teaching a Tuesday–Thursday class, so I'm hightailing it out of here on Sunday. But I'll still try to come back for a Friday-through-Monday block or two. I think Paul can do pretty much as he pleases first semester, so he'll no doubt hang around for good once I'm gone, until everybody else has vamoosed. When did Bill think he'd get here?"

"He wasn't sure, but he thought around the middle of the month."

"Good deal. Of course, you're coming back to Chadron with Paul later this month for rendezvous, aren't you? Buck Creek's an international holiday for us Plains rockeologists. Any fieldwork still underway that late in the season shuts down for at least three or four days."

"You bet I am. I look forward to observing you in your natural habitat. Are there other critters like you wandering the Pine Ridge?"

"Nope, I'm the last of the breed. Once I go, we're extinct as a species."

"Bummer," Clifford said, chuckling.

Just as he began telling Hillary about his visit with his folks, loud voices erupted on the other side of the bar.

"I did *not* hide that point!" Peter Ashton yelled.

"Well, then, where did it go?" said a worked-up John Riley. "Where's it at?"

"I have no idea."

"You lying son-of-a-bitch. You've been lying about that half the summer. I was watching you with binoculars that day you were a couple miles, maybe two and half miles, up the canyon. I saw you pick up a shiny black tool of some kind as plain as day, then toss it into a bush—for safekeeping, I'm thinking. I wonder what other evidence you've trashed or hidden up there, and why?"

With that, Ashton lashed out with his right fist at the wiry young cowboy, who dodged the swing and came back to slam his opponent's gut with a left of his own. Ashton folded and hit the floor. Hillary and Clifford sprang to action. The former subdued Riley by locking his arms behind his back, while Clifford put the same move on Ashton once he stood up looking for more.

"Boys! That's enough!" Paul Barlow appeared from his corner of the bar, where he'd been playing Texas hold 'em with several others. "What's this about?"

"Ashton here has been doing some pirate archaeology up Sleeping Dog Canyon on his own," Riley said, "and hiding his findings."

"Have not!" said Ashton.

"Okay, let's get this sorted out later," Barlow steamed. Then he raised his voice, looking stern. "Everybody. Time to get back to camp. I expect you all at your posts at the usual time tomorrow, and that's going to come mighty early for some of you. I don't want Riley or Ashton, either one, driving back. Jefferson, you're pretty much yourself, so you drive Riley's truck. And Mary, you handle Ashton here. I'm sure you won't mind that. Who else has had too much tequila? Let's see a show of hands, children."

Danny Ho, Harry Oldcomb, and Josie MacDonald all raised their arms in the air.

Calming down some, Barlow nodded. "Okay, the rest of you guys and gals figure it out amongst yourselves, but don't any of you three drive. We don't want any more tragedies around here this summer."

He paused then cast his eye over the whole group. "Look, I'm exceptionally pleased and proud of the work you young people have done this summer. And with how you've conducted yourselves both on and off the site. I hope you've gotten some good out of the experience, too. I want you to know I'm grateful to each and every one of you. I don't want this to end on a sour note, that's all. Let's get on home, and I'll see you in the morning."

"Oh, boy," Clifford heard Danny Ho muttering as they all filed out through the framed doorway of the Tired Puppy, "Barlow was really pissed."

27

INTO THE COLD AND DARK

Though the autumn equinox was a few days away, fall had settled on the Big Horn country. Bursts of red and burnt-orange brush burnished the foothills and leaves of faded yellow danced on the cottonwoods overhanging Sleeping Dog Creek.

During his extended leave, Clifford discovered, another crew romance had blossomed, or at least come out of the closet—Mary O'Donnell and Peter Ashton, apparently negating Hillary's suspicions about the female grad student's sexual preferences. He understood then why Barlow had speculated that O'Donnell wouldn't mind taking care of the inebriated and angry Ashton back at the Tired Puppy the previous week.

What a perfectly matched couple. By now, they're off together in Texas somewhere.

Additional changes had come about during Clifford's absence. All three of Galen Davies' cabins had been vacated, so Clifford transferred his gear from the farmhouse attic into the easternmost hut and took up housekeeping. The excavations had grown larger and deeper; the floor sat a full twelve feet below ground surface. Tall ladders, jury-rigged by Ben Reed and Tom Jefferson from lengths of lodgepole pine, were now required to get in and out. Cooler weather, coupled with the deeper excavations and lowering angle of the sun in the sky, had permitted the skeleton crew to go back to working eight hours straight, with just a half-hour break for lunch. Now, even with the shortening days of September, calling the workday quits at four-thirty left Clifford plenty of daylight for knocking around the canyons and foothills to search for artifacts and spiritual guidance. And for clues or impressions that might lead to him solving the mystery of Bobbi

Alder's murder. From what Clifford had been told, the sheriff and his boys had made little progress in the investigation.

It was on such a post-work hike that Clifford set out twelve days after returning from his road trip to the Midwest. As he strode along, he thought about Hillary, wondering how his first week of classes at Chadron State had gone. He reflected on some of the folks he'd worked with for much of the summer, now gone back to their other lives. He wondered if he would see Danny Ho again, or Chuy Padilla, now a senior at the University of New Mexico.

Probably so. Like Hillary says, the world of Plains and Rocky Mountain archaeology is small and tight.

Carrying a light supper, a camera, and a few other items in his daypack, Clifford made his way up to the merging of the dry and wet fork canyons of Sleeping Dog Creek, a mile above where he'd found Bobbi's body on that horrific day in mid-August. From there, he veered left to continue following the creek as the dry fork canyon branched southeastward.

After another mile-plus, the topography of the Sand Burr escarpment mellowed considerably. Clifford began ambling upward more or less at random, lost amid a discordant landscape of foothill slopes hosting sagebrush and an abundance of sandstone fins and concentric, low-slung outcrops of the same rock.

Petrified dung heaps shat by giant prehistoric bison. Clifford giggled at the thought.

Savoring the pungent scent of juniper and sage, he watched as a group of four mule deer does stotted up a steep hillside and out of sight.

Clifford focused on utilizing all his available senses; on opening up to any and every possibility around him. He paused, climbing up to sit atop an impressive block of sandstone that radiated warmth even though the chilly air of early evening had set in. Listening, he thought he heard and felt in his chest the vibrating "whoomp!" of a diving nighthawk.

It reminded Clifford of jogging in the canyon with Bobbi several weeks earlier, when together they had heard the same distinctive sound.

The night Bobbi told me she liked me.

Thanks to the tough work he'd been performing over the summer, combined with endless hours of exposure to the sun and dry air, Clifford looked and felt as hard and dark as the ageless rock supporting him. For a brief and lucid, yet largely unconscious moment, he felt physically connected to the sandstone block on which he reposed. It reminded him of how he had felt himself to be part of the big old poplar the night of the powwow at the Crow Fair.

Clifford stood and resumed wandering, going farther, higher. He imagined himself packing into one of those southern Utah labyrinthine settings pictured in the Sierra Club calendars that had adorned the walls of his dorm rooms at UM over the years: box canyons, broad expanses of slickrock, narrow slot notches, tall redrock walls. He watched bats darting low and high in the sky, availing themselves of a late-season insect hatch. He felt the palpable presence of the ancients here, where men and women had trodden four hundred, two thousand, ten thousand years ago. He couldn't help thinking again about Hillary's pet peeve, those mega-pickups sporting "Wyoming Native" bumper stickers. Like the gray-headed hippie-yippie had proclaimed back in May, those bozos' ancestors had landed in the Big Horn country decades, if not centuries, after his own people had.

This is *my home.*

Estimating that there was an hour of daylight remaining, Clifford figured he had time to hike south from where he now stood, back down into the canyon of the wet fork. He put the total distance back to the site at around five miles, meaning he'd have to descend at a rapid clip. But the final mile would be creekside, over a route he knew so well that he could manage it blindfolded and walking backwards if he had to.

His plan, in theory, was to descend from the rim immediately above where the creek took its southeasterly turn—a mile upstream of the site, the very spot where he'd found Bobbi's lifeless body. He knew of a tight gap carved into the rim there, which he had used once before to negotiate his way down to the creek bottom.

But Clifford had overestimated the amount of daylight remaining, and night fell before he could descend from the rim. The last-quarter moon had yet to rise. When he came to the cliff edge hanging high above the cleft of the creek, the darkness was nearly absolute. A multitude of distant stars dotting the black sky overhead provided the only light.

Clifford acknowledged that he would be spending an unplanned night outdoors, his first-ever bivouac. Then he chuckled at his own cleverness. For just such an eventuality he always carried in his daypack the lightweight sleeping sack handmade by the female half of the couple who owned the Big Horn Outfitters sporting goods store in Worland. The sack consisted of a pair of thick sheets sewn together, each wrapped with a heat-reflective panel of aluminized plastic, the entire affair sandwiched between layers of water-resistant, rip-stop nylon. Weighing only a pound, the sack as advertised would make for comfortable sleeping on a forty-degree night, and might make a zero-degree night outdoors survivable.

It'll probably dip well below freezing by morning.

Clifford understood, despite his cleverness, that he was in for a chilly and restless night. He felt his way over the ground to a low sandstone wall, exercising caution to avoid taking the big step into the canyon of Sleeping Dog Creek. Or a smaller step into a "kiss tank" filled by a recent rainfall; no need to add to his forthcoming misery by soaking his feet in frigid water. He crawled into what his fingers informed him was a small, cave-like depression, praying that he wouldn't disturb any snakes, packrats, or owls.

Gotta add a flashlight to my pack; that would make things a whole lot easier.

Like the sandstone block he had rested upon a couple of hours earlier, these rocks retained warmth from the day's intense sunshine. So, his night afield started out quite comfortably, despite the hard rock bed supporting him. By three a.m., though, Clifford's sedimentary mattress had surrendered all its stored heat to the cold night air. Wide awake and shivering, he rubbed his upper arms and torso to generate warmth. He felt in his pack for the Snickers bar he knew to be there and sat up to gobble it down. Then, lying back down, to take his mind off the cold he concentrated on identifying as many sounds as he could. The wild clamor of yip-yammering coyotes; the lonesome, haunting hoot of a great-horned owl. But a couple of other weird sounds he didn't recognize, and the fact made him uneasy.

I don't know all the noises a bear can make, or a mountain lion.
Daylight couldn't come too soon for Clifford's liking.

He had a lot of time to think during the next three hours. One of his trains of thought carried him back to a place he could see and smell and hear; a place he recalled with intense clarity and which he had missed far more than he realized until this very moment: the Red Earth High School gymnasium. It was a place filled with the scent of adolescent sweat, the sound of uninhibited laughter, and the emotions of young men crying real tears, shedding authentic rage, and sharing unencumbered joy.

He remembered one morning lying face up on the bleachers, alone, waiting for his companions to show. Looking up, he'd attempted to trace a speck of dust drifting around the upper reaches of the high ceiling as the day's first sunlight hit the iron-bar-protected, east-facing windows. He heard his best old buddy, Andy Johnsson, and his other teammates bursting one by one through the locker-room door; Johnsson shouting, "Morning, Clifford, you frickin' dork!"; the peace-shattering song of tautly pumped Wilson basketballs resounding off shellacked maple slats and exploding against metal backboards... all the sounds echoing and coalescing and ricocheting off the gymnasium's cement-block walls and lofty tiled ceiling.

Clifford finally fell asleep to what sounded like the snorting of a horse in the near distance.

***

Light began filtering into Clifford's makeshift den at just before six-thirty a.m. His watch told him he had been in that black void for ten hours, but it seemed more like ten days. He recalled the sound of the horse, but he wasn't sure if it he had actually heard it or just dreamt it. Emerging from his cocoon, stiff and fully dressed, he stretched and jumped up and down a few times, happy to be moving again and able to see his surroundings.

After scouting the cliff rim a hundred yards to the south, Clifford concluded that he hadn't ended up where he thought he had the night before. Any nearby drop-off point appeared too precipitous for safe navigation. He didn't even know if he was to the west or to the east of his intended route of descent. He guessed the former and began hiking up the ridge toward the mountains. This took him through alternating stands of scattered juniper, where the footing was sandy and good, and jumbles of cracked sandstone boulders, which reduced him to crawling and scrambling. All the while he remained as far south on the high rim as he could, in an effort not to miss finding the key notch.

After forty minutes, Clifford came to the obvious head of a mini-drainage. Not the one he'd anticipated finding, but a different one that appeared negotiable. He saw stunted pines and junipers growing up out of the gash, potential handholds should the tug of gravity require the aid they could provide.

Clifford estimated that he had two hundred feet of elevation to lose before setting foot on the narrow canyon floor. Summoning his somewhat depleted reservoir of strength, he crab-crawled his way down on all fours, feet first and face and chest pointing upward and outward. After ten minutes and just one slip, which he'd immediately arrested by snatching onto a stout juniper trunk, he stood on level ground. Yet he remained within a fissure, which penetrated the cliffside far more deeply than he would have guessed. He couldn't understand how he'd managed to miss seeing such a major crevice on at least one of his countless canyon forays over the past few months.

On gaining the creek and the two-track path paralleling it, Clifford recognized exactly where he was, at a point two and a half miles above the dig site and half a mile upstream of the meeting place of the wet and dry forks. He gazed back at the rim. From here, due to the aspect of the gash and the rock walls and shrubbery camouflaging it, the crevice looked like nothing more than a minor rift in the cliff face.

Clifford walked back toward the mouth of the deep alcove, pacing off the distance.

Fifty yards.

Then he re-entered the rift to view its interior from a new perspective. Approximately ten feet into the narrow mini-canyon, looking down at the base of its west-facing wall, he glimpsed what appeared to be disturbed ground. Stepping over to investigate, he verified his suspicion.

"Weird," he muttered.

Beneath a fractured overhang approximately five feet above Clifford's head, soil on the ground had been removed and piled up. The excavation had uncovered what appeared to be part of a slab once belonging to the overhang above—not unlike the situation back at the site, when Hillary had busted through the fallen cornice of sandstone with the backhoe bucket.

I suppose this slab also broke off decades ago. Centuries maybe.

Clifford knelt at the leading edge of the fallen rock. He sifted with his hands beneath the slab through unconsolidated soil that he guessed had been dug out and shoveled back in. About a foot back under the six-inch-thick slab, he felt a narrow protrusion, hard and cold, like… bone. After scratching out and scooping away fill with his cupped-together hands, he positioned his left eye at ground level and squinted in under the slab to have a look as best he could.

Looks like the pointed tine of a deer or elk antler.

Reaching in and digging deeper with both hands, he felt something cool and roundish, like a large bone.

The animal's skull? Dang, wish I had that flashlight.

Though it seemed misplaced relative to the angle of the antler, he realized things could well have broken apart and ended up out of context if the poor animal had been unfortunate enough to be occupying this spot when the big sandstone slab came loose.

Still lying on the ground, Clifford glanced over at a ceanothus bush a few feet to his right. Something glimmered at its base. He crawled over, reached in, and pulled out a side-notched obsidian arrowhead.

Strange… could this be the point Riley was fuming about, the one he says he saw Ashton toss into the brush?

Clifford dated it as Late Prehistoric and pegged it as almost identical to the arrowhead he'd found nestled between the mano and metate in the Blackburn Draw dunes west of Worland. He stuffed it into the pocket of his jeans.

A glance at his wristwatch told Clifford it was eight o'clock. Tom Jefferson, Josie MacDonald, and Marge Paavno would just be getting to work. They'd also be wondering where in the heck he had gotten himself to this time. After pushing the loose dirt back into the hole and covering the antler tip, he stood and began walking down canyon.

I'll be back soon enough, that's for sure.

Feeling the hair on his neck bristling, Clifford stopped and shuddered. He sensed something, or someone, watching him. He looked around, everywhere, but saw nothing—no cougar, no bear, no human. He resumed his downstream travel, jogging to make time.

28
AN ARREST

A loud knock rattled the flimsy front door of Helen Richardson's cramped, yellow-walled quarters above the Coast-to-Coast hardware store in downtown Worland.

"Open up. It's the sheriff."

"Shit!" Dan Oberlin exclaimed. "How'd he know we were here? Well, you'd better let him in, Helen."

Richardson stood up from her seat on the floor, took two steps, and opened the door. "Sheriff," she said. "What's up?"

Sheriff Hendrickson stepped in and removed his Stetson to reveal a shock of faded red hair. He surveyed the room's occupants. The bald Oberlin glared back at him, while Alan Alvarez, Jimmy Fanslow, and the others in the room avoided eye contact with the sheriff altogether.

"Dan Oberlin," Hendrickson declared, "I'm taking you in for questioning in regard to the murder of Miss Bobbi Alder on August the fifteenth."

"What?" Oberlin said. "What, do you think I'm crazy?"

Expressions of disbelief colored the faces of his companions.

"I've learned from reliable sources that your truck's been seen on the south mesa above Sleeping Dog Canyon several times this summer, including early on the morning of Miss Alder's death. And a couple of my men have been looking into your CAUSE group's activities in other parts of the West. We know you want the cattle out of that drainage. We suspect you'd just as soon be rid of the archaeologists, too."

"Well, yeah, that's true. But I'm no murderer."

"Time will tell," Hendrickson said, opening the door for his ward to walk through. "But before you say any more, I suggest you obtain the services of an attorney.

"You..." Hendrickson said, aiming his gaze at the Hispanic youth in the corner. "You're Alan Alvarez, right?"

"Yes, sir."

"There's some folks down in New Mexico looking for you. I'm not taking you into custody now, but don't make yourself too scarce over the next couple of days. And you," he added, looking at another of the young men in the room, "aren't you one of Paul Barlow's archaeologists out there at the site?"

"Yes," said the young man, with a hangdog look. "I was until a few days ago, anyway."

"What's your name again?"

"Ashton. Peter Ashton."

"What are you doing with this bunch?"

"Well, I got to know them this summer and just enjoy spending time with them," Ashton said.

His demeanor informed Hendrickson there was more to it than that.

"I'll have to tell Dr. Barlow I found you here," Hendrickson told him.

"Yeah, I suppose you will," Ashton said, his head lowered.

***

Sheriff Hendrickson pulled up to the Sleeping Dog site at just after nine the next morning and found the much-reduced archaeological crew hard at it.

"Mornin', Dr. Barlow," said the sheriff, looking down into the pit. "Boys, ma'am."

He tipped his hat in greeting to Marge Paavno and Josie MacDonald. At the sheriff's request, all five excavators climbed, one by one, out of the pit.

"Now, you haven't heard this, but I arrested a person late yesterday on suspicion of murder. Bobbi Alder's murder."

Clifford did a quick double-take, then spoke before Barlow had a chance to. "You really think this person did it?" he asked, eyes wide. "Who is he?"

"Well, it's a 'he' all right, but I can't reveal his identity just yet. And yes, I do believe he did it. There's too many things pointing his way."

Marge Paavno chimed in: "Did you find the weapon?"

"No, not yet, but you better believe we're looking for it."

"Well, what's his motive?" inquired Barlow. He had returned to the site minutes earlier himself, after a quick overnight trip to a cattle sale in Cody with Galen Davies.

"I can't talk too much about that, either, but he's part of that anti-grazing group. CAUSE, they call themselves. I guess they think that's a cute name. Stands for 'Citizens Against Unfair Stockgrower Entitlements.' What a mouthful that is. Arrogant. They're radicals. Seems they'd do just about anything to get cattle out of this canyon and sheep off the mountain. And murder an innocent fellow human being, it seems, to try and scare you folks out of here.

"But I've already said more than I should," Hendrickson continued. "I just wanted to let you know. I think it's safe to say you all can rest a little easier now. I'll keep you posted."

With that, the sheriff turned around and walked over to his white Ford Bronco. But before opening the door he stopped and reversed direction.

"By the way, one of your workmates from the summer is hanging out with that CAUSE bunch."

"What?" Barlow exclaimed, frowning. "Who?"

"Peter Ashton."

"What... the hell?"

Barlow looked at Clifford, who shrugged his shoulders.

"I thought he was in Texas," Clifford said.

"Well, he's not," Hendrickson said. "He's in Wyoming. We'll get that straightened out, too."

With that, he jumped into the Bronco and sped away, kicking up a ghost of dust on the dry gravel road.

"What do you think?" Clifford asked of no one in particular, as they all watched Hendrickson drive away.

"I think I'm not going to rest easier until I have more information," Barlow said. "They might have the right person, but I don't have a world of confidence in Hendrickson and his boys. And what in God's name is Ashton doing back here with that bunch of yahoos?"

"That's the question of the day, all right," Clifford agreed. "But back to Bobbi—I have a lot of trouble believing anyone would kill her just to make a point about cows, or archaeologists. I mean, sure, they might be radicals, but that doesn't mean they're insane. Maybe Bill Parsons can figure it out when he gets here tomorrow."

"I thought Conrad said he wasn't coming 'til October," Barlow said.

"That's right, he wasn't, but the Forest Service asked him to come out to work a couple of weeks early this fall. Something to do with a special archery hunt for elk in the Absarokas. I had a message waiting for me at the Puppy last night to call him, which I did. Said he'd be able to hang around here for a week or so."

***

Later that day, Clifford partook of a rare treat: a home-cooked dinner served in the dining room of the low-slung, brick-faced ranch house of Galen and Twinstar Davies. Joining them at the table was their daughter Janie, who was headed back to college in Laramie the very next morning. Clifford loved going to the Davies' home, in no small part because he considered Twinstar a real lady, in every positive sense of the word. She could rope, brand, and pull calves with the best of cowhands, but could also set a fine table and create an ambiance that made Clifford feel like invited royalty. And on this evening, in his estimation, Twinstar had outdone herself, with oven-roasted homegrown chicken, mashed potatoes with gravy, green beans and beets from the garden, and cherry pie made from the early summer bounty of the trees growing outside the kitchen door.

"Twinstar, thanks so much for dinner," Clifford said, after everyone had finished dessert. "You make me realize how much I miss my mom's cooking back on the farm. Thank you, too, Galen, and Janie, for having me over."

"You're welcome, Clifford," Janie said. "It was fun."

"Yep," said Galen. "Sure was. Say, let's go for a walk out back before you vamoose outta here."

Clifford strolled with Davies toward the back pasture. The older man, Clifford had noticed, had seemed uncharacteristically distant during supper, preoccupied. The pair had become well acquainted over the long, hot summer. Clifford liked Davies and, when time permitted, had helped him out by bucking hay bales and moving irrigation pipe.

"What's up, Galen?" Clifford asked, kicking a small rock across the gravel-covered ranch yard.

Davies looked up at the taller Clifford. "Aah, it's them damn environmentalists."

Clifford took no offense, though he considered himself a moderate member of that breed.

"The ranger got another letter today from the Sierra Club regional director. They keep bitching about my lease to graze cattle on the forest lands in upper Sleeping Dog and high up the Bear Creek drainage." As he spoke, Davies' irritation intensified. "They said the cows are trampling wildflowers. Can you believe that?"

To Clifford, Davies' face looked redder than the sideburns growing below his Stetson.

About the same shade as the beets we had for supper.

"Why, they even complained about my cattle crapping in the streams!" With that, Davies bent over, picked up piece of dried cow dung, and, to Clifford's astonishment, stuffed it into his mouth.

"Ain uthin' b' glurt," is what came out of Davies' mouth next. It took Clifford a second to translate it as "It ain't nothin' but dirt."

"I hope it *was* them CAUSE people that killed Bobbi Alder!" Davies said, speaking clearly again.

Clifford winced. "Geez, Galen, we've already had dessert. And it may be just dirt, but cowpie can't compare to Twinstar's cherry pie."

Davies looked at Clifford with a remorseful expression, then started spitting and sputtering. He calmed down some. "You're right, Clifford. It is just dirt. Anyway, I hope so. But I have to admit, this dirt don't taste all that good. And I'm really sorry. I shouldn't've said that about Bobbi. I know how you felt about her. Paul told me. I can be a real son of a bitch sometimes. Musta put my chaps on backwards this morning. But I don't care for that Oberlin fellow coming around calling on Janie," he added, heating up again. "Damn environmental-ists, anyway."

"Oberlin's one of these CAUSE guys, right?"

Is that who Hendrickson's taken into custody?

"Yes, damn 'em." He lapsed into an uneasy silence.

"I guess you and Paul have been close pretty much all your life, huh?" Clifford said, aiming to change the subject.

Davies snorted, then chuckled. "Well, that's just about right. You know we were reared on adjacent ranches over in the Ten Sleep country. Both our dads had good land sprawling out from the foothills down there. Paul's is still in his family; I sold mine to buy up here from my uncle in the late forties. We're just three months apart in age, Paul and me. He's the older. My mother tells me we were playin' together and communicatin' before either of us could speak words adults could comprehend. Later on, when we weren't workin' for our dads, we camped together in summer, fishing the high lakes for browns and rainbows. During the fall we'd play football and, come weekends, hunt on and off horseback for trophy bulls up there in them Big Horn north-slope fir thickets."

Davies gazed at the distant forested mountain slopes.

"Even on particularly promising, new-snow school days," he added, his eyes dancing with the memories. "Damn, we had us some times. He's the finest man I've ever known. I'd kill to protect his hide if I had to."

The statement startled Clifford, but he retained his cool. "I never asked before, did you go to college?"

"No, my dad died just before we graduated high school, so I stayed home to run the ranch. I'd been accepted at Laramie, but it didn't work out. Anyway, I'd of studied ag, and I've surely gotten my fill of that regardless. Paul went back to the University of Nebraska, where he went all the way through the doctorate program in archaeology. I s'pose you knew that already. 'Course I spent those three years in the Army during the war… You know, as boys, Paul and I were surrounded by evidence of prehistoric Indians. We were both fascinated by the subject—Paul on a more academic level than me, obviously. I'd say going into archaeology for Paul was as natural as it was for me to stay home and ranch. He has a wonderful imagination. He told me once that the deceased residents of the past several thousand years in the Big Horns and the basin seem almost as real to him as its present occupants. I thought it was kind of a strange thing to say at the time, but I think I'm finally startin' to understand what he meant. As my wife likes to point out, I'm a little slow on the uptake sometimes."

"Could've fooled me, Galen," Clifford said. "You seem about as sharp as anyone I know."

29
TRACKING

Bill Parsons pulled up to the soggy site late the next afternoon, sitting behind the wheel of his big brown half-ton Chevy pickup with an Alaskan pop-up camper mounted in the bed. He spotted Clifford on the farmhouse porch, out of the rain, eating dinner with his trio of fellow remaining crew members.

"Ho, Clifford Gustafson!" Parsons bellowed out the truck's window after turning off the engine.

"Welcome, Bill!" Clifford yelled, grinning. He rose and ran over to shake hands with their guest. "Come on up to the porch and meet my friends. You hungry? We got quite a bit of chili still bubbling on the stove inside." Clifford wiped raindrops from his forehead with the back of his hand. "I'll go get you some."

"Sounds good."

Parsons walked over to the porch and introduced himself to the others. After Clifford returned with a steaming bowl of chili, Parsons sat down on the porch floor to eat.

"So, what's new?" he asked through his bushy, pale-blonde beard.

"You mean 'what's old?' don't you?" Clifford joked. "We're still plugging away. We've now uncovered a total of five-dozen occupation levels, from historic Crow down to Folsom, a Paleoindian culture of more than ten thousand years ago. Dr. Barlow says it's the most continuous record of human habitation he's seen in the northern or central Rockies. It's almost complete, except for that pesky missing thousand years or so of Late Plains Archaic. We've even found postholes at the Paleo level, indicating structures of some kind. A rare find, Barlow says."

"Yeah, your work's been getting a lot of ink. I've been reading about it even back in Iowa."

Clifford wanted to tell Parsons about his up-canyon discovery of earlier in the week, but he bit his tongue. No one else on the crew knew about it and, for now at least, he wanted to keep it between himself and Parsons.

"Come on, Bill," Clifford said, after they'd finished eating. "I'll give you a tour of the site."

As the pair wandered up toward the excavation area in a soft drizzle, Clifford filled Parsons in on, among other things, the arrest Sheriff Hendrickson had made in the Bobbi Alder case.

"We don't know who it is," Clifford said. "The sheriff couldn't reveal that yet."

"Interesting."

"Bill, tomorrow's Saturday, so I don't have to work. I'd like to take you up the canyon to poke around. I'll show you something unusual I found."

"Poking around is what I'm here for, Clifford. It's what I do best."

"Good deal. Before it gets dark why don't you grab what you need and bunk up in my cabin? I've got a spare bed."

"Thanks, but if it's all the same, I'll just stay in my camper. It's my home away from home. If I drive a ways up the canyon there, can I find a good spot to park near the creek?"

"Oh, yeah, there's plenty of good campsites. Maybe you'll catch some important vibes. You'll pass Dr. Barlow's trailer about a half mile from the site. Anywhere upstream of him, over the next quarter mile or so, should be fine."

"My vibe-ro-phone is up and running," Parsons said, laughing. "Tuned and ready to go."

"Outstanding."

***

The morning broke cloudy and cool, with the temperature in the low forties. When Clifford stuck his nose out the cabin's door he sensed impending rain, a repeat of the previous day's weather—another noble attempt by the Big Horn Basin's arid climatology to help recharge the Wind River Aquifer.

After brushing his teeth and pulling on his clothes, Clifford donned a storm jacket and grabbed his daypack, then headed up Sleeping Dog Creek to join Parsons for their eight o'clock breakfast date. He spotted the camp a couple of hundred yards above Barlow's trailer and found Parsons outside cooking over a Coleman stove perched on a waist-high cottonwood stump.

Mmm, the smell of bacon frying in the great outdoors.

He saw flapjacks were also on the menu.

"Morning, Bill!" Clifford yelled.

"G' mornin', Clifford." Parsons' bellow disrupted the morning quiet, yet to Clifford's ears its richness and resonance blended into the natural surroundings as seamlessly as a hawk's whistle. "So, what's this surprise you're going to show me?"

"Well, it really is still a surprise, because I've only uncovered the very tip of it, literally. It's the tip of an antler. Deer, I think, but maybe elk, lying under a big sandstone slab. I'm guessing the animal must've died when the slab broke away from the overhanging cliff, who knows how long ago. I'm not the first one to find it, either. The soil there had been disturbed when I came across it Wednesday morning. Fairly recently, I think. I'm a little bit of an outlaw, digging unauthorized up there, but I don't think it's an archaeological site as such, just a freak accident site. I could be wrong, of course."

"Speaking of outlaws, have you heard from the Pennington County Sheriff? Sherman?" Parsons asked. "I talked to him, and also to George Summers, superintendent of the Black Hills National Forest, and persuaded them to dismiss the federal charges. They'll recommend to the judge that he sentence you to some trail work over in Custer State Park next spring to pay your dues. They've already donated the eagle feathers to tribal elders down on the Pine Ridge Reservation. They were mighty pleased to get them, so you can feel good about that. But you shouldn't feel good about leaving that male eagle without a mate."

"I don't, Bill. I feel like a real butt. Or worse. I really do want to do something to try and make up for it. And, no, I haven't heard from Sheriff Sherman. I'm supposed to check in with him on October tenth, so maybe he'll give me the good news then. Thank you for doing that, Bill. Thanks so much."

Breakfasts consumed and appetites satiated, Clifford Gustafson and Bill Parsons headed side by side upstream along Sleeping Dog Creek, walking mostly in silence through the autumn color. Each gust of wind blew hundreds of cottonwood leaves loose from their branches, turning them into earthward-twirling bursts of yellow and gold destined to cover the ground in a deepening, soft carpet. Every breath they took carried the rich, earthy scent of decay. The creek still ran strong, its soft gurgling amplified in the cool, cloudy confines of the muted fall morning. As they rounded the bend a few hundred yards above Parsons' camp, they scared up a small flock of Canada geese that had been bobbing on slow, shallow waters lapping against the creek's bank. Their flapping and honking shattered the calm.

"Bill, this is where Bobbi was killed," Clifford said quietly, pointing to the spot. "Right over there. Lying face down with the arrow sticking out of her back."

"You're assuming something that might not be, Cliff."

"What? Whaddaya mean?"

"I mean, you said Bobbi was killed here. True, this may be where you found her, but she could have been killed somewhere else."

"Oh, I see. But we didn't find any footprints or drag tracks."

"Well, clever killers know how to get rid of things like that, or how to avoid making them in the first place. I'll take a closer look around here later. Right now, I'm anxious to see that deer you found. Plus, you don't want to hang around here too long. I noticed your mood go downhill as we got here."

"Yeah. You're probably right."

A mile farther upstream, where the wet and dry forks merged, Clifford and Parsons veered left to stay alongside the creek. After another half mile, Clifford led the way north from the creek into the slot canyon he had descended the morning after his recent unplanned bivouac.

"God!" he gasped, on finding what there was to see. Or not to see.

"What's 'a matter, Cliff?"

"Look at that hole! Damn. It's gone. That's where the deer was. Who's been up here?"

Whoever had been digging at the spot hadn't bothered backfilling and had left behind a depression roughly two feet deep and three feet wide. As best as the pair of them could determine, the excavation extended under the broken-off slab for at least five feet, west to east. The flashlight Clifford had added to his rucksack made the final measurement possible.

"This is too weird, Bill. Like I told you, the ground had already been tampered with when I first came across this on Wednesday morning. I wonder if whoever did that got scared off by something the first time they were digging here? Like, by me? Or maybe they knew I'd found their discovery, so they went ahead and removed it because of that?"

"It's a mystery for the time being, Clifford. Have you been above here, up that slot?"

"Yeah, that's how I happened across this in the first place. Like I said, I had to sleep out up above after getting caught in the dark. The next morning I came down to the creek through this crack."

"What's the terrain like? Could a person drive relatively close to this point up above here?"

"No way. It's a jumbled mass of boulders, sand and trees, prickly pear. And steep. The only way to drive anywhere close to here, as far as I know, would be on the track paralleling the creek. But I don't see how anyone could have done that without being spotted by me or by Dr. Barlow or some other crew member."

Clifford looked up at Parsons, then scratched his head.

"But, then, how do I know that one of the other crew members *didn't* see them, and just hasn't mentioned it? Or maybe, even, it was one of them that came up here. Dr. Barlow was away from his trailer Wednesday night—off on a cattle-buying escapade with our buddy Galen Davies—and that person would have known that."

"Show me the route you followed, will you? Think we can climb up the notch?"

"Yeah. There's good trees for handholds. But watch out for cactus. It's thick and nasty."

With a soft mist falling, Clifford led the way as he and Parsons reversed the younger man's previous hike into the high badlands overlooking Sleeping Dog Creek, eastward along the Sand Burr Rim, and back down into the wet fork about a half mile upstream of where they'd left the creek.

***

Four hours after starting up the steep notch, Clifford and Parsons arrived, drenched, back at the site. They found a small group gathered around Sheriff Hendrickson's white Bronco. They all wore solemn expressions.

"What's up?" Clifford asked, as he and Parsons fell in with the others.

Paul Barlow spoke first. "I'm afraid a couple of your friends were killed in a car accident night before last. Outside Basin."

"Friends?" Clifford asked, concerned. "Who?"

"I was just telling the others here," said the sheriff, "that I would have come out sooner, but we had to get definite IDs. Justin Willits and Jamie Newhouse were their names, from up on the Northern Cheyenne Reservation in Montana. Had tattoos on their arms, saying 'DSR.' Dr. Barlow says you knew them. What's DSR stand for?"

"Dog Soldiers Resurrected. Yeah, I knew them. What the heck happened? And what were they doing down here?"

"Newhouse ran his Road Runner off the highway and slammed into a power pole, doin' better than eighty, we think. The oddest thing is what they had in the trunk, and that's what I was just now telling Dr. Barlow and the others about."

"What was it?" Clifford asked.

"A couple 'a skeletons. One of a buck deer and the other one human. They were sort of all intertwined together. Big hole on the side of the human skull; looks like it was old and not a result of the car crash."

Clifford's eyes met Parsons'. Both men looked at Barlow when he began speaking.

"From Sheriff Hendrickson's description of the skeletons, this is no recent death. I'm going into Worland with him to have a look. If it's old, as in prehistoric, I'll try to get John Mills out from Minneapolis. He was wanting to visit us this fall, anyway. He's the best I know at aging remains and figuring out how an individual died. Maybe he'll come up with a clue that'll help us learn where the body came from."

Again, Clifford glanced at Parsons.

"They also had an old-fashioned willow bow and a bunch of arrows in their car," the sheriff continued. "The arrows aren't quite like the modern homemade one that killed Bobbi Alder, but it's mighty suspicious all the same. Suspicious enough that, combined with some other information I learned this morning, I'm letting Dan Oberlin out of the can this afternoon."

"Dan Oberlin? The anti-grazing guy you hauled in?" Barlow asked.

"That's right," said the sheriff. "CAUSE."

"He's also the guy Galen didn't like coming around visiting Janie," Clifford said.

"Yep, Galen mentioned that to me," said Barlow.

Clifford noticed that Parsons seemed totally lost in thought.

"You guys look cold," Barlow said. "Clifford, you're shivering. You better get over to your cabin and start a fire. I don't want you coming down with pneumonia."

"Sure thing, Dr. Barlow. Thanks."

On their way to the cabin, Clifford spoke quietly to Parsons. "What were you thinking back there, Bill?"

Parsons replied in a low, deliberate tone. "What it was, but didn't want to say in front of the others, is a hunch I have. And my hunches often prove out, if I do say so myself. There are some things you know by feel, without learning—that's one of my guiding principles. It occurred to me before, Clifford, and now I'm beginning to feel it's for certain. It wasn't the anti-grazing bunch at all, or the DSR boys, who were responsible for Bobbi's murder."

"Then who was it?"

"I'll tell you this, Cliff, but please don't tell anyone else just yet: There are too many similarities between Miss Alder's death and that of a poacher whose body I found two autumns ago in the Yellowstone border country. In the Teton Wilderness, high up there above the confluence of Thorofare Creek and the Yellowstone River. Definitely murder, though it still has me and the Forest Service baffled. There's just too much similarity here for it to be a coincidence."

"How do you know the poacher wasn't killed by one of these groups, either CAUSE or DSR?"

"Well, Dog Soldiers Resurrected makes no sense whatsoever. And Citizens Against… what is it… Unfair Stock Entitlements? I don't think so. No grazing permits are allotted up there in the Thorofare country. No, something else is going on here, Cliff, something more sinister. And it's up to you and me to figure out what it is."

30
LONE BEAR

The solitary figure twiddled with a strand of his long, black, greasy hair, thinking things over. All angles and protruding joints, and as skinny as a coyote, he was blanketed in tattered flannel and worn-out khaki. Bare of foot, and with his head covered in a dirty, misshapen Panama, he looked more like a scarecrow than a man. The hat was pulled low over a mat of stringy hair and a thick black beard hid everything below the nose. Cold gray eyes peering through the tangle were all that could be made of his face.

Back in Walla Walla, where he grew up, he'd been known as Stuart. But today he thought of himself only as Lone Bear. And, save for the rare occasion when the only person in the world that he trusted paid him a visit, he spoke to no one but himself.

Lone Bear had taught himself to be an unseen observer. For this he possessed an innate talent, and he had honed the skill during his time in the jungles of Southeast Asia. In many ways, he reminded himself often, Lone Bear was more like a cougar than a bear.

He'd been there that morning, hunkered down on the south side of the creek at the base of the slope, where the desiccating sunrays rarely reach and the brush grows thick. Now he willed himself back to the scene, reliving it, wishing to relish the pleasure and turn it over in his mind…

***

Lone Bear watches the gray-haired hippie with Ben Franklin glasses. The angler curses after getting a bite but hooking no fish.

How inept!

The man swears, then pulls a metal object from his back pocket and places the shiny item on a large boulder north of the creek. Lone Bear considers taking the old man, but then thinks better of it. The potential price is too high. Lone Bear knows he has it good. Except for his one friend, no one suspects he is here; he knows this is so because no one has been looking for him. Had they been, he would be the first to know. If he took the aging hippie, his privacy would become a thing of the past. Lone Bear prizes his solitude, requires it. He does not appreciate outsiders entering his domain, coming so close to his home. It's nothing but a shallow cave, but home all the same. Merely a cleft in the cliffside a couple of miles upstream of where he now watches the old man. High on a rocky hillside, its opening is well camouflaged with rock slabs and brush.

After the gray-haired man has gone away, Lone Bear lies down for a nap. At his side rests his bow, a stout weapon he has carved and crafted from a thick juniper branch he harvested a year earlier just a couple of hundred yards upslope from where he now lies. Also beside him is his deer-hide quiver, filled with half a dozen arrows.

Lone Bear tells himself he will make further plans on awakening.

Drifting toward sleep, Lone Bear reflects on times gone by. He hadn't even tried to save the others after the first explosion hit. He, too, would have died, as they did, had he been with them on the road detail instead of in the jungle being sick. Seeing the bloody remains of his former friends and workmates had caused him to panic. Getting himself out of the country had been difficult. It had taken days, or weeks; maybe months. He'd had to kill several gooks to make it happen. He doesn't remember exactly how many. In fact, he doesn't even recall getting out. It is like a dream, or a nightmare, with no beginning and no end. He remembers little, other than vague impressions, from the time the explosion hit until he woke up in a hospital bed in Seattle.

Lone Bear awakens from his nap not on his own terms; rather, he is stirred awake by a female's voice, humming. On seeing the owner of the pleasant voice, he is pushed over the edge. This is too much. The enemy is getting too close to Lone Bear's home, and there are too many of them.

She is such an easy target that he almost feels ashamed; in fact, for a moment, he does sense an actual pang of human regret. She is so young, so pretty. But that feeling is overtaken by one of pure excitement. Lone Bear hasn't killed in, oh, how long has it been? A few summers have passed. He has killed before, many times, mostly in the jungle, with a rifle or by strangling or slitting throats. But not once has he performed the act on a human since living here, high in the desert foothills.

Occasionally, Lone Bear has killed a deer. He has running stream water nearby. He makes knives of chipped stone, and arrows of willow branches, turkey feathers, deer sinew, and his cache of razor-sharp manufactured arrowheads. His friend has offered to bring him other store-bought tools and weapons, but this is the way Lone Bear wants it. He has everything he needs. Except for an infrequent hunter, cattle wrangler, or government employee, no one has trespassed into his homeland. Other than his friend… that is, until recently, until earlier in the summer. Now Lone Bear's domain is being invaded almost daily.

A familiar, calm thrill encompasses him as he pulls back the deer-tendon bowstring, takes aim, and lets the arrow fly.

"Lone Bear is a good hunter," he proclaims. "An excellent warrior."

***

…Yes, it was a good memory, but now, just a few weeks later, anger and concern consumed Lone Bear in his rock shelter. His act had served only to increase the number of invaders in his territory. Just days earlier, hidden in the brush, he had watched a handsome young Indian man standing near the creek at a point between Lone Bear's abode and where he had taken the young woman's life. He thought about taking him, too, but did not. Lone Bear reminded himself that he had already done the wrong thing once, permitting his excitement for the kill to consume him.

What is Lone Bear to do?

He had considered migrating back by night to the only other place he had felt safe in recent years, to the thick timber of the high country south and east of Yellowstone National Park, to what some people called the Teton Wilderness, but which he had rechristened the Lone Bear Province. However, as he had told the only human being he trusted, the only other person he ever spoke to, the deep snows of winter in the Lone Bear Province had proved too daunting.

"Ah, now Lone Bear remembers," he whispered aloud. "That is where I last killed." In fact, they may still be looking for him in the Lone Bear Province.

He sat on the sand floor, eating deer tenderloin he'd cooked over a fire in his cliff overhang late the previous evening, after the skies had blackened. Lone Bear never burned a fire during the light of day or in the early evening, knowing that smoke emanating from his quarters might reveal his whereabouts. Sniffling and snorting, he closed his mouth and pushed his right thumb against his right nostril and then blew out, clearing his left nostril of its clogging snot. The mucus wad hit the dirt floor with a soft puff. He wiped the ground with his greasy hands, then ran them through his long, stringy hair. He had to urinate, which he always did in the creek, like a dog, to prevent the buildup of stench. Not because the smell would bother him, but because it might lead to his camp being discovered by the enemy.

Lone Bear crawled out through the cave's narrow passageway and stood, squinting in the light of day, which was blindingly bright compared to the dark harbor of his lair. After his eyes had adjusted, he began the quarter-mile scramble down to the creek.

31
A MYSTERY NO MORE

Despite nausea and throbbing headaches, or maybe because of them, Clifford and Parsons awoke early, the latter having opted to spend the night in Clifford's spare bed. Their initial fireside brandy toast the prior evening had tasted so good, and warmed them so well, that they'd had another. Then another. And so on.

"Okay, Cliff, are we gonna do it, or was it just the liquor talking?" Parsons asked, his deep voice sounding hoarser than usual.

"You mean tell Dr. Barlow? You bet we're going to do it. You're darn right."

"Well, let's then. Like you said, we can stop by his trailer and confab, then spend the rest of the day pushing up the canyon. It's the fall equinox. Looks like a beautiful day. I guess Mother Nature got the rain out of her system yesterday."

After devouring the contents of a pair of small orange juice cartons and large bowls of Grape-Nuts with milk and frozen huckleberries out of Clifford's small refrigerator-freezer, he and Parsons started up the canyon. They arrived at Paul Barlow's trailer a few minutes later. Clifford knocked on the door.

"Yeah, who is it?" came the sleepy-sounding voice from within.

"Oh, great," Clifford whispered. "Not only do we have bad news, but we woke him up." He cleared his throat. "It's Clifford, Dr. Barlow. And Bill Parsons."

The trailer shook and emitted muffled banging noises, then the door swung open.

"What is it, boys?" asked Barlow, outfitted in boxer shorts and a sleeveless T-shirt. He looked a mess. "It's Sunday morning. Don't you sleep in on Sunday?"

"It's almost nine, Dr. Barlow," Parsons said.

"You gotta be kidding me. I was supposed to be at church in Worland at nine-thirty. Guess I'll have to worship in God's great outdoor cathedral today. Ah, well, it's always better that way, anyhow. I wonder what happened to my alarm clock? I set–"

"Uh, Dr. Barlow," Clifford interrupted, "we've got something to tell you. And you're probably not gonna like it."

Barlow's forehead crinkled as he looked at Clifford over the top of his spectacles. Then he scratched his unshaven chin. "Come on in, fellas. Squeeze in around the kitchen table there. I'll start a pot of coffee. Here, chomp on these."

He laid a long rectangular cardboard box full of white powder donuts on the table, along with a stack of pink paper napkins.

"So, fire away," Barlow instructed once they were all seated.

"Well," Clifford began, "you know that deer and human skeleton that were in the trunk of my Cheyenne acquaintances' car?"

"Sure, of course. I inspected them late yesterday. They're old, all right. Got right on the phone to Mills. He wants to be sure you'll be around when he gets here this coming week, late Tuesday or early Wednesday. You will be, won't you? He's flying into Billings and renting a car."

"Yeah, I'm not planning on going anywhere, unless you fire me," Clifford said, only half kidding.

"That's not likely. We can all three drive over to Chadron together in Mills' rental car for the rendezvous. Of course, you're more than welcome to come along, too, Bill. There'll be room for you. Now, what about these skeletons?"

"Well, I was poking around up in the canyon last week, Wednesday morning, and I found them, buried under a rock slab. I dug around and found the tip of the deer's antler and could also feel what I thought was a skull. Anyway, I assume it's those same skeletons. And someone had been digging not long before I got there. The disturbed soil is what got my attention in the first place."

"What makes you think it was the same find?" Barlow asked, looking hard at Clifford. "I mean, a lot of deer have died over time, and you didn't see the human remains, you say?"

"Right," Clifford said, looking over at Parsons. "But when I took Bill up there yesterday morning to show him what I'd found, there was just a big hole where the deer had been. I'd planned on excavating it further with him. Then, when we got back to the site, Sheriff Hendrickson was there telling you all the story about what he'd found in the back of the wrecked car. A pretty easy two and two to put together."

"What day was it again that you made your find?" Barlow asked.

"Early Wednesday. The morning after I had to camp out above on the rim."

"Let's see. The car wreck happened Thursday night. I was here then, but I wasn't the night before. If those boys came up the canyon and dug up those remains, it would have to have been later on Wednesday. But you or one of the others would've seen them during the day. It's hard to believe they could have driven up there at night without anyone noticing. Why would they do that, anyway? How would they even know about the skeletons? It would have to have been planned in advance and not just a chance discovery, right? Anyway, I don't think a guy could drive a Dodge hot rod up that far, night or day. He'd bottom out, tear it up. Did you see any tire tracks yesterday?"

"No," Parsons said, "but the trail's pretty well covered in leaves. And, it's been raining. But, like you, I don't think they could have driven up there, regardless. I'm thinkin' they must've come down from above, to the south."

"Plymouth," chimed in Clifford.

"Huh?" said Barlow.

"It was a Plymouth hot rod, not a Dodge."

"Oh. Yeah. Gotcha."

"Jamie Newhouse told me it was not only his car, but his pickup truck, his jeep, and so on," Clifford said. "And I think some mythology is involved. A legend. And that's what my DSR friends were doing here. In fact—and I haven't even let you in on this yet, Bill—a friend of theirs named Amy Looksbehind told me that Jamie told her about some Cheyenne elders, including his uncle, who were searching around here for something much like what he and Justin Willits had in the back of their car when they had their wreck. I believe she said that was four or five years ago. Sal Calderara, the BLM arky in Worland, was with them, too."

"Calderara!" Barlow exclaimed. "What the hell was he… and, Gustafson, what the hell were you doing digging around up there in the first place? You know my number one rule is no private excavations. We're a team of scientists, not a bunch of hooligans. And what is it DSR stands for again?"

"Dog Soldiers Resurrected. I know, Dr. Barlow. I'm really sorry. But seeing that someone else had been poking around already… well, I guess I just couldn't help myself."

"It's okay. I can see why you were intrigued. I don't always practice what I preach, either. Archaeology's in our blood. Hell, I pot hunted with the best of 'em before I went to college and got enlightenment. Do you think those boys who were killed in the crash knew you'd found their prize? Or were they already planning on coming in here and taking possession?"

"That," Parsons said, "is one of several sixty-four-thousand dollar questions. I don't know if we'll ever learn the answer. There's some other baffling stuff going on, too. Unrelated? Maybe, maybe not."

"Like what?" Barlow asked.

"The way Bobbi Alder was killed. The modus appears way too similar to a case I was on two years ago in the Thorofare country outside Yellowstone. Like I told Clifford, I was tracking a poacher up there, a man I'd already tentatively ID'd through talking to some hunters camped nearby. I found him, all right. Dead, up on the north flank of a low peak called Hawks Rest, face down with an arrow in his back. A handcrafted job, but tipped with a machined broadhead. I haven't seen the one that killed Miss Alder, but I'll wager it's a spittin' image."

"It has a big metal head, but the shaft's made of willow," Barlow said.

"That's what Clifford told me."

"Dr. Barlow?" Clifford said. "Bill and I are gonna go do some more looking around up the canyon this morning. Would you care to join us?"

"That I would, boys, that I would. Let me get together some food and water. Are you packing lunches?"

"Yep," Clifford said, "we're all set."

Inside of five minutes the trio was sauntering upstream. Clifford gave a running commentary on his theory of how the deer may have been killed when a slab of sandstone broke off from the cliff above. "But if the man was there, too, that might change things. Do you think he was?"

"Well," Barlow responded, "it sure looks that way. Both appear to have died a violent death, by the looks of their crushed skeletons. There were a few fresh marks from the car crash, but most of the breaks and scratches are weathered and old. The man has a big hole in the side of his skull that is definitely not new. But it doesn't appear to be the sort of damage a big rock slab would do. More like a piercing wound."

"Here's where we leave the creek," Clifford said, forty minutes into their hike.

He pointed north at the notch in the Sand Burr Rim. Parsons, two steps ahead, was already aimed that way. When all three had arrived at the excavation, they studied the ground around them.

"Look at that." Parsons pointed at a smooth, shallow depression in the dirt. A bare human footprint. Then he pointed at another, and another. "Someone's been up here since you and I were here yesterday, Cliff. This whole deal keeps getting more and more interesting. I think we'd better start watching each others' backs."

***

Lone Bear was beside himself. Someone had been digging in his canyon. Even worse, an invader had gotten close to his lair, possibly even been inside it. He had never seen such a thing. It was the beginning of the end, he told himself. More and more of the enemy would come now that he had killed again.

Lone Bear had learned in the jungle, and later improved his skills in the Lone Bear Province, how to avoid leaving signs of where he traveled. But in his mounting desperation earlier that morning, he had neglected to follow his cardinal rule of stepping backwards when in soft, impressionable soil, and dusting away his footprints with a pine or juniper bough. To compound matters, rather than returning to his cave by way of the hard sandstone surface at the base of the slope south of the creek, he had simply walked up the path paralleling the stream to the north. Then, two miles upstream of where he had killed the girl, he had veered north to climb the quarter mile to his hidden shelter.

Now, at what Lone Bear estimated to be high noon, he understood the magnitude of his mistakes. Panic set in. He grabbed his bow and arrow-filled quiver and departed from his cave. He returned to the creek, crossed it, and inched his way up to a favorite game overlook, a cliffside platform of sandstone just large enough for him to comfortably sit cross-legged. He would be well hidden amid the bursts of chokecherry, serviceberry, and juniper growing out of the surrounding cracks and depressions. There, fifty vertical feet above creek level, he would wait to see if additional intruders invaded his territory on this day. If they did, and if they provided him the opportunity, he would kill again. He had no other option remaining.

***

Bill Parsons, the tracker, led the way as the three men pushed upstream alongside Sleeping Dog Creek.

"Whoever it is, he's been walking up this track, and not long ago," Parsons said. "I'm ninety-nine percent sure it's a 'he' and not a 'she' because of the size of the foot."

After slowly tracing the tracks in the damp, leaf-strewn path for several more minutes, Parsons stopped.

"They're gone. No more prints."

Clifford scratched his head and looked at Barlow, who shrugged his shoulders. Neither of them had been able to discern the prints even when, according to Parsons, they'd been following them.

"He must've crossed the creek here," Parsons said. "Or, he might have headed north. See how I don't leave any prints when I leave the path and walk on this pebbly hardpan?"

"*Aaaaaaahhhhhhhhhh!*" A mournful, human-like scream shook the men from their study.

Parsons instinctively hit the ground; Clifford and Barlow followed suit. Looking up to the southeast, in the direction from which the shriek had come, they watched as an apparition, a ragged specter, fell earthward away from the rock face. To Clifford, the creature appeared to be half man and half animal.

About a sand wedge away, maybe seventy-five yards.

The thing hit the ground with an audible thump, slid a short distance, and came to a stop on the buttressed talus slope not fifty yards above them. It lay motionless on the scree, at the point where gravity and friction had come to an understanding.

The three men made their cautious way up toward whatever it was awaiting them.

"Hullo!"

The men froze at the shout of greeting—or was it a warning?—that came to them from the east.

"Pete?" exclaimed Barlow. "Pete Patterson? What the…"

Pete Patterson leaned into the slope, climbing toward the three men as they stood up. It amazed Clifford that Barlow had recognized him. The big man, who was carrying a bow, wore camouflage from head to toe and his face was painted with black and brown stripes and blotches.

"I may have just saved one of your lives," Patterson said, on reaching them. "But I'm not sure which. This guy had an arrow ready to release, probably as soon as you passed below him. I beat him to it, pegged him from forty yards out."

Parsons knelt beside the supine body and checked for vital signs.

"Dead," he said.

"Pete, how…?" Barlow began, but faltered again.

"I've been up here, and higher up above, since Friday hunting black bear. It's the only Wyoming big-game species I haven't taken with this gear. Finally killed my bison bull over in Gillette earlier in the month."

"Well, you may not have killed your bear yet, but you've bagged a *Homo sapiens*," Parsons said, with nary a hint of humor.

"Yes," said Patterson, with equal gravity. "That's one trophy I never planned on taking."

"That was one helluva a shot with a recurve bow," Parsons added.

"Well, thanks. I guess. It's my Fred Bear Super Kodiak. I also carry this wounded-bear insurance." He patted the .357 magnum Colt Python holstered on his right hip. "But believe it or not, I'm actually more deadly with the archery gear."

"So, did you just happen to be in this very vicinity this morning, or what?" Clifford asked. "Or did you know something was going down?"

"Early this morning I stumbled across a cave shelter up in that draw." Patterson pointed north at a drainage notch climbing away from the creek. "It's being lived in—or was until very recently." He looked down at the dead man lying on the ground. "It's camouflaged with brush. Chock-full of stuff, like a modern-day stone-age shelter. Obsidian knives, willow-wand arrow shafts…"

"I'd say we've found the killer," interrupted Parsons. "See that arrow? Looks just like the one that killed Bobbi Alder, right?"

The arrow, strung in the bow still in the dead man's hand, appeared to be a homemade-looking job, but was tipped with a machined arrowhead.

"Sure does to me," Barlow said.

"A couple of us better get to town and call the sheriff," Parsons said. "Paul, would you mind going? And—Mr. Patterson, is it?—you should accompany him, and stick close. The sheriff will want to get your testimony. Clifford and I will hang out here. We want to be sure this guy doesn't go anywhere, and the way things have been happening… well, you never know."

"Sounds like a plan, Bill," said the senior archaeologist. "We'll try to get back inside a couple of hours, in the Jeep. And Pete? Thank you. Thank you very much."

Barlow held out his hand to his longtime non-friend. The two held each other in a tight grasp while making unwavering eye contact. Then Clifford and Parsons took turns shaking hands with their William Tell of a savior.

Before they could part company, however, the quartet heard men's voices drifting in from the west. Rounding the corner came Sheriff Hendrickson and a bald, younger man.

"Well, what do we have here?" asked Hendrickson, after he and his companion had climbed the slope to join them and saw the body on the ground.

"He's dead," Barlow said.

"Oh, no," the bald man said, falling to his knees. "Why, Stuart? Why?"

"Stuart?" Parsons asked.

"Yep," said Hendrickson. "Stuart Cassidy, according to what Mr. Dan Oberlin here has been telling me on our little walk. Seems they go way back."

"We grew up together in Walla Walla, Washington," Oberlin said. He got back to his feet. "Stuart saved my life when we were just ten. I almost drowned in an irrigation canal. He went to the war in Vietnam after high school and came back a different person. But he had his lucid moments, like when I helped him get set up in this canyon almost two years ago. I knew he was off-kilter, anti-social, but I didn't think he was dangerous. Or at least I convinced myself I thought that. I brought him provisions now and then, but that got a lot harder to do after you archaeologists set up camp down below."

Oberlin sighed before going on. "I tried for a while to ignore it after the girl was killed. Still in denial, I guess. But then the sheriff accused me of her murder, and then the Indian boys who died in the car wreck last week... well, it was time to tell the sheriff what I knew."

"Did Stuart live over in the Teton Wilderness near Yellowstone before he came here?" asked Parsons. "Say, two years ago?"

"Yep, in a similar kind of arrangement," Oberlin confirmed. "He was there for more than a year. How did you know that? Except up there he lived in a canvas hunter's tent, way back in the woods. I never knew why, but all of a sudden one day when I was bringing him food and some other stuff he told me he had to move, fast. That's when I drove him over here and helped him get set up."

"Well, I've investigated a similar case over there," Parsons said. "A murdered poacher. I would have thought you'd have heard or read about that and tied the loose ends together. I think your friend committed that one, too."

"Damn!" Oberlin exclaimed, looking down at the body. "Damn it, Stuart. No, I hadn't heard about that. I'm kind of an obsessive avoider of newspapers and other media. Did it happen at about the same time? Fall of seventy-one?"

"That's right," said Parsons.

"How did you come to start your CAUSE chapter here?" Clifford asked.

"Well, I do hate seeing those damn cattle hammering this beautiful canyon. I haven't totally explored it like I want to, but I've known and loved this place for eight years now. That's how I knew it would make a good home for Stuart. And it did. For a while, anyway. For two years. I can't believe it's been that long already."

PART 4
SENSING THE FUTURE

32
BUCK CREEK RENDEZVOUS

"Pretty sporty, John," Paul Barlow said, running his eyes over the Chevrolet Impala John Mills had rented in Billings.

He hopped into the front right black-leather bucket seat of the white, four-door hardtop, joining Mills, at the wheel, and Parsons and Clifford, sitting in the back. Departing the Sleeping Dog site early on Thursday, September 27, they intended to drive the three hundred-plus miles to Chadron in one go, stopping only for gas, pee breaks, beer, and other necessities. Barlow knew activity at the Buck Creek Rendezvous would be heating up fast and he wanted to have camp organized by late afternoon.

The sun edged over the eastern horizon as Mills geared down for the descent from Powder River Pass into Buffalo. Its glare made it difficult for him to see with his one good eye.

"Paul," he started, "you already know this, but Clifford probably doesn't—I don't know about you, Bill—but the northwest corner of Nebraska is one of America's best-kept secrets. I absolutely love it there. Prairie yields to the Pine Ridge, a surprising terrain of buttes and breaks and timbered ridgelines. It's maybe a hundred miles long and twenty or so wide." Mills stopped speaking long enough to adjust the elastic band holding his eye patch in place. "The Pine Ridge appears to be a small upthrust range, but in fact it was carved out of high plains that had built up from sediments washing down as the Rockies and Black Hills uplifted. It's actually a forested badlands of bisected sedimentary layers. What do you think about that?"

"I think you're still in professor mode," said Barlow. "Me, I'm ready for some Kentucky Kool-Aid."

As the men drove southeast out of Newcastle toward the Nebraska state line, Clifford reminisced aloud about the crazy summer he had just been through. He spoke partly for the benefit of Mills and Parsons, who hadn't been there to share it, and in part simply to debrief himself.

"I can't wait to see Conrad," he said in closing. "It's only been three weeks, but I miss the crusty old fart." He grinned and looked over at the bearded Parsons.

"Yeah, he's a different thing, all right," Parsons agreed. "Any resemblance between him and a human being is purely coincidental."

On reaching U.S. Route 20, Mills steered the Chevy east toward Chadron.

"Just a few miles that way," he said, pointing behind him to the west, "is Fort Robinson. Maybe we can go there on the way back. It's an old frontier military post. Lots of history. It's where Crazy Horse was killed in 1877," he added, glancing over his shoulder at Clifford. "He was being held captive and, so the story goes, tried to escape. A lot of folks think it's just that—a story. Later, the fort served as a POW camp during World War II."

In Chadron, Mills pulled the car into the Safeway parking lot and shut the motor down. All four men piled out of the car and marched into the store, each with his list of things to find. Clifford was responsible for grabbing chips and cookies, Mills for dairy products, and so on. Next stop: Bert's Booze-tique, where the men procured more than enough beer to last the weekend, along with three fifths of Jim Beam to support Barlow's annual bender.

Having gassed up, Mills drove back to the west edge of town and went south onto U.S. Route 385. Fifteen miles later he turned west onto a dirt road, nursing the low-clearance Chevy up a steep track cutting through a wide drainage in a ponderosa pine forest. Clifford's attention was caught by a lone tree to the right, branching out against the horizon; to him, it appeared to be magically sprouting from the top of a flat, rocky bluff. Closer in, atop a lower ridge, he studied a block of sediment shaped like a hawk's head. Then he spotted a Clark's nutcracker flying over the barrens toward timber. The arid terrain supported an abundance of cacti resembling the prickly pear so common in the rocky, sandy foothills above Sleeping Dog Creek.

Mills crested a ridge and all four men looked down on the grounds of the Buck Creek Rendezvous.

"Wow!" Clifford exclaimed. "Unbelievably groovy."

The older men were no less taken with it, even Mills and Barlow, who had attended numerous rendezvous over the years.

"This reminds me a whole lot of when I first laid eyes on Crow Fair last month," Clifford said. "I think it's gonna be fun."

After negotiating the gnarly two-track into camp they rolled past an assortment of temporary accommodations, which ranged from small travel trailers and large canvas shelters to tiny pup tents and hide-covered tipis.

"Ahoy there! It's the sleeping dogs!" The cry of a hoarse but familiar voice came in through Barlow's open window.

Conrad Hillary, yellow can of Coors in hand, waved with his free left hand from where he knelt in front of a big bonfire. Mills stopped the car and Hillary came over.

"I saved you a good site right next to ours," he said. "Lemme show you the way."

He proceeded up the track, swinging his free arm in a full circle as a sign for Mills to follow. After walking about a hundred yards, passing encampments full of people and campfires the entire way, Hillary veered left onto an even rougher track, leading the newcomers into a protective grove of tall ponderosas. At once they recognized Hillary's eighteen-foot Moonraker trailer. Beside it sat a very old and battered green Ford pickup truck. On the other side of the small clearing Tom Jefferson, Marge Paavno, and Josie MacDonald were busy setting up a big, beige-colored wall tent.

"What time did you all get here, Marge?" Barlow yelled out the window.

"Only about an hour ago. We got out of Buffalo later than I'd hoped. I wasn't sure about getting the New Yorker over this rough track, so Conrad helped out by driving it in for me."

"How'd you get that big trailer way back in here?" Mills inquired, slowing the Chevy to a stop.

"Carefully, very carefully," Hillary said. He paused to cough and spit. "I'm an extremely skilled trailer backer-upper. One of my countless hidden talents."

"Great to see you, Rad!" Clifford said, popping out of the car.

"Likewise, Jeofredo," Hillary grinned, giving Clifford a big pat on the back and a hearty handshake. "How 'bout a libation, gentlemen?" The other three already had open cans sitting on makeshift tables of firewood rounds.

"You bet," Clifford answered for the foursome.

The bespectacled, gray-haired hippie disappeared inside his trailer and clanged around for a few seconds, then emerged holding five cans of Coors.

"Five o'clock. You guys got here just in time. Manny Ortiz from Colorado U. gave a bison-skinning and butchering demonstration earlier this afternoon. He used flint knives he knapped on the spot. It was something to see, but that's not the best part. The best part is that he's been slow-roasting the backstrap for the last couple of hours and we're all invited to go help him eat it at around six. What a treat! It'll go great with your Jim Beam, Paul." Hillary grinned at his longtime friend and colleague.

"I bet it will, Conrad." Barlow said. "Certain twentieth-century luxuries I'm mighty appreciative of."

"Beam me up, Scotty," added Mills.

Barlow stared blankly at him, not grasping the *Star Trek* reference. Only Clifford, Jefferson, and Josie got it and laughed.

The four new arrivals spent the next forty minutes setting up camp as Hillary stood idly by drinking beer, smoking Camel straights, and barking misleading instructions. Jefferson, Marge, and Josie had wandered over to the main bonfire area. The trickiest task turned out to be erecting Barlow's big canvas safari tent. He'd packed most of the stakes and smaller poles in the car trunk but had to send Clifford and Parsons out on a mission to find four straight, eight-foot-long poles to serve as the main supporting cross pieces. The poles milled for the purpose, still lying under Barlow's trailer in Sleeping Dog Canyon, were too long to fit into the Chevy's trunk. Barlow had suggested lashing them to the roof, but Mills had nixed the idea.

At suppertime, the four men accompanied Hillary back through the central encampment to an opening where a couple of dozen men and women milled around a large, crackling pine-log fire.

"Paul, John, you know Manny Ortiz," said Hillary, "out of Boulder. Manny, this is Clifford Gustafson. And over here we have Bill Parsons."

"Ah, the famous tracker," Ortiz said, grinning. "Nice to meet you, Bill. And Clifford, was it?"

"Yep. Clifford Gustafson," he said, shaking hands. Clifford noticed a bandage covering Ortiz's left hand.

"Sorry you missed my show this afternoon," Ortiz said, "but I'm glad you made it in time for the feast. As you can see, I butchered my hand a bit making the tools. I wonder what the prehistorics used for gauze and adhesive tape? Moss and pine pitch, maybe?"

Supper was a memorable affair, quite unlike anything Clifford had experienced. Bison backstrap with plenty of salt and pepper and steak sauce; big Idaho russet potatoes wrapped in aluminum foil and baked in the fire, then smothered in sour cream, chives, and fried-bacon pieces. There were also baked beans slow-cooked in a Dutch oven over coals, along with potato salad, huckleberry-and-cherry pie, fudge brownies... It all was eaten off paper plates with plastic utensils and washed down, in Clifford's case, with a boilermaker—a can of Coors enriched with a shot of Jim Beam.

"Isn't that Sal Calderara over there with Dr. Barlow?" Clifford asked Hillary, who was sitting beside him on a log bench.

"Yep, that's the Bureau of Land Mismanagement archaeologist all right," Hillary confirmed. "Not a bad guy, really. You weren't there when he came out to the site a few weeks ago. He sort of spilled his beans to Paul and me, admitting he'd been wasting a lot of time and energy seething. Seems he'd been feeling covetous of the two of us and our work at Sleeping Dog. And of our lofty Ph.D. labels. He actually told Paul he's decided to return to Colorado U. to earn his own Ph.D. Said he'd even quit his government job if necessary, although he thinks it's likely the BLM will give him a professional leave of absence."

With dinner finished, Clifford wandered over to where Barlow stood beside Calderara in his wheelchair.

"Mr. Calderara? I'm Clifford Gustafson. I've been working all summer at the Sleeping Dog site."

"Sure, hi, Clifford. I remember seeing you at the young lady's memorial service in Mercerville. Are you still out there with the skeleton crew?"

"Yep. They tell me we might be working through most of October."

"Fine, I'll come out and visit you."

"Hey," Clifford said a moment later, "those two young Cheyenne men that were killed in the car crash last week?"

"Yes?"

"You knew them, or at least some of their relatives up near Lame Deer?"

"Yes, I knew the uncle of one of them."

"I got to know Jamie Newhouse and Justin Willits in August. I learned, not from Jamie but from another of his friends, that you spent time with some Cheyenne elders looking around Sleeping Dog Canyon for a burial of some sort a few summers back?"

"That's right," Calderara said. "That's when I got to know Jamie's uncle. But we never found anything. Or I never saw it, anyway. We also searched other west-slope canyons—Shell, Bear, Stinking Springs. There's a long-standing legend among the Northern Cheyenne that the remains of some variety of deer-human hybrid were buried in one of those foothill canyons. It relates to the Dog Soldiers, not unlike a creation story."

"Well, the legend seems to be true. You do know about the intertwined skeletons of a man and deer that were in the trunk of Jamie's car?"

"Sure do. That's what got me thinking maybe the Indians did find the burial, or whatever you want to call it, when we were investigating up there in sixty-nine... and that they just 'neglected' to tell the government archaeologist about it."

"Wow. This thing gets more and more interesting."

"That it does," Calderara said.

***

As the evening progressed darkness displaced daylight and the huge bonfire threw sparks into the black sky, illuminating the immediate surroundings. Clifford approached an attractive, twenty-something woman with long black hair, green eyes, and dark skin peppered with light-brown freckles. Her features struck Clifford as unusual.

Most people I know with freckles have fair complexions.

"Hi, I'm Clifford Gustafson," he said, extending his right arm.

"Nezzy Farson. Pleased to meet you, Clifford."

"Nezzy? That's different."

She laughed. "It's a nickname. My real name is Jennifer, but my college friends started calling me 'Nezzy,' and I kind of liked it."

Clifford sensed an element of wildness in her voice, like the prairie wind washing over him.

Weird.

"Where's the name come from?"

"I'm one-eighth Nez Perce, or thereabouts. Though I know you wouldn't guess it by looking at me. When one of my undergraduate anthro classmates found that out, he gave me the nickname as a joke, I think. But there it is. I'm a Ph.D. candidate at the University of Nebraska," she added. "I'm writing my thesis on the ceremonial use of volcanic glass from Obsidian Cliff in Yellowstone. It's turned into an even bigger project than I'd imagined. Seems there are very few places in North America where some of that obsidian hasn't show up at one time or another in the archaeological record. It was typically used for utilitarian purposes, but also quite often for ceremonial or sacred use. Of course, it's not always easy to distinguish the utilitarian from the ceremonial."

"I'm sure you know we've uncovered our share of it at the Sleeping Dog site," Clifford said. "But that's no surprise, as close to Yellowstone as we are."

"No, no surprises there. But what a site you folks have on your hands!"

"Mmm… uh, Miss Farson?" Clifford started, following up on a gut feeling.

"Jennifer," she corrected him, smiling. "Or, better yet, Nezzy."

"Nezzy," Clifford asked, his voice growing softer, "what would come to your mind if you found a perfectly made obsidian point—say, a Plains side-notched—out in the middle of a north-central Wyoming sand-dune desert, lying nestled between a mano and metate? A mano and metate that appeared not to have been moved in decades, or centuries?"

"Did you find such a thing?"

"Yes, I did. It's still out there. Anyway, I assume it is, because I left it as I found it. An extraordinary thing to see."

"I should think so. I've heard from amateur archaeologists who've said they've come across similar finds, but I've never seen one myself. I would say that the projectile point was very, very important to someone at some time in the past. Maybe it saved a life by killing a threatening animal or person. Maybe it held some magic. Perhaps it still does."

"Do you believe in such things?"

"Yes. I believe in magic." Then, after a pause, she continued. "You know, Jamie Newhouse and Justin Willits *were* resurrected Dog Soldiers."

"Huh? You knew them? What do you mean by that?"

"Yes, I knew them. And they were not bad men, either. They were not without some magic themselves—or, put another way, special skills." Nezzy Farson locked eyes with Clifford.

"How do you know this?" Clifford asked.

"Their special skills are what they called upon to travel into the canyon and retrieve the skeletons undetected."

"You're weirding me out, Nezzy," Clifford said, chuckling nervously. "How do you know these things?"

"I just do. And one more thing—an important connection exists between the arrowhead you found in the dune desert and the skeletons that were removed from Sleeping Dog Canyon."

Silence fell between them.

"Wow," Clifford managed to mutter at last.

"And you, Clifford Whitetail, you are the one who will figure out what that is."

"What? Seriously, who are you, Nezzy? How do you know my birth name?"

"Let's just say I'm someone who is interested in what's going on," she said, then paused again. "And in you. I've been watching over you for a long time, Clifford. Off and on for your entire life."

"What?"

"And know this, Clifford: so many males of your people have forgotten how to be men. More to the point, they are often left feeling there is no way for them to be men in the Indian way while living in the modern world. I want you to be a man. And I believe you're off to a very good start."

Astonished, Clifford could think of nothing to say in reply.

"One more thing, Clifford."

"Y-yes?"

"She is in a good place."

"Who is?"

"Bobbi Alder. She wants you to go on exactly as you've been doing, and never forget her. To let her memory steer you, but not drive you."

"How-"

"Hey, Pedro, come over here for a minute, will you?"

The sound of the gravelly voice coming from the far side of the fire interrupted them. Clifford looked intently at Nezzy Farson.

"Hold that thought, okay? Conrad needs me."

He skirted around to the other side of the big bonfire and found his gray-haired friend. "What is it, Rad?"

"I don't have a flashlight, Jeofredo, and I don't see so well in the dark any more. Especially when I'm seeing double. Would you mind running down to our camp and grabbing that topo map that's rolled up in a tube behind the seat of my truck? And the flashlight out of the glove box? I want to show Manny and these other guys the lay of the land at Sleeping Dog."

"Sure, okay. No problem."

Clifford hurried off in the direction of their camp. When he returned to the fire moments later, Nezzy Farson had vanished.

"Rad," he said, handing Hillary the items he'd retrieved from the truck, "did you see where that young woman I was talking to went? Twenty-five-ish, dark hair?"

"No, Cliff, sorry. I didn't. The only time I saw you over there, you seemed to be alone. I thought you looked kind of spaced out."

"Weird. Totally weird. Well, I'll find her tomorrow, I suppose. She told me some things you won't believe… But I'll fill you in the morning. I've had it. You old farts are impossible to keep up with. I'm heading for the tent."

"Okay, chief, see you in the a.m. Don't feel bad. We old farts have had years of training. We're like finely tuned Olympians."

On his way to the campsite, something caught Clifford's eye that he hadn't noticed when covering the same ground a couple of minutes earlier—a big horse, tethered to a horse trailer behind a pickup truck. He couldn't tell for certain in the dark, but he thought it looked like an Appaloosa.

"Strange. I didn't see you before," Clifford whispered, walking over to the horse.

He gave the animal a couple of firm, friendly pats on the forehead. The horse nickered, then nodded its head up and down as if to say, "Yes, I like that."

33
FATE

"Dr. Barlow," asked Clifford, sitting at the wheel of John Mills' rental car as they drove away from the rendezvous, "what can you tell me about that gal Jennifer Farson—or 'Nezzy' she said they call her at school?"

Barlow turned in the passenger seat next to him.

"Who's that, Clifford? I don't recall the name."

"She said she's working on her Ph.D. at Nebraska. Documenting the prehistoric distribution and use of volcanic glass from Obsidian Cliff?"

"I have no grad students by that name, nor anyone working on that topic. What'd she look like?"

"Dark hair, slender, maybe five foot six. Freckles?"

Barlow paused, thinking. "Sorry, Clifford. I just can't think who that would be."

Clifford gripped the steering wheel tighter, furrowing his brow. Had he dreamt it all up, dozed off while standing without realizing he was asleep? He'd never done that before, at least not to his knowledge. Yet, Hillary had said he hadn't seen Nezzy Farson at the fire that night. And Barlow had never heard of her. He himself hadn't encountered her again over the rest of the weekend…

But she was so real. I felt her soft, warm skin when we shook hands.

A few moments later he shook his head sadly. "What a waste."

"What's that, Clifford?" asked Barlow.

"Bobbi's death. Totally senseless."

"Yes, it was. Is. I'm afraid we have more of those walking-wounded fellows around than anyone knows, or cares to admit. I supported the war in Vietnam early on, but I got over that real quick. A tragic course of events in many ways. We'll be paying for it, unfortunately, for many years to come."

The four men who had driven together to Buck Creek Rendezvous from the Sleeping Dog site were exhausted. The event had taken its toll: three days of hearty partying and making long hikes up and down the Pine Ridge, not to mention honing up on primitive skills like taking target practice with atlatl-flung spears and tanning Manny Ortiz's bison hide with the animal's own brain tissue. Owing to Clifford's youth and energy level, he was the only one bright-eyed enough early on this Monday, the first day of October, to be trusted at the wheel of the car. The other three remained in various stages of unconsciousness until Newcastle. By then, all had caught up to some degree on their beauty sleep. Mills took over the wheel to give Clifford a chance to rest, but with all the others now alert, he felt more like talking.

"Dr. Barlow? Paul?"

"Yes, Clifford?"

"I've been thinking. I really like the archaeology we've been doing. Excavating midden heaps and cooking fires; finding points, knives, butchered animal bones… the whole works."

"Well, I figured you've been enjoying it. You're good at it, you know. You've demonstrated skill, and that you have some intuition."

"Thanks. But what really gets me excited, for some reason, is the idea of finding human remains. That intertwined deer-man combo, that was something else. Incredible. Do you think I could get into the osteology end of things? Become sort of a physical anthropological detective?"

"I don't know why not. There are men and women who do just that. Are you thinking modern cases, or old?"

"Definitely old ones. Prehistoric. Maybe older historic cases, but not current ones. I want to help reconstruct the past through the study of human remains."

"In this country, in the Plains and northern Rockies, burials are about as rare as sage hens' teeth, you know."

"Yeah, well. Has anyone put together a comprehensive survey of exactly what has been found here, in terms of prehistoric remains?"

"The closest I'm aware of are the studies compiled by Dr. Maryanna Hartfield, up in Alberta. Her work in the Canadian plains and Rockies does spill into Montana some, but it doesn't come this far south."

"Why couldn't I do something like that covering our region for my master's project? Once I go to grad school, that is."

"Would you want to come and study with me in Lincoln?"

"Is that an invitation?" Clifford asked, sitting up. "If it is, my answer is definitely yes. There's nowhere I'd rather go, and no one I'd rather study under. Other than Conrad, of course, or you, John. But for me U-Minnie is a little too upper-Midwest and Great Lakes oriented. And, as you know, Chadron State doesn't offer a master's program. But Nebraska? I feel myself turning red. Go 'huskers!"

"When would you want to start?"

"How about second semester? In January?"

"It's a done deal. You know, we'll need to put some geographic constraints on your study area, both to help keep you sane and to maintain regional integrity. I'd say something like from the hundredth meridian, where, as our friend Wally Stegner points out, the arid West begins, to the Continental Divide. West of the Divide, as you're aware, you start getting into more Great Basin and Pacific Northwest cultures. And north to south? Probably from right around the Canadian border to midway through Colorado. Montana, Wyoming, northern Colorado. Where we're still in the Plains and before we start getting into the Anasazis and Fremonts and Puebloans of the greater Four Corners. And stretching east a ways also, into the western Dakotas, Nebraska, Kansas."

"That sounds reasonable to me."

"What are you doing between now and then? I mean, after we close up shop for the season at Sleeping Dog?"

"Well," Bill Parsons interjected. "I hadn't done so yet, but I was planning to ask Clifford if he'd like to come over and accompany me for a week or two on some horseback forays into the Absarokas. We might bag a poacher or two, or we may just have to settle for riding through some of most godawful gorgeous country on Earth."

"Hey, thanks, Bill," Clifford exclaimed. "I think I would like to do that. But I have to tell you, I'm not much of a horseman."

"I'll get you on a good mare and pointed in the right direction."

"That'll take you—what?—into mid-November?" Barlow asked.

"That's about right," Parsons said.

"I assume you'll be wanting to go home to your parents' place for Christmas," Barlow said.

"Right on," Clifford confirmed.

"So then, you've got at least a month to fill before late December. If you're game, I could try to get you a temporary appointment at the Northern Cheyennes' museum up in Ashland. I happen to know they're starting the search for a tribal historic preservation officer, but they don't plan on filling the post permanently until spring. They might be interested in bringing you on for a few weeks, just to start getting their collection into some semblance of order. It's in quite a mess, from what I've seen and heard."

"That sounds like a fantastic opportunity!"

"It would be. And you'll be interested to know they have a fair number of human skeletal remains—including some of Dull Knife's people, individuals who froze to death late in 1876 after their village in the Powder River country was destroyed by the cavalry. You, being Northern Cheyenne yourself, might even be able to do a little bone-scratching."

"Wow, outstanding!"

"I understand they even have artifacts and a few remains from Custer's battle at the Little Bighorn. That happened just a few months before the Dull Knife event. Custer's bloody defeat was the chief reason the government boosted troop numbers in the Wyoming Territory, which is what led to Dull Knife's undoing."

"That'd be unbelievable, working with Little Bighorn materials," Clifford said.

Maybe I'll track down some living relatives of my own while I'm at it.

A few moments of silence passed before Barlow resumed speaking.

"I have to admit, I have an ulterior motive in trying to get you positioned up there."

"What's that?" Clifford asked.

"I'd like to persuade you to sniff around a little bit in the archives and with the elders, the old-timers. You should able to ferret out information that an old white man like me can't. Something pretty interesting's going on."

"What? What do you mean?"

"Well, we've solved one mystery all right—that of Bobbi's murder. Or maybe I should say it solved itself. But we still have this other one. See if you can't learn where the name 'Sleeping Dog' came from."

Clifford chewed his lip for a moment before speaking. "I think I already know, Dr. Barlow. Or, anyway, I have a theory that I'm more and more coming to believe."

"What is it?"

"That human skeleton in the trunk of Jamie Newhouse's Road Runner? I think it belonged to a Cheyenne, who, along with the deer, at some point in time became a symbol, or totem, for the Dog Soldiers. We don't know when they died, of course, but even if it was before the Dog Soldiers became a full-blown military society—in what, the 1830s?—I believe they may have somehow come to consider him one of them; a *sleeping* Dog Soldier."

"Huh, interesting," Barlow said. "Of course, like you pointed out earlier, the elders and Sal Calderera were looking for something rumored to be in one of the west-slope Big Horn canyons. That it would be a 'sleeping Dog' makes some sense. But it would have to have been uncovered before, way back sometime. Then re-covered with dirt?"

"Or maybe he was with others when he died, and the legend passed forward from them. Or his people found him later. Maybe they even 'helped' the rock overhang to fall as sort of a ritual burial?"

"That's an intriguing theory, Clifford. I like the way you think. I do believe the rock art Galen uncovered looks too sharp to be extremely old. A hundred years, maybe two hundred? If you're right, the carvings and pictographs may have marked the entrance to the upper canyon where the sacred site is located. How did you come to this conclusion, or hypothesis?"

"I dreamt it to begin with, if you can believe that. I've been having a lot of strange dreams lately, and I think they're trying to tell me something. Then I just started thinking more and more about it and putting together things various people told me, like Sal Calderara just this weekend. And Nezzy Farson..." Clifford didn't finish the sentence.

"So, you think this is how your friends in the Dodge hot rod knew about the man and the deer? That it's Cheyenne lore, and lots of folks are aware of it?"

"Plymouth."

"Huh?"

"It was a Plymouth Road Runner, not a Dodge."

"Oh, yeah. I can't seem to get that through my thick skull."

"Well, enough of them knew about it, anyway. It could be that it was a protected secret, relatively speaking, one revealed only to certain people who would respect and not violate the site. That is, until the DSR—I'm speculating here, of course—started worrying that we archaeologists would find it as we branched out from the main site, surveying up the canyon."

"Clifford, theories are approximately eighty-five percent of what archaeology is about. And yours sounds tenable. Dreams are not to be discounted, either. I've had similar visions while sleeping that turned out to be prescient. I'll go along with you for the time being, but see if you can't learn more if we do manage to get you in at the Ashland museum. I'll make a phone call or two tomorrow."

"Speaking of that," said Parsons, "there's something I've been meaning to ask you, Clifford. Something that's been nagging at me. I hope you don't mind me bringing it up in front of Paul and John."

"What's that, Bill?"

"A week ago yesterday, before you and I and Paul walked up the canyon and had that thrilling little caper with the deranged mountain man..."

"Yeah?"

"You told Paul and me for the first time about a conversation you'd had with Amy... what's her name?"

"Looksbehind."

"That's right. Amy Looksbehind. You said she was the one who told you about the Cheyenne party poking around Sleeping Dog Canyon with Calderera?"

"Yes?" Clifford said, hesitation in his voice.

"As you were explaining it, you said something like, 'I haven't even told you about this yet, Bill.' Why was that? You seemed excited about having me help you out, so why would you keep a potentially important piece of information like that to yourself?"

"Oh, yeah. That was stupid, wasn't it? Well, no, I don't mind saying this in front of Paul and John. I think they'll understand.

You see, Bill, it was a Cheyenne—Amy Looksbehind—telling another Cheyenne—that would be me—about a matter concerning Cheyennes both living and dead. A sense I had, or maybe you'd call it a little voice, told me I shouldn't let that bit out beyond the circle. I am an Indian, you know, or at least trying to learn how to be one. Can you understand what I'm getting at?"

"I think so, Cliff."

"But in the end I did decide it was a dumb thing to do. To keep it to myself, that is. That's why I told you and Paul about it that morning. I realized it needed to be let out."

"Okay," Parsons said. "Case closed."

After a few moments of silence, Clifford introduced a new topic. "Dr. Barlow, Paul, what are you going to do about Peter Ashton?"

"That son of a bitch really has slipped off to Texas now," Barlow said. "Anyway, that's what Sheriff Hendrickson told me when I rang him up on the phone from Chadron yesterday. It will be my secondary mission over the coming months to track him down and have a little talk with him. Probably get his father involved. Now that we know Ashton's mixed up with that anti-grazing group, I'm thinking that's what induced him to persuade his dad to secure him a spot on the crew this summer in the first place. What do you think about that?"

"I think I agree," Clifford said.

"Me too," said Parsons.

"I can't say he's done anything illegal, but he's sure as hell acted unethically. I'll catch up with Ashton, find out what in God's name he was thinking, and keep you all apprised as to his state of atonement."

"One way or the other, we'll be seeing more of him in the future," Parsons predicted. "I know his type too well."

"What's your primary mission, Paul?" asked John Mills.

"Huh?"

"You said dealing with Ashton was your secondary mission. You must have a primary?"

"Oh, I see. Yes. It's trying to figure out the mystery of why we're lacking only the Late Plains Archaic in the archaeological record at Sleeping Dog. That fact, that one missing piece of the puzzle, is driving Conrad and me to distraction. It means, or probably means, that no indigenous populations were living in the canyon for a minimum of a thousand years, between twenty-five hundred and fifteen hundred years before the present. At least. Where'd they go, and why did they come back? To borrow from our rock-knocking friends in the geology world, it's like an archaeological unconformity."

34
HUNTING

Clifford rose early on the morning following the crew's return from the Buck Creek Rendezvous. After showering, he headed up the canyon to keep a breakfast date with Paul Barlow and Bill Parsons, who, after wolfing down his bacon and French toast, would be leaving to report for his hunting-and-gathering duties in the Absaroka Range.

"Good morning!" Clifford hailed on his arrival at Parsons' campsite. The famous tracker was standing over his Coleman stove. Barlow sat on a stump nearby, sipping coffee.

"Morning, Clifford!" said Parsons.

"Bill, you're a federal government employee when you do what you're going to do, right?" Clifford asked after he had sat down.

"Yep, temporary GS-9. The pay's not great, but the benefits are out of this world. Riding a government horse, staying in a government cabin, using government tack and rifles, eating government food. It's like a paid vacation, really. Occasionally there's real work to be done, and even less often some real danger involved. Like the time I dragged that mauled hunter's corpse out of a grizzly bear cache off Stipper's Butte. And, as you might expect, poachers themselves aren't always the most upstanding of citizens, not always good guys who respect us enforcers of the law. Still, it's a nice break from slopping the hogs."

"I imagine so," Clifford said, chuckling. "Even a grizzly bear's den couldn't smell as ripe as an Iowa hog lot. I can get over there around the nineteenth, Bill, if that works for you."

"Sure. I pretty much set my own schedule, unless something comes up. I'll plan to be back at my cabin from the field a couple days before that, just in case you're early—on the seventeenth, which is, let's see, a Wednesday. I'll mark the location for you on a spare forest visitor's map I have in the truck there. It also has the phone number for the Supervisor's Office in Cody, where we can leave messages for each other if need be. The cabin's easy to find, really. From Cody you follow the road southwest to where it ends at the Washakie Wilderness boundary. That was designated just last summer, by the way. They combined the Stratified Primitive Area and the South Absaroka Wilderness into the Washakie Wilderness. Has a nice ring to it, don't you think? As you probably know, Washakie was a great chief and warrior of the Shoshone people-"

"Clifford," Barlow interrupted, "we'd better help Bill get these dishes cleaned up and hightail it back to the site. Josie and Marge and Jefferson will be cussing us."

"Check, myte," Clifford said, in his best Aussie accent.

Barlow half laughed and half grunted, wagging his head at his boy wonder.

After shaking hands with Parsons and bidding their farewells, the two archaeologists headed down canyon, Clifford cupping a crisp new Shoshone National Forest map in his hand. As an afterthought, he turned around and yelled back at Parsons.

"Bill, I'm gonna try hunting myself this weekend, over on Beaver Butte outside Greybull. I've been seeing quite a few mulies over there this summer. Don't worry, though, I've got a license. I'm legal. And I bought myself a used Winchester thirty-thirty in Worland that I meant to show you."

"Sounds good, Cliff," Parsons said, his deep baritone booming in the cold morning air. "Be careful, and good luck. See you in a couple of weeks."

***

Clifford looked down on the Big Horn River, its snaking course marked by a yellow procession of autumn-fired cottonwood trees. Even from half a mile away, he could see that its flow was a trickle of what it had been when he'd first set foot in the basin four months before.

Between Clifford and the river's floodplain sprawled the Rye Creek alluvial fan. Its lower portions supported alfalfa hay, nourished by a system of rough canals, while the upper reaches persevered in a semi-wild state—although, he noticed, that pit bull of a noxious weed leafy spurge had gained an invasive toehold. During the long autumn night, water pulsing from irrigation pipes had frozen on the hard ground of the hay field, sealing it in ice.

Clifford looked up at the impossibly deep-blue sky framing the willows lining Rye Creek. And he thought about Bobbi—beautiful, kind, vibrant Bobbi.

The love of my life.

Resuming his hike, Clifford inched upward along one of the nameless, brush-filled draws creasing the autumn-drab foothills. He watched as the daybreaking sun hit the top of the butte above, backlighting the oranges, golds, and reds of aspen and mountain maple. He stopped and turned around. In the far western distance, he saw the summits of the high Absarokas, likewise set ablaze by the first rays of the morning sun.

Parsons is over there, somewhere.

Clifford thrust his arm into the air and threw his friend a big wave.

Up, up, up. Clifford looked at his watch. Half-past eight. He inhaled the powerful, earthy aroma of leaves decaying in the buckbrush coulee beside him. A sage grouse erupted in a frenzy of wing-flapping, scaring Clifford and producing a rush of adrenaline. It made him think of the thunderous racket made by Sir Ralph the Wonder Dog when he shook his floppy ears hard against his broad skull.

On a whim, Clifford lay down, back to the cold, hard ground. Staring into an infinite sea of blue, he pinpointed a red-tailed hawk that was illuminated on one side by the rising sun. He followed the bird as it soared high, higher still, finally losing sight of it. Then he relocated the raptor, drew a sure bead on it, and willed his spirit to sink its talons into the hawk's flank. Together they soared, high and fast, and for the next few moments Clifford was thoughtless and free.

His reverie was broken when he realized he was shivering from the cold and that his feet were numb. He stood, grunting, and took off his gloves, then massaged his trunk and torso with bare hands. Imagining himself back on the Red Earth High football field he popped fifty jumping jacks—his long raven ponytail flapping a half beat behind the metronomic rhythm of his arms and legs—and then fifty squat-thrusts. In his mind he heard Coach Hennessey barking the count, "ONE-two-three-four, TWO-two-three-four..." That soon warmed him right up.

Clifford grabbed his daypack from the ground and reached his arms through the straps. He re-slung his Winchester carbine over his shoulder and continued on his way. As he progressed he looked around carefully, inspecting everything he could think of inspecting—the dusty earth for fresh tracks or scat, the clacking leaves of arrowleaf balsamroot, brittle in the breeze, for a trace of deer hair... A couple of ravens flew overhead.

Anticipating a steaming gut pile, perhaps?

Clifford moved through a terrain of transition, where the mountain surrendered its slopes to an undulating sea of short grass and the mule deer's rocky, sparsely timbered foothills overlapped with the pronghorn's grasslands. After wiping the sweat from his brow with the sleeve of his Woolrich, he stopped to remove the jacket and stuff it into his rucksack.

Stepping as quietly as possible amid the crackling autumn leaves, he inched up alongside a serviceberry-choked draw crumpling the northwest flank of Beaver Butte. Finally, he reached the lowest copse of aspen on the first bench, more than a thousand vertical feet above the valley floor where he'd begun his trek. A massive, four-point mule deer exploded from the thicket above. Like an apparition the buck vanished, almost before its presence had registered in Clifford's mind.

He stared in startled wonder at where the deer had been.

He went higher still, the gradient steepening with every step. By the time he had gained another thousand feet of elevation and reached the grove of ancient Douglas firs he had visited several times over the summer, Clifford had flushed out three more mule deer. His mood went further downhill with every deer he missed, even as his altitude increased. The third deer, a doe, had him swearing out loud with aggravation.

"God dammit!"

He heard the doe wheeze somewhere out of sight.

She's snorting at my incompetence.

A few seconds later, he heard her wheeze again, a bit further away.

Now she's rubbing it in.

He couldn't stay angry for long. The deliciously warm Indian summer sun drew his face and body to it, seducing him. He stumbled drowsily across the broad top of the butte and into an open park of fat-trunked ponderosa pines. Choosing the beefiest tree in sight, Clifford leaned his rifle against it, removed his rucksack, and crashed to the fertile duff, nestling his backside against the tree's rusty-cinnamon base. It made him think again of the August evening at Crow Fair when he'd propped himself against that cottonwood trunk and become one with the tree, a prelude to his purification through the drumming and singing that continued far into the night.

Clifford emptied the contents of his pack onto the ground, then unwrapped and tucked into his sandwich of chunky peanut butter and raspberry jam on a hamburger bun. To wash it down and quell his mighty thirst, he guzzled the entire contents of his plastic quart water bottle.

It was a comfortable place to be, an oasis of autumn. The air felt cool and dry, the sun warm on his skin. No mosquitoes or flies buzzed around, biting or otherwise annoying him.

Any recent hatches no doubt got themselves flash-frozen last night.

The bright sunlight made Clifford squint. He found it easier keeping his eyes closed, but that rendered him helpless to resist slipping into the strange gray world bridging sleep and wakefulness. A fleeting thought told him, though he wasn't yet sleeping, that at this juncture he couldn't return to the world of the conscious if he tried.

Dreaming now, Clifford joined the hawk whose T-shaped profile he'd spied earlier against the lofty cloud-free sky. Sinking deeper, he *became* the raptor. Angling outspread wings just so, Clifford Gustafson the hawk caught a spectacular thermal that lifted him high into the sky, higher still. Permitting the wind to push him hard to the northeast, he soared across the Big Horn Mountains' desiccated western foothills, over the prehistoric Medicine Wheel, above the Castle Buttes of the Pryor Range. Looking down, he recognized a dot on the landscape as the homestead of the great Crow chief Plenty Coups, a place he had visited just months earlier, though it seemed like half a lifetime ago.

Continuing his airborne journey, Clifford the red-tailed hawk soared upstream along the course of the Tongue River. After gliding over a windswept corrugation of rippled dry ridges, he crossed the divide into the watershed of the Rosebud and began losing elevation. In no time, and through no effort of his own, he touched down a couple of miles north of Lame Deer, Montana—where, nearly two decades ago, in a horror of heat and flames, Clifford had been torn from the Cheyenne Indian Way. Almost forever. He could see the fire, feel its heat. He smelled the smoke and his own singed eyebrows. Screams pierced his skull.

The latter part of this vision Clifford had dreamt countless times over the years, a fact he semi-understood when trapped inside the dream. But never on awakening could he conjure any details. Rather, a hazy apparition would encompass him like a ground fog—undeniably there, but impossible to grab hold of…

Until now.

***

Clifford woke with a start.

"What?"

What was this dream that remained so vivid? He clearly recalled watching a grown man and woman, Indians both of them, running into a burning house.

My parents? Was that child I saw waddling out of the woods, dragging a blanket—me?

Clifford had no way of knowing the answer, but he *was* struck with a surprising revelation of certainty: he had been going about things in altogether the wrong way. He should be pursuing game with bow and arrow when out hunting solo like this. And not just any arrow, but an arrow tipped with the magical obsidian point he had found in the dune desert west of Worland, the one he believed still to be nested between the beautiful mano and metate.

Clifford stood, relishing this fresh sense of clarity. He knew exactly what he had to do. And it would be an easy task to carry out, because he would be spared the need to make decisions. He had received from his dream the gift of direction.

Clifford slipped his arms through his pack, grabbed the lever-action Winchester and checked the safety, then hightailed it off the top of Beaver Butte in a barely controlled fall. About a third of the way down, he stopped to rest. He removed his pack and sat cross-legged on the sage-covered ground about a hundred yards north of a sandstone outcrop he'd eyeballed two or three times over the summer. As he sat staring at it, he realized he had never taken a close-up look at the isolated block of stone, which appeared to be about thirty feet long and wide, ten or twelve feet high.

Aiming to remedy the situation, Clifford stood, grabbed his pack and rifle, and made his way to a previously unviewed side of the big rock. He sensed in advance what he would see next. About eight feet above the ground, or a couple of feet above Clifford's head, was a fine line of faded pictographs drawn in blues and reds on the rock's face. No man or bighorn sheep, but a row of six dogs—or wolves or coyotes, perhaps—all curled up, apparently sleeping. They were so similar to the ones uncovered by Galen Davies with his John Deere, the find that had precipitated the past summer's excavations and the historic discoveries made by the crew at the Sleeping Dog site. The animals' heads, Clifford noted, were pointed south-southeast, in the approximate direction of the site.

How cool is this?

Back at the fire-engine-red state truck, Clifford checked his watch again. One-thirty.

Time enough to drive out to the dune field, retrieve the point, get back to my cabin, and make some weapons.

He would be back on Beaver Butte early the next morning, he vowed, bow in hand.

"Wait," Clifford said aloud as he reached to fire up the truck's engine. "I'd better double-check."

He reached for the hunting regulations brochure lying on the floor in front of the passenger seat. Leafing through it, he stopped on page twelve and pointed with his index finger.

"That's what I thought," he mumbled to himself. "The archery season goes through to the twelfth, Friday."

As the truck bounced along the rugged dirt access road, Clifford laid out his plans. On his way through Worland he would stop to pick up a few items and buy an archery tag at Big Horn Outfitters. He hadn't attained Wyoming residency so, just like his firearms license, the tag would be rather costly. But he'd managed to save a fair amount of cash over the summer.

This is one expenditure I know will be worth it... won't be getting no Caddy, though.

He chortled at the memory of Hillary's coughing fit back in May, triggered by his suggestion that he might buy a Cadillac with his summer earnings.

***

Clifford walked into the towering dunes where a month earlier he'd come across his remarkable find. He feared he would have trouble relocating it. As it turned out, it seemed that he was guided back to the mano and metate by something other than his own orienteering skills.

He lifted the hand stone for a second time.

What the...?

The obsidian point was still there, but now its point faced in a slightly different direction. He was sure he hadn't touched the arrowhead on his earlier visit. And he was certain he had set the mano back down gently enough to leave the arrowhead undisturbed. He could see the faded outline of the point's former orientation on the flat surface of the metate, where it had no doubt rested for decades, or centuries.

Who, or what, altered the point's position? And why?

It was just another of life's little mysteries, but truly a weird one.

I wonder if Nezzy Farson, whoever she is, had something to do with it?

He retrieved from his pocket the obsidian point he'd found in Sleeping Dog Canyon the morning after his unplanned bivouac and held it next to the point lying on the grinding stone.

"The same," he murmured. "Identical twins."

He returned the Sleeping Dog Canyon point into the right-hand pocket of his jeans.

On a whim, leaving the other point exposed, Clifford jogged back to the truck and pulled from behind the seat a cardboard tube holding several topographic maps, including the Worland and Basin 1:100,000 scale topos. He also grabbed the tripod and Brunton compass, along with a notebook and pencil and the crew's Nikon. Then he returned to his ancient discovery.

He laid the two maps side by side on the ground, orienting them along a north–south axis. Next, he screwed the threads of the compass into the threaded receptacle on the top of the tripod and set the three legs on the ground so that they straddled the metate. He aimed the compass in the direction the arrowhead had pointed in its previous position and recorded in the notebook its reading of seventy-eight degrees. Next, he shot a line over the arrowhead in its present position. Forty-two degrees. He scribbled that in the notebook, too. Finally, he removed the compass from the tripod and set it on the ground at the westernmost edge of the Worland topo map, then used it to shoot in a pair of bearings. Triangulating, he drew two long lines across the map, using the side of his notebook as a straightedge. Both lines originated at his current location, one extending out at forty-two degrees and the other at seventy-eight. One of the lines passed through the location of the Sleeping Dog site; the other, over the north end of Beaver Butte.

As I suspected.

Before packing up, Clifford shot a photo of the exposed arrowhead, then picked it up and stuck it in the left-hand pocket of his pants

"Left pocket dune point, right pocket Sleeping Dog," he whispered, then repeated it over in his mind several times, like a mantra.

***

It was still dark on Sunday morning when Clifford slipped out of the pickup parked at the foot of Beaver Butte. He closed the truck door without making a sound, holding the handle up while pushing on the door to secure its latch. His strategy was to do exactly as he had done the day before—cover the same route, at the same pace—except with his self-crafted bow in hand rather than a rifle slung over his shoulder.

As he crept along, Clifford's mind centered on the present. Only once did he catch it wandering. And even then it meandered back only as far as the previous evening, as he sat in his cabin working a willow shaft. After heating the shaft over the flame of his Coleman stove, Clifford had run it up and down the groove of an ancient soapstone arrow straightener. Young Ben Reed had discovered the artifact a few weeks earlier in the dry fork canyon of Sleeping Dog Creek. He no doubt regretted bringing it back to show off to the others, because Hillary had immediately insisted it be added to the tools collection and not go home with Reed.

It had been fine work, hafting the obsidian point from the dune field to a notch cut into one end of the straightened shaft, using sections of light fishing line to secure it in place. To the other end, he had attached segments of bird feathers he had collected during the summer, using model-car cement to hold them in the three grooves he'd cut lengthwise into the base of the shaft. He had also cut out a small notch in the base end to secure the arrow to the bowstring.

When finished with these tasks, and with crafting a bow from a curved juniper branch and a length of waxed cord, Clifford had marveled at his handiwork. Never had he attempted making such items. In fact, he'd witnessed the process only once, just days earlier, performed by a Montana State University grad student at the Buck Creek Rendezvous. Yet Clifford's creations looked wonderful and very functional; perhaps even more so than Shelby Smith's had.

It was as if someone else's experience and skill had been channeled through Clifford's fingers and hands…

He had repeated the arrow-building process, using a second willow shaft and the projectile point he'd found in Sleeping Dog Canyon. This arrow, readily distinguishable from the other by the darker shades of the feathers at its base, was a backup piece of weaponry he believed he would not need.

Now, two hours out and halfway up, Clifford entered the lowest scattering of pine on the west side of Beaver Butte. He sensed that he was getting near, so he drew his bow. A heavy-bodied, four-point mule deer—the same one he'd flushed out the day before, he was quite sure—exploded from the thicket above. It stopped and looked back at Clifford, who released his arrow just as the deer flexed to flee uphill. The projectile hit the buck in the heart-lung area of its left side, forcing an audible wheeze from the animal. It staggered for three or four huge strides upward before crashing down into a bramble of serviceberry.

Slowly, Clifford walked up to the deer, giving it time to die. When he reached the body, he squeezed the buck's eyelids shut with his thumb and forefinger.

What would Jamie Newhouse say?

"Thank you, brother deer, for sacrificing your life so that I may sustain mine."

Something like that, anyway.

With the sharply honed blade of his foldable Buck knife he made a shallow slice on the deer's underside, beginning at the neck and ending at the anus. He had never field-dressed an animal, but he'd studied how to do it and asked questions of others who had. But none of that mattered, as this task, too, came without thought or effort. As if something other than his own brain guided his hands.

After completing the bloody work of gutting the deer, Clifford removed the heavy canvas tarp from his pack. He spread it out on the ground and rolled the deer over onto it. Then he wrapped up the dead animal, running a stout nylon rope through the grommet holes in the tarp and pulling the two ends taut. These he knotted together around the front of his torso, placing his Woolrich jacket between his belly and the rope to protect his skin from friction. He proceeded to drag the heavy buck downhill toward the truck.

Clifford found himself sweating in the sunny, seventy-degree heat of early October. Halfway to the truck, he stopped for a breather, when he realized he was feeling a remarkable sense of liberation.

"Lordy, lordy," he said, gazing out across the immensity of the Big Horn Basin, "how I've come to love this country!"

35
APPARITIONS

Late on Tuesday morning Clifford stood in the excavation block with his three workmates, whistling and concentrating on mapping stratigraphy. A voice from above startled him—familiar, though not quite right.

"Clifford Gustafson?"

"Yeah?" he said, looking up. "Aaaaaah!" He fell to his knees. "Bobbi!"

The wraith shook her head. "Oh, no. I'm awfully sorry to surprise you like this. It's Billie. Billie Alder."

Clifford stared up at her for a moment. "Are you Bobbi's twin, or what?"

"No, I'm a year younger. But they've always said we could be twins."

Clifford climbed up the wooden ladder out of the deep excavation to stand face to face with his visitor. Her eyes were as green as Bobbi's had been, her smile as wide and white, her hair as brown and silky, her figure… Clifford struggled to speak.

"I… Bobbi talked a lot about her younger sister, but she never said anything about the similarity in appearance." Clifford felt altogether freaked out, transported to a dream world. Even betrayed in a sense. Finally, he gathered himself and offered his hand. "To answer your question, yes, I am Clifford Gustafson. You've heard of me?"

She laughed and took his hand. "Billie Alder. Pleased to meet you, Clifford. Yes, I heard about you at length. That was Bobbi. Always 'neglecting' to tell people she had a spittin'-image sister, on the outside chance an opportunity would come around to pull a prank on them. She kept the secret in reserve, in her bag of tricks. I don't know if you learned this about her, but she could be quite the practical joker.

I guess I can be, too. And there are all kinds of tricks sisters who look alike can play on people who don't know the whole story."

"I didn't think Mormons had a sense of humor," Clifford blurted out. "What?"

Clifford read a mixture of hurt and surprise in her tone and facial expression.

"I-I'm sorry," he stammered. "An old friend of mine told me that, but I know it's not true. It was awful of me to say it."

Damn, that was dumb. Why does Hillary brainwash me with his anti-Mormon stuff?

"You know, Clifford," Billie Alder said, "Bobbi really enjoyed her work here. She would tell me about it in letters and on the phone. It got me kind of interested, too."

"Yeah?"

"Yes." She smiled at him, her green eyes engaging his and bringing forth a flood of emotions—regret, excitement, nostalgia, joy, confusion, sadness.

"So... what are you doing here?" he asked.

"Oh, I'm here with my parents. My mother and father have been in close contact with Sheriff Hendrickson and your Dr. Barlow the last couple of months. They're at his trailer now. We're staying in Worland. I—we—would like to take you out to dinner tonight, if you're free. We could drive you into Worland and then bring you back."

Clifford considered it for a moment. "I appreciate it and I'll be happy to accept the invitation. But I can use a state truck, so you don't need to drive all the way out here again tonight."

The way the sunlight hit Billie's T-shirt, the way her eyes sparkled, her voice—it all reminded Clifford so much of the last time he had seen Bobbi alive.

***

Clifford enjoyed a wonderful dinner with the Alders at Mack's Steak House. The rest of Bobbi and Billie's family—their mother, father, and teenage brother, Buddy—were all such congenial people that it made him feel even guiltier for some of the things he'd said about Latter-day

Saints in recent months. In fact, spending the evening with them turned out to be both therapeutic and energizing.

"This was great, folks," he told them as he prepared to leave. "Thank you. I feel like I know Bobbi even better now."

After Clifford had said goodbye to the others, leaving them in the restaurant foyer, Billie accompanied him to his truck. The streetlamps and the moon overhead provided the only illumination in the darkness of the early autumn evening.

"Clifford?" Billie said. "Like Dad told you, we're heading back to Star Valley in the morning. But I'd like to see you again sometime. Soon. I miss my sister more than I can say. I can see that you do, too. It would be nice to spend some time with you and talk about her."

"It's a promise, Billie," Clifford said, smiling and holding her hand in parting. "Uh, there's something I'd like to tell you."

"Sure, go ahead."

"Bobbi and I were more than friends. We were-"

Billie put her index finger to her lips to silence him. "I know. There were *no* secrets between us." She smiled. "She told me, 'Clifford Gustafson is the finest young man I've ever met... the finest person.'"

"The feeling was mutual. *Is* mutual."

With that, he got into the pickup truck and drove away, watching Billie Alder getting smaller in the rearview mirror until she disappeared.

***

Clifford pulled into Mercerville at ten past eight, still dizzy from the day's disclosures but settling down some. He wasn't surprised to see the other state rig parked in front of the Tired Puppy. He parked beside it, then strolled through the tavern door. Inside he found his three remaining fellow crew members, along with Paul Barlow, Galen Davies, and Pete Patterson. They were hard at it, drinking beer and watching the fuzzy signal from KTWO in Casper on the television mounted above the bar. As Clifford pulled up a chair, the local sports announcer appeared on the screen, previewing what he would be reporting on during the ten o'clock news.

"How about those Mets?" he said, alluding to the World Series slated to kick off over the coming weekend. After the airing of a commercial for laundry detergent, an episode of *Gunsmoke* resumed.

"Well, you know what the Mets' manager, Yogi Berra, says about baseball, don't you?" Patterson said.

"What's that?" asked Clifford.

"It's ninety percent mental, and the other half is physical."

That brought a round of laughter, which precipitated another round of beers.

"How was supper with the Alders?" Barlow asked.

"It was great," Clifford said. "I understand you've been talking to them some?"

"That's right, I have. I hadn't told you because I didn't want to stir up your thoughts any more than necessary."

"I appreciate that, Dr. Barlow. But I'm okay now."

"Good to hear it. I was floored to see that Bobbi's younger sister looks so much like her. I bet you were, too."

"You can say that again. I almost passed out. Literally floored."

"Hey, I almost forgot. Bonnie took a call from your mother earlier today. Here, she gave me this note to give to you."

Barlow reached into the pocket of his coffee-stained cowboy shirt and pulled out a small scrap of white paper. He handed it over to Clifford, who unfolded it and found a message penned in Bonnie Anderson's neat handwriting.

"Clifford: Your mother called late this afternoon from Minnesota. No emergency, but she said you had received a call from a Mary Terreton in Los Angeles, California. She'd like you to call her as soon as possible, collect, on the number below."

Clifford glanced at his watch. Eight-thirty. "California's an hour earlier than here, right? That makes it just seven-thirty over there... I'll be right back, comrades. I'm just gonna go make this call."

Wondering who Mary Terreton was and why she would be calling him, Clifford jogged outside and across the street. He swung open the folding door of what, over the course of the summer, had earned the moniker "Mercerville Phone Booth National Monument." The nickname underscored the vital role the pay phone had played as the crew members' primary link to the world beyond Sleeping Dog Canyon and the burg of Mercerville. He dropped in a dime, dialed the operator, and read her the number off the piece of paper.

"Reverse the charges, please," he said. "My name's Clifford Gustafson."

He heard the phone ring once, twice, three times. Then a click and the voice of a girl, or a young woman. "Hello?"

"Will you accept a collect call from Clifford Gustafson?"

"Yes, operator."

"Go ahead, sir."

"Uh, hello. This is Clifford Gustafson. In Wyoming. My mother back in Minnesota said you called?"

"Oh, yes, hi. Umm…"

The pause continued for so long that Clifford began wondering if she had hung up.

"So… why did you have me call you? Do I know you?"

"Clifford? I'm Mary Terreton. Uh, Mary Whitetail. Your sister…"

***

Later that evening, back in his cabin, Clifford reflected on what an incredible day he had just experienced. And what an amazing summer. Adding to this day's highlights, late in the afternoon on his way to Worland for dinner he had swung by the post office in the Big Horn Mercantile to see if anything had arrived for him via General Delivery. There was just one piece of mail, a letter from his college buddy Hal Whitworth III, informing Clifford that he had landed a position with the National Park Service in Yellowstone. He would begin the job in April.

"Hot dang, that's great!" Clifford whispered to himself, grinning.

Whitworth's joining me in God's country—after school is out at Nebraska, anyway, and I'm back here next summer. Oh, I also need to schedule that trail work in the Black Hills. Gotta remember to call the sheriff tomorrow.

Later still, as he lay in bed sleeping and through no choice of his own, Clifford slipped into another round of cathartic dreaming—a swirling mishmash of visions, a bizarre and inextricable jumble intermingling countless experiences and characters Clifford had known in his twenty-two years. Running with Ralphie along empty Red Earth County rural roads. Going nine holes with his father at the Bobby Wilson Golf Course. Skinny-dipping in the frigid waters of Sleeping Dog Creek with the finest girl he'd known. Hunting with primitive tools he had crafted himself, while being guided by something other than his own knowledge or skill. A long-ago house fire. An Appaloosa mare watching over him. And something hazy and strange involving an ancient ancestor, a buck deer, and a pair of obsidian arrowheads.

EPILOGUE: LATE SUMMER, CIRCA 1800

Whistling Elk sensed something sacred in the air; a voice in his head or an ancestor speaking to his heart. After eating he grabbed his gear and told Saw-Whet Peak he was going to go look around for a while.

"Good luck" she answered, avoiding eye contact.

An hour later Whistling Elk slipped noiselessly around an outcrop of dark-yellow sandstone the size of a skin lodge. In the high-desert nightfall, he could feel the release of heat inhaled by the stone during the long hot summer day. Under his cool palm the rock felt warm and alive. He thought for a moment about the dream he had dreamt the night before and on several other occasions during the previous few weeks. It involved a ghost horse that would run away if summoned but remain annoyingly close if Whistling Elk tried chasing it away. The dream meant something special for him, but he hadn't yet figured out what.

Such dreams guided Whistling Elk's very being, his actions driven by a firm belief in supernatural entities and signs.

In the land of steamy summers and big lakes, in the direction from which the sun came daily, where Whistling Elk's great-grandfather's grandfather had lived and hunted, the sun took daylight with it. Or so Whistling Elk had been told. But here in the arid foothills angling up toward the lofty peak so often embraced in thick cloud, the light lingered long after sunset. On this evening the sun had left the visible world some time ago, yet enough light still filtered in from the west to permit Whistling Elk to see clearly.

In his left palm he held his juniper bow by its soft leather hand-hold. The gut bowstring rubbed against his inner arm as he crept around the big rock, which he hugged with his right arm to steady himself. The warm, pervasive scent of sage and juniper dominated his olfactory senses.

From his great-grandfather, who had been impossibly ancient by the time Whistling Elk was old enough to make sense of his stories, he had learned how the Tsitsistas' ancestors had come from the earthlodge river country. And how before that, back at the beginning of time, they had been created from the rich duff of the country of inland freshwater seas and thick boreal forests where there were no horses and only rarely bison.

Despite hearing them from the indisputable source that was his great-grandfather, the tales of a fantastic land where water and trees covered nearly everything tested Whistling Elk's imagination to the limit. In the world he knew, trees covered very little and water even less. He had stored the vision away in the back of his mind, where it rested with other legends passed along to him; things that surely were realities at some time in the long-ago past of the Tsitsistas but which related to his life today only in distant spiritual ways.

Yet it had been impossible for Whistling Elk to believe a time existed when the People possessed no horses to hunt the far-ranging bison herds; he had been certain his ancestors had always hunted the buffalo on horseback. At least in their dreams, for that simply is the way of the Tsitsistas. It had been impossible to believe, that was, until three summers ago, when Whistling Elk had begun, after receiving direction in a dream, to head out by himself on evening deer hunts like this.

Whistling Elk savored hunting solo, one-on-one with his prey, despite the fact that stalking and killing a lone buck or doe was not essential. He and his family had plenty of dried bison meat remaining from the successful horseback drives of the previous weeks. It had come naturally to Whistling Elk, this sort of hunting his great-grandfather had told him magical stories about—the kind of hunting at which Whistling Elk's great-grandfather's grandfather and his fellow Tsitsistas were adept before the Ojibwa obtained weapons from the white man and became a fighting force with which the People could not reckon. That had been before the Tsitsistas traveled west by foot to the big river country, where they acquired the horses that gave them the means to travel farther west, and to harvest large numbers of animals in the crazy bison drives.

Ah, he ruminated, the bison drives. Necessary, but dangerous and wild. Whistling Elk didn't enjoy them, although he pretended to with great gusto in front of the other warriors, and they considered him a fearless and skilled hunter.

Life was good. Ever since he was a small boy Whistling Elk had excelled in nearly every sort of game and skill important to the People, readily bettering most of his age-mates in all of them. At nine years of age he had become the youngest boy in the band ever to capture an eagle by hand. With a flat, pointed stick young Whistling Elk had excavated a shallow round depression in the dirt, five feet across and two feet deep, along a low sage-covered ridge jutting above a twist in the Madman River. With a three-day-dead jackrabbit as an odiferous companion he had curled into the hole, covered himself with leafy chokecherry branches he'd cut from below and hauled up to the spot, and reached back through it to lay the stinking long-ears atop the bramble. Even now, as he closed his eyes and concentrated, Whistling Elk could smell the rotting rabbit and feel the womb-like sensation of being enclosed by Earth. There he had waited eleven hours; first cold hours and then hot hours, a period that would have seemed an eternity to most nine-year-olds—screaming to scare away ravens on several occasions, before finally a golden eagle had swooped down for the carrion. When it did, Whistling Elk had reached up and grabbed her by the talons, simultaneously bursting out of his cover of branches to thrust his chert knife through the furious flapping of feathers and slice the screaming raptor's jugular vein.

Whistling Elk's endurance appeared limitless. Occasionally, for no reason other than it felt right, he headed for hours out across the desert basin, running at times and walking at others. The wanderings began when only stars filled the eastern sky and ended long after the sun had bloodied the western horizon.

Because of his stamina and athletic prowess, his bison-hunting skills, and his legendary eagle capture, and with thirty-four winters under his belt, Whistling Elk was the most esteemed individual in his band. With great pride he wore the prestigious hairstyle of the Fox military society.

Whistling Elk's time on Earth was a period of pride and power for the Tsitsistas. They were strong and in good favor with the spirits that guided their destiny. He found it offensive and confusing that the Sioux referred to the Tsitsistas as "Sha-hi'-ye-na"—aliens who speak a strange language—when in fact the Tsitsistas were the People and the Sioux an odd anomaly.

Life was so interesting, Whistling Elk reflected. So many things he had seen and heard, learned and experienced. One thing he had heard about but never seen was a white man, though he had spoken with Tsitsistas who had encountered them. He himself wore a band around his left wrist of sparkling glass beads said to have come from the white man's world.

It had cooled enough for the warm updraft of afternoon to reverse direction, and Whistling Elk knew he was downwind from a deer standing above him. He couldn't see the animal for the thick brush, but he sensed its presence. Maybe the soft breeze carried to him the deer's scent, or perhaps he had heard the deer exhaling or snapping a twig with its foot. He was certain it was there; he had come to trust his intuition in such matters.

Crawling on all fours in a low depression between two large sandstone blocks, Whistling Elk paused, advanced five feet, and paused again. For luck and for confidence he fingered the projectile point tipping his willow-shaft arrow. He thought back to when he had discovered the point, and another just like it, two summers earlier. He had found them lying side by side, protruding from the leeward base of a large pile of wind-drift sand far out in the basin. He often came across stone tools in similar locations while on his long-distance wanderings. This pair of twin points, fashioned in the unmistakable style of the People, he believed to be neither particularly old nor particularly new. They were in excellent condition; the one he took with him he had to touch up with his bone chipping tool only slightly to make it perfect. The other point he had likewise touched up and left as an offering, hiding it in a special place, close to where he had discovered the pair. He sensed that both points contained great magic, that a powerful hunter and skilled stone worker had created them. He also knew that the black volcanic glass of which they were fashioned had grown from the earth in the high, terrifying country of steaming waters, fumaroles, and bubbling mud pots a few days' travel to the west.

Whistling Elk had embellished the opposite end of his arrow with the tips of feathers from the golden eagle he had captured twenty-five years earlier. A special arrow, he understood, to be used only when he sensed something sacred in the air, as he had sensed this evening— which was why, in the first place, he had told Saw-Whet Peak he was going to go look around for a while.

Whistling Elk crawled atop the crumbling sandstone boulder to his left. He spied the mule-deer buck twenty yards upslope, browsing on wild rose, moving his mouth, and flicking his ears. Whistling Elk heard the nearby creek singing its song of life. He knelt, caught his breath, drew the bowstring back, and aimed the arrow at the buck, a stout animal wearing a silky dark-brown coat. He released the arrow. With a dull thud, it found its mark just behind the deer's left front shoulder. The buck wheezed, jumped, looked around crazily with eyeballs rolling, then took several giant strides. Whistling Elk heard it, but didn't see it, crash into the scrub and go silent.

He inched toward the deer, finding that it had ended up in a cave-like depression beneath a low sandstone overhang jutting out not far above Whistling Elk's head when he stood. He knelt at the deer's side, squeezed its eyes shut, whispered a prayer of gratitude, and sprinkled dried kinnikinnick over its wet black nose. He inspected where the arrow had hit; then, with great force, he removed it. He felt warm red blood oozing from the wound. He stood, walked over to the boulder, and put the arrow on top of it for safekeeping while he finished his job. Lifting his chert knife from its hide pouch, Whistling Elk began gutting the deer at its brisket end, his face inches away from the massive, antlered head of the buck. It smelled musky and of the earth.

Without warning, the buck's neck violently flexed in the animal's final death spasm. The front tine of its left antler drove deep into Whistling Elk's skull, smashing through his temple. Shortly thereafter, his spirit too departed the world of the living. Man and beast, hunter and prey in life, had in death become as one.

ACKNOWLEDGMENTS AND DISCLAIMERS

Some of the locations in this story are real places with real names, some are actual places with made-up names, and others are fictitious places with fabricated names. All characters are products of the author's imagination.

I would like to thank those who reviewed the manuscript in advance. They include Jamie Schoen, recently retired archaeologist on the Bridger-Teton National Forest in western Wyoming; Ramsey Bentley, senior geologist with the Carbon Management Institute at the University of Wyoming (also newly retired); and, most importantly, my wife, Nancy McCullough-McCoy. She made valuable suggestions over the course of the many years and numerous drafts it took to get this story into print.

Any blunders remaining are mine, not theirs.

Also, I would be remiss not to acknowledge my sister-in-law, Susan Cook, for her persistence. For eons, her first question for me, whether on the phone or meeting up in person, has been, "How's the novel coming?"

Muchas gracias to the folks at Sastrugi Press for taking on this project and permitting me to tell my tale. With any luck, we'll be teaming up again to highlight the continuing adventures of Clifford Gustafson.

Finally, I want to offer my heartfelt gratitude to God, or the Great Spirit, for making Wyoming and the greater northern Rockies and northern plains what they are.

CPSIA information can be obtained
at www.ICGtesting.com
Printed in the USA
FSOW02n1441080218
44254FS